ENCOUNTER AT CARAWAY

All around me, the forest lay white and black and silent, the snow sparkling in the light of a white, round moon that sailed above the treetops.

Someone said softly "Calanthe." I froze, helpless in blind panic. A knife blade kissed my throat with its sharpest point. I could not turn my head without risking injury, but I knew it was Jafit standing beside me.

He grabbed my hair, his thickly-gloved hand yanking my face close to his own. He shook his head as if in sadness. "I'm disappointed in you, my dear," he said.

"Then you were a fool to trust me," I replied, finding my voice.

"Where's my Panthera?"

"Not *yours*, Jafit."

"Be quiet. You are surrounded. You have no chance. Just hand him over, Calanthe, and I might let you off with a beating."

I laughed in his face. "You can drop dead, pimp! Panthera and I will die before you can take him back to Piristil!"

"Oh, how touching. Search the area!" Jafit ordered, with a tasty mouthful of satisfaction.

"That won't be necessary, Jafit." The voice was cool, and there was Panthera with his back to a fallen pine, looking as mean and deadly as a she-cat about to defend her young. He held a slim-barrelled gun in his hands, which was pointed directly at Jafit's head.

Tor Books by Storm Constantine

STORM CONSTANTINE
THE FULFILMENTS OF FATE AND DESIRE

TOR
fantasy

A TOM DOHERTY ASSOCIATES BOOK
NEW YORK

THE FULFILMENTS OF FATE AND DESIRE

Copyright © 1988 by Storm Constantine

Reprinted by arrangement with Macdonald & Co. (Publishers) Ltd.

A Tor Book
Published by Tom Doherty Associates, Inc.
49 West 24th Street
New York, N.Y. 10010

Cover art by Sam Rakeland

ISBN: 0-812-50558-1

First Tor edition: March 1991

Printed in the United States of America

0 9 8 7 6 5 4 3 2 1

This book is dedicated to Roy Wood who 'discovered' me in Andromeda and to whom I am deeply grateful for his help, advice and encouragement.

With thanks to Sue Eley for her swift correcting pen and critical eye, and also for the map, glossary and character guide; Jeanne Wheeler, Alison Perry, Steve Allman and Jag for contributory ideas; Steve Waters for illumination about androgyny, and the remaining Wraeththu-ites who were brave enough to be filmed as such; Jayle Summers, Phillipa Cotterell, Richard Clews, Sharon O'Hara, and John Matley.

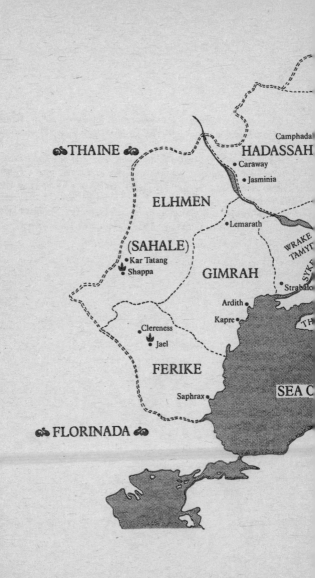

⚘ THAINE ⚘

HADASSAH

Camphadal

• Caraway

• Jasminia

ELHMEN

• Lemarath

(SAHALE)

• Kar Tatang

♣ Shappa

GIMRAH

WRAKE TAMYD

SYKE

• Strabalo

• Ardith

• Kapre

TH

• Clereness

♣ Jael

FERIKE

SEA C

• Saphrax

⚘ FLORINADA ⚘

THE
TRIBES of JADDAYOTH

Prologue

One day, a time will come when all that we are pioneering, praying (preying?), cultivating, is history. The past. It shall be analysed; a subject for earnest scholars to pore over and dissect. Trivial events, accidents, coincidences, shall be imbued with great meaning. I can already hear the voices raised, confident they know it all. Oh yes, I can see it now; our far descendants, all gathered together, clothed in their perfect flesh. One shall say; 'The first Wraeththu, of course, were little other than barbarians, hectic in their search for truth and so far from it, eh? All they could grasp at was their sexuality. What a shock it must have been! They were human to start with, after all. What a shock to find they were half-female after centuries of despising that sex.' Ha, ha, ha. They will all laugh together smugly. Then another bright spark, perhaps younger or more controversial in his views, might venture; 'But surely the reason they couldn't see the truth was because they were so shrouded in self-deception. Knowledge was so close, and yet ... they couldn't see it through the shroud. How sad.' Here, I feel, one of the older Hara, stern-faced, will deliver a subtle reprimand.

'The first Wraeththu were without *discipline*, too outspoken perhaps, before considering what, in fact, they were *really* saying.' This will be said with relish and the younger Har will feel humiliated. He may look down abashed, he may not. But whatever, those sentiments may well be right, and half of me is inclined to hope so. If those highly advanced Hara never *do* come to exist, if our race remains static or even slips backwards to the ways of men, then the struggle really was all for nothing. A cosmic joke. The biggest case of self-delusion in the history of the planet — and there have been many, let's face it. We were just mutants, freaks; end of story. Not saviours, not ultra-men, not sons of angels or deities — just accidents. The gods weren't looking; it just happened. And yes I have to admit it, the other half of me is lying back, sipping good liquor, with its feet up, thinking; 'Yeah, fuck the heavy stuff. Let it all be — just this!' I don't think this earth should ever countenance a future scorn for what we are — what *I* am — for, after all, our descendants can never be here, now. They will never know us as we are or why we do things. The bloody times, the horror, will just be history to them, words on a page, so how will they dare to judge? Very easily, I should imagine. Will it ever be said that, in spite of everything, we all lived to the best of our ability? If life is a battle, then my inner scars are medals for valour, for swiftness, for courage, for passion. Evil is the dark-haired brother of Good; they walk hand in hand — always. And by the way, whatever it sounds like, that is not an excuse …

Fallsend: Its Mud Patch
'The burnt out end of smoky days ...'

T.S. Eliot, Preludes

The years were numbered ai-cara from the time when Pellaz came to power in Immanion. Sorry, that should of course read, Pellaz-Har-Aralis, as lesser beings must refer to him. I am a lesser being, best forgotten, best reviled. I have no part in the future of kings. I lost my sense of chivalry an age ago. Thank God! This is my story and perhaps it will be the truth, for I suspect that there will be an awful lot of untruth spoken about me. I realize it's unlikely anyone will ever read it; more likely that it will lie forever in some unhallowed spot, deep in the earth, clasped to my shrivelled breast. Who knows? (Who cares?) Will someone bury me when I die? Are demons allowed that privilege? This began as a diary but lost its way. This began as a confession and developed a life of its own. This is me.

I shall start in the middle of the story. That is a bad place to start, and because of that, the best one for me. Here goes.

And it came to pass, gentle reader, that I found myself sliding down the black, mud channel they call a road, into Fallsend, a town of reputation but not repute, in the tail end of the year ai-cara 27. Time to rest. Time to reflect. Time to get rat-arsed drunk and stop dissecting the past in my head. Some hope. My first impression of Fallsend was simply to register it as a cold town in a cold country where it always seemed to be late autumn. Never winter. This more or less reflected my rather down-hearted mood at the time, and later had to be revised when it started snowing. Fallsend never looks pretty. It's built on the side of a hill and the floor of a valley the shape of a teacup. After being incarcerated here for a few weeks it begins to feel roughly the same size as well. The name that the country used to have around here has fallen into disuse. Everyone forgot it. Now, it's a northerly, ill-policed fragment of Almagabra known as Thaine. Nowadays, Hara (nice ones) don't want to stay here long enough to think about where they are — if they have any sense. I've never had any sense. Presumably, that's why I'm here. That and the fact I wandered into the place without finery or finance and my horse was about to die on me, or more accurately, beneath me. OK, I'll look on the bright side. I'd managed at long last to shake off the shadow that had been following me to this godforsaken place, but that's about as bright as it's going to get for a while, my friend.

Fallsend is damp and made a little of stone, but mostly of wood, which rots at a merry pace. There are lots of steps, most of them likely to collapse beneath the feet of the unwarily drunken. Planks across the puddles which are collared with scum and the occasional dead creature. Little colour. It's depressing. Just about every Wraeththu criminal, lunatic or honest-to-goodness misfit has passed through this little town, heading east to Jaddayoth. Today, from where I'm sitting, it looks like most of them stayed here. Uptown, they call it Glitter, it will convince nobody. Up here, those sweet souls who make this shit-hole pay have high, gothic houses and you can buy almost anything here. Drugs to make you sane. Drugs to make you insane. Waters of forgetfulness, powders of remembrance. They have white-skinned, moon-eyed Harlings of the Colurastes tribe up here somewhere, bought and sold like meat, kept in the dark. Two spinners buys you one as a whore for a night in the shadows. I heard some of them have their tongues cut out so they'll never scream. We are the race of peaceful equality, remember.

Now for the social comment. I suppose it's necessary, though tiring when you've heard it and thought it a thousand times. Back west, children, the supremely superior tribe of Gelaming have scoured the home country of evil, or so I've heard. As a matter of fact, it was still pretty suspect when I was last there, but I admit that was some time ago. Things might have changed. Everything changes on the surface. (But does it change inside? Can it?) The Gelaming also control the south-western part of this continent as well, where it's sunny all the time, I suppose. I've worked out they swept all their rubbish east and it ended up here. Someone built a town on it. Fallsend. Not a place you'd want to die in.

I'd had to leave Morass, a settlement some ten miles west of Fallsend pretty quickly. Painful as it is to recall, I'd got involved in some sordid argument concerning someone's virgin son, which had all got unpleasantly out of hand. I shine at quick getaways, but as I was drunk, I don't remember too much about it. I lie a lot and sometimes get found out when I'm drunk. After forcing my ailing mount over several miles of boggy ground, I was actually relieved to catch sight of the glum pall of smoke that always hangs over Fallsend. Of course, I'd heard about the place. Every town I'd passed through was full of horror stories about it. What could happen to the unwary traveller there; rumours of abduction, slavery, murder — all anathema to upstanding, Wraeththu-kind. After some of the throw-back, puritan woodpiles I'd visited, it sounded like a welcome relief. 'Well,' I thought to myself, threatening the horse with death if it dared to stumble, 'here it is; a town named for yourself. Have I stopped falling now? Is Fallsend rock bottom?'

After half an hour of wandering aimlessly about, taking in the sights, I took a room in a leaning, listing hostel in the south of the town. Its proprietor didn't work out that I couldn't pay him at first. I sold what was left of my horse to a Har that didn't ask any questions, and to further my investigations of the place, went for a walk through the streets. Nobody looks at you in Fallsend. This is because you may well be a homicidal (or should that be Haricidal?) maniac with a sensitive spot about prying eyes. Nobody wants to take that risk. I bought a bowl of nondescript gruel in a shady tavern — puddles on the floor, blotted by heaps of soggy sawdust, that sort of thing — and asked the regular patrons about where I could find work. At first, they were reluctant to answer me at all, but because I have a deceptively honest face, they eventually plucked up enough courage to laugh. Someone took pity on me. 'What can you do?' I was asked.

'Ah well,' I answered, 'I'm pretty good at killing people, or just fucking up their lives if you can't afford that ...'

This was not a remark to be met with humour, which was how I'd hoped it would be. They told me gravely that there was really quite a glut of killers in Fallsend and that there was too much travelling involved, even if you could get work of that kind. Nobody wants to pay travelling expenses to a murderer, it seems. I tried not to look downhearted. The way I was feeling at that time, I'd have welcomed the chance to throttle the life out of someone, even for free! More pity came my way. Someone said, 'You're quite a looker. Skinny, but some people aren't fussy. If you're not fussy, you'll find work in Glitter ...' I'm fussy. I half-starved for a week before I reviewed my morals.

Because this is the beginning of a book, I think it is a good time to talk about the concept of Wraeththu, if indeed there is one. I can't say it's something I think about often — how many of us in this confused world are allowed the luxury of time to think anyway — and I'm not sure if it is important or not, but for the sake of posterity, I'll say what I think. I am Har, a member of the race that came after man. Came *from* man. We are the race that solved that niggling problem of sexual inequality, not to mention sexual orientation, by evolving into one sex; Hara. I have a female temperament at times and masculine strength at times. Usually these things manifest themselves at the wrong time. Masculine temperament coupled with female strength are guaranteed to land you in hot water, so we all have our problems, no matter how complete and whole we smugly say we feel. Most Hara will tell you that all Wraeththu are beautiful, but this is not entirely true — and how boring if it was! What is inside a person nearly always influences what is outside. The most beautiful Hara are the truly evil, the most powerful and the most clever. Don't believe it if you are told all Hara are good. I've never met a thoroughly good Har and I don't want to. Not even the Gelaming are all good, although I'm sure they like to think so. They are certainly the most beautiful, so draw your own inferences.

Philosophers might tell you that Wraeththu are a race of sorcerors and mystics, supposedly created to rid the world of evil. Now we have a United Council of Tribes desperately trying to convince themselves that this aim has been achieved, but, like I said before, the rubbish was merely pushed east. Northeast, to be exact. In the west, we have the large countries of Almagabra, Erminia, Cordagne and Fereng. In the middle, Thaine, which is where I am now. East of that lies Jaddayoth, but when I first arrived in Thaine I knew very little about Jaddayoth. Let's imagine a line drawn down this continent from pole to pole. West of the line we find law and order, the ability to get the world on its feet again and tranquillity. East of the line is a delightful trip back to the Middle Ages and chaos. South on both sides of the line, we have a huge, hot country we now call Olathe. Humans fucked it up very thoroughly by tossing nuclear weapons around, before Wraeththu spread east from another great continent, Megalithica. Well, that's the essential geography of my tale.

I came from Megalithica originally, and I've been dodging the apparitions of my conscience around Fereng and Thaine for what I think must be several years. It's all very alcohol-fogged, I'm afraid. I don't look any older and I know it's impossible for me to feel any older than I do now. All I want to do is keep running and lose myself in the chaos I know lies east. Sexual inequality may well be a thing of the past, but believe me, there were a host of other, equally irresistible inequalities that had just been busting a gut waiting to take its place. The strong enslave the weak. That about sums it up. Rewind history. Replay. *Ad infinitum*. Oh, I'm sure that there's a warm hearth yearning to give me comfort in Jaddayoth!

Anyway, as I was explaining before, I starved for quite a time after reaching Fallsend, and then the hostel-keeper began to get suspicious. Mainly, this was because I never ate in the (dare I call it this?) dining-room with the other residents. It was a cash for meals arrangement in there you see, and as I quickly got through the money I'd made from selling my horse, the dining-room was deprived of my enlightening presence. On the sixth day, just when

I was convincing myself that I liked eating out of trash cans and had nearly finished my last bottle of liquor, money was demanded for my room. The hostel keeper and I argued in a civilized manner for about half an hour, until he lost patience and had me thrown out, keeping my meagre bundle of luggage as security until I could pay him what I owed. It was all quite undignified. Sprawled in a black, stinking puddle, sniffed at by a stray, mangy hound, I shouted that I used to be the consort of a prince, which was rather an exaggeration on my part, but I had no fear of being found out in that place. It failed to impress my friend the hostel keeper, however. He told me to piss off back west and claim alimony if that was the case. I acknowledged defeat and abandoned the argument. Too many people had gathered to watch, and even numbed by alcohol I hate feeling embarassed.

Remembering the conversation I'd had about finding work some days before, I quickly examined my feelings on seeking employment in Glitter. Strangely, I found I had none whatsoever. Hunger and misery do odd things to your principles. Dusting myself off or sludging myself off which is more to the point, I walked up town and knocked on the prettiest door I could find. It had a string of coloured lights all around it. Tacky, I know, but I appreciated that the occupants were trying to make an effort at decoration in the face of such overwhelming squalor. I had no idea if I'd chosen the best house. A musenda was a musenda to me. Men once called such things whorehouses. After some minutes of repeated knocking on my part, the door was opened by a Har who looked like something out of my past. That is to say he looked clean, attractive and wore jewellery and cosmetics. It had been so long since I'd seen anyone wearing either, that I spared a brief, wistful thought for the days when I'd been adorned with them myself. I said, 'Someone in town sent me up here. They said there's work ...'

'There are no spare places here in Piristil,' the Har said frostily, trying to close the door.

I pushed it open again. 'Look, I know I'm a mess at the moment, but I've had a hard time recently. I've no money, no place to stay. If I don't get work, I'll die of cold, of hunger and the stink of the

16

town. Could you live with that on your conscience?'

'Have you had experience in this line of work?' he snapped.

'No, I've never been a kanene, I've never even set foot in a musenda before, but I swear to you, if you let me stay, you won't regret it. It's a line of work I'm eminently suited to if you'll let me prove it.'

The Har looked at me with about the same amount of enthusiasm (and belief) as he'd look on a turd telling him it was a diamond. We suffered in silence for an eternity, staring at each other. I sensed a growing refusal. He said, 'You're filthy,' which I presumed meant my appearance.

I shrugged. 'Yeah, I know, but I've told you, I've had a run of bad luck. Clean me up and the Aghama will have to shield the angels' eyes from my wondrous beauty.'

He wasn't convinced, although he allowed the corner of his mouth to twitch a little. It was then that I realized I'd have to do that thing I'd just about forgotten how to. It had always worked like magic. I felt my face crack and, for a moment, I was scared it was my skin. But it wasn't. Just dirt. It was my last hope: I smiled. The Har blinked at me, a little dazed. Poor creature, poor sucker. He opened the door wider. 'You'd better come in,' he said.

And that, my friends, is how Calanthe, lover of kings and princes, slayer of friends, charlatan of wit, beauty and refinement, a legend in his own time in fact, became a whore. How much lower could I fall?

The house in Fallsend

*'... prowling hungry down the night
    lanes.'*

Robert Graves, A jealous man

*I am living two lives. I am not mad. Perhaps that is my punishment.
Yesterday is two places, each memory convincing, each incident clear as
ice-water. I am fourteen years old. Seel is with me, younger, eager, dog-like
in his trusting simplicity. The air smells bad around here. It is a dead part of
the city. They say that the Wraeththu live here. We have come to see. Seel's
trousers are ripped, his knees grazed. He is nervous. I am merely numb. It is
the only way for us. The others, the world, our families, what is left of the
establishment on this wasteland earth are on to us. We are so young. We are
afraid yet brave, our courage is a kind of contaminated innocence; we are
human and we are lovers. In the wake of various hysterias, our love is
outlawed. We risk death every day. (The first thrown stone; others would
follow.) No-one must know about us. It is a danger even to look at one
another, in case the warmth of our eyes betrays us. So little warmth in this
world; we must stand next to it when we can. Flesh pressed too long to ice
brings death; death of the soul. Many soulless people walk this land. Every
other house stands empty in our street now. Doors and windows silent,
sagging, vomiting desolation. Our trysting places. We first made love
amongst the rubble, the sound of wailing outside, far away, in the sunlight. A
sharp report of gunfire. Summertime. Dogs barking on the hot asphalt but no
children playing. Seel shuddered and closed his eyes. We both knew. There is
no place for us in the grave of Mankind. Always smoke on the horizon and
the stink of recent carnage. Frightened eyes, sealed mouths. Mankind are a*

frightened people. Demons without, demons within. They can see the door closing on them, shutting off the light forever. It is the end.

There is a hole in the ground. A house once stood here. This was the cellar. Seel and I look at each other. We are so young; we know that. Our hearts ache with nostalgia for other summertimes, simple pleasures, a mother's voice calling from the shade. We look back at the city. I see us as children, happy in that forgotten sunlight, and I know that Seel sees it too. He smiles and puts his hand on my arm. We both look into the hole in the ground. There is a musky smell as would issue from the lair of a beast. Wraeththu live beneath the city. What are they? We have heard they can take our humanity away from us. Take us in. It is our only hope. We can no longer live above the ground. I take the first step and still look back. Seel is a silhouette against the white, summer sky. He reaches for my hand. 'We are together,' he says and his lovely eyes are full of fear.

'Yes,' I say, and he follows me . . .

The name of Piristil irresistably conjures to mind a fairy-tale palace, a haunt of witches and brooding, satanic lords, but despite its pathetic gaudiness, there was little glamour to be found within the house. I learned it was occupied by eight kanene, including Astarth who had let me in. There was also a staff of four, including a cook, a stablehand and the owner of the establishment, a thin, mean-looking Har named Jafit. Astarth was the favourite of Jafit and virtually ran the place.

He shut the door behind me and I stood, drooping and dripping, in the hall looking around myself. There was a grand staircase leading to a gallery that ran round the three sides of Piristil opposite the door. The light was gloomy, trailing plants looped desperately over a table, somewhere a clock was ticking. I could have been back in Megalithica, a hundred years before.

'Well,' my host began, 'I am Astarth. I suppose I'd better get you cleaned up. Jafit can see you later. I hope you've told me the truth.'

I didn't answer. He took me upstairs, and several inquisitive pairs of eyes peered round open doors.

'Charge him double, Astarth!' someone called cheerfully.

'Haven't you any belongings?' Astarth asked, above the laughter that accompanied that last remark.

I shook my head. 'I prefer to travel light.'

He shrugged. 'OK, in here. This is my room. Don't dirty it.'

I was gratefully surprised by the warmth. There was a huge fire burning in the grate across the room. I could smell soot. Another Har was sitting on the floor by the fire painting his toenails.

'Ezhno, get out!' Astarth spat unpleasantly.

'No, my fire's gone out. The chimney's fucked. Get it fixed, Astarth. That's your job, isn't it?' Ezhno looked at me. 'Hello filthy one,' he said and resumed painting his nails. 'Who's your friend, Astarth?'

'My name's Calanthe,' I said lightly and walked over to the fire, holding out shaking, white and grey hands to the heat.

'Well, hello Calanthe, in that case,' Ezhno said, shying fastidiously away from the filthy rags dangling from my outstretched arms. When I squatted down, I could smell his cleanliness; clean hair and tooth polish. He had narrow, crafty eyes, a startling blue.

'The bathroom's through here,' Astarth said, and I realized that was an order.

The rooms in Piristil are comfortable, but worn. They look better in lamplight, but all have carpets on the floor. Unfortunately, all the water is heated by the fires and it appeared that everyone had just taken a bath that day.

'I hope you don't mind the water being cool,' Astarth said, in a voice that showed he didn't care whether I did or not.

'No, I don't mind.'

He watched me rip off my rags, standing with folded arms and expressionless face across the room. When I stood there, naked and shivering, he said, 'I think these old garments should be burnt, don't you?' I agreed. After I had lowered myself gingerly into the tepid water, Astarth emptied a bag of fragrant crystals over me and asked, 'Well, who was it that told you to come here then?'

'No-one really,' I confessed. 'The lights outside impressed me, that's all.'

Astarth smiled grimly and rolled up his sleeves. I was happy to let him scrub at my hair.

'Don't let Jafit know you're inexperienced,' he said.

I laughed. 'There's no way I'd ever describe myself as that!'

Astarth did not share my amusement.

'Everyone thinks that before they're a kanene.'

That sounded ominous. I studied him through a tangle of soapy hair. Astarth has the face of an impudent female and the body of a young god. Some angry part of him makes him hack his bright red hair off very short. He affects a noncommittal attitude to everything, which I quickly realized was a complete sham. Many things hurt him, but he'd never show it. Because of his relatively elevated position in the house, the other kanene make his life a misery at times. I hate to think what miserable set of circumstances brought him to Piristil and kept him there. It's not something you can ask. Kanene don't talk about their history if they can help it. No-one would be doing this if there was an alternative. Wraeththu culture is nothing like Mankind's. Our attitude to sex is utterly different. Obviously, it would have to be, but there should be no need for kanene in a Wraeththu world. This may give some kind of intimation of the sort of hara who do business in a musenda. If ordinary aruna is available to everyone for free, what kind of Har wants to pay for it? What does he expect for his money? Sitting in that luke-warm bath, it was about the third thing that came into my mind, after comforting ones of food and sleep.

Astarth shrugged off my question about it. 'No-one gets hurt,' he answered enigmatically.

'Now why doesn't that comfort me?'

'You wanted the job,' Astarth pointed out reasonably.

I'd become so paranoid over the last couple of years, that I was dreading someone asking me questions about myself. It was a needless fear. Nobody in Piristil asks personal questions — or answers them. I suppose everyone had something to hide. Astarth brought me a plate of food from the kitchen (cold potatoes and lumps of fatty meat), and he and Ezhno watched me eat it. It tasted like nectar to my deprived tongue. There seemed little to say. When you meet a person for the first time, it is customary to strike up conversation by asking them about themselves. This could not occur on either side in Piristil. Any questions about the house or the work were answered by, 'Jafit will tell you the rules.'

'You eat like an animal,' Ezhno said at last, as the sound of my frenzied chewing echoed round the room.

'That's because I feel like an animal,' I answered, with my mouth full.

Astarth sorted out some clothes for me from his own wardrobe. We were roughly the same size. Clean, fed and clothed, I was already much more optimistic about my future. Ezhno was eager to paint my face, enthusing over my cheekbones and eyelids. He combed out my hair, and it felt like I lost a good deal of it in the process, if the pain was anything to go by. I regarded his handiwork in Astarth's mirror.

'I look like a whore,' I said.

'That's the idea,' Astarth answered drily.

Jafit arrived home in the early evening. He had been drinking the afternoon away with friends down in Fallsend. Astarth wasted no time in taking me to see him, mainly because he said that Jafit would probably soon fall into a deep and unwakeable sleep. Jafit's office is on the ground floor to the left of the front door. It is where he generally entertains his best (richest) clients before Astarth shows them upstairs. Astarth knocked on the door and opened it just as Jafit was saying, 'Come!' I could tell by first glance that Jafit is not a Har easily fooled. Astarth had given me some advice on how to bullshit my way through this interview, but one glance into those shrewd, yellow eyes had me doubting myself.

'So, you're looking for work,' he said, after Astarth had explained how I'd arrived. I murmured some assent. 'Thank you, Astarth,' Jafit said meaningfully, and Astarth backed out, closing the door gently behind him. Jafit offered me a drink and I poured myself gracefully into a chair. I could see the spinner-light crashing round Jafit's eyes like a cash-till while he looked at me. He handed me a glass of tart wine.

'And where have you worked before then, er, Calanthe?'

'Oh, in Wesla, Persis ... places like that.'

'You are familiar then with the advanced practices of chaitra and pelcia?'

Astarth had told me to say yes when Jafit asked me that. 'I've had no trouble before,' I answered carefully.

'Forgive my asking, but how come you're so far east? I detect a trace of Megalithican in your accent. You don't look like a kanerie. I get the feeling that you're the sort of person who doesn't need to be one, either!'

I shrugged, pulled a wry face. 'You flatter me. I did come from Megalithica originally, yes. There are reasons why I'm doing this work, which I'd rather not go into. But they won't cause you any hassle, I can promise you that.'

Jafit grinned. 'They'd better not. I don't relish the thought of angry pursuers materializing on my doorstep. You'd better tell me now if you're in any kind of trouble. That doesn't mean I won't give you a place, so don't be frightened.'

'I'm not in trouble,' I said. 'Nobody's after me.'

'Good.' Jafit slapped his legs and stood up. 'OK Calanthe, I admit I like the look of you. I'll let Astarth take you over the rails for a week or two and then you can come to me. If you pass my test, and it's rigourous, I promise you, we'll set you to work. Payment is seven spinners a week, plus bed and board. You'll live here, of course. There won't be any need for you to do domestic duties, we have a staff for that, so you can sit and rub lemon juice into those torn hands of yours every night to get them soft again. One thing; don't abuse the staff! They have to work for a living too. Don't get cigarette burns in the furniture. Don't waste fuel or food and don't go poking around in any areas of the house that are off limits to you. Got that? Any other rules of the house, Astarth can tell you about. Learn as you go along; they're mostly a good bunch here. They'll help you. Any questions?'

I shook my head. 'No, it all seems clear.'

'Good. Now one thing, Calanthe, that I have to say to all newcomers and I only say it once, so remember it well. I look after my Hara. I look after them very well. So you work well for me, do you hear? If anyone pulls a fast one on me, they're dead. No questions asked. Got it?' I nodded. Jafit reached forward and shook my hand. 'I'm sure you do, Calanthe, I'm sure you do. Now, once a week, I like us all to have dinner together, so I'll see you again then. Listen to Astarth; he knows his job. You'll learn well and quickly from him. I make sure my kanene are the best around here.' He waved a hand at me and I stood up. Jafit didn't speak again.

I went out, my mind reeling. What had I got myself into? Jafit's little empire. What, in the Aghama's name, were pelcia and chaitra?

Astarth was waiting for me in the hall. He asked no questions, but told me that I would have to wait a few days until I could have a room of my own. Apparently, all the spare rooms were in varying states of decay, so one would have to be redecorated and furnished for me. At my request, Astarth reluctantly took me on a tour of the house. It is much larger inside than it appears from the front, and rather haphazard in design. It is constructed in a rough square around a central courtyard. Three-storied on two sides, where the main rooms and living quarters of the kanene are to be found, and two-storied on the remaining sides, which comprise the kitchens, domestic quarters and the stables. I heard that it could all get very fragrant out in the courtyard come summer. Refuse collection is not one of Fallsend's strong points. What community council exists is more interested in feathering its own nest rather than the welfare of the people, or so Astarth told me. I can belive it. In fact, I was rather surprised that Fallsend had a community council at all, however corrupt.

A bitter wind worried round the courtyard as Astarth and myself, standing in a kitchen doorway, studied the rear vista of Piristil. Astarth wanted to make it brief. Shivering and exclaiming, he began to close the door. 'Wait!' I said, staying his hand. I pointed out into the gloom, towards the right of the house. There, the top storey's windows were shuttered, in a disturbingly permanent-looking manner. Several were reinforced with iron bars. Light was leaking around the shutters. 'And what's kept up there?' I asked lightly. 'A mad consort of Jafit perhaps? A deranged kanene?'

'What do you mean?' Astarth responded frostily.

'Well, you have to admit, it does rather look as if something's being ... *kept in* up there, or hidden at least. Very gothic, Astarth, a nice touch.'

My laughter did not amuse him however. His face had assumed a curiously blank expression.

'You must be tired, Calanthe. Sleep is what you need now, I think,' he said, and the door was firmly closed.

That first night in Piristil, I succumbed to an exhausted slumber, stretched out on the floor in Astarth's room. In the morning, I awoke with my feet uncovered, freezing cold, my neck complaining fiercely because I'd rolled off the pallet in the night and slept on the hard floor. Across the room, I could see Astarth looking blissfully comfortable, up to the ears in thick quilts, his head buried in a mound of white pillows. As soon as I looked at him, he woke up. He has the instincts of a wild animal.

'Well, I'm glad you look different. You were telling the truth, it seems. You *are* beautiful,' he said.

Normally, such words would be taken as a compliment, but Astarth delivered them without feeling. Nothing for me to work on there!

'You will never catch me lying,' I said.

Astarth ignored this remark. 'At least your training will be that much more pleasurable, well *bearable*, for me. As a rule, ugliness revolts me,' he said profoundly. His conceit amused me. Piristil was certainly a little world of its own.

'Training,' I said, without inflection, somewhat affronted, somewhat amused. I didn't know Astarth's age, but I estimated that he was anything between thirty and fifty years younger than me; a second generation Wraeththu Har. 'It will be interesting to see what you can teach me.' The matter would clearly have to be dealt with on a scientific basis. Astarth didn't answer. Secure as a princeling of his own little kingdom, he sat up in the bed and lifted aside the curtains to glance out of the window. 'Rain again,' he said.

'Well, what a surprise!'

'I would like to live in a warmer country, but Jafit thinks I would find it uncomfortable,' he continued vaguely. 'Orpah will be bringing our breakfast in soon. You'd better dress. You don't want the servants seeing you in that state.'

I groaned and lifted my cursing body off the floor. Astarth brushed me with a fleeting glance.

'Oh, scars,' he said.

'A few. Will that increase or decrease my value?'

'Neither.'

'I hope I'm not going to regret any of this,' I said, in a cheerful tone, pulling a shirt over my head.

'Hmmm,' Astarth said.

'Have you?' I asked. 'Regrets I mean . . .'

Astarth stared at me. I had offended him, asked a question he did not want to answer. I put up my hands in a gesture of apology.

'I don't intend to stay in this place for long,' I said. Astarth was silent. He rose from the bed, crossed to the mirror, touched his face, stretched.

'Jafit is impressed by you,' he said.

I am Uigenna. This is the tribe that took us in. Uigenna. We had no way of knowing one tribe from another; we did not know they have different beliefs, different ways, different breath. Inception was ghastly. A fire-lit cellar, leaping flame shadows on the walls, a stink of filth. Inception room. Their hienama wore feathers and fur, stripes daubed across his face and chest. He took glass, a shard of glass in his hands. Someone held me down. I felt the painless, sickening kiss of sharpness against weak flesh. A transfusion of Wraeththu blood. We'd heard it was something like that. Hienama and me. His blood into my veins, humanity dripping out of me onto sand and sawdust, with a halo of whimpering. I heard Seel crying, far away, nearby, in my head. Yes, in my head. Seel would not accept inception to this tribe. I had already made up my mind. The past was powerless to persuade me otherwise, whether through love or hate. Even in my pain and fear, I did not regret. Not once. Not ever. For the next few days, whilst my body churned and changed, it was that one, fierce thought that kept me alive. It was what I wanted. I would face death to get it; and I did. And now is the time . . .

Now is the time for this virgin body to flower. I have arisen, shining, from althaia to a waiting hunger. The leader of this Uigenna tribe is known as Manticker the Seventy. This is because he once slew seventy armed human soldiers in one frenzied outburst. I can believe it. He is scarred and muscled, his femininity betrayed by his temper, his inner strength. I have only been here for a short while, yet already it is clear Manticker is being rivalled for control of the tribe. His contender is one Wraxilan, a great favourite of the warriors. He is rash and careless, but fearless and strong and quick. He carries few scars. His blond hair is shorn at the sides of his head, but as the rest of it is so thick, he still carries a splendid mane. He is also known as the Lion of Oomar, which is how our branch of the tribe is named. Wraxilan has the broad shoulders of a man, the slim hips of a dancer, the hands and neck of a graceful Amazon, the shapely legs of a whore. He laughs nearly all the time. Like all the others, I am passionately intrigued by him. Slightly afraid, yes, but that is a wise precaution. Now, I lie waiting in the straw, by the light of a single candle, in a dank cellar. I am waiting for the one who will come to me, awaken my new, female crevices, seal the pact that I have made with Wraeththu. As he comes towards me, it is his hair that I recognize first. 'You,' I say, and in my voice I hear the echoes of welcome and fear.

'You think I would let anyone else have you, Cal?' he answers, smiling. 'You're the best we've had for a long time. Lie back. I will make this good for you.'

The Lion of Oomar. He says, 'I am your first. You must remember this.'

'No,' I answer, 'you are not the first. It was Seel.'

He laughs and cups my chin with his hand, squeezes hard. I wince.

'No, my darling, that was before. All that is gone, do you hear? I am your first. Me!' As he says that, he plunges into me. Ouana-lim, the phallus of Wraeththu. Bone and petals, with the tongue of a snake. He enjoys my weeping. He licks the tears from my face, and even in pain, I cannot resist the rising delight of aruna. That is the way of it. Irresistible. At the end, he takes my head in his hands once more.

'What am I?' he asks, and through a haze of tears, half-delirious, I say, 'You are the first. The first.'

'And will you ever forget that?'

'Never. I swear it. Never.'

He pushes me back into the straw. Stands up. Rearranges his clothes. As I lie there with tears falling down my face into the straw, I can hear him whistling as he strolls away from me.

Breakfast in Piristil is necessarily a light meal. This is because most kanene rise late in the morning and the mid-day meal follows soon after. It is customary for most of the kanene to meet at lunch-times, in the dark and elegant dining-room on the ground floor. Astarth told me I could use his cosmetics until I had some of my own.

'Is it really necessary at this time of day?' I asked.

'It is always necessary,' Astarth replied in a stony voice. 'You had better get into the habit of it quickly.'

He was strangely modest about displaying his body and even reprimanded me about my own carefree attitude towards nakedness. 'Your body is the tool of your trade,' he said. 'Get used to the idea that it is to be flaunted only in the presence of paying clients. If you like, this is a psychological exercise in maintaining a certain mystery about what we do.'

I did not bother to argue. It was a minor point.

About an hour later, we heard the chime of a gong from downstairs 'That is for lunch,' Astarth said. 'Come on. Hurry up.' I was still fighting with my hair in the mirror, not possessing Ezhno's quick knack of arranging it. I followed Astarth downstairs. It is quite amusing how the kanene look upon themselves as creatures of quality. All day, they maintain this genteel code of manners and behaviour that would have been more at home in an upper-class girls' boarding-school of perhaps a century before. They are obviously not blind to their station in life, hence the need for a pretence of class and etiquette. Downstairs, I was formally introduced to the other kanene. Several of them were natives of the fabled land of Jaddayoth. Salandril and Rihana, languid creatures, came from the cat-worshipping tribe of Kalamah in eastern Jaddayoth; Yasmeen, Nahele and Ezhno from the gregarious Hadassah; and a gaunt, forbidding-looking creature named Flounah from the Maudrah.

After polite greetings, I took my place at the table, between a delightful imp named Lolotea and Ezhno. Of course, as before, the usual ways of starting a conversation were taboo, and it seemed my presence inhibited the sharing of gossip, so I opted for a safe subject, and one in which I had a deep interest: Jaddayoth. Nobody was loath to talk about it. I learned that there are twelve tribes of Jaddayoth and, from what I could gather, they were all equally eccentric in one way or another. Most of them had formed from groups splitting off from the Gelaming, who wanted to develop their own brand of Gelaming philosophy and lifestyle, whilst others had grown from bands of refugees fleeing Megalithica at the time of the Varrish defeat. Of course, during that time, many Hara were reluctant to live under Gelaming rule. This would, naturally, have meant their giving up such practices as murdering, looting, raping and conquering, and most of the hierarchy of the Varrs and their chief allies, the Uigenna, did not welcome the prospect of a world of peace and plenty. Their rituals were too steeped in the previously mentioned depravities for that. In Jaddayoth, such a vast and empty place, they had been able to hide and lick their wounds, eventually emerging as new tribes. The Gelaming, true to their all-powerful reputation, do keep a cursory eye on what goes on in Jaddayoth. Several of the tribes are, in fact, still closely allied to Almagabra, but on the whole, it is still an unsupervised country, where new societies can blossom unmolested. All natives of Jaddayoth are surprisingly patriotic about the place, even those who, for dark and untold reasons, have obviously had to leave it, such as the kanene. Obvious too was the fact that Jaddayoth is a rising star in terms of affluence and trade. In Piristil, we eat Gimrah meat and vegetables off Hadassah plates. Our perfumes and cosmetics come from Kalamah, our oil and carpets from Emunah, our wine from Natawni. It didn't take long for one clear and radiant idea to settle within me. Once I'd saved enough of my immoral earnings, Jaddayoth was the place I'd go. Privacy and freedom; what more could I want?

After lunch, Astarth excused us both from the company and took me upstairs again. 'Take a bath,' he said. 'The water should be hot now.'

'Again?' I protested. One bath a month had been luxury to me for the past couple of years.

'Yes, again,' Astarth replied. 'I want you thoroughly clean, if you don't mind.'

I thought, 'Ah, training,' and complied without further argument.

Sitting in a deliciously warm bath, soaking in bubbles and steam, I found a package of cigarettes on a reachable table, plus a couple of yellowed but professionally-produced newspapers. I lit a cigarette and lay back to examine one of the papers. It had apparently come from Maudrah. This was obviously the top cockerel in the pecking order of Jaddayoth tribes. I read with inter-est. It was mostly propaganda stuff; how marvellous the govern-ment was, etc. About every five sentences the name of the Archon cropped up. Ariaric, Lord of Oomadrah, first city of Maudrah. If ever an election was held in Heaven, this Ariaric would definitely be confident enough to run a campaign against God. From what I read, he certainly seemed powerful enough. There were a couple of muddy photographs, showing an individual whose face held the same expression and air of potential destruction as the blade of an axe. I smiled to myself. Whiffs of Terzian, I thought. Astarth came bustling in.

'What are you doing in here? We haven't got all day!'

'Who is this character?' I asked, dripping soapy water all over the paper.

Astarth took it from my hands and wiped it. 'Ah, Ariaric,' he said. 'I've only been in Maudrah once. I've never actually seen him in the flesh.'

'Now there's someone I would like to meet!' I declared with relish, putting my arms behind my head, blowing a series of smoke-rings at the ceiling. 'He sounds just my type. Rich and powerful.'

'And complete with royal consort,' Astarth added sharply. 'You certainly have a high opinion of yourself, Calanthe, I'll say that.'

'Certainly not. I am perfectly at home in royal houses.'

'Yes, well, you're not in a royal house now! You are a lowly kanene, that is all. It might interest you to know that Ariaric's consort Elisyin is a Har of the Ferike tribe, whose wit, charm, intelligence and breeding transcends all others. You think you will ever get to Maudrah? Ha!' He laughed coldly. 'You think you'll ever get near such Hara as the royal family of Ariaric? You are mad, Calanthe. Chances are you'll never see the outside of Thaine!'

'OK, OK, don't distress yourself,' I said, rising from the water. Astarth stonily handed me a towel. Obviously, I had hit a raw spot. It didn't take much to work out what that was. Bitterness. Astarth looked around the four walls of that bathroom as if they were a prison. Perhaps they were.

He stalked coldly back into the bedroom while I dried myself. 'Ill-humour!' I thought and expected a cold reception when I rejoined him, some moments later. He was sitting on his bed, pensive in the grey afternoon light. A winsome sight. He looked up and saw me. 'Come here,' he said, and held out his hand. I took this as an apology for his sharp words. 'Well, let's see what you can do, Calanthe.' I sat down beside him and he put his arms around me, for a brief second favouring me with the pressure of his bright head upon my shoulder. It was short-lived. The flavour of that afternoon in Piristil shall stay with me forever, I think. The damp air, the sound of rain on the windows, the half-darkness of a grey, hopeless day. Little warmth reached us from the fire. I had never partaken in such a passionless, empty coupling. Aruna should never be like that. Astarth seemed dead to pleasure, his mind buried deep within his head. There was no touching of souls, no sensation of shared thoughts; nothing. Confused. I tried to change things, to bring us closer. It seemed so long since I had touched another Har. I wanted it to be good. Astarth pulled my hair. 'What are you doing?' he asked coldly. How those words, delivered so emotionlessly, stung is hard to convey. I had always come alive during aruna. Perhaps it is my outstanding ability. Perhaps that was why I thought I'd make a good kanene. I was wrong. Astarth and his kind are not proficient at aruna, no way. If sex is a machine, then kanene are good mechanics, but there is no way I will call what they do aruna again. It isn't. Now, I'm glad about that.

'It seems you have a lot to learn,' Astarth told me resignedly.

'I'm not sure I want to,' I replied. He smiled cynically.

'There are two types of pain. Pelcia and chaitra. Now I will teach them to you. Forget what you know. That is no use to you here. No use at all.'

Pelcia is a corruption of the word pelki, which means violation. It involves learning how to put up a convincing resistance to the sex act. I must allow myself to be raped. Is that possible? Chaitra, simply, is the same service performed for a client. They want pain, whether delivered or received. That is what they pay for.

'Learn,' Astarth said. 'They don't know much. There are a hundred ways to deceive, a hundred short-cuts to the desired result. As long as they hear you squeal, they will be content.'

I sat up in bed. I actually thought about leaving. Staring out of the window, I could see the depressing vista of Fallsend dropping away into a murky mist. Where could I go next? I had no money, no horse, not even any clothes of my own. It was the closest I had come to despair for a long time. Now, some of Astarth's bitterness when I'd been waffling on about going to Maudrah began to take on deeper meaning. I was trapped in a vicious circle. Unwelcome memories were coming dangerously close to the surface of my mind.

'Astarth, I have to think,' I said. 'All of this is going to take a little getting used to.'

'Of course,' he answered unctuously, as if we'd just been discussing a business venture of an entirely dissimilar kind. 'Think all you want. I will see you later.'

I wandered downstairs, looking for warmth, looking for company, and went into the sitting-room that led off the dining-room. Only one other person was in there, sitting close to the fire. Once I'd shut the door behind me, cheerfulness invaded the room. 'Hi there, come in. Sit down.' It was Lolotea. I smiled dimly and sat down in the window seat, my knees up, my chin on my knees, brooding sourly at the yard beyond.

'Hey,' Lolotea said softly. He came and drew the curtains in front of my face. 'Don't sit there. It's cold.'

'Is it possible to be warm here?' I asked.

Lolotea didn't reply. He led me to the fireside and poured me a cup of coffee from a pot standing in the grate. He studied me for a moment. 'In a week, you'll forget you ever felt like this.'

'Like what?'

'Like the expression on your face. Don't worry. You'll get used to it. We all did.'

'I can't think of anywhere else to go,' I said bitterly, unwilling to accept those last words.

'There can't *be* anywhere, that's why. I'm sure you wouldn't be here if there was. None of us would.'

'I think I've failed Astarth's test. Perhaps I'll be asked to leave anyway.'

Lolotea shrugged. 'Hmm, maybe. But if I were you, I'd sit down here for a while, warm up, smoke a few cigarettes, have a few more cups of coffee, then go upstairs and put that right. You're not stupid, are you? Just put it right.'

We smiled at each other; conspirators.

'Advise me.'

Lolotea smiled into his cup. 'Astarth has a way of intimidating people. He looks down on everyone if they give him half a chance. This is the result of a rather large and heavy chip on his shoulder. Don't let him look down on you. Get in the first blow, so to speak. Surprise is the key to success.'

'Hmm, already I feel I've learned more from you than Astarth could ever teach me,' I said.

Lolotea gave another expressive shrug. 'That is because I'm not trying to impose authority over you.'

'Is that what Astarth's trying to do then? Just that?'

'I would think so. Astarth will be jealous of you. You spoke of plans to leave here, plans for the future. That would anger him. He resents ambition in others, mainly because he's too lazy or complacent to do anything himself. Dog in the manger syndrome. Don't you think so?'

'I can't say,' I answered diplomatically, aware that any careless remarks might be repeated as gossip. 'I haven't been here long enough to judge anybody's character.'

Lolotea smiled politely. As he suggested, after a few more cups of coffee, I went back upstairs.

Astarth was tidying his room, something he seems to spend an awful lot of time doing, mainly moving things from one end of the room to the other. He looked up at me with annoyance. Perhaps I'd disturbed some precious, private revery. 'Yes, what is it?' he snapped.

'I've been teaching myself,' I answered. Luckily, I was angry. My whole, miserable set of circumstances was making me angry. Astarth's caustic, condescending tone was the final straw. I half threw him across the room. He landed with a clatter amongst some of his precious belongings. That, at least, wiped the hauteur from his face. I *do* know how to be wild. It is not something I'm proud of and I don't care to remember it most of the time, especially how and where I learnt it. When I'd finished with Astarth, he looked as if he'd just fought off the Hounds of Hell. He lay on the floor, staring up at me, dazed, and not a little frightened. I squatted down and put my face close to his. 'Now remember this, my friend. It is something I want you to think about very deeply. One day, while you're still here, working on your back, I shall be back up there amongst the royal houses. Don't doubt it for a second, my darling. I don't know what keeps you here, and I don't want to, but believe me, I've lived in royal houses, I've been right up there among the angels, and I intend to get there again! Not you, your sarcasm, or your little world of sin is going to stop me. Is that clear? I'm not a whore, Astarth. I never will be. This is just a stepping stone. Got that?'

Astarth put up his hands. 'OK,' he said placatingly. It was the beginning of a certain mutual respect between us.

That evening, instead of staying in Piristil for the evening meal, Lolotea suggested that he and I should go down into Fallsend for a 'bite to eat, a skinful of good liquor and a change of scenery'. He guessed that my first day in the establishment had been a little harrowing.

'No work tonight then?' I enquired.

Lolotea pulled a face. 'Well, just one, as it happens, but I managed to farm it off to Rihana. I thought you needed the company more.'

We trudged down the muddy streets, past the grey and brown stalls selling grey and brown merchandise, to a tavern that Lolotea called 'passable'. If the food wasn't exactly haute cuisine, at least it felt warm and friendly inside and the ale was decent. Lolotea had kindly lent me the money that I owed the hostel-keeper who had kept my belongings. Knowing the labyrinthine streets of the town as well as he did, we had only had to take a short detour to call in there on the way to the tavern. After we'd finished eating and the pot-Har had removed our plates, I emptied the contents of my bag onto the table, to examine what mementos I had left of my past.

Lolotea picked up a small, jewelled pin and inspected it with interest. 'Hmm, this looks Varrish,' he said, before he could stop himself.

'It is,' I answered, taking it off him. Terzian had given it to me. Holding it, I could see once more the imposing outline of his house. Forever, feel the warmth of its hearths, smell the sandalwood perfume of its rooms. There was a moment's silence while I relived those memories, all the more painful because of the contrast between what I'd been then and what I'd become. My grief must have been unmistakable. In sympathy, Lolotea broke the first rule of Piristil.

'I came from Megalithica,' he said at last.

'Me too,' I replied in a thick voice, although I knew Lolotea had already guessed that.

'Look, don't answer this if you don't want to,' he ventured, 'but are you, were you, a *Varr*?' I looked up at him, unable to speak. He mistook my silence for something else. 'I'm only asking, well, because . . . I was Varrish once.'

I smiled. 'Yes, I too was a Varr for a time. In Galhea.'

Lolotea rolled his eyes. 'Ah, *Galhea*! The nest of all intrigue! Terzian's stronghold was in Galhea, wasn't it?' This was a rhetorical question of course, but I still nodded.

'It was.'

Lolotea laughed nervously. 'Oh, it seems stupid, doesn't it. All this secrecy about ourselves!'

'Not if you happened to be a Varr in Megalithica round about the time I left there,' I answered.

'Yes, but what does it matter now? It's over and done with, isn't it?'

'I suppose so,' I agreed cautiously, 'but you have to remember that the Varrs had a lot to answer for once. I expect that there are quite a few blood-debts left hanging around, even over here in Thaine. I don't think anyone will forget completely all that happened.'

'Yeah, you're right, but I think most of them in Piristil have worse secrets to hide than they once used to be Varrs!' he said fiercely. 'I must admit, I feel quite a sham keeping it quiet really. Look around you. The chances are nearly everyone in Fallsend had some connection with the Varrs at one time. I bet Astarth, for one, has several dark secrets lurking in his past!'

I agreed readily to that, mostly because I still hadn't forgiven Astarth for trying to humiliate me.

'I lived north of Galhea,' Lolotea continued. 'I once saw Terzian when he rode through on his way to Fulminir. What a hero! Everybody was virtually falling down and kissing the ground as he went by!' I laughed at this, visualizing it easily. 'Did you ever see him, close to?' Lolotea queried, still tentative. 'I mean, living in Galhea and all, I suppose you must have, but, well, we often used to wonder what he was really like ...'

'I saw him,' I said. I hadn't meant to put all that feeling into those words. It wasn't a deliberate clue so that I could show off to Lolotea. I just couldn't deny the feelings inside me.

'And what about Cobweb, the famous consort, or should I say the famous *first* consort? Did you ever get to see him too? Is he as beautiful as people say?'

I made an exclamation, remembering. 'Oh yes! You could say that Cobweb and I actually got to cross swords a couple of times!'

'Really?' Lolotea was not sure whether to believe me or not.

'I suppose I'm saying too much,' I said.

'No! Not at all. Please go on.' He wasn't stupid.

'It may just be stories. How do you know I'm not making it up?'

'I'll take that risk. It's entertaining anyway, even if it is bullshit.'

'What do you want to know?'

'Cal ...'

'No, *Calanthe*,' I butted in.

'Calanthe,' he said thoughtfully, staring at me very hard. I could see a certain dawning of realization creeping over his face, but it was too wonderful a coincidence for him to believe at first. He said casually, 'Wasn't ... wasn't Terzian's second consort, you know, the one that caused all the trouble in Forever, named Cal? He had yellow hair too, didn't he ... like yours.'

'He was called Cal, yes, among other things,' I replied, filled with a weird kind of relief. I wanted him to know. I didn't know why. Lolotea raised his glass at me and smiled.

'It's not a common name,' he said and drank thoughtfully. 'Well, I'm not even going to attempt to work out why the consort of Terzian the Varr is working as a kanene in a dead-end pit like Fallsend ... er, if he is doing so, of course! I thought that all of Terzian's family came under the protection of the Gelaming after

Fulminir fell. Terzian's son went over to the Gelaming, didn't he? Swift, wasn't it? As I recall, he came out of it all very well! Some say *too* well.'

'You don't know the circumstances,' I said, defending Swift who certainly deserved it. 'He acted in the only way possible. Galhea must be quite a mighty metropolis by this time, I would imagine.'

'I don't know,' Lolotea said. 'I came over to Thaine before the Gelaming ever really got a hold on Megalithica. It seems we're both old crows together, doesn't it! Maybe one day, I'll tell you my story. If you tell me the rest of yours, of course!'

'That's a deal!' I said, having no intention of ever doing so. We clinked glasses, laughed, and drank. Now I had a friend. Perhaps things were not as bad as I'd thought.

Body for Sale
'I have been one acquainted with the
night.'
Robert Frost, Acquainted with the night

3

I am Uigenna. I am sixteen years old. The world has gone now, the world that I knew. My family is probably dead. I don't care. I really don't. I tell myself they never liked me. I still don't know if that is true. Seel went to the Unneah. That was because the Uigenna were too wild for him, too ferocious. We meet sometimes, on those crazy borderlands that exist in cities like this. It has changed so much in such a short space of time. I feel like I've lived for a hundred years. There is Wraeththu blood in my veins and I feel like God. Human life means nothing to me. They are so small. I hate them. I have to kill. Every time I kill, I see a mocking, threatening face. Such faces followed me in the past. Such faces drove me to what I have become. They shouted out to me, menacing, vulgar, ugly. But no more. They are dead and those that still live shall die. In the shadows of perpetual night, in the light of dancing flames, I meet a Har named Zackala. We intrigue each other in an outlandish courtship. Our nuptial bed is a heap of debris, broken window-frames, wreckage of love. He bites me. We laugh. Pain makes me strong. I live in this place. It is always with me. At night, I do not dream. I just remember. There are no nightmares.

Lolotea and I returned to Piristil very late. There were several minutes of drunken giggling as we tried to sneak up the creaking stairs.

Lolotea paused by his door. 'You'd better go to Astarth,' he said.

I pulled a sorrowful face. 'I suppose I'd better.'

'Goodnight Calanthe.' He closed the door on me. Astarth was asleep when I went in. I did not wake him. I curled myself in blankets on the floor and lay staring at the ceiling until I fell asleep.

The following day, Astarth informed me, with unmistakable relief, that he would be working until the evening. My training session would have to wait until then. At lunch, I took the opportunity to examine in more detail the other occupants of the house. I entertained myself conjecturing whether their eating habits gave any clues as to their personalities. Flounah glared at his food, eyeing it with suspicion and chewing distastefully. Ezhno read a book throughout the meal, shovelling forkfuls into his mouth abstractedly. Both Salandril and Rihana sorted out their food, before eating, into piles of what they liked and what they wouldn't touch. This, of course, was the only fitting behaviour for Hara whose tribe were reputed to be innately catlike. All of them were of averagely lovely Wraeththu appearance, which to me signified that they must all be villains of one colour or another. Astarth sat at the head of the table, moodily ignoring his food and taking only wine. I had been surprised by the quality of the wine, which was excellent. Piristil was a place of contrasts.

There was a knock at the front door, which we all ignored. It came again. Sighing, Astarth fastidiously wiped his mouth with a napkin and graciously rose from the table. 'Orpah!' he yelled unnecessarily as he left the room.

I had come to realize in a relatively short space of time that the staff of Piristil were inordinately apathetic about many of their duties, answering the door being one of them. Presumably, this was why Jafit had seen fit to caution me about my attitude towards them. Apart from Orpah, there were three others in the house; Wuwa, Tirigan and Jancis, who was the cook. All of them had that half-finished appearance of the unsuccessfully incepted. Relations between the staff and the kanene were not of the warmest kind.

'You have ruffled Astarth's feathers,' Ezhno remarked to me as Orpah put his head round the door and said, 'What?' We ignored him. I made no comment on Ezhno's observation. 'Don't pull his hair too hard, that's all,' he continued mildly. 'Astarth is lord of the hearth in this place. He won't like it if you challenge his authority too much.'

'I didn't realize I had,' I said, wondering how much Lolotea had been blabbing to the others.

'Astarth perceives challenges to his authority in all kinds of innocent behaviour,' Flounah pointed out morbidly. Of them all, he was the most bewitching creature. Pale, attenuated, with smooth black hair like a sheet of silk. His slanted eyes must be the envy of the Kalamah. He is not to be trusted, however.

On my way upstairs that afternoon, I had my first glimpse of one of Piristil's customers. He was coming out of Jafit's office, accompanied by Jafit himself. I'm not sure what kind of monster I'd been expecting, but from what I could see, the Har looked merely ordinary. No manic eyes, no clawed hands anxious to do business with the flesh of a kanene. I had seen many such Hara as warriors in my late consort's army. This Har looked no different, dressed in black, scuffed leather, his hair tied behind his head, his eyes tired.

'Kruin, I'd like you to meet our latest arrival,' Jafit said indulgently, as if bestowing a great honour. I bowed appropriately.

The Har named Kruin inclined his head awkwardly and said, 'Er . . . hello.'

'Be so good as to summon Rihana,' Jafit ordered, so I called 'Rihana!' and went upstairs to find Lolotea.

He was in his room and invited me inside. 'Comfortable!' I said.

'I try. Do you want to go into Fallsend again?'

I could tell from his voice that he hoped I didn't. 'No, I don't think so. What do you usually do to keep entertained when you're not working?'

'Sleep!'

'That boring, huh?'

Lolotea lay down on his bed and stretched and groaned. 'Not really. We could be artistic and paint pictures, we could tell each other stories or we could get very drunk.'

'The last of those suggestions seems the most promising,' I said.

'I agree. What do you want, wine or betica?'

'I've never drunk betica, so I'll have that.'

'You sure?' Lolotea laughed, but sprang off his bed and poured us both a large drink. The liquor was yellow and its taste better left undescribed. However, after half a glass, the mouth is sufficiently numbed not to be alarmed by it. Lolotea flopped down on his bed again. 'God, I'll be glad when you get paid, Calanthe! I don't suppose you've got any cigarettes, have you!'

'No, but you have.' I helped myself.

Lolotea laughed but did not protest. 'So, mysterious one, tell me about life in Galhea.'

'Oh, it's not that interesting,' I said. Everything that happened to me in Galhea was, naturally, intensely interesting, but I didn't like talking about it.

Lolotea thought for a moment, stroking the rim of his glass. He looked enchanting and mischievous. 'Is Terzian really dead?' he asked, 'or is that an indelicate question?'

He was pleased with himself for being shocking. Kindly, I tried to appear shocked. 'Foully indelicate!' I answered. Lolotea raised his eyebrows. 'Yes, he's dead ...' I sat down on the bed beside him. 'And no, I'm not grieving for him, before you ask. I must admit, I do sort of miss Galhea though. I had a good life there. Besides, I was rich in Galhea, I lived in a grand house; now look at me!'

'You look just fine to me, Calanthe,' Lolotea remarked. I was not sure of his motive in that. He might possess a perspicacity I'd not given him credit for.

'I'm a survivor,' I said.

'You will need to be here,' he answered, although I didn't agree. Piristil, in its way, is just as womblike as Forever had been. No outside world. I would have liked to enlighten Lolotea about just what real survival entailed, but there was little point, and I didn't want to reveal that much about myself. Instead, because I like to turn and turn and trample in a new nest to make it comfortable, I said, 'Lolotea, I would like to take aruna with you this afternoon.'

Lolotea laughed and I'm quite sure that his first reaction was to ask, 'why?', but it was not part of the image that he wanted me to have of him. 'I hope you don't want to try out your newly acquired skills of pelcia and chaitra on me,' he said with a smile.

'Is that an answer?'

'You didn't ask a question.'

'OK, will you? I know it's probably not the sort of thing you do for relaxation around here, but the truth is, I'm desperate for a cuddle and need my faith restoring in physical contact.'

Lolotea pulled a face. 'Do you know, when I think about it, I haven't taken aruna for years, not *proper* aruna. I suppose we get kind of sexless, what with our work being what it is.' He looked at me. 'Maybe I need my faith restoring too. Faith! Ha!' He threw one hand over his face and laughed coldly. 'What did all our dreams come to, Calanthe? Have we realized any of them? Look at us! My self-development went right out of the window as soon as my need to earn a crust for myself came in! Were we kidding ourselves that it was all going to be better? Are we really better than men?'

'Oh, give it a rest, Teah!' I said. 'Leave the heavy bullshit for those who've got the time to worry about it. Right now, I want you. That's magic. No amount of failed dreams can take that away from us.'

He sighed. 'You're right. Undress me. And do it slowly. Let's make the best of it.'

We did.

Maybe taking aruna with Lolotea woke up parts of me that had been sleeping (or catatonic), I don't know. But I remember how when I left his room that evening, the sun had struggled from its mantle of clouds; the hall and stairs of Piristil were bathed in a beautiful sunset glow. I could feel my senses, lifted with the kinder light, waking up, sniffing, looking around and thinking, 'Ah yes, time for work to begin again.' For too long I'd been aimlessly shuffling around the countryside, with no direction in mind, abandoning my skills, living like a scavenger. Look what it had brought me to! I might as well have been human. OK, I'd got a whole book of excuses for what might be termed my 'breakdown', but the time of healing was over. No more excuses. From here, it's one way: up.

I went to Astarth. 'Reporting for training,' I said, with a smart and sassy salute.

Astarth shook his head and nearly smiled. 'I can teach you

nothing, Calanthe. From now until your room's ready, sleep with Lolotea. He can train you instead. I've asked Jafit, so it's alright. In a few days, I'll see what you've learned. OK?'

'Very OK,' I said. And that was that.

We come to a place where humans still have control. It is not a large city, but from where we are stationed on the hill, it appears to cover the entire valley floor beneath us. Zack holds up his knife to the hazy sun. The clouds have not yet lifted. Pale ribbons lead into the town below us; empty roads. There is smoke rising and little sound. We begin to descend the hill. There are maybe just over a hundred of us, well-rested, well-fed. Now our leader is Wraxilan; Manticker the Seventy is no more. Wraxilan, Lion of Oomar rides a slim, brown horse that tosses its head impatiently as it picks its way down the narrow path. The Lion's hair flows yellow down his back, like girl's hair, beneath a metal helmet that covers nearly all of his head, giving him the face of some feral, gleaming animal. We trot like wolves and, before us, we can now see the barricades that have been built around the town. Feeble fortifications. Do they really think they can hold us back, stem the relentless waves of Wraeththu? We that beat patiently, like water, licking like flames, like fire. Unbeatable. Weak sunlight picks out the deadly nozzles poking through the makeshift wall before us. Tumbled automobiles, masonry and skeletal woodwork, all clothed by a rotting flesh of torn fabric. They have plundered the body of the town; she will not aid them. I allow myself to laugh. What we are doing is merely as tiresome as having to rub the sleep from our eyes in the morning, and perhaps not even as dangerous. We can smell their fear because they will have heard the tales. Just the presence of their meagre defences speaks of the fact that they have not entirely believed them. If they had, they would have run and run fast, north into the great forests where it is still possible to hide — for the time being. Instead, the fools have chosen to stay and defend their territory. Just ahead of me, the Lion of Oomar reins in his mincing horse and raises his hand. We halt. His generals confer. Half-naked, their skin shining like oiled leather, their hair arranged in savage crests, they are proud beings, the cream of Uigenna. Now the humans will be thinking, 'Oh, they are so exposed, hardly shielded, unarmoured', and their spirits, their paltry hopes will begin to rise. I can feel it rising, like a weak mist over the town, so soon to be burnt to extinction. The light is getting stronger now. An order is given. We pull ourselves up straight and, around me, I can see a

43

hundred pairs of eyes light up. Nothing can quell the hysteria of potential conquest, not even when it is so easily achieved. We begin to move once more and now I can hear the voices coming from the town, half heard-shouts, the clank of metal. They will wait until we are closer before they begin to fire. Now our shaman walks before the Lion's horse. He is robed in pale, floating stuff, his hair unbound, his arms raised. I can see, where his sleeves have fallen back, the sunlight glinting off the golden hairs on his arms. He is famed among Uigenna. His powerful voice is famous. We can hear him crooning. There is an order being given behind the barricade. 'Fire!' There is a sound, it is true. It is the sound of the earth cracking, the earth stretching, the call of the fire serpents deep in their earthy lairs, but it is not the sound of gunfire. We need no further order. Wolves again, we bay and lope quickly towards the town. As I leap the barricade, I look quickly into a pair of wide and stricken eyes, looking up. My knife obliterates their expression and, for the first time that day, my skin is sprayed with blood. They cannot fight us for our shaman has poisoned them with fear. Like children, they whimper and cower. Like corn, we cut them down. There can be no pity.

The shambles of the town opens up before us. It is another vista of decay and putrefaction. There are lights that will no longer shine, shops with broken windows, whose wares have long since been looted or burned. Cars sag dismally along cracked streets, their insides gutted as if picked at by carrion-eaters, the lamps that were their eyes dimmed for eternity. Of course, humanity had turned upon their own a long time ago. We pass human corpses dangling from the lamp posts. We pass slogans of despair scrawled across walls. And still we run. 'This town must be cleansed,' our leader tells us and we know that. We know that so thoroughly, so lovingly. I howl and kill like the rest. Even as I plunge metal into flesh, I think, 'A pity; there will be little food here.' By evening, it is over. All the surviving young males have been rounded up and now stand shivering in pools of their own piss and vomit, next to the fire we have built. It is a good fire, large and potent. The magic still eats away at the hearts of the remaining man-children. They cannot lift a finger to help themselves, but even so, we look upon this as sport. Wraxilan has already chosen the best. The boy is dragged forward, weeping, kicking the dirt. I choke on despising, even though I know his mind is not his own. I never blink as his flesh is cut, nor wince as he screams, screaming still as our beloved leader's blood is instilled into the wound. A small libation, but enough. When the transformation is complete, the Lion shall take him, but

*not before. We are not barbarians. We know the rituals, respect the
Changing. We shall tend the Incepted and help them in their passing from
humanity. This town is depressing. I shall be glad to leave it. The Changing
takes three days. Then the inception is fixed forever by the sanctity of aruna.
The newly incepted will have haunted eyes for a while, but then they will
Accept and the power shall course through their once feeble bodies. This the
ways of things. This is what we have to do to the world; cleanse it. Change it.
We are young, yes. Our cultures are young, yes. But the world is ready for us,
you see. She wants us. She has waited a long time for our coming. She hates
humankind. They have raped her and beaten her nearly to death. We are her
angels and we are the voice of vengeance. The lights go out forever all over
this blighted country and the Earth shall claim back what is hers and we
shall be given what is ours and the temples shall be sanctified with blood . . .*

The next two weeks passed very quickly for me, while at the same
time instilling within me the sense that I had been in Piristil for a
long, long time. Its routines became my routines; it no longer smelt
strange to me. At night I slept in Lolotea's bed (he was excused
'night duty' for the time being with the clientele), and it was from
him that I received my initiation into the rites of a kanene. Most of
it was absurd. We did it, but then got drunk and laughed about it.

After a week, my room was ready for occupation. Orpah and
Wuwa had been responsible for the decoration, so it was with no
surprise that Lolotea and I found paint smears on the window and
across several of the floorboards round the edge of the room. My
bed hid a bald patch in the carpet. On the day that I finally moved
into that room, I stared at the bed for quite some time, trying to
envisage what I must eventually do in it. I wished I had a different
place to sleep in. I did not want my personal nest to be crowded by
ghosts. I resolved to try and do most of my business on the carpet. I
sat down on the bed and thought, 'And how long is this to be my
little world?' I couldn't help adding to it though, striving to make it
some kind of home, however temporary. Out of my meagre wages,
I resolved to save at least half. Clothes, food, cosmetics, I would not
have to worry about buying myself. Jafit footed the bill for those.
Liquor was always available about the house. So all I would have to
spend my money on was small comforts for myself. Fallsend has

quite a good market, selling merchandise from Jaddayoth and sometimes from Almagabra. I decided that as soon as I could afford it, I would buy some patterned rugs to hang on the walls and to disguise the tired appearance of the carpet. It might also help to keep the room warm. Occasionally, the open fire belched unwelcome clouds of thick smoke back out of the chimney. You see, I was thinking in terms of a certain permanency. Dangerous. I should have kept the discomfort and saved *all* my money. At first, the place smelt damp.

The Dire Time was drawing near. Sometimes, I would pass customers on the stairs, or come across them in the two sitting-rooms we had on the ground floor. I had quickly adapted to the Piristil tradition of deeply loathing those that came to buy, and was only frostily polite to anyone that spoke to me. Only in the bedroom, Lolotea told me, do we have to put on The Act. 'They don't pay for us to like them, after all!'

Near the end of my first two weeks, Astarth summoned me to his room again. It was another dreary evening. Astarth looked miserable and uncomfortable. 'Now, we shall have to see …' he muttered, convulsively wringing his hands. Maybe he was psyching himself up to find out what I'd learned. Guessing this, I infuriated him by talking about the weather, a subject which holds not the slightest fascination for either of us. 'Calanthe, listen!' he cried at last. 'You know why you're here. Let's get on with it, OK? I shall take the part of a client. I have to see how you will react.'

In the light of the fire, stalking me, he looked feline and dangerous; his tension was power. 'I can see the Wraeththu in you now,' I said, and I could, for perhaps the first time. Astarth made a noise like the fire crackling. When he put his hand on my shoulder, I could feel thin, hard ropes of muscle trembling up his palm.

'Begin. Speak!' he said.

'Have you already paid for me?'

'Jafit takes the money before anyone comes upstairs.'

'How much?'

'Not your concern. Never ask about money.' He squatted down before me, where I sat on the carpet. 'They will begin by saying something like; "You don't want me here, do you?" How will you answer?'

I laughed. 'Well, that's obvious. I shall say; "Yes, that's true." it won't be a lie, after all.'

Astarth shook his head. 'Somehow, I don't think you'll look frightened saying that, Calanthe.'

'I don't think I can be frightened. Alright, I know the game. Don't look like that. I shall say, "Please Tiahaar, don't hurt me." Will that do?'

Astarth smiled grimly. 'Simpering and lisping do not become you, but they pay for the sex, not a command performance.' He put his other hand upon me. 'Say it then.'

I looked grave and said, 'Astarth, I don't want you to hurt me.' He looked strange and old in the firelight (had I been wrong about his age?), holding my eyes with a steady, flickerless gaze.

'I won't,' he said, and dropped his eyes. He stood up, walked backwards two paces, turned his back, flinched and wheeled around. Before I knew what had hit me, I was half-way across the room, stars in front of my eyes. Astarth was only a stooped, carnivorous shadow against the window. I crouched into a position of defence, quite instinctively. I could see him moving. 'My God, I think he means this,' I thought. Had Astarth been waiting for the right moment to attack me ever since the aftermath of our first training session?

'Don't move!' he said. I didn't answer. He came at me quickly, like some monstrous spider, kicking out sideways so that my shoulder slammed against the wall. He'd been well-trained at some point, but it must have been a long time ago. Already I could see his weaknesses. I waited, then thought clearly, 'Right! Now!' and retaliated. He was unguarded. Surely no client would leave his neck exposed like that? I don't know. We're not supposed to fight back in this role, are we? My fingers clamped around Astarth's windpipe, forcing his head back. He clawed at me, but sensibly gave that up when my other hand punched him in the stomach. Now we are both snarling, rolling like frenzied wildcats across the floor. It *was* exhilarating. Astarth gasped, 'What in hell are you doing, Calanthe?' but in the dim light, I could see him grinning.

'It's no good,' I said, pinning him carefully to the floor. 'I just can't let anyone kick the shit out of me and not fight back. Perhaps, when I'm provoked, I can give pain, but I can't lie back happily and receive it.'

'You're a fool!' he said. I could feel the bones grinding in his wrists.

'Enjoying it, aren't you!' I replied. That set him off snarling and spitting and twisting and flailing. I let go of his arms, let him rave for a while before slicing him under the ribs with the edge of my hand. That shut him up. I carried him to the bed and dropped him on it. He lay silent, breathing heavily, one hand across his stomach. His eyes were glass, staring out of the open curtains at a sky where there was no moon. I sat down on the edge of the bed to catch my breath. Clearly, I was far from fit myself.

'I don't think I'm going to be of any use here,' I said.

'You must!' he answered vehemently and then coughed for quite some time.

I politely allowed him to finish before saying, 'And what is it to you, Astarth?'

'Nothing. But Jafit will be displeased if you don't work out, that's all. He wants you here, Calanthe, not me.'

'And yet it was you who was stupid enough to let me in.'

He ignored that. 'It's not that difficult to learn,' he said. 'We all had to. It doesn't come naturally, I know, but you *do* need the money.'

'Yes.' I sighed and rubbed at my face. 'The problem is, I've always believed in aruna, Astarth. I know its magic. This pelcia and chaitra business is an obscenity. It turns my stomach.'

'I know. Just don't look on it as aruna. There are other things we have to do with those parts of our bodies. Look on it as that.'

'Succinctly put,' I said, impressed. 'And yet, I get the feeling, Astarth, that … how can I put this? It seems to me you perhaps don't feel the same about it as I do.'

'You mean I enjoy it?' he asked in a clipped voice without any hint of shame. 'Perhaps I do. It lets the anger out, doesn't it? Sometimes I feel like I want to be beaten to death. Sometimes I want to kill. You have your dreams to sustain you, don't you? I can't dream like that anymore.' He turned his head away from me.

I put my hand on his shoulder and felt the flesh tense beneath it. 'You want me to finish what I started?' I asked. There was a silence. 'Come on!' I chided and poked him in the ribs. 'Come on, Astarth!' I tickled him under the arms and he couldn't help laughing. Astarth likes it rough, it's true, but I look upon him as a kind of highly strung horse. Treat him the right way, gain his trust and you can mount him, no problem. Crude comparison, I know, but that's what living in a whorehouse does to people.

Later, we drank a bottle of wine and Astarth advised me how to behave with Jafit.

'Just get drunk,' he said. 'Rave like a banshee. Think female; it helps!'

'I'll try.'

'Sure you will. You'll starve out there in the winter if you don't. Anyway, Jafit likes you. He won't kick you out.'

I had been careful in my buttering up of the patron of this establishment. I had only met him properly twice since my first interview and that was when everyone else was there, when we all ate together. Not oblivious to the extent of my acting ability in respect of the boudoir, I realized it was important to seem indispensible to Jafit, if only for my looks. He always complimented me and I always sparkled with wit and charm in return; I squirm with shame to think about it. As Astarth and I sat by his fire, staring into the flames, sipping our drinks, Astarth said, 'Don't forget the royal house of Maudrah now, will you!' I appreciated all that he meant by that.

'Thank you for your faith in me,' I said. We drank to that.

The summons came next evening. Following Astarth's advice, I consumed an entire bottle of betica in the space of just over an hour. Rihana, Salandril and Lolotea watched me carefully as I did so. None of them felt capable of remarking on it. I was thinking about the few times I'd spoken with Jafit. Of course, I'd studied him keenly on all occasions, but I still couldn't work out what kind of reception I would get from him. He treated his kanene indulgently, like favoured pets. He stroked their hair and pinched their limbs. They did not dislike him. I had learnt, though, that he could deal harshly with anyone who did not perform their duties properly. He always carefully examined any complaints received from the clients, although he didn't believe that the customer was always right. Lolotea said that Jafit could always tell when you were lying to him. Pickled in betica, but able to control movements and voice through years of experience of being in that state, I went to Jafit's office.

There, he offered me another drink and said, 'If I appear to insult you, I don't want you to take it personally, but I suppose you know what to expect by now, don't you?'

I grinned at him helplessly.

'Take me upstairs,' he said.

In my room, he sat down and looked at the table, where I saw a bottle of wine had been left opened next to two glasses. The cork lay beside the bottle. I offered him a drink, which he accepted. When I did not pour myself one, he said, 'Please, join me, Calanthe,' and I had to force down yet another measure of alcohol. I was dressed in a black lace robe that Lolotea had given me. It was virtually transparent. A wide, soft leather belt hung with net and chains swathed my hips. Jafit stared at me with approval. He asked me to undress, which I did.

'You have a warrior's body,' he said.

'I've lived rough for a while,' I admitted.

'I expect you want to be left alone now, huh?'

'What?' He didn't look at me. It was part of the performance.

'Yes,' I said with convincing bitterness. 'I want to be left alone.'

'Why, is no-one good enough for you?' he asked and I looked at him sharply. His eyes warned me to silence before I spoke.

I smiled to myself, tapping the table with idle fingers. 'No, as a matter of fact, they're not,' I agreed.

Jafit nodded appreciatively and for a brief time, we smiled together. 'You're just filth,' he said.

'You think so?'

'I'm going to show you just how much I think so.'

I decided to scream. Jafit nearly laughed. Then he lunged at me. He didn't really hurt me, just pushed me around a little. We ended up on the bed, me struggling, him trying not to laugh at my amateurish lamentations and then, half-way through, forgot what we were supposed to be doing and started enjoying ourselves. I remember saying, 'Why Jafit, you're not so much of a rat as I thought!'

'We all just try to make a living Calanthe,' he answered, 'but you're no kanene, that's for sure. What the hell are you doing here?'

I shrugged. 'Being employed by you, I hope.'

He shook his head. 'Alright. I'm not sure what I can do with you yet, but you're beautiful enough to be given a chance. Just don't fuck up, that's all! Piristil's clientele can be very pernickety.'

'I'll try,' I said, meaning it, surprisingly.

In the morning, Jafit stayed with me for breakfast. I still thought he looked mean. He is dark-skinned and wears his black hair short. I bet he too had rather a colourful history. He dipped hot, buttered muffins in his coffee, and said, 'You're going to be bored a lot of the time, I think.'

'Oh, I've decided to write my life story,' I answered airily.

'Really! As your employer, I think I shall have to demand that you show me every thing you write.'

'And what makes you think my life story is worth reading?'

'Last night,' he answered. 'Your veiled mind. I'm curious about what's going on in there.'

'Mmm, well, talking of veils, Jafit, why are *you* here? Is it just that you've always wanted to be a pimp? Have your realized your life's ambition here in Piristil?'

He laughed good humouredly. 'Why are any of us here? It's a bolt-hole isn't it? I hope you're not going to record any of this conversation for posterity.'

'Not if you'd rather I didn't,' I lied.

'The Gelaming want to ask me a few questions ...' he said darkly, which was all he had to say.

I nodded to show my understanding. 'Ah well, come to think of it, I suppose Fallsend is quite a charming place to retire in,' I said.

It is late in the day when the summons comes. A young Har stumbles in through the broken door, tripping over the rubble; bricks, cloth, bones. Zack and I are eating dogmeat that we have roasted in the fire. Our companions hurl gentle obscenities at the newcomer. His face reddens. He says, 'The Lion sent me.' That shuts us all up. We are all thinking, 'Have I transgressed at all? Have I?' It is rare that Wraxilan bothers with any Har save his own elite.

'Which of you is Cal?' asks the messenger in a brave voice. He is one of Wraxilan's body-servants. We both envy and despise him.

'What do you want with him?' I ask.

'A message . . .'

'I'll take it!' Zack springs up and snatches the rolled missive from the young Har's hand. The messenger protests, but Zack just pushes him aside. He unrolls the note.

'But it is for the yellow-haired alone!' squeals the messenger.

'What does it say?' I ask, my body heavy with dread.

Zack makes a sneering, angry sound and throws the note to me.

'What does it say?' our companions ask, all leaning forward. I stand up.

'That easy, is it?' Zack asks coldly. 'He calls, you go. That easy?'

I am silent. I have been summoned, that's all, but I am silent. I buckle on my belt, which carries my knives and darts. Zack picks up a bone from the floor. 'See this?' He says. 'Dog-meat! Ha!' he throws the bone into the fire, where it sizzles for a while. We stare at each other.

'See you later,' I say, and walk away. There is no sound from those sprawled around the fire, but I am quite sure, once I am out of earshot, they will begin to talk.

The Lion of Oomar has made his headquarters inside an old supermarket. I have never thought it a good choice, but apparently the liquor shelves were well stocked when his company moved in. A warehouse and storerooms at the back are the private living quarters of the elite. I am shown within. The Lion is there with a bunch of sleek Hara, all sitting round a fire. They are laughing together. Wraxilan does not look up when I approach, but he knows I'm there, alright. He says, 'Take him to the inner room', and the Har who is my guide, grabs hold of my arm and drags me off. It is most unnecessary. I am locked in an unlit cell. I sit down on the floor to wait. He is not that cruel. He comes very soon. He comes in alone and sits with his back against the wall opposite me.

'I am glad you came,' he says, as if I'd had a choice. I say nothing. He is *magnificent, in the way that all conquering heroes are magnificent; intimidating, confident, strong. 'Give me your knife,' he says and I comply. It is not my best blade, however. Wraxilan makes a small cut in his palm, holds out his hand to show me. 'See this, Cal,' he says. 'This is yours.'*

'My blade? My wound?'

'No; your blood. Here, take it.' Warily, I put my hand in his. He squeezes it. 'Outside, the shamen are waiting. The ritual will not take long.'

'Hey!' I pull my hand away, hug it to my chest. 'What are you talking about? What ritual?'

'Don't be afraid, Cal. Don't you remember? I marked you a long, long time ago. The Nahir-Nuri of the north were here some days ago. They are pleased with my progress. Soon, I shall have my caste level raised again. You know what that means? Soon, I may activate the real magic, the one we're not that sure about yet. Can we conceive new life within our own bodies? That will be the test, won't it! If we're wrong, then we might as well give up and leave what's left of the world to Mankind. It is the test, Cal. I need a vessel. The best. I need a consort. The best. I need you.'

During this speech, I have backed right up against the wall, trying to push my body through solid concrete. I have never felt such fear. I know he means what he says. The Lion always means what he says. True magic. No-one has achieved it yet. If it is possible at all, it may kill me. We know so little. We have never been women. These things are mysteries to us. Trial and error. We may be wrong.

'Come on now,' Wraxilan says in a reasonable voice. He stands up and wipes his hands on his chest. 'Cal, come on!'

'No.' It is such a small sound. I don't think Wraxilan believes he has heard it at first.

'What?!'

My voice becomes stronger. 'I said no, Wraxilan.' I too stand up.

'Do you know what you are saying? I am your leader, Cal. You can't just say no! I've decided your future.'

'No, you haven't.' I back towards the door, still nursing the hand that has touched his blood, as if it were me that had been cut.

'Don't you understand what I'm saying?'

'Yes. I understand.'

'Then ...'

'I don't want to do it.'

'I could have you killed.'

'I know.' For some reason there are tears in my eyes. We fight like men, we weep like women. 'I know.'

I reach the door. There is a brief, electric silence. He can now give the order if he wants to. He can shout, 'Kill him!' but he doesn't. He says, 'If you will not agree to this, you know you must leave, don't you.'

Banishment, in these times, is not as trivial as it sounds. It is important, very important, to have the protection of a strong tribe behind you. Life is a gamble, dangerous, deadly. I nod my head. I understand.

'It is your choice,' he says in a soft, venomous voice. If he could have said different words, if he could have . . . but no. We are Wraeththu. All that lies dead in the world of men. I walk away. By the time I reach Zack and the others, I am weeping openly. I am afraid of the Outside. I tell Zack we have to leave. He says nothing, but gathers up our belongings. Within an hour, Wraxilan's guards have burst into the ruin that is our home.

'To the perimeter, you!' one of them snarls at me and swipes me across the shoulder with the barrel of his gun. Zack puts his arm around me. We walk away and the guards follow us to the edge of the safe zone. 'No Uigenna will take you in,' they say. 'Get going! Now!' They fire at our feet. Humiliated, we have to trot away. No Uigenna. We are unthrist; tribeless. We go to Seel, of course. The Unneah know more of the ways of peace than the Uigenna. It is not that bad. Sometimes at night, I think of the Lion. I see his face. One day, when I am older, I might recognize that expression as being the one of hurt, of rejection, but not for a long while yet. Throughout my life, this scenario shall be replayed several times. In Terzian I loved the Lion. An exorcism? Maybe, but it is not over yet . . .

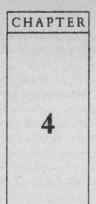

CHAPTER

4

Discovery of the Big Cat
'And in the idle darkness comes the bite
Of all the burning serpents of remorse;
Dreams seethe, and fretful infelicities
Are swarming in my overburdened soul.'
Maurice Bearing (from the Russian
of A. Pushkin) Remembrance

I have been writing now for over a week. I find it cleansing, refreshing; it is good for me. Perhaps I have grown stronger because now I am facing the biggest, blackest door in my mind and am prepared to open it a little. I must continue to heal myself by facing the past. Lolotea thinks he has discovered my secret and that it is Galhea and all that happened there, but the truth is my real secrets come from a time way before I'd ever heard of Terzian. The biggest of them remains yet undiscovered, unspoken. Once, in Galhea, Cobweb, who is a true mystic, had a vision. He spoke these words; 'I shall be left alone and there will be a time of glass, like shattering, like shards of light, and the past shall come back like a shimmering veil … I shall be left alone, but not for long …' At the time, I thought he uttered those words for himself, but now I know better. It was spoken for me.

Once Jafit knew about my desire to write in my spare time, he presented me with utensils for the task. The pen has my name on it; how sweet. I think he must have had a glowing report about me from my first customer. It was luck rather than effort. He was yet another refugee from Megalithica. He asked me to twist his neck. I barely paused before obliging. Jafit obviously considers it safer to use me for chaitra rather than pelcia. Perhaps he guesses my inability to accept pain gladly. Part of me dreads that I may come to actually like it, like Astarth. I didn't tell the Har I'd once lived with Terzian, although his name was mentioned. Terzian's name is always mentioned when speaking of Megalithica, even after all this time. Terzian was good to me. I must take care not to abuse his memory.

Last night, I was woken up by a terrible noise in the house. By the time I'd sat up in bed, it had faded away. I was still and silent, straining to hear more, wondering if it had just been part of a dream. Lolotea's room is next to mine. I thought about banging on the wall. Had he heard it too? But perhaps it was just another of the kanene entertaining a client. Although Jafit prefers most of them to be kicked out before we go to sleep, special customers sometimes stay all night. I lay awake for a few minutes, listening. The sound did not come again. It had sounded like an animal in pain; hair-raising. One single, desperate wail, cut off. The darkness around me seemed very thick, almost breathing. Outside, it was no longer raining, but I could hear loud dripping sounds in the yard. Whatever water fell there must be black, or red.

It was colder the next day. Winter is approaching fast. Soon, I hope, the cheerless appearance of Fallsend shall be covered with a cosmetic blanket of snow and ice. It had taken me a week to get round to writing again; I'd been rather preoccupied.

When I first woke up, I'd forgotten about the eerie howl in the night. I took my breakfast into Lolotea's room and we started some idle conversation about going into the town later on.

'By Aghama, but it's cold!' Lolotea said. 'It's enough to freeze the howl in a dog's throat!' That reminded me.

'That reminds me, Teah,' I said. 'Last night, I was woken up by the most godawful noise. Is the place haunted or something? Did you hear it?'

'What kind of noise?' he asked, somewhat too warily, I thought.

'Well, it was rather like the complaint you might make if you'd discovered someone had just cut your throat. You know, kind of spooky, and, well, *despairing*.'

Lolotea laughed. 'How melodramatic! Can't say I heard it and no, the place isn't haunted. Must have been a dream.'

'I'm sure it wasn't.'

Lolotea shrugged. I felt he was hiding something.

Strangely enough, nobody else appeared to have heard it either.

'Probably just a cat in the yard.' Ezhno said. 'Why let it bother you?'

But, by this time, my senses were alerted and I wouldn't let it rest. I'd not lived this long in the wilds, in war-torn cities and wastelands not to recognize a Harish scream when I heard one. I don't like to be in a situation where things are kept hidden from me. It's dangerous. Because of that, it was no coincidence that my feet led me in the direction of those shuttered rooms I'd seen above the kitchens. Piristil is a confusing place to explore. I kept finding myself in dead ends off corridors that led nowhere. Retracing my steps several times, I eventually emerged into a passage that had barred windows on the righthand side, looking out over the yard. This was more like it. Several of doors I tried were locked. I turned a corner to the left. Here, the passage was darker. I came across another door, almost by accident, in the shadows. I reached for the handle, turned it. It was unlocked. Just as I was about to push it open, a voice shouted, 'Hey!' and a heavy hand landed on my shoulder. Ducking, I pulled away. Behind me, a tall and impressively muscled Har seemed to fill the passageway.

'What are you doing here?' he demanded, in a manner that was unmistakably hostile.

'I live here,' I said, suitably affronted.

'Not in this wing you don't. Now get out!'

'Why? What's going on in here?' I did not expect enlightenment and was not disappointed.

The Har waved an enormous fist in my face, quite menacingly. 'Out!' he growled.

I stood my ground for a moment, before walking back the way I'd come. This branch of investigation was obviously proving fruitless.

I went looking for Astarth. He was in the kitchens, menu in hand, supervising the dinner arrangements.

'I've just been accosted!' I said. He raised an eyebrow and politely listened to my outraged explanation; I know how to act when I need to.

'I'm sorry that happened, Calanthe,' he said, 'but I should have warned you. Don't wander about up there.'

'Why not?'

'That's Jafit's business.'

'Oh, a house secret!' I cried, as if delighted. 'How marvellous!'

'Don't go meddling,' Astarth said. 'Jafit will not be pleased.'

What was behind the locked doors? I did not sense danger, not exactly. It was just another flavour of the house; Piristil of soot and perfume and forlorn, leftover food. The corridors were cold here. Someone howling in the night. A sound like an animal, becoming clearer in my mind all the time. It was not despair; it was anger. I would find out why eventually.

Kruin was my second customer, and one destined to become a regular. The first time he set foot in my room, I could tell that half of him hates coming to this place. He was uneasy, giving off whiffs of profound guilt and self-loathing. I wondered what he wanted of me. I think I warmed to him because he looks Varrish; the same ropy, muscled look, tawny hair, restlessness. 'I am Natawni,' he told me. The name was familiar; a Jaddayoth tribe.

'You'll wear a hole in my carpet,' I said. He ceased striding up and down.

'I have to explain before we ... well, in my tribe, some aspects of aruna are forbidden to us.'

'The delights of pelcia and chaitra? Don't worry. They are forbidden to just about every tribe.'

He shook his head in irritation. 'No.'

'Then please explain.'

'It is because of our god,' he said hesitantly. 'The Skylording. Like us, he is the two in one; bisexual. His priests, the Skyles speak with Him often and He has decreed that for the warriors of the tribe, there should be a special code. Our affinity with each principle, either male or female, must change with the seasons. Thus, in spring and summer, we are female, and on the cusp of the changing season, the procreation of Harlings takes place as our sexuality shifts towards the male. For the autumn and winter, we are masculine. It is the curse of the warrior caste! We must not deviate from our decreed affinity lest we harm the blood of our children. The other Hara of the tribe respect this code; they would never transgress it. Why should they? It is not their problem. It is early winter here. I am in the masculine phase. I desire warmth. I desire ... submission ...'

'You desire to be soume,' I finished for him.

He smiled timidly. 'Of course, you find nothing unusual in that. Don't mock me, Calanthe! The code of my tribe runs very deep within me. By this transgression, I taint my love of the Skylording. I risk the lives of future Harlings.'

I doubt it, I thought, but kept it quiet. 'You must be very weak-willed, Kruin,' I said. 'I've seen you here often.'

He bristled visibly. 'I'm a long way from home. I have no friends in Fallsend. I do not have to justify myself to you!'

'No, of course not.' I shoved a drink in his hand. 'Here. How come you're in Fallsend anyway?' I sat him on my bed and began to unlace his jacket. The workmanship was exceedingly fine, the leather soft as living skin.

'Trade,' he said. 'I come from Orligia, a town in southern Natawni. Once a year, we bring leatherwork to the market in Fallsend. That way, we pick up trade that might otherwise be missed if we operated only in Jaddayoth. The Emunah export to Fallsend, but of course, we would lose a lot of profit using them as brokers.'

'How many of you are there?'

'Four. The others don't know I come here. They think I visit a Har in some corner of the town, but they don't suspect it might be a kanene. If they did, they'd draw their own conclusions, of course.'

It was clear why Jafit had sent Kruin to me, for he wasn't seeking the ultimate in pain and repletion, but merely aruna in its simplest and most pleasing form. I took delight in his lean, hard body, which is how I prefer them. Lolotea and Astarth were sleek, it is true, but they had a certain *softness* about them, which came from their easy existence. Kruin had warm skin. His limbs were supple and our melding was harmonious. His tribe are also called the People of the Bones. He wore thorns of bone in his ears. I learned he was anxious to return home before the snows became too deep. 'Jaddayoth can be a harsh place in Winter,' he said. Before he left me that night, he gave me one of his earrings, placing it in my ear himself. Half-way through the night, it woke me up because it had happily burrowed itself into the side of my neck. That was the first time blood stained my bedsheets; hopefully the last!

We leave debts in every town. We are notorious. Our lives have become a sort of daring, a desire to tempt Fate. Perhaps we feel immortal. The Unneah are far behind us now; we had little in common with them. Hara are looking for us, some to settle scores, some to ask for our services. We have a lot of money because of that. Zack grows more beautiful every day. He blooms like a strong, dark-petalled flower on a grave; what sustains him, sleekens him, is probably corrupt. I am half afraid of him. He is too wild, too reckless, too ephemeral. Flowers only bloom for a short time, don't they? It is night-time and this city is damp. Yellow lights flicker, but don't dispel the shadows. There are noises in every alley. We are armed with knives and guns; we are sleek. There is a red light above the door to a bar, lending an alien cast to those that stand beneath it. They part to let us pass within. The place is packed with Hara, the air dense with smoke. Much noise; music. Zack sits down at a table and begins to clean his nails with the point of a knife. I go to the bar. Someone speaks to me there. They tell me something important. I give Zack a beer and tell him we have enemies in this place. He shrugs and smiles. We drink. We talk of where we shall go next. Zack's teeth are very white and feral in the livid light. Someone comes to our table. Zack doesn't stop smiling, although we alert each other with our eyes. There is a conversation and, during this conversation, I pull out a gun. There is a shot, the ripping of flesh and bone, a red spray. Those seated behind us make noises of disgust and annoyance, as the body falls across their table; glasses, liquor flying all over the place. Everyone is looking at us, some smiling, some shocked and, inevitably, some angry. People have died before in this bar. What I've done is not that unusual but Zack still thinks we should leave. I agree. There are too many of the dead Har's friends here. We walk to the door and, once outside, begin to run. We run through the wet, dark streets. Zack is laughing out loud. We become aware of footsteps behind us, running, echoing. The city seems empty. A car prowls by emptily; black, silent and shining. We do not know this place, but we are not afraid. We run. And . . .

They corner us at the end of a dismal, filthy alley. There are trashcans, boxes everywhere; a dead dog with an open mouth. Zack turns panting. A distant light reflects off the blade of his raised knife. The wall before us is high, but it is our only way out. Zack puts the knife between his teeth. 'On my shoulders!' he mumbles, past the blade. 'Hurry!' I tuck my gun into my belt and scramble up his body. His muscles are trembling. 'Hurry, for fuck's sake, Cal! They're nearly here!'

'OK!' My hands curl over the top of the wall. It is wet and slimy. I don't feel strong enough to pull myself up, as if all my strength is draining out of my feet. Should we stay and fight? We will die, almost certainly, but can we escape? Is there enough time, is there?

'Cal, for God's sake!' Zack is angry. He pushes me up and I lie on my belly on the wall. There is a clatter. My gun drops down on the other side.

'Oh, fuck it!'

'Cal?' Zack's voice is low. I look up the alley we have just come down. A gang of Hara is approaching. They are now only feet away from us. They have stopped running. Their breath is steaming. They are so silent. Then one of them begins to move.

Zack turns his face up to me. 'Pull me up!' he says and reaches towards me. There is no time. I have no weapon. There is not enough time. 'Cal!' One by one, behind him, the predators begin to move. Some of them are smiling. They look so furtive. 'Pull me up! For fuck's sake, Cal, pull me up! What's wrong with you?!' There is disbelief in Zack's voice, a certain crack, a certain realization that I cannot, will not help him. 'Cal!'

I stand on the wall. It is just seconds, but seconds that pass like hours. Everything is so slow. I am turning. Below me, on the other side of the wall, is safety and another alley. Just seconds. I am turning, so slowly, steam-light, neon, damp, viscous walls. A distant shout. I am turning. Noises below me are the howls of the pack.

'Cal!'

At last, desperation. He is afraid. I love you, Zack. I pull myself up, to jump.

'You fucking bastard! Cal!'

He can't believe I'm turning away. But then, he does believe. I feel something hit my arm. A brick. A dead dog. A curse. Who knows? I have heard many curses. I land on the other side of the wall, closing my ears to the sounds; the sickening, dull sounds of flesh under attack. I land on feet and hands and my arm buckles. I look. I am wet and warm. It is blood; Zack's knife in my arm, to the hilt. With a sad, desperate cry, I wrench it from the flesh. I can feel nothing. I stumble, I start to run. I keep on running.

We thought we were immortal. Now we are both dead ...

Jafit sent for me the next day. 'Kruin speaks well of you,' he said, sitting behind his desk, looking authoritative.

'Perhaps I've found my vocation then.'

Jafit smiled thinly. 'Sit down, Calanthe,' he said. I did so. He leaned forward over his desk. 'Now, Astarth tells me you've been asking one or two awkward questions, nosing around in places where you shouldn't be.'

'Well, I ... er ...' I raised my hands in vexation, pulled an apologetic face.

'Hmph. Quite the curious cat, aren't you!'

The fateful proverb paraded before my mind's eye. 'Mysteries intrigue me, perhaps. But if you want to rap my knuckles, Jafit, please go ahead.'

'Does that mean you won't try to find out what's up there now?'

'I didn't say that! What's the matter? Don't you trust me?'

He laughed. 'Trust you? That's a good one! We're both Hara of maturity, Calanthe. Is there a place for trust in this day and age?'

'If there is, it is certainly south of Thaine,' I said.

'Quite so!' Jafit agreed. 'No, I don't trust you, Calanthe, but I'll let you in on the secret. You've been here long enough. Anyway, it's not that terrible a thing.'

'I'm all ears.'

'Drink?'

'If you like.'

He went to his cupboard. 'There *is* a Har up there, you're right,' he said, filling two glasses with betica. 'Want to know why I keep him locked up? OK here.' I took the glass. 'Three years ago, I travelled to Meris, a town in Emunah. It is not a journey I make often, but some merchandise is only available to us inside Jaddayoth. Astarth had given me a list this long,' he made an appropriate gesture, 'of things to buy. Now, as you know, slavery is outlawed everywhere that the Gelaming's claws can burrow into, but if there is going to be such a thing, Emunah is the place to find it. I got wind of a black market slave auction. My contact was going along and he asked me if I wanted to take a look. I was curious. I went with him. Now, normally, I'd never even consider accruing kanene in that way. Slaves are more trouble than they're worth. They rarely provide a good service, but ...'

'Ah, something out of the ordinary?'

Jafit smiled and sat down again. 'You could say that. This one particular Har ... I'd never seen anything like him. Obvious that he had Kalamah blood, but there was something more. Beauty didn't come into it.'

'How romantic!' I said. 'Of course, you bought him.'

Jafit nodded, smiling. 'Cleaned me out, naturally! Astarth was most put out! I came back to Piristil with nothing but a slave.'

'So what went wrong? Why the bars?'

'Hmm, well, it was a nightmare from the start! I wasn't surprised that he was unco-operative — that was only to be expected — but his ferocity and sheer madness, that was not something any of us were prepared for. The first client I sent him barely escaped with his life. He lost an eye!' Jafit shook his head miserably at the recollection. 'Could have been nasty, more than that, money completely wasted. Then Astarth came up with an answer. We would use the slave's violent nature as an attraction. Some Hara pay me dearly for that kind of sport. And here was a kanene who did not have to act! His name is Panthera, by the way. I sell him for the fight.'

'And he still has to be locked in?'

'God, I should say so! He escaped three times in the beginning. Three times I had to pay trackers to bring him back. In every instance, they barely succeeded. Panthera is half-Kalamah and half-Ferike. Because of that, he possesses brains, stealth and cunning to an exceptional degree. The Har you discovered in the corridor up there is a Mojag. I have three of them on my payroll. Mojags are the most fearless, warlike tribe of Jaddayoth. Only they can keep Panthera in Piristil.'

'So, an insane beauty kept in chains,' I said. 'It really *is* romantic.'

'There is little romance about Panthera,' Jafit replied drily. 'He is sullen, uncommunicative and vicious … but lovely. Some Hara pay me just for the privilege of looking at him.'

'Well thanks for telling me, Jafit,' I said 'It was a great story.'

'Don't thank me yet,' he replied. 'There was a reason. The staff won't go near Panthera. Astarth and the other kanene see to his needs. They don't like it but that's just tough. Consider yourself in, Calanthe. If any one can handle that wildcat, I think it's you.'

'From whore to housemaiden in a single step! Is this a promotion?'

Jafit smiled without humour. 'You'd better meet him,' he said. 'I'll take you now.'

Nobody had ever created a pedestal for Panthera, but from the moment I first saw him, I created one there and then out of pure thought-form, and put him right on it. Wreaththu have spawned many legends. I remember the ones I've known; the Varrish Cobweb, the Kakkahaar viper Ulaume and, of course, Pellaz, Tigron of the Gelaming. Men had their goddesses, women named as the most beautiful and potent creatures that god could create. Wraeththu surpass all that. In them, beauty is complete because it is both male and female; the way it should be. Jafit knocked on Panthera's door and one of the Mojags opened it to us. I could see the other two sitting at a table engrossed in some kind of board-game.

'Well, there you are,' Jafit said. 'Feast your eyes on that.'

Panthera sat apart from the others, straight backed, on a stool, looking down into the yard through the bars of the window. The room was very light, tastefully decorated, pale hangings on the walls, soft, pale carpet underfoot. Panthera turned and examined us carefully for a moment, as a cat may examine a movement in the corner of a room. His green eyes were as cold as stone, his wild, thick hair tied up, his shoulders bare and bruised. I noted that his hands clutched each other in his lap. He was chained to the wall. He was, as had been implied, incredibly lovely.

'Well, there you have it,' Jafit said, 'A Wraeththu legend.' Panthera turned away quickly. 'How's he been today?' Jafit asked the Mojags, Huge things, they were, magnificent and deadly.

'Quiet, I'd say. Quiet,' One of them said and the other two laughed.

'What's all that?' Jafit enquired, pointing to Panthera's bruised shoulders. The Mojags shrugged. They did not think it was any of their business. 'Here, let me see that.' Jafit went and put one tentative hand on Panthera's arm. Panthera did not resist. He ignored Jafit. Jafit pulled the material of Panthera's robe down to reveal his back. He made an angry noise. 'Look at this!' he said. 'This is too much! What do they think they pay me for?'

I sauntered forward to have a look. It seemed like Panthera had been mauled by a pack of wolves. Some days ago, too, by the look of the damage. The bruises were yellowing, the scratches dark and crusty.

'Well that's somebody who won't be coming here again!' Jafit decided.

'What do you expect us to do about it?' one of the Mojags asked gruffly, sensing criticism of their work. Jafit shook his head. He brushed the comment away with a brusque wave of his hand. Panthera looked as if he was on another planet for all the notice he took of what was going on.

'I'll let you rest for a while,' Jafit told him. Panthera still did not respond. I looked on in amazement. 'Panthera, this is Calanthe,' Jafit said as if speaking to an imbecile. 'He's going to help look after you.' Panthera actually looked at me. His disdain was withering. He sighed through his nose and turned away again. 'Come on, Calanthe,' Jafit said. 'You can start your duties in a day or two.'

Outside the room, I said, 'Jafit, that isn't slavery. That's a life sentence in hell.'

'Oh come on, everywhere in the world is somebody's sentence, somebody's hell,' Jafit replied equably. 'Don't be squeamish Cal, it could be you sitting there. Count your blessings.'

'Maybe' I said. 'And the name's Calanthe, nothing else.'

Jafit smiled. We walked away.

It could be me sitting there … A sobering thought. I really should not care about anybody else but myself. Why put myself in danger? What would it be like to be chained to a wall? That night a Har came to my room seeking chaitra. I gave it to him alright. His was the miserable face of someone given all the gifts of God, who was throwing them back without gratitude. His was the face of perfection turned to corruption. His was the face of Fallsend. I knew it couldn't be the Har who'd rearranged the flesh of Panthera's back, but it helped to pretend it was. He left me a chastened creature. I lay on the bed and smiled. There were no gifts for me that night.

Red sand. Red pony. I ride away from those that succoured me. I am healed — in body. The desert has power; Mankind has barely touched it. It is soothing. After a few days, I ride into a one-horse peasant town. I have a feeling something will happen here. It does. I see him, framed in a doorway. Peasant boy, all hair and eyes, but such eyes! They know so little here. They do not know what I am. I watch him constantly. Here is beauty, I think. Yes, here it is. A healing loveliness, but human. 'I am Pellaz,' he tells me and he smiles; a nervous, bright smile of the uncorrupted. I am death, little child. I will lie to you. I cannot let you know me because I want you. I ride through the mist on a steamy afternoon, through red mud on a red pony, stolen money in my pocket, a stolen smile on my face. I ride towards him and he tells me his name. The first, fateful magic. Now I will have you, little one. It is so easy. I steal him away, like the money, like the pony, into the wilderness, that is not just a waste of stone and sand, but a wilderness of the spirit because he is leaving the world he knows. He looks back and I think, he will go back. He has realized, and he will go back. But he merely sighs and follows me. There is something powerful and untrained inside him. He must become Har — and quickly. Seel has a stronghold in the desert mountains. I shall take him there. He shall be made Wraeththu. Then he will be mine. Healing balm, healing feelings; his innocence shall cleanse me and make me whole. I'll wake up and the world shall be new and my smile shall come from the inside, black memories forgotten. Please don't let him see me kill.

'Tell me about Jaddayoth,' I said to Kruin.

He smiled. 'It wouldn't mean anything to you.'

'How do you know that?'

He shrugged. 'You're a kanene. Part of the Wraeththu rubbish heap. There are no kanene in Jaddayoth. No Fallsend.'

I was stung. 'You know nothing about me!'

'Only what I need to know.'

'Fuck you, Natawni. Fuck you!' He laughed and I stood up, pulled aside the curtain to my window. Across the yard, a yellow light burned in Panthera's window. 'Look at that,' I said. I felt Kruin's warmth before he touched me. He kissed my neck. 'Look at that.'

He looked. 'What?'

'The light. Do you know what they keep in there?'

'Yes; doesn't everybody?'

'I'm not part of that.'

'You don't have to be here.'

'That's where you are wrong my friend, I do.'

He sighed and went to lie down again on the bed, pouring himself a glass of wine. 'I don't care, Calanthe. I don't want to know.'

I threw some more logs on the fire. All the light in the room was orange-red. Kruin didn't want to know about me because he despised me. It was I that broke his tribal code; not him. The scapegoat. Rubbish. God, I shall not stay here long, I thought.

'Tell me about Maudrah?' I said.

'What about Maudrah?'

'Ariaric.' I was thinking of Terzian again.

'You wouldn't like Maudrah,' Kruin said. 'It's a gaunt, severe place. It's people are gaunt and severe. They have no sense of humour.'

'Then I will feel very at home there. I'm rapidly losing my sense of humour!'

'Stick to fantasising about the big cats in this place, if I were you! Forget the Lion!'

'What do you mean?' (Why did I go cold?)

'Ariaric. Panthera; you know. Panthera's half-Kalamah; his name comes from panther. They call Ariaric the Lion ...'

I did not hear what else he said. My mind was singing with white noise. When I came out of it, Kruin was saying, 'Soon I shall be going home, thank God!'

It was a coincidence, surely ... *surely*. I shivered.

'I wish you'd known me before, Kruin,' I said.

* * *

Later, I woke up from a terrible dream. I was standing before a huge dam, which began to crack. I knew I was going to drown, but the dam was so huge and I was so small. There was nowhere I could run to. The flood-gates to the past have been opened. It has found me. I never thought I could think of Pell, but I have. I have written his name and our beginning. Something I have been afraid to admit, but now I will; they are watching me constantly. The Gelaming. In daytime, I rarely think that, but at night ... I can almost *feel them*. I am not afraid of Pellaz, but I know I would run if he appeared before me. It was all so long ago. Now he is Tigron and I committed murder because I lost him. No-one here knows this. No-one ever shall. Perhaps it's all part of an absurd dream I once had. Pellaz; we knew each other once.

Morning. I awoke with a thick head and Astarth ripping aside my curtains to let a brutal light into the room. 'Come on, get up!' he said. 'What's this? Two empty betica bottles? You're disgusting, Calanthe! Come on; up! Get dressed! We have work to do!'

'What time is it?' I croaked, squinting at my clock. 'Jesus! It's the middle of the fucking night, Astarth! What the hell are you doing here?'

'Language!' Astarth corrected mildly. 'Zoo duty. Come on.'

My turn to help wait on Panthera. It woke me up a little. Still putting on my clothes, I followed Astarth who was stalking down the corridor. He carried a tray of food. 'The staff are afraid of Panthera,' he told me, when I caught up with him.

'Why's that? Blacks their eyes does he?'

Astarth laughed. 'No, worse than that. He spits out very convincing curses.'

'And as we despicable kanene consider ourselves cursed already, his words cannot harm us, eh?'

'Something like that. Hardfaced creatures, aren't we.'

'I feel honoured!'

'Don't be. Panthera will hate you as he hates all of us.'

We turned the corner into the long, shuttered corridor.

'What do you think of him, Astarth?' I asked.

Astarth raised a thoughtful eyebrow. 'He's beautiful. What else can I say? If you look like that, being conceited, arrogant and insulting doesn't really matter, does it!'

No pity on Astarth's part, obviously.

The Mojags opened the door to us. Two of them were going off duty. 'Don't envy you today,' said the third. 'We've not dared let him loose yet. He's got killing eyes today!'

'Oh, come now Outher,' Astarth said lightly, 'surely you're not afraid of our little pussy cat.'

'See this?' Outher said to me, displaying a splendid scar on his neck.

'It's not fear; it's respect.' I smiled politely.

'OK, take a break, Outher,' Astarth commanded. 'Calanthe and I can handle it.'

There were curtains around the bed, blowing softly in a cold, light breeze. One of the windows was open. The bars beyond it were glistening with ice. I could see my breath. The room was freezing. Astarth pulled the curtains apart. On the bed Panthera lay spreadeagled, tied by ankles and wrists to the bedposts. It was not the most elegant of positions. His skin was dead white.

'I thought Jafit said he was going to let Panthera rest for a while,' I said.

'He has! Panthera has to earn his keep too, you know,' Astarth replied, rubbing his hands. 'I'll get a fire going. God! It's like hell in here. Shut the window, will you.'

It was stuck fast with ice. It had been a while since I had used any of my special abilities. I thought 'warm' and was just successful enough to shift it. Standing back, wiping my hands, I felt a soft, hesitant mind touch. 'You've taken the cold away …' I looked sharply behind me. Outher had gone out. Astarth was busying himself at the grate. I looked at the bed, straight into the direct gaze of a pair of green eyes. 'The others have forgotten how to do this. You're not one of them, are you?' I flicked a quick glance towards Astarth. It was obvious he had sensed nothing of this silent conversation. To me it was like having someone confirm that, yes, I was alive — at least not brain dead. I had thought my ability to communicate in this uniquely harish manner had rotted through disuse, but apparently not. It reinforced my views about the pedestal. Panthera, I could love you.

Astarth wandered back to the bed, brushing wood dust off his hands. 'OK, big cat, I'm going to untie you now. Just don't try anything stupid.'

Panthera didn't answer. He was still just staring at me. I went over and untied his wrists. The flesh was like corpse flesh; icy. Half his long fingernails were broken off, raggedly, viciously. Once free, he sat up and rubbed his wrists. I realized he must have been tied up like that all night, yet how detached from it he seemed. As if it was nothing. Astarth handed him a robe which he wrapped around himself. Without a word, he went into the bathroom and, presently, I heard water running.

'He'll have a bath now,' Astarth said.

'Does he ever ... speak?'

'Sometimes. He's so arrogant, so high and mighty. It's not our fault he's here, is it! Some of us tried to help him, you know, make friends at first, but he didn't want to know. He's happy to stay in his tower of ice.'

'Perhaps he'd be insane if he wasn't.' I looked towards the bathroom. 'I think I'll try and talk to him.'

Astarth laughed. 'You're wasting your time,' he said. 'We've got to clean up in here. Don't be long.'

Panthera lay back in his bath, facing the door. His eyes were closed.

'They are not true Wraeththu here,' he said at once, again through direct contact to the brain.

I sat down on the edge of the bed. 'So how do you know I'm so different?' I asked aloud.

Panthera opened his eyes. 'They do talk a lot you know. I know all about you. You've got them guessing. I know you want to leave here.'

'Can't you speak aloud?'

'It is dangerous. You'll know why when you understand what I have to say. I knew you'd be sent in here eventually. I've been waiting. You shouldn't confide in Lolotea, Calanthe, you really shouldn't.'

I didn't comment. There was nothing I'd told Lolotea that I didn't want anyone else to know.

'Get me out of here, Calanthe . . .' A silver arrow of thought.

'What? Are you mad?'

'Not at all. I've thought about it very carefully. I'm not going to die here. I've tried every other way of escaping. I need help from the outside now.'

'You can get lost!' I said, standing up. He *was* mad.

'No', he said silently. 'I can't. That's why I need help, you fool. You are leaving eventually anyway. You're a Varr, Calanthe. You can get me out.' He closed his eyes once more. 'Come back. Talk to me.'

'You've forgotten how to talk, I think.'

Panthera speaks mostly with his eyes. I knew I'd help him. He knew it too. It was something that had been subliminally decided from the moment I first saw him.

'One more thing,' he said. 'It will interest you to know; my family will pay highly for my safe return to them.' He smiled. 'Until we meet again, Calanthe.' He slid under the water, all his hair floating around him like weed, his eyes open, staring up through the water.

I went through the door. 'Goddam!' I said. 'Goddam!'

'I didn't hear him answering you', Astarth said smugly.

'Oh, he whispered!'

Astarth laughed. 'Oh dear! Got to you has it? We've all been through it, Calanthe. We've all wanted him. He has that power.'

'And where are your powers Astarth?' I asked.

There was a silence. Astarth uncovered the tray of food. 'There is a price to pay for everything,' he said.

CHAPTER

5

The Beginning of Plans

'Tell me:
Which is the way I take;
Out of what door do I go,
Where and to whom?'

Theodore Reethke, The Flight

I could have told Jafit, of course. I could have gone straight to his office and said, 'Guess what, Panthera has asked me to help him escape!' and, no doubt, we'd have both laughed about it. There were two reasons why I didn't do that. The first was that I hated what I was having to do to earn money, and Panthera had mentioned a substantial reward. The second was that I thought it would help me considerably to be in the company of a native Jaddayothite when I first went there. The fact that Panthera was irresistably lovely had nothing at all to do with it. It would not be an easy thing to accomplish though. Panthera was guarded night and day. We'd need horses, money ... Someone outside Piristil. Now then, who did I know who was also a native of Jaddayoth, who had horses and money and who was planning to return home soon? Kruin. I'd have to start working on him, and fast.

That afternoon, I went into Fallsend with Lolotea and Flounah. My mind was buzzing with plans. Lolotea said I was preoccupied. 'What's the matter?' he asked.

'I know,' Founah said darkly. I looked at him quickly. He smiled. 'It's Panthera, isn't it? It bothered me too at first. At least I live this life by choice!'

I smiled carefully. Flounah nodded to himself. He understood quite a lot. We took wine together in a small inn near the market.

Lolotea went off to buy himself some Gimrah cheese. Flounah glared at the passersby through the window, taking small, bird-like sips of his wine.

'So, tell me,' I said, 'what's it like in Maudrah at this time of year?'

Flounah grimaced. 'Cold. The weather is the one thing that Ariaric has no control over.'

'Ah yes,' I said casually, 'Ariaric. He sounds a fascinating character. What is it they call him? The Lion ... or something?'

'The Lion of Oomadrah, yes. He is thought of as a god ... lucky for him ...'

Suddenly, I didn't want to hear any more. It was too much of a coincidence, that was all. How many self-styled leaders of Wraeththu tribes might identify themselves with the king of the beasts? Many. I broke quickly into Flounah's conversation, not wanting to hear anything that might confirm or deny my suspicions. 'Why can't you go back there?' This was, of course, breaking the Piristil tradition, but Flounah didn't appear to object.

'What makes you think I want to?' he said.

'Well, working in Piristil is hardly a worthy way to spend your life.'

'No, of course it isn't! Let's just say I'm licking my wounds here. Maudrah is not for me. I wanted to get away more than had to. In the summer I intend to head west, maybe south-west to Almagabra. I need money.' I could sympathize with that. 'Hara like Lolotea and the others, they will be here forever,' Flounah continued, without malice. 'They lack spirit. You, on the other hand, would be wise to wait until the spring before you leave here.'

'You think I'm planning on leaving then?'

He gave me a stripping glance. 'Oh yes, I think you are. Don't be hasty.' I wondered how much he knew, or had guessed. Perhaps not all of the kanene were as helpless as I'd thought.

I nearly said, 'OK, but I haven't got that long,' but managed to check myself in time. For all I knew, Flounah might have been instructed by Jafit to question me. 'I'm not planning on going anywhere yet,' I said. 'I want to save at least fifty spinners. That's at least seven weeks, if I don't spend a single fillaret. You think I'd head off into the great unknown with no money and winter coming on? You think I'm that crazy?' I shook my head, smiling. 'No, I'm not leaving.' Flounah raised his brows, sipped thoughtfully. Thankfully, Lolotea chose that moment to return. He offered us some of his cheese. It was really quite exquisite.

'I want to buy some,' I said.

'I thought you were saving every fillaret of your money,' Flounah mentioned accusingly.

'Oh, buy some!' Lolotea said cheerfully. 'Don't be such a misery, Flounah!'

Flounah will watch me now. I'm certain of it. He doesn't know me. None of them know me. Once, long ago, I'd learned how to escape. That time, I'd left a lover behind me to die. I still haven't paid that debt. Maybe now is the time. I raised my glass and stared Flounah in the eye.

'To my cheese,' I said.

Kruin came to me again two nights later. I'd been waiting for him, panicking, thinking, 'Oh God, I upset him. He'll never come back again!' But he did. He came in through the door and said.

'I've been thinking of you, Calanthe. I was hard on you last time. I'm sorry. Here.' He gave me a necklace of polished stones.

'Don't be silly,' I said, putting it round my neck. 'Thank you, Kruin. I like it. You look nice today too.'

'Oh, come on!' Kruin sat down on my bed and kicked off his boots. 'This town is a hole. Neither of us should be here.'

'No,' I agreed. 'Wine?'

'Mmmm.' He looked thoughtful. 'I enjoy being with you, you know. Don't think that I don't.'

'I'm glad. Get your money's worth, Kruin. It's always better if you enjoy it.'

'I don't know how you do it; you're always so cheerful.'

'Of course. I'm here to please. Drink up!'

I really worked hard for my money that night. Every possible permutation of pleasure, however small, I lavished on Kruin with convincing sincerity.

'Stay with me tonight,' I said.

'I can't. It's not allowed.'

'They won't know. We'll be quiet. Stay. Please.' It didn't take long to persuade him, but then, it was cold outside and a long way back to the inn where he was staying. We lay together, on my new rug by the fire. I smoothed his animal skin, murmuring endearments. He lapped it up. 'Be ouana for me,' I said, 'I want to know you that way.'

'It's not what I come here for,' he answered, but I knew he was pleased. I sneaked him out in the early morning through the kitchens. We had hardly slept. Because I had the following evening free, I asked him to meet me in Fallsend. He hesitated and took my hand. 'Where is this leading, Calanthe?' he asked, not totally stupid.

'I like you, Kruin.'

'It's not just that, is it.'

'Will you meet me?'

He rubbed his eyes with one hand, sighed. 'Alright, but you must tell me what you're up to. I wasn't born blind, Calanthe.'

I kissed him. 'Trust me,' I said.

He shook his head, smiling. 'I hope I don't regret this,' he said, and trudged away, pulling his collar higher up his neck against the cold air.

I learn from him constantly. His goodness rubs off on me like an ointment, into my skin. The blackness just sinks in deeper. Pell has Thiede's blood in his veins now. Thiede the mysterious; too powerful, too cunning. What interest does he have in Pell? I shouldn't have let it happen, but Seel thought I was being too paranoid. 'Pell will be incepted by Thiede,' he said to me and then couldn't understand my fears. 'Won't this be an honour?' 'No, a travesty!' a voice screams inside me, but only inside. Now my Pellaz is Wraeththu, but he is Thiede too and I am afraid for him. He possesses a taint of ancient wisdom, a taint of feyness. In the moonlight he appears transparent, touched by death. I am mirrored in his eyes; pure and clean. Oh Pell, we must be together always. Without you, I might go back. No, no, not that, not the darkness, the time of blood. And now I mount the stairs in Seel's house, dressed in white. Dusk is past us; now is the night. I have bathed in milk and perfumed oil. I have been blessed, kissed with sacramental balm upon lips and breast and phallus. My part of the inception is nigh. Pellaz is waiting for me. I have sat for an hour with Seel on the window-sill at the back of the house. The air was warm there. Seel smoked a cigarette, which was torture for me because I could not. Until this is over no stimulant, of any kind, must pass my lips. Seel and I were once chesna; perhaps we were remembering those times, although we did not speak our thoughts aloud. But memory certainly prompted the remark, 'He seems so small, Cal, so fragile. Be careful not to hurt him. This is not the City.' I did not answer him. Seel is wrong. I am incapable of hurting Pellaz. Not in that way. Now the bare wood of the stairs is creaking beneath my feet and I enter his room, and shut the world away from us. In our universe Pellaz is a radiant star, luminous skin, lambent eyes, power that leaks from his pores. I have been yearning to touch him for so long, now the moment must be savoured, prolonged before I do. His body surrenders for the first time, and I watch him discover the delights of his new being. He forgets he was once human, forgets he was once male. We take aruna and we are invading each other, cautiously and reverently. This is not the city. Zack is dead. My flesh twinges at the memory of the savage bite. I hear laughter, but it is far away. Now I will weep inside because of the simple, giving pleasure we enjoy. There is nothing beyond Saltrock. This is sanctuary. It is not safe to leave. I vow to keep us there.

We will stay in Saltrock for just twenty-two months.

It was my turn to take 'zoo duty' again that day. Lolotea was with me. This time, Panthera wasn't tied to the bed. He was still asleep, or pretending to be, flags of dark hair spread around him on the pillows. One Mojag was on guard duty; the other two slumbering peacefully in an adjoining room.

Lolotea gave Panthera a shake. 'Wake up. We have to change the bed,' he said, beginning to pull at the sheets.

Panthera stretched and looked at me. It was a glance that had my common sense struggling to keep my libido under control. Fluid as quicksilver, Panthera rose from the bed and stalked arrogantly to the window. He must spend an awful lot of time gazing out of that window. How many fruitless plans had been hatched there?

'I'll run your bath,' I said.

Panthera did not look at me or say anything, although Lolotea glanced up sharply, shaking his head and smiling to himself. I went into the bathroom with its high, pale walls and started to run water into the pale, high bath. Panthera came in silently behind me.

'Well?' he asked at once, in a voiceless arrow to my brain. 'Have you thought about what I said?' He'd obviously been thinking about it, perhaps worried that my answer would be 'no'.

'I've said nothing to Jafit, if that's what you mean,' I answered.

Lolotea must not hear us. We conversed by mind-touch alone. I felt Panthera's uncontrollable relief pass through me like a breeze. He glided past me and let his robe fall to the floor. The threat of being struck by blindness could not have stopped me from looking at him; this he refused to acknowledge, although I could tell he derived a certain satisfaction from it. His body is like Seel's, almost too slim, but malleable. He lowered himself into the water and closed his eyes.

'You mustn't stay in here long,' he said. 'The fool out there might get suspicious. I have no contact with any of them if I can help it.'

I sat down on the edge of the bath. 'I have been thinking, Panthera,' I said, 'and, if I can, I will try to help you. But it won't be easy. Too much for me alone. I'm going to need help from outside Piristil.'

Panthera's eyes snapped open. 'Who?! Nobody can be trusted.'

'You had to trust me.'

He sighed. 'Alright, but be careful.'

'You know you don't have to worry about that. You wouldn't have approached me if you didn't.'

'True. Now remember, if we succeed, you will be well paid.'

'That is not the only item of concern.'

'No, of course not. You want to get into Jaddayoth; preferably into a royal house. See how much I know about you? I have royal blood ...'

'I don't doubt that for a moment, Panthera!'

He smiled. 'You're a mercenary, aren't you. You can be bought. Have you made any plans yet?'

'A few sketches. I'm working on it.'

Panthera leaned forward with vehemence. 'Make it soon!' he said. 'I've waited long enough.'

I met Kruin in a small tavern near his lodgings. He was sitting at a table in a corner of the room with an ashtray full of cigarette ends on one side of him and three empty glasses on the other. As I sat down, he fumbled to light another cigarette and began to look mournfully at the bar.

'I'll get them,' I said, to give him a few more moments to compose himself. I bought him a beer and one for myself. It was warm and rancid, and left an unwelcome deposit of slime in the back of the mouth. I asked Kruin why he was so nervous.

'I prefer you to be ... *contained*,' he answered furtively. 'The part of my life you represent should remain locked in Piristil.'

'Let's have less of the "locked", if you don't mind!'

Kruin smiled at the table, stubbed out his cigarette and lit another one. 'Well, why do you want to see me?'

'Maybe I just like you.'

'Maybe. Like I said, why do you want to see me?'

I leaned back in my seat; a perilous action, it wobbled dangerously. 'Hmmm, now tell me; you are a warrior? Brave, courageous, fearless, all that?'

He laughed. 'Calanthe, what is this?'

'Are you?'

'I've escorted three wittering merchants from Natawni, that's all. It's hardly the stuff of heroism. OK, back home, I've been involved in scuffles with the Maudrah, nothing serious. Why are you asking? Are you trying to hire me?' He laughed again, nervously, his eyes scanning the faces in the crowd behind us, in case his travelling companions should show up.

'In a way, yes. When you leave Fallsend, Kruin, I want to come with you.'

'What?! No! A kanene? Do you realize ...'

I broke into his furious splutterings. 'Shut up! The minute I leave Piristil, I'm no longer a kanene. In fact, I'm not even one now! Do you understand?'

He looked into my eyes, silenced by the tone of my voice, sighed and shook his head. 'You don't look like a whore, Calanthe,' he said, at last.

'Good, then stop being so worried about being seen with me.'

He pulled an apologetic face. 'That obvious?'

'Rather, yes.'

'I'm sorry. Let's start again, OK?'

I rejoiced in the moment when my friend Kruin stopped seeing me as meat and started seeing me as Har.

'Now then,' he said, 'I get a feeling it may not be a good idea to get involved in whatever scheme you have in mind. There *is* some reason behind all this, isn't there?'

'Could be that I just want you to take me back to your tribe. Could be that I'd ask to become chesna-bond with you; you're quite a catch, Kruin.'

'Yeah, and hard nuts like you don't have any finer feelings, Calanthe. Let's not play games. What is it you want?'

'You're suspicious aren't you!'

'Ever looked in the mirror, tiahaar?'

'At least a dozen times a day, sometimes more, depending on the weather.'

'Ever noticed your eyes never smile? That's what tells me to be careful!'

'Survival's a caustic process,' I agreed. If his observations were supposed to disquiet me, he was badly misguided. No-one knew more than me how thorough my defences were. 'Back to what you were saying,' I said. 'You're probably right that it might be bad for you to get involved with me. Worse than that it may be terribly bad. You may never be able to set foot in Fallsend again ... safely.'

Kruin raised his hands. 'Forget it!'

'Sssh, just listen. There's money to be made ...'

'Oh?' He raised his brows, drank some beer, grimaced. 'Go on.'

'It concerns the Har kept locked in Piristil, you know, Panthera.'

'Mmmm.' Deeper suspicions began to cloud his eyes. He drank again, lit another cigarette.

'I've been approached, Kruin. Panthera wants out. There's a substantial reward waiting for someone who can get him home.'

Kruin did not over-react as I'd expected.

'Too risky, Calanthe. What is this? Social justice on your part? I doubt it! Must be one hell of a big reward!'

'You lack subtlety, Kruin.'

'Yeah, maybe. But how the hell do you think we can blast our way through those Mojags? It'll need more than two of us!' He whistled through his teeth, shook his head. 'No, Jafit's security is impeccable. It will take more than brute force.'

'Well done, Kruin!' I said, somewhat sourly. 'The power of seduction accomplishes far more than blazing guns.'

'You've got a plan then? A watertight plan?'

'Are you in with me or not?'

He shrugged. 'Tell me how you're going to do it first. I don't see how you'll get away with it.'

'If I set my mind on something, I always get away with it!'

'Convince me then!'

'I'm still working on it. Come to Piristil tomorrow night.'

'Again?! This is going to cost me a fortune!'

'But it will be worth it,' I said, and leaned forward to pat his cheek.

The Beauty of Poison

'Sure to taste sweetly, — is that poison too!'
Robert Browning, The laboratory

Pell and I are in Galhea. Terzian is lord here and we are in his house. Flashbacks to another time. Terzian is a powerful Har. He likes me. He says, 'Don't you get sick of travelling around, Cal?' Of course I do, but how can I explain that we are running, just ahead of something and that something is huge and dangerous. We don't even know what it is. 'It's because of Pell,' I say, and that's all I can say. 'We have to ... keep going.'

'We?' Terzian smiles. 'you don't have to surely!' He wants me to stay with him. He wants me to have his sons. Such an offer. This is not a burnt-out wasteland; this is real living. Comfort, security, affluence. But then, there is Pell. And there is memories. It was not easy when Zack and I were kicked out of the Uigenna. I was younger then. We suffered for a while until we reached the sanctuary of the Unneah. Terzian cannot banish me. I don't belong here. He doesn't own me. This time, when I say no, it will be because I have the power; not him.

'Cal, don't leave me,' he says. 'Don't.' When I am sure he loves me, I walk out of the door. It is not a happy triumph. Empty victory. Pell and I ride towards the south. The clouds are gathering.

I scuffed back to Piristil, through the bleak, moist cold, wrapping my woollen cloak more tightly around me, head down against the wind, sucking on a sour cigarette clasped between rigid fingers. I thought about Panthera. Occasionally honest with myself, I questioned my motives in wanting to help him get away. What he said was true, of course. I did want to leave Piristil, and I did want to get into Jaddayoth, but it is also true that I could probably have persuaded Kruin to take me back to Natawni with him, without the added hassle of liberating Panthera. I am not a person easily bewitched. Not now. I have learned· to recognize the sweet, unsubtle pangs of desire when they assault me and never euphemize them with titles of love and longing. I also know that no beauty, however thrilling, is worth risking life and limb for. What the hell am I doing? Money, freedom, desire ... I looked up the hill towards Glitter. Narrow buildings seemed to lean towards me, all crippled, all hopeless. A light shone down through the darkness, making the damp streets gleam. It was an arcane, eerie and almost stimulating scene. The town was hushed. I stood for a moment in the empty, almost gully-like street and absorbed the ambience. Perhaps I was waiting for an omen. I looked up, pulling the grey wool closer to my neck. I felt as if I was clamped in the jaws of Fate. I was being manipulated, things were getting beyond my control. It is not a comforting feeling. Very well, if Fate was involved, I would just wait. If it was meant to be, coincidence would bring me a way to free Panthera. 'Do your worst,' I said aloud. From the darkness of the sky, a single, spiralling mote fell to earth, practically at my feet. I watched its descent, watched its rapid merging with the flesh and bones of Fallsend. 'Soon,' I thought, 'everything will look different.' I raised my head once more and the sky above me was creeping with movement. After a moment, I continued to climb the hill. Around me, snow fell silently.

My room was cold when I returned; the fire had died. Winter suffused the place. It was squatting there waiting for me and what chill I brought in with me merged with it eagerly. Before going to find Orpah or Wuwa to light the fire, I crossed the darkened room and glanced quickly through the window, seeking the light in Panthera's room. It glowed as usual, but there were no shadows crossing the bars. Everywhere seemed unusually hushed that evening. The house was too quiet, creaking as if it thought it was alone. I wandered along to the kitchens, thinking only about my fire. Jancis the cook stopped me at the threshold. 'You'd better get back upstairs,' he said ominously, with expressionless face.

'Why?'

'There's been an incident. Jafit says everyone is to stay in their rooms for now.'

I felt chilled. 'Incident? What kind of incident? What's happened?'

Jancis began to close the door in my face. He smiled. 'A death,' he said. 'A killing.'

'What?! Jancis! Who? Jancis!' The kitchen door had slammed in my face. I heard him turn the key inside. I heard him chuckling.

Panicking, I bolted straight to Panthera's quarters. If anyone was going to get himself murdered around here, he was the most likely candidate. Outher was standing guard outside the door. I feared the worst. 'What's happened?' I asked.

'Trouble!' he answered. 'Comes with the job, I suppose.'

'Panthera?' I cried, horrified. Outher shook his head.

'Oh, *he's* alright,' he said. 'God, as if anyone could get away with murdering him!'

'Can I go in?'

Outher thought about it for a moment. 'I guess that'll be alright.' He opened the door for me.

I put my hand on his arm. 'Thanks, Outher. I appreciate it.'

The Mojag actually flushed. 'S'alright, Calanthe,' he said. 'You got a thing going with our pussy-cat, have you?'

I laughed, but did not answer.

Panthera was surprised to see me and uncommonly natural because of it. It made me realize what a creature of artifice he can be at times. I asked him if he knew what was going on.

'No,' he answered. 'All I know is that all clients have been cancelled for the night and that two of the Mojags have been summoned to Jafit's office.'

'Damn!' I said, annoyed enough to hit the wall. 'If only this could have happened later! It's almost too good an opportunity to miss. One Mojag and the house nearly empty! Damn!'

'You mean we could ... *leave* now?' Panthera sounded uncertain.

'We could have, but unfortunately we're not prepared and neither is Kruin.'

'Kruin. Who's Kruin?'

I explained. Panthera sat down on the bed. 'I hope Ferike and Natawni are on friendly terms at the moment. Things might have changed since I left home.'

'Relations that flimsy between the tribes then?'

'Can be. It's hard to say. It all depends on Maudrah really.' He smiled beautifully at me. 'Still, this Kruin doesn't seem to be worried. It will cause problems in another way though. The Natawni's route home can't possibly take him anywhere near Ferike. Surely, if he drags the merchants south with him, they're going to want to share the reward.'

'God, Panthera, that's a minor point. Let's just get out of here intact before we start quibbling over details. That's Kruin's problem.'

Panthera looked at me archly, but said nothing.

'I suppose I'd better go and find out what's going on,' I said.

'Not yet,' Panthera decided. 'Stay. Have some coffee.'

'Lonely for company are you?'

'No. I'm used to not having any; you know that. I was just thinking we have to talk about our plans and there won't be many opportunities like this one.' He stalked over to the fire and picked up a coffee pot. Only then did I notice the long, silver chains.

'Are those uncomfortable?' I asked him, pointing.

'Not as much as they were, no,' he answered.

I asked him about Ferike. 'It is beautiful,' he said. 'There are woods everywhere, hills and mountains. All I live for is to see it again. All the noble families live in great, stone castles. Jael, my father's domain, is quite near the Clerewater and the shoreside town of Clereness. Look, I'll show you.'

He preceded me over to a low table where sheets of paper and coloured pens were laid out. I picked up a drawing; dark and disturbing scribbles of torture. 'Yours?' Panthera snatched it from my hand.

'Yes. Look, I will draw you a plan of Jaddayoth.' I watched his slim, hard arm skim quickly over the paper. 'Here is Natawni in the north, you see? Both Hadassah and Gimrah separate it from Ferike. The quickest route to Natawni is north from Fallsend, out of

Thaine, into Fereng and from there to Jaddayoth. That's probably the way your friend Kruin would go home. Now, Jafit will expect us to go south towards Elhmen, so I think we should go north.'

'It will be a much longer journey,' I said, studying the map.

'Yes, but safer'.

'OK what ever you say.' Without thinking, I put my hand on his shoulder. Ah, such warmth, such strength, such softness and hardness! These are the most succulent sweetmeats in the market of life and often the ones most dear. Panthera shrugged me off and gave me a hard glance. I was irresistably reminded of Cobweb.

'You must not stay too long,' Panthera said, and thus concluded our conversation.

Plans were beginning to formulate in my head. After I left Panthera, I paused to share a cigarette with the Mojag. He could offer me no information concerning the identity of the murder victim. If it wasn't Panthera, I decided I wasn't really bothered who it was. 'Don't worry yourself with that,' Outher said. 'Stay here for a while. We could ... talk.'

'We could, but ... Do you get any time off from this job?'

'Tomorrow afternoon is free,' he said, without a tremor.

'Fine. We'll talk tomorrow then.' I had a feeling that friendship with Outher might prove useful.

I didn't know what action Jafit would take over the killing, but I was surprised when I found him still at home. I knocked on his office door and Astarth opened it to me (so it wasn't him lying dead somewhere). The room was full of smoke, opened bottles on the desk, Jafit sitting behind it with his feet up. He didn't look exactly grief-stricken, although Astarth was a little green about the gills. The Mojags were sitting awkwardly in small chairs, clutching glasses of betica in their large fists.

'What's happened?' I asked.

'Come in. Sit down, if you can find a seat,' Jafit replied.

Astarth clutched my arm. 'Lolotea is gone,' he said.

'Lolotea?' I said softly. 'No ...' It stunned me. Of all the kanene Lolotea was the least deserving of such a sordid end. Over the years, I have become inured to the death of friends, but it still shocked me. Astarth sat me down. 'How?' I asked 'How, Jafit?' A full glass was pushed into my hand. Jafit was comfortably exhibiting unconcern. 'Don't you care?' My voice was near to breaking.

'Of course I care,' Jafit answered sharply. 'It was a Har named Arno Demell, from the town. Don't worry, it will be dealt with.'

'Has this sort of thing happened before?' I asked. Jafit made a noncommittal gesture.

'Yes it has,' Astarth told me bitterly. I was satisfied to note that he looked quite ill.

'There are risks in every walk of life,' Jafit said. Astarth sneered at that and I don't blame him.

'What are you going to do?'

Jafit smiled at my question. 'Do, Calanthe? Why we're going to kill the fucking bastard, aren't we my dears?' The Mojags grunted uncomfortably in assent.

A voice sounded in the room. It said. 'No, Jafit, you don't have to. I will.' I was surprised to find it was mine.

'You?' Astarth said. 'Why?'

Why indeed? I wasn't sure myself, but the feeling was there, gut-strong. Jafit didn't give a damn really; I did. They wanted reasons, so I gave them. 'He was my friend. I liked him a lot. Let me deal with it. Don't you think I'm capable?'

Jafit smiled and poured himself another drink. 'Capable? Oh my dear, you are obviously eminently capable. But you don't know Fallsend, do you? Think you could find Demell?'

'No he couldn't,' Astarth said, and I turned round to protest, but before I spoke, he continued. 'But I could. Calanthe is right in this, Jafit. It is our blood debt. It could have been any one of us up there.' He looked at me. 'Get your coat, Calanthe. I'll meet you in the hall.'

'Astarth, do you know what you are doing?' Jafit asked, highly amused.

'Yes, give me some money. Twenty spinners should do it.'

'OK, but you realize it will be too late to get help from us if you fail. Demell will be in hiding, I should think.'

'We'll find him, Jafit.' Astarth took the money that Jafit had taken from the drawer. 'Come on Calanthe.'

I went to fetch my coat, pausing in the corridor outside Lolotea's room. If I'd been in there ... If I hadn't gone to see Kruin

... I shook my head. A life for a life for a life; never-ending. I opened the door and went inside. It was not ghoulish curiosity or even because I wanted to fuel the fire of the vengeance lust. I just went in. Someone had thrown a sheet over the body; a pathetic huddle on the floor. The light was on, the fire roaring away merrily in the grate. There was little sign of a struggle. I lifted the sheet. Whoever had done this was not on a blood and guts kick. Lolotea's neck was neatly broken with little other damage. He stared in surprise at the ceiling, his hands above his head. I squatted down and closed his eyes. Someone should have already done that. It was wrong that he should just be left lying there. I lifted the body in my arms and laid it on the bed. It was limp and cooling in my arms. The feeling of dead flesh is like no other; it is disorientating. The body of Lolotea was as empty as the clothes hanging in the cupboard. I opened the window, put a robe over the mirror and murmured a few soothing prayers to help the spirit on its way, although strangely I could feel no inkling of its presence. Someone or something had come for it quickly. I shivered, suddenly cold with the sense of being watched. Of course, I am always watched. Perhaps to Lolotea's advantage in this case.

Astarth had scrubbed his face and dressed in dark, sober clothes. This was not the hard-bitten tart I knew. He looked very different; determined, competent. He paused, one hand on the door, looked at me hard. 'Were you trying to shame me?' he said. I shook my head. 'You know I wouldn't be doing this if it wasn't for what you said.'

I shrugged. 'Does it matter?'

'It should.' He shook his head fiercely, swore under his breath, and opened the door. We went outside into the muffled snow-darkness and Astarth closed the door behind us, pulling on thick, woollen gloves in a manner that implied he meant business. We trudged down the hill towards the town. Tiahaar Arno Demell, I learned, was usually to be found draped over the bar and the pot-Hara in the Red Hog Inn. Astarth suggested we go there first, although neither of us had much hope of finding Demell there.

'Jafit doesn't seem that upset about this,' I said.

'No he doesn't,' Astarth agreed in an uncommunicative tone.

'Would he have done anything?' I persisted.

Astarth stopped trudging. He turned to face me. 'Oh Demell would've been banned from the establishment, but not much else, no. If Jafit persisted, he may have been able to get financial compensation from him. That, by the way, was what he meant by "killing the bastard". A momentary killing. Arno Demell is not a rich Har. Don't you see, Calanthe, there is not that much of a difference between pelcia and murder. Sometimes a client will get carried away. Once they've paid their money to Jafit, he has little control over what goes on in those rooms.'

'Astarth, that's … that's …' I could not think of a strong enough word.

'Yes, isn't it!' We carried on walking.

'Why are you doing this?' I asked. 'Why are you here, Astarth? What kind of life is this?'

'Don't ask! Don't ask!' He started running through the quickly deepening snow. I followed him and we did not speak of it again. We didn't have to. After all, it's no kind of life, is it?

We searched and we searched. From inn to musenda to inn. Astarth asked questions, paid for information. Every lead we gained led to a dead end. I was beginning to give up. Demell could be miles from Fallsend by now. Astarth was more persistent. At another musenda, we spoke with a kanene who had a stitched wound all across his face and neck. Luck was looking us right in the eye; he knew where Demell was. Apparently, our prey had turned up there some while ago, being a close friend of the owner of the place.

'He was obviously in a bit of a state about something,' our informant told us. 'OK, we weren't supposed to know what was going on, but, let's just say we're more resourceful than our keeper gave us credit for.' He smiled and the scar wriggled horribly on his cheek. '87 Canalside Row. Remember that. It's where you'll find him.' He pressed the handle of a long, barbed knife into my hand. 'Give Demell one for me,' he said, running a finger down his scar. 'Tiahaar Demell's a regular customer here; you see?' I tucked the knife into my belt. Yes, I could see.

Outside, I laughed and brandished the knife in a threatening manner. Astarth put his hand over my wrist and shook his head at me. 'No,' he said. 'The punishment has to fit the crime. Come on.' I followed him up another narrow streetlet that was slippery with snow. We went into a large and noisy inn named The Stone. Astarth said that many of the Jaddayoth traders frequented it; some even stayed there. The Stone did look more affluent than the majority of Fallsend establishments. I wouldn't have minded pausing for a mug of ale there myself. Astarth said we didn't have enough time. I watched him asking a few questions of people, wondering what he was up to. We knew where Demell was now. Someone directed him to a thin-faced Har wearing dark, purple clothes. He was leaning on the bar, smoking a long-stemmed pipe, staring at the crowd as if deep in thought. He inclined his head towards Astarth semi-interestedly. A brief conversation took place, and then the pair of them went outside. Astarth motioned me to wait in the bar for him. Never a person to miss opportunities, I bought myself a drink and sat down. Astarth was only gone a few minutes. He rejoined me looking furtive and edgy, manifesting dire impatience as I finished my drink. Outside, the freezing cold was as welcome as a hangover and just as mind-numbing.

'Well Astarth,' I said, 'what shady business were you up to in there?'

'The Har I talked to was the Garridan Liss-am-Caar,' he replied with reverent tones of dread. 'He sold me this.' A twist of paper was held out for me to inspect. I had seen such things before and opened it cautiously, sniffed the contents. This was something the Uigenna had once been most famous for; poison. 'The Garridan deal in toxins and venoms,' Astarth explained, taking the twist of paper back. Shades of Uigenna, I thought. Yes, definitely. We hurried through the streets to the place where we'd been told Demell had secreted himself. It was an unimposing house, close to the canal that was one of the trade routes between Thaine and Jaddayoth.

'Well, what do we do now?' I asked Astarth who had appeared to have assumed command. 'Go up and knock on the door?'

'We wait awhile.' It was terribly cold and uncomfortable. I smoked four cigarettes and then the door to the house we were watching opened. A solitary figure stepped out into the street, glancing this way and that. I saw the flare of a match. 'It's him,' Astarth breathed.

Arno Demell walked towards the canal. He exhibited no signs of worry, or fear that he was being watched. An average kind of Har, unremarkable in appearance. He stood at the water's edge and threw something into the shifting, oily blackness. I'll never know what. For a moment, he continued to stare into the water. Then we jumped him. It would have been easy just to have thrown him into the canal; the freezing cold would have finished him off pretty quickly, but Astarth wanted to shake that packet of crystals into the poor fool's mouth. It was his moment of glory and I wasn't going to deprive him of it. I don't know whether he was genuinely grieved by what had happened to Lolotea, it was difficult to tell, but he certainly enjoyed making Demell suffer for it. The victim didn't ask who we were; he knew. Of course, he may have seen our faces before in Piristil, but I saw that resigned acceptance of doom as he witnessed Astarth's bared teeth and patient execution of vengeance. Demell knew what he had done and now accepted he had to pay the forfeit; in this case, death. The law of the jungle, the law of the world. Few poisons can affect a Harish frame. We are a resilient race. We left Demell gasping and writhing at the edge of the water. I expect he eventually did fall in, but we didn't stay to watch.

We walked back to Piristil in silence, both of us wrapped in our own thoughts. Perhaps Astarth was thinking that one death can't pay for years of degradation, I don't know, but I was thinking of the Garridan. It was possible that they were derived from Uigenna stock. Suddenly, my mind was alight with ideas. This was it. Panthera's liberation was suddenly so much nearer.

The following day, a predictable pall of gloom and despondency hung heavily in the air in Piristil. The air smelt greasy; the air was cold. The kanene passed each other on the stairs with barely a greeting. We dressed in black and bound up our hair. There is a hill about half a mile away from the house. It is reached by a steep, muddy path. That is where Lolotea lies buried. There are no hienama in the town of Fallsend, no priests. Jafit, who had made no mention of Arno Demell and his fate, spoke a few hackneyed words over the open grave as Orpah and Wuwa lowered the rough, unadorned wooden box containing the remains of the murdered one into the ground. The rest of us stood around, numb from cold and, in some cases, shock. Some of them wept. Flounah veiled himself in grey and stood with his back to the grave. Ezhno held onto my arm, looking aggressive. There was no-one of Lolotea's blood to mourn him there. No-one would ever even know he was dead; a group of desperate whores the only thing he had close to a family. It was pathetic really, but me, I felt detached. I've experienced worse things.

After a dreary lunch, shared with Jafit and the others in Jafit's personal dining-room, I went to find Outher. 'I have to go into Fallsend,' I said. 'Want to come with me?' I think this rather disappointed him as he'd been planning to spend the afternoon with me in a more secluded place. 'We can eat in my room tonight, if you like,' I added. That convinced him.

As we walked down the hill into the town, snow seeping through my boots, I was deep in thought. My mind was racing, but I strove not to show it. I remember forcing some inane chatter onto Outher. He must have thought me as empty-headed as the rest. Once the streets levelled off, I mentioned that I would like to go for a drink in The Stone. 'It seems it's the best this lousy town has to offer,' I said, and Outher agreed.

He took my arm. 'It will make me proud to walk in there with you,' he said. How gallant.

Unlike the previous evening, The Stone was relatively quiet when we got there. A sumptuously painted Har was draped over the bar waiting for custom. Outher offered to buy me a drink. I must not move too soon. I smiled and nodded and asked for a beer. As he strolled up to the bar, I reflected that it was almost a pity that I would have to leave Piristil this way. I'd made good friends whose company I would miss, not the least of which, Lolotea. That resolved me. The sooner I left the better. I scanned the room. Being large, it appeared emptier than it actually was. I could see no face that I recognized. Outher came over to the table I had chosen with the drinks. I smiled. He sat down.

'Panthera seems to have taken to you,' he said. 'I've never seen that before.'

'Oh, I don't know about that,' I said. 'I just get on well with anybody.'

'I don't think I've ever heard him speak to any of the others.'

'Have you *heard* us speak then?'

'No, but . . .'

I inclined my head. 'Well then!'

'You know what I mean, Calanthe,' he laughed. 'By Aghama, you're a cagey creature — just like Panthera.'

'Cagey are the beasts kept in cages,' I replied lightly, while surreptitiously glancing over Outher's shoulder. I drained my glass. 'My round, I believe.'

Outher looked at his half-full glass in surprise. 'You are thirsty, Calanthe!'

'Yes, burying is thirsty work.' Outher had the grace to look abashed. I said no more and went to the bar. The pot-Har slouched over to me after leaving me waiting for maybe a minute. I watched him fulfil my order with the same amount of enthusiasm. Ale splashed over my hands as he handed me the glasses. 'Tell me,' I said, 'is the Garridan Liss-am-Caar staying here?'

The pot-Har gazed at me stupidly. I sighed and threw a spinner onto the bar where it rolled for a full insulting twelve seconds before lying still. The pot-Har continued to stare.

'Well?' I enquired sweetly.

'Who wants to know?' he said at last.

'I do.'

'And who are you?'

'A potential customer of his wares.'

The pot-Har continued to eye me with suspicion. 'And what wares are those?' he asked, with undiminished surliness.

'Look.' I said. 'I haven't much time. Just tell him, will you! You don't have to be afraid. I'm not Gelaming. I'm a Varr. I just want to buy. No questions either side. Do you understand?' The pot-Har stared me in the eye. I stared back.

'You want I should send him to your table?'

'No!' I hissed emphatically. 'Have you a yard here?'

The pot-Har pointed sullenly to a half concealed door to the right of the bar.

'Ten minutes,' I said. The pot-Har shrugged.

'If he's in. I'll have to try his room.'

'Yes, you do that!'

I took the drinks back to the table. Outher asked what I'd been doing. I lied glibly about some flirtation with the pot-Har. Outher grinned at me engagingly. Such a simple soul. I watched the clock above the bar. Nearly time. After nine minutes, Outher said, 'Calanthe, you really are special.'

'Yes, thank you,' I said. 'Look I just have to buy a couple of things. Hang on here for me, will you?'

'But I ...' Obviously more profound sentiments were about to erupt.

'I won't be long.'

'That's alright. I'll come with you. It's no bother.'

'No! I mean, no, don't trouble yourself. Anyway, I want to buy something for us to eat tonight. It's going to be a surprise.'

Outher smiled. He really is quite handsome. 'OK, if you're sure.'

I smiled and held up my hand. 'Five minutes,' I said.

I thought it safer to leave The Stone by the front door and hope that there was another way into the yard from out front. I had to be careful not to arouse any suspicions in Outher. Luckily, there were a couple of Hara carrying barrels of ale through an open door in the wall. I followed them into the yard. It had been cleared of snow and strewn with ashes. I stood stamping and shivering for what seemed an eternity before a light touch on my shoulder made me spin round, half-afraid it would be Outher. It wasn't. In daylight, the lean face of the Garridan seemed even crueler, more snake-like, but seeringly attractive. I could see easily the mark of his Uigenna history in his eyes. Perhaps we had even met before. It was possible. Inspired, I held out my hand and said, 'In meetings hearts beat closer', which was an old, clichéd but authentically-Uigenna catch-phrase. Liss-am-Caar raised his brow fastidiously.

'In blood, brother', he responded. 'You're a long way from home, friend.'

'As are many,' I replied. Now, I hoped he would not try to cheat me.

He asked my business.

'Should you ask?' I replied.

He smiled thinly. 'Only the result, my friend, only the result.'

'Not death,' I said.

Liss–am–Caar registered no expression. 'Then I can only offer Bloodshade, Diamanda and Rauspic.' Only two of those names were familiar to me, and I was also familiar with their side-effects. Death may even be preferable.

'I need sleepers not shriekers,' I said mildly. 'What is this Diamanda?'

'Perhaps what you require, although the sleep is deep. The dosage is crucial, for heavy-handedness whilst dosing could initiate a sleep deeper than might be required.'

'That should suffice. How much?'

'That depends upon how much you want.'

'Enough for ten, I think.'

The Garridan did not flicker. 'A hundred spinners then.'

'What!'

He shrugged. 'Sleepers are more expensive. I could sell you Acridil for a mere three spinners and you could administer maybe a hundred doses.'

I reflected for a few moments. Should I? No. I remembered the shadow that had been on my tail through Thaine. Chances were, once out of Fallsend and in the open country, vigilance on the part of my pursuers would be stepped up. I could not risk causing another death. I'd already been through enough for the ones I'd initiated in the past. Arno Demell was more than enough for one town. 'Diamanda for three, a light dose; how much?'

'A light dose? Should be thirty, but I'll give it to you for twenty-five.'

Sighing, I handed over the better part of my savings. The Garridan counted it thoughtfully. He opened his bag and gave me three twists of paper. 'This is a child's dose,' he said, holding up one twist.

'And how will that affect a fully grown Mojag?' I asked.

The Garridan whistled through his teeth. 'Ah, you're cutting close to the bone there! A light doze for half an hour, maybe.'

I sighed again. It would just have to be enough.

'The advantage is, of course,' the Garridan continued, 'that should anyone wake up from a Diamanda sleep, they'll be groggy for ten minutes or so, no matter how light the dose.'

'Thanks!' I said, glumly.

'Pleased to do business with you!' Liss-am-Caar touched his brow politely and turned away.

'Oh, one more thing, Tiahaar,' I said. He turned.

'Yes.'

'Who is the Lion of Oomadrah?' There was an electric silence. The Garridan's face was stony. He looked briefly round the yard.

'A changed person, my friend,' he said. 'In view of your history, you would do well to stay out of Maudrah. The Lion has sharpened his claws, but he never laughs nowadays. If you're looking for old friends, come to Garridan. Here, have my card.'

I took it. 'Thanks again,' I said.

'Any time, my friend. Goodbye.' He went back indoors.

I hurried back into the street and recklessly spent a further three spinners at the food stalls. Outher was looking very harried when I went back into The Stone, perhaps afraid I'd ditched him. 'A long five minutes,' he said.

'I'm sorry,' I purred. 'Listen, I have the whole day free. Do you want to go back to Piristil now?' That brought the smile back to his face; he didn't know I was thinking how much more preferable it would have been making that offer to the Garridan Liss-am-Caar.

We sat and talked beside my fire, mostly about what I was going to prepare for our meal; an engrossing topic, as you can imagine. I was still indulging in casual fantasies about the Garridan, even as I discussed with Outher the superiority of Fallsend chicken-meat to Fallsend pork. After what I considered to be a suitable time, I went to sit on Outher's lap to share breath with him. He cupped my face with his hand. 'You're too good for this place,' he said.

'Yes,' I agreed and slipped my hand inside his leather shirt. 'No, don't do that now,' he said gently. 'Calanthe, I have something to say to you. In the spring, I'm going back to Mojag. Someone else will take my place here. I'd like you to come home with me.'

I laughed. 'Outher, this session is for free, OK. You don't have to say things like that!'

He flushed angrily. 'I'm not joking, Calanthe! I want you, but not just for a sordid night. I want you forever. It's terrible thinking of what you have to do here. Tell me now, will you or won't you? There won't be many chances for you like this here.'

'Oh, I know that! But this is unexpected, Outher. So quick. Have I made such an impression upon you this afternoon?'

'You are laughing at me.'

'Well, you must admit, it's hard to take your suggestion seriously. After all, we've only just met really.'

He looked perplexed, wondering how to convince me. I resolved to let him suffer for a while. How could I be so lucky? I felt like leaping up and dancing round the room, but not for the reason Outher would want.

'It sounds so corny,' he said, 'but I wanted you from the moment I first saw you.' He was right; it did sound corny.

I smiled. 'Do you think I'll like life in Mojag?'

'Anything's better than this, surely!'

I lay back on the rug and stretched. I made him wait for as long as possible before saying, 'Alright, if you're sure you mean it. This isn't going to be retracted after tonight, is it?'

Outher stood up. 'Now you've said yes, there won't be a tonight,' he said. 'When we take aruna together, it will be when this place is far behind you!'

'Fine,' I said, thinking, you get away from that door, idiot; you don't get away that easily. 'Look, you don't have to go just because we're not going to leap in the bed or runkle the carpet! Let's get to know each other a little, shall we? Tell me about Mojag. Come on, sit down. I've got all this wretched food now and there's some wine chilling on the window-sill.' I snuggled up against him again and let him bore me stiff rambling on about Mojag, a place that seemed tedious to the point of incredibility. I made a mental note never to go there. I've met many Hara who are more masculine than they should be; sometimes they can carry it off pretty well. Mojags reminded me of the worst type of men who were probably (and thankfully) the first to be removed neatly from the face of the earth when Wraeththu rose up and splatted the humans. Mojags are a complete waste of Harish time. Sorry Outher, you've been put together very nicely physically but your brain would be more at home floating, chopped up, in soup. After he'd exhausted himself talking, we sat quietly and watched the fire. He thought we were sharing a peaceful, silent moment together, but my mind was racing, planning, trying to take advantage of this incredibly fortuitous event. Outher was my key for Panthera's locked room. 'What do you do in the evenings?' I asked.

'Drink mostly!' He laughed and I tittered impishly, flapping my eyelashes in what Kruin would have thought was a demented manner. 'There's little entertainment to be found here,' he continued woefully. 'Most nights we have to listen to what goes on in Panthera's room. You have to get drunk to put up with that!'

'Ah, but you have me now,' I said, nuzzling his face. His rapture at this behaviour was laughable. Even an imbecile could see I was hamming it up so much you could virtually taste the salad too. 'Do you have the same nights off as Panthera?'

He looked sour. 'In a way. We take it in turns. Jafit won't ever let Panthera stay unguarded.'

'How many nights off a week does Panthera get?'

'Only one, and he never knows which one that will be.'

'Do you?'

'Yes, of course. We have to organize our duties round it.'

'And when's the next one?'

'Four days' time. Why? What is it to you?' He didn't have an ounce of suspicion in him, however.

'I just want to know, because that night, I'll send you a present. I don't want you having to be all alert and on duty while you're enjoying it.'

'You're lovely,' he said tenderly.

'Deadly,' I replied and he laughed.

So, tonight is the night. No more waiting. Goodbye vulgar clients, hello freedom. When I write again, it will be to state whether our plans were successful or not. If they're not, I may not be able to write again! A less than cheering thought. The Mojags are to be drugged with the Diamanda, which will be diluted in the large carafe of expensive wine that I'm sending to Outher for him to share with his companions. Once they're asleep, Kruin will scale the wall outside and try to remove the bars. He has obtained a corrodant which takes about fifteen minutes to work. Panthera and myself will leave Piristil through the window, into the yard, where Kruin will have the horses waiting, loaded with supplies. This venture has cost Kruin and myself nearly all the money we have. Kruin, to get rid of his duty towards the merchants, even had to hire another guide to get them safely back to Natawni. The planning is all finished; we'll just have to pray we're successful. It all hangs on Outher's trust in me and whether he's generous enough to share the wine as I'll suggest. I've had to endure four days of his dull wooing, made more vile by the fact that it required convincing responses. Imagine, we've even been discussing names for children! Every moment he has, he swears undying love to me; I have to take it all in without laughing. The fool's so easy to deceive it's embarrassing to take advantage of it. I could almost serve him a dose of Acridil for being such a stupid bore. People have died for less, as they say.

Flight towards Hadassah
*'Where but to think is to be full of sorrow
And leaden-eyed despair.'*

J. Keats, Ode to a Nightingale

*D*ampness, warmth, rising steam. The sound of moisture dripping from
leaf to leaf. Birds are silenced; our horses pushing through greenery.
Ahead of us the trees are thinning. Pell is in front of me. I am filled with
feelings that I cannot describe. It is as if Fate himself is looming above the
trees, filling the sky. At the time, I am not afraid nor even do I try to fight it.
A town has appeared. It is quiet, no smoke rising, no movement; the trees
have peeled back to reveal it. The town is red, the trees are green. We walk
our horses upon the road. 'Pell,' I say, 'let me go first. It might be dangerous.'
Pell shakes his head. We are both powerless, but we know nothing, only that
we love. We do not realize that all the time something has been following us,
leading us, directing us. I should have known. God, I should have known.
Love blinds me. Now the time for such teasing has come to an end. Pell can
play at life no more and my time of sanity is over. Back to the time of blood.
The end. We are not aware of what controls us because, for a time, we were
innocent and incapable of thinking about, let alone comprehending, a thing
so huge, so terrifying, so corrupt. We can only see each other and that is enough.

The bullet, when it comes, surprises me only by its sharp, exploding
sound. Pell is killed instantly. I see him jerk, fall from the trembling horse.
What's happened? It takes a moment to sink in. My face is stinging. Why?
Has a sharp twig snapped up and scratched me? What is it? Pell, what's
happened? He doesn't answer. He can't. Never again. Never. I watch my life
explode in a spray of blood and a scream; a horse's scream). Then madness

99

takes me and everything is cold, cold, cold. I look at him lying there, his fingers twitching. Screaming horses. Death. The smell of burning. There is light above the trees, taking him from me. A cold light. I am crying out because I'm sure it is the end.

If only it had been.

Jaddayoth is near. We are high up in the hills and the sharp, chill air is free of the stink of Fallsend, which is now far behind us. A fox with silver fur was watching me some moments ago as I wrote in the light of our campfire. His eyes were disks of gold. He watched me. Was he really a fox? Kruin and Panthera are asleep, rolled uncomfortably in blankets under the canopy of rock behind me. I have to take my gloves off to write and it is bitterly cold, but if I don't get it down on paper soon, I will begin to forget and the narrative will lose its edge. We have been travelling for a week, with, as yet, no sign of pursuit. I should have begun this before.

I'd been worried that some of the others in Piristil were suspicious of me, perhaps anticipating my plans — Flounah especially. For days I'd had to try and behave normally, not let anything slip, no matter how trivial, endure Outher's plodding and serious attempts at wooing me, prevent myself from packing away my belongings too soon. We weren't as prepared as I'd hoped we could be. There were too many areas in our plans where things could go drastically wrong, that we had no control over. I was concerned that we had so little Diamanda. It would be so much safer (and would improve our chances of success) if most of Piristil's occupants were slumbering peacefully as we made our getaway. On the actual night, obstacles arose like the fingers of a corpse who would not stay dead. It had taken careful machinations to nudge our time of escape onto a night when neither Panthera or I would be working. Suddenly, after dinner, Jafit told me he wanted me to see a client; a last minute arrangement. Flummoxed for a moment, I had to pretend to be ill, which also meant that Jafit relieved me of my duty of taking Panthera his dinner that night. Panicking furiously, I imagined Panthera would think our plans had been discovered if anyone else took my place of attending him. He might even do something rash. I thought it would be too risky and too suspicious to try and get a message to him. I'd just have to trust his faith in me and try to sneak into his room later. The drugged wine had already been delivered to Outher and his friends with a suitably simpering note. Timing was crucial. After the wine knocked them out, we had about half an hour to get out. I knew that Outher and the other Mojags usually ate their dinner about nine o'clock on nights when Panthera wasn't working. They would drink the wine after that. That gave me about two hours to get in there. I shut myself in my room and paced it from end to end for half an hour. Then Flounah knocked on my door and asked if I was alright. He'd heard the floor creaking. Irritably, I answered that I'd just got a stomach-ache; I'd be alright soon. He asked if I needed anything and I tried to calm myself by answering slowly. No, I didn't need anything, thank you. I would go to bed very shortly. I could sense him waiting on the landing outside my door for several minutes before he padded off. Did he suspect anything? Then Jafit came up, knocked and demanded to be let in. Feverishly, I opened the door.

'You look ghastly,' he said, touching my face. 'You should be lying down. Should I fetch a physician? Would you like one of the others to sit with you?'

I shook my head. 'No, I'll be fine, honestly. I get this complaint sometimes.' Once, such things would have been utterly plausible. But that was when I'd been human. Physical illness is not as common in Hara. Perhaps I'd been foolish expecting that they'd leave me alone. Jafit continued to fuss and I could barely restrain my temper. The thought, 'Look, will you just fuck off!' was dangerously close to becoming a spoken reality. Eventually, after I'd uttered more than enough reassurances that I would be fine in the morning, he left.

I locked the door again and sat down on the bed. I turned off the light and stood up again, crept to the window, gazed over at Panthera's dim lights. I tried to see if Kruin was lurking in the yard yet, but of course, it was too early for that. I fretted the time away, checking and rechecking the clock as its hands crawled lazily round the dial. I smoked seventeen cigarettes, but refrained from consuming either of the bottles of wine standing on the window-sill. I would be needing a clear head. My bags were packed and standing together on the carpet. I regretted having to leave the rugs behind.

Twenty minutes past nine o'clock, I put my ear to the door. All seemed silent outside. Working kanene would be busy in their rooms. Those who were off duty would either be in Fallsend or in one of the sitting rooms on the ground floor. Jafit, as far as I knew, was conveniently visiting a friend down town. I opened the door, looked out, and there was Flounah advancing down the corridor. *(Quickly, throw bags, coat behind me).*

'Oh, Calanthe,' he said, 'are you feeling better now?' I hoped the stricken feeling of horror inside me had not manifested on my face.

'A little,' I said weakly. 'I was just going to the bathroom.'

'The bathroom's that way,' Flounah said, pointing behind me.

'And to get a drink of milk from the kitchen,' I added stonily. Flounah smiled and walked past me. Seething with annoyance, I had to walk past the corridor that led to Panthera's wing and go downstairs. Now I would have to go back to my room to pick up my luggage. Nuisance, nuisance; damn these stupid whores! Lurking in the shadows of the hall, waiting to see if Flounah should come back again, I was surprised by Ezhno.

'Calanthe, are you alright?' he asked, as I physically jumped about two feet. Perhaps he thought I was delirious, standing there in the dark, peering up the stairs.

'Oh fine!' I said, 'Much better.'

'What are you doing here? Why have you got your outdoor clothes on?'

'I was cold,' I answered. 'I just came down to get a drink of water.'

'Why didn't you get one from the bathroom?' (Thank the Aghama my room didn't have its own water tap; what excuse could I have given then?)

'There was somebody in the bathroom!' I said, through gritted teeth. I longed to turn and smack him in the jaw, but knew he'd make too much noise.

'Why are you looking up the stairs?' He joined me, peering.

'That's none of your business, Ezhno!'

'What are you up to?'

I sighed, turned and looked at him for a few moments, sifting, discarding desires of murder. 'Ezhno, come with me,' 'I'll tell you.'

Putting my arm around his shoulders, I led him up the stairs. He said nothing as I went back to my room, hoisted my bag, grabbed my coat and silently closed the door. Said nothing, but stared at me all the time. I think he'd realized that I wasn't (nor had been) in the least bit ill, but had perhaps lost my sanity. Wise in the more cunning avenues of self-preservation, Ezhno, dumb little tart, kept his mouth shut. Luckily, there was no further sign of Flounah. Panthera's corridor was in darkness. There didn't appear to be a Mojag in sight, but the shadows seemed alive with potential adversaries. With panicking heart and a desperate urge to flee struggling inside me like a startled, cornered horse, I knocked on Panthera's door. Softly, briskly, Panthera called out, hissed out, 'Who is it?'

'Cal,' I answered, forgetting the new form of my name in my urgency. I think that was the moment when Calanthe disappeared into oblivion for ever. Some disguise. To the people I tried to hide from, names mean nothing. I heard a key turn in the lock and the door opened, spilling yellow light into the corridor. I dragged a protesting, wide-eyed Ezhno into the room with me quickly and Panthera closed the door behind us, turning the key in the lock. Panthera, thrumming with an energy that had bleached his face, turned his eyes to dark, animal disks, looked at Ezhno with distaste.

'What's this?' he asked me.

'What the hell is going on?' Ezhno squeaked, trying to struggle away from me. Worry had broken through his sensible silence. His eyes darted round the room, seeking bolt-holes.

I gripped his shoulder painfully. 'Keep your mouth shut!' I advised, giving him a small, warning shake.

Ezhno glared at me, but complied. He wasn't stupid.

'Oh wonderful!' Panthera spat. 'What do we do with this? And keep your voice down; you'll wake the Mojags.'

Behind him, I could see Outher and his companions around the table, all unconscious. One had slipped to the floor, while Outher and the other slept with their heads cradled in their arms on the table. They had suspected nothing.

'What kept you?' Panthera hissed. 'I nearly died when Astarth came in tonight. I thought we'd been found out and the Mojags had already started to drink the wine. I wondered whether your friend Kruin and I would have to leave Piristil without you.'

'Leave Piristil!' Ezhno had found his voice again. I twisted his arm until he yelped.

'He needs silencing,' Panthera observed. Ezhno made some further noise of disgruntlement so Panthera spun lightly round and kicked him in the side of the neck. Quite a feat. Ezhno was still pretty close to me. All I felt was the wind of Panthera's passing foot. Ezhno crumpled to the ground without a murmur. I had an idea that he might sleep a little longer than the Mojags. Panthera was dressed in black and still had the remains of the silver chains round his ankles. I could tell he felt completely confident about all this.

'Any sign of Kruin yet?' I asked and went to the window. With superb timing, Kruin's face popped up and we both jumped, Kruin nearly to his death in the yard below. He waved a fist at me.

'Hurry up!' I mouthed. Panthera was pulling on a pair of boots behind me, which I supposed he must have stolen from the Mojags. They did look a little loose on him, but it was too cold outside for sandals or soft slippers; he had no heavy shoes of his own.

'They keep moving,' he said, cocking his head at the table.

'Hmm, I'm not surprised. It was a light dose. (*Too light? No, don't think that*). God, I hope we have enough time. Come on, Kruin.'

Kruin did not hear me. He was busily applying a smoking liquid to the bars of the window, a scarf tied over his face.

'Think we could take these three on?' Panthera enquired. I looked at him, then at the powerful, lightly slumbering forms of the Mojags. Sometimes, the willowy Panthera can look surprisingly menacing, a creature who could kill by stealth rather than strength.

'Not three, no,' I said. 'Not even with your high kicks!' I continued to gesture encouragement at Kruin. Panthera opened the window, the sash squealing dreadfully, and overpowering, foul fumes began to drift into the room. Kruin pulled a forlorn face over his scarf as both Panthera and I began to cough.

'Shut the window!' Kruin ordered. 'If the smoke reaches the Mojags, they'll probably wake up.'

The window was swiftly closed. We looked through it anxiously. Kruin kept trying to break the bars, but they appeared unmovable. Eventually, after what seemed at least an hour, one of them moved in his hand.

'Thank the Aghama!' Panthera murmured beside me. His fear, anxiety had released an enticing Panthera-type aroma from his pores; a delicious scent of cinnamon and smoke. Even under such conditions of stress I couldn't help noticing it, wanting to fill my lungs with it, wipe out the corrosion-stink. All Hara have their own, bewitching perfume; passions of any kind can release it. Panthera became aware of my subliminal interest. He moved away from me and the moment was lost.

Just as Kruin was tugging and wrenching at the third bar, whose removal would give Panthera and myself enough room to squeeze through, there was a noise behind us. The door. I wheeled around and saw the key hanging from the lock, trembling, rattling. It fell, landing with a dull plop on the carpet. Whoever was on the other side of that door had the master key. Panthera and I exchanged an agonized glance. To both of us, a monster Jafit was waiting out there. Panthera swore and threw the window up on its sashes. More foul smoke billowed into the room. Behind us the door swung open. Not Jafit; Astarth. An Astarth with a key in his hand, looking right at me. His face was expressionless.

As air and fumes rushed into the room, Outher uttered a groan and began to lift his head, shake it, make further noises. 'Come on!' Kruin urged, panicking. He disappeared, dropping to the courtyard below. Outher was lurching towards us, looking about twenty feet tall, one hand over his eyes, unsure of what was happening. Astarth was feeling his way carefully into the room, one hand over his mouth and nose. It was getting very murky; smoke everywhere. Another Mojag began to stir and rise, the third still lay unconscious on the floor.

'Get going, Cal!' Panthera said. He was grinning from ear to ear, positively vibrating with force.

Suddenly movement seemed to erupt around us. The second Mojag scuttled forward, growling. Outher shook his head clearer, saw us properly and roared. Astarth ran forward, a bottle held purposefully in his raised hand. Panthera tried to push me out of the window, throwing our baggage down before me. Just as I jumped, I saw Astarth smash the bottle down onto the second Mojag's head, then I landed with a sickening jolt in the yard. Looking up, I could see Panthera poised on the windowsill. Silhouetted behind him was the lumbering form of Outher. Kruin helped me up, looking anxiously at Panthera. It was bitterly cold out there, our hot, steaming breath almost clouding the scene on the window-ledge.

'Jump!' Kruin called, but not too loudly for fear of attracting further attention. Pushing off, with an exhuberant cry, Panthera effortlessly kicked Outher in the throat, kicked him senseless back into the room, and soared backwards through the air, to land on all fours beside me. Astarth ran to the window, put his hands on the sill, leaned down. We stared at each other. I could not understand his motives. I could not speak.

'Get going,' he said, 'and good luck. Give my love to Jaddayoth.'

'Astarth?'

'Go on, quickly!' He smiled. 'Jafit will come after you, Calanthe. Don't let him beat you. Don't. Now go!'

'But Jafit will know what you did in there! He'll kill you!' An impulsive idea followed. 'Come with us, Astarth. Jump!'

He was still smiling at me, shaking his head. 'Would Jafit kill me for protecting his prize pussy-cat? It looked like the Mojags were attacking him, didn't it? Difficult to tell with the room all full of smoke. No, I didn't know what was going on, Calanthe. Don't worry about me; I'm indispensible. Just get going will you! Now!'

Then light was spilling out into the yard as the kitchen door opened. I heard Jancis' voice cry out.

'What's going on?'

I grabbed Panthera's arm and we ran after Kruin, both of us laughing hysterically in our mad panic. Our bags bumped into our legs, the one containing my notebooks thumping painfully against my back.

'Come on!' Kruin shouted. He was in the gateway to the street, already on horseback. Two other horses were prancing in the snow beside him. I could see the rolling whites of their eyes. Panthera, unbelievably, jumped on the nearest horse by vaulting over the tail.

I chose a more conventional method by using the stirrup, slinging my bags over the saddle. Behind us, activity in the yard became louder. We didn't look back. We shrieked and kicked the animals' flanks and skidded, slipped, half-galloped up the road, north out of Fallsend. Kruin had bought Gimrah horses and had to borrow money from the merchants for that purpose. Gimrah horses are fast, very fast. We were away before Jafit could follow us. Of course, we knew he would hire trackers to bring us back, or try to, as he had done when Panthera had escaped before, but we counted on him thinking we would opt for the quickest route, which was south. Obviously trained trackers wouldn't take long to realize that was the wrong way, but it could give us a little more time, a little more lead. Filled with the exhilaration of our success, I felt that what we had achieved that night was more of a memorial to Lolotea than what I'd accomplished with Astarth the previous week. We galloped madly past the forlorn, funeral hill. I waved into the snow-lit darkness. 'We did it, Teah!' Panthera's laugh echoed my cry.

'May Jafit drown in his own blood!' he said, and we all whooped and cheered as it began to snow once more. If it snowed thickly and quickly enough, our trail would be covered. We estimated that it would take some time for Jafit to engage the trackers — if we were lucky, as much as a couple of hours. We headed towards the main road out of the town so that our trail would be more difficult to follow. Few Hara were travelling at this hour, but the main road had been strewn with ashes all the same. What Hara we passed looked at us curiously for we were still travelling fast. Although this did attract attention, we felt that speed was more advisable than caution in this case. We rode all night, punishing the horses. By dawn, we were well into the hills north of Fallsend. All towns that we passed were deserted and overgrown. Kruin was familiar with this territory. 'We must keep north for a few more miles,' he said, 'and then head east towards Jaddayoth, following the River Scarm upstream. It should be more sheltered.'

As morning began to seep a red mist over the land, the cold crept back into our bones. Camp-fires would not be enough to keep us warm. It was going to be a long, uncomfortable journey.

A Tale by the Fire
Two roads diverged in a wood,
And I —
I took the one less travelled by

Robert Frost, The road not taken

Fereng will soon be behind us. We have had to cut across its corner to reach Jaddayoth. Here, the air is dry and bitterly cold, making our lungs ache and our eyelashes and nostrils frost over. There is no sign of pursuit from Fallsend yet, but we are not so complacent as to think they're not behind us somewhere. Up here, in the spiky, clean air, it becomes impossible to remember the details of life in Piristil; such things should never be possible. But if I can forget it with ease, I do not think the same can be said for Panthera. After the first flush of excitement and triumph, he became very subdued. Initially, I thought the weather conditions were getting to him. Kruin complained aloud and dreamed of the warm hearths of Natawni. I could not envisage the future, and I am used to cold (cold of heart and cold of body). All I could think of was putting enough distance between ourselves and Jafit.

One night, Panthera and I sat huddled round a meagre fire and he began to talk. Kruin was asleep behind us.

'I can't believe I'm free,' Panthera said.

'We're not yet!' I told him. 'We're only free when we reach Jael and the protection of your family.'

'Ah yes, my family,' Panthera said in a soft, cold voice, staring at the fire. 'They must think I'm dead.'

'What happened?' I asked. 'How come you were up for sale in Emunah anyway? Do you want to talk about it?'

'I'm not that sensitive about it, if that's what you think!' he said. 'If you really want to know; I'll tell you.'

'The night is long,' I replied, waving a hand towards the hard, starry sky. 'We're cold, without the support of alcohol or good food. Tell me your story, my pantherine. It may help to pass the time.'

Panthera shrugged. 'You're a ham,' he said, settling his chin comfortably on his knees. 'OK, here goes. First the background stuff. I was born to the family Jael in the land of Jaddayoth, among the forest hills of Ferike. My sire is the Ferike Castlethane Ferminfex Jael and my hostling an imported Kalamah named Lahela.' He smiled wistfully at the fire. 'Talk about myself? Very soon; maybe. Now I'll speak of my family, which is a story in itself. People back home write poems about my parents' courtship; I can't remember them though. But I do remember my father telling me about it, how one day, he was invited to the Kalamah city of Zaltana, by the Fanchon, its lord, and there it all began ...'

It was not just a sweet tale of romance as Panthera implied, but also a sneak preview of the Jaddayoth I intended to squeeze myself into; the world of the royal families. Round about the time Ferminfex received his missive from the Fanchon, Zaltana was nearing completion. Panthera said that the Kalamah work very slowly (lots of time for refreshments etc), but their architecture is splendid. Zaltana is a diamond of Wraeththu cities. The Fanchon wanted the history of its construction documented, his own accomplishments immortalized by written word — well-written word. The Ferike are the scholars and artists of Jaddayoth tribes. They are often called upon to undertake such work. Ferminfex set sail.

Zaltana is made of creamy, peachy marble and stands upon the coast. Ferminfex was immediately impressed by the wonderful, perfumed air of the place; hanging gardens of riotous, exotic blooms flavoured and coloured the city streets. He was in awe of the grand, lazy grace of the soaring buildings and the languid, feline beauty of its people. Day after day, Ferminfex would sit in the great library of the Fanchon's palace, working at his papers. He had been given a blond, pinewood desk still smelling of the forest, and as he sat there sunlight would fall on his hands through the open windows. Pausing from his work now and again to drink citrus cordial or smoke a musky, greenleaf cigarette, he would gaze out of the window at the langourous activities of the Kalamah.

In the late afternoons, before the early evening meal, the sons of the Fanchon would come to the tiled terrace beneath the library windows. They would sit on plump, tasselled cushions around their teacher who taught them to play strange, meowing music upon strangely clawed stringed instruments. Ferminfex would gaze down at them, as he took another drink, and be reminded of a pride of young lions from the land of Olathe. They always had their cats with them, purring and chirruping in cat voices to their small, feline companions. Delightful, artless creatures they were, with tawny, streaky hair like manes, and slim, supple bodies. Lahela was the eldest of them, past Feybraiha but seemingly unattached, and of such loveliness that even the austere and normally unmovable Ferminfex could not help but fall desperately in love with him. Every day, while watching Lahela, he would put aside the dry, dusty business of praising the Fanchon's achievements, to write long, passion-laden poems instead; hymns to the Fanchon's eldest son. Occasionally, Lahela would glance up at the library window and smile at him. He was not a proud creature. Perhaps Ferminfex even let one or two of his desperate odes float down to the terrace below, who knows. Panthera didn't say. I like to think he did.

The time came when the Fanchon asked Ferminfex to name his payment for the work he had completed. Without hesitation, the Ferike requested that he be given Lahela as his consort and be allowed to return with him to Jael. For a Ferike, this was not an unusual request; theirs is a tribe that often sells children to others who might want to improve their bloodlines. But it was not the custom in Zaltana. For a while, the Fanchon was quite taken aback, even affronted, by what he thought was Ferminfex's audacity. Lahela himself solved the problem by telling his father he was wholly agreeable to the arrangement. They were bonded in blood without hardly ever having spoken a word to each other.

'Romantic, isn't it,' Panthera said, at the end of his tale, 'and quite removed from what happened to me! My parents adore each other! True, the Jaels were annoyed by Lahela's Kalamah ways when he first came to Ferike, but I suppose they've got used to it now.'

'Your home is a happy one then?' I asked.

'Very.' Panthera frowned. His violation and degradation might offend that happiness.

'So, you've spoken mainly of Jael,' I said, too heartily, 'what about how you came to be in Emunah? I presume your family didn't sell you to slavers.'

Panthera laughed. 'No, but they were selling me in a way. That's what made it happen.'

'Oh?'

'Yes. I was approaching my Feybraiha, you see, and they were all concerned about who would be "the one" for me then, and all mixed up with that was Lahela thinking I should spend some time in Kalamah, because I was half-Kalamah, after all, and being cooped up in Ferike was denying me half my heritage, if not half my family. They came up with a cosy arrangement between them. The Fanchon had a spare cousin of mine knocking about who was quite a lot older than me but in need of a suitable consort. He was due to take over some far-flung Kalamah settlement on the Emunah border. Guess who was picked for him.' I pointed at him silently. Panthera nodded. 'Correct. Never mind the fact that I loved Ferike and didn't want to leave; that was irrelevant. "Panthera, you will be more at home in Kalamah," Lahela kept telling me. I knew he was wrong. I'm not that much like him; much more Ferike. I want cold and dark and trees all around me. I tried to protest but it was useless. Ferminfex said that I'd be able to come home whenever I wanted to; a chesna-bond was not imprisonment. "Aghama willing, you may like each other," he said, but I didn't hold out much hope. Cousin Namir. How I hated the name! To me it sounded cunning and sneaky. The name of a thief!

'I can remember the day we set out from Jael so well. It was autumntide and very misty and dank, Ferike looking its best to see me off and make me feel worse. I was being accomapnied by a guard of ten Hara, all armed with Maudrah weapons, all capable of being competent and deadly, should the need arise. First we were going to Gimrah to pick up a present for the Fanchon, a group of racing-steeds. Then we'd take a ship from the coast of Gimrah, straight to Kalamah. The guards barely spoke to me. I was full of anger. Even more so when I discovered they weren't nearly so efficient as my parents had thought. Crossing the plains of Gimrah, we were overpowered by a large gang of Emunah slavers. It was over in a trice. Me and three others were carted off to Meris; the rest of my escort was dead. For weeks, I existed in a kind of stunned trance. Things like this just don't happen to sons of castlethanes, surely? But they do. No rescue. No respite. Dignity stripped away until all that's left is self-loathing. And there were no Feybraiha garlands for me either, oh no! By sheer luck, I think, I remained untouched until Jafit got me back to Thaine. Then I lost my virginity to a half-formed Har who paid Jafit a lot of money for the privilege.' He shook his head. 'Vileness! Never again. Never. If my family searched for me, they found no clue to my whereabouts. No-one to tell them. No-one to care. The last three years have been more than hell for me, Cal. Much more. I'm not going back there. Ever. I'll die first. I mean that.'

'It's OK,' I soothed, reaching to touch his hand. He pulled away from me.

'No, it isn't OK!' he said angrily. 'You know how aruna is so important for us! All that is just a dim, dark memory of a possibility for me. Anyway, you're so keen to interrogate me, what about yourself? What secrets are you hiding, Cal?'

I don't think he expected me to answer truthfully. I shrugged. 'I may not be safe anymore. Not out in the open.'

'Is that all you're going to say?'

'It's all I can say. I don't feel anything yet, but I'm sure it will come. Fallsend was just a refuge. I could hide there, but not forever. There's no way I can hide out here; too big, too wide.'

Panthera looked puzzled by that answer. 'Who's after you?' he asked.

'I'm not sure. It could be one of several people. It could be many.

I don't know.'

Panthera leaned towards me, searching my eyes, which he would find empty of clues. 'What have you done, Cal? Why are you being followed?'

I smiled. 'Now, now, my pantherine, don't pry,' I said lightly. 'Have you considered that it might be because, not of what I've done in the past, but what they'd have me do in the future?'

Panthera narrowed his eyes. 'You speak in riddles. Why?'

'To protect you. I don't want to involve anyone else.'

'That's an excuse!'

'No, it's not.'

'You don't trust me. I told you everything.'

'It's not a question of trust, Panthera. Really it isn't. I can't explain. Please leave it be.'

He fell silent, moody because he had been denied something he wanted. We were sitting by an inadequate fire, both wary of pursuit. That night, we did not sleep.

CHAPTER

9

In Hadassah
*'Reprieve the doomed devil —
Has he not died enough?'*
Robert Graves, A jealous man

*O*f course, Seel is being very civilized about all this. There can't be many
times he's had a houseguest go for the throat of his best friend, but Seel
is, after all, a diplomat. Orien has gone home, nursing a bruised throat; Flick
is hiding in the kitchens, very silently. 'What do you know?' I say to Seel. Seel
shrugs, lighting a cigarette. 'Nothing, Cal, nothing. Have I ever lied to you?'
He is testing our friendship. I would like to believe him. I would like to
believe them all; they that claim to know nothing about Pell's death. Do they
really think I've forgotten Thiede came to Saltrock for Pell's inception? How
did Thiede know . . . unless he was told?

'You're not well, Cal,' Seel says to me. 'You haven't been well for a long
time, have you?'

'Always so goddam wise aren't you Seel!'

He smiles; tolerant. 'Who knows you better than I, Cal?'

Oh, he can look right through me to the black and rotten core, I'm sure.
Now I will avoid his eyes.

'Bed!' I say, standing up. It is late. There are wine bottles on the floor; I
knock one over. Seel stoops to put it on the table; as he stands he lays his hand
on my arm. 'Alone,' I say.

'You sure?' I'm sure; there's no way I could sleep next to those eyes. He
kisses me on the lips. 'Sleep well, Cal.'

Sleep? What's sleep? I grab two opened bottles of wine off the dresser on
my way out of the room.

My room is in darkness and I don't want to change that. I sit on the bed, drinking wine from the bottle. What the hell am I doing here? Saltrock can never be home to me now; too many memories. I drink, fumbling for a cigarette in the dark. Matches spill over the floor, the bed. Damn! Damn, damn, damn. I'm on the floor, grovelling, snatching at nothing. Then I'm curled up weeping; no violence, no punching the ground; just weeping. When someone comes into the room, I am beyond objecting. It feels as if I have no bones as they lay me on the bed. God, how I hate to cry. It hurts, contorts, makes me so vulnerable. Someone says, 'There was nothing I could say, Cal. Truly, there was nothing.' It is Orien. He's come back. He's come back because he cares. I look up, uncurl, at the sound of his voice.

'God, how I want to believe you,' I say. I am aware how I must look to him. Red eyes; childlike, helpless. He sits down on the bed, strokes my wet face.

'Then do believe it.'

'Oh, you knew, Orien; I'm convinced you did. Why didn't you warn us?'

He never stops looking at me, yet there is no guilt, no furtiveness in his eyes. 'There was no need,' he says. 'There was nothing I could tell Pell that he didn't know already.'

'What do you mean?'

'Just what I said. If he said nothing to you, that's not my fault. Or Seel's or Flick's or anybody else's . . . is it now.'

I want to say, don't you patronize me, but I just bury my face in the bedspread. Orien stands up to leave. I look up. He's standing there all lean and tawny and gentle; perfect Wraeththu. God, how I want to believe him; I can't stop thinking that. 'Don't go,' I say.

He hesitates, looks once at the door. It is a long moment. He smiles into my eyes and it's a slow, sad smile. He pushes his hair back from his face. 'If you need me, I'll stay,' he says.

'I need you.' Come to me, Orien, come to me. Let me feel your warmth; penetrate my eternal cold. Please. Oh, I am so desperate; I want to melt. Is he surprised by my desire? Yes, he is. Maybe, he thinks it's irreverent because of my grief, but he complies all the same. Soothing, slow, languorous; that's Orien. A skilled lover. Afterwards, I sit up in bed to watch him fall asleep. One arm is thrown above his head; blankets thrown off to below his waist. He looks like the son of God. After a while I get out of bed and squat down in the corner of the room, still watching him. He barely moves; just the rise and *fall of his chest. Moonlight is falling through the window to burn me, my knees hunched up nearly to my ears. I don't feel well. My insides are aching. The room is black and white; no colour at all. How come I'm dressed like this, dressed to leave? I don't remember. How come my bag is packed and standing by the door? Have I been awake for a long time? Have I blacked out? How come there's a long-bladed knife in my hand? My hands are trembling; the sharpness catches the moonlight and shivers between my fingers. Slowly, I run the back of my left hand over the blade. So sharp. Hand to mouth; blood upon my tongue. Salt. Salt. I am not afraid of death. Are you, Orien? Are you afraid of death? He looks perfect. I stand up; the room tumbles, bars of black and white across my face, my hands. Adepts fear nothing. If he wakes up he'll take the knife away from me, won't he? His eyes will command me. There's nothing to fear, but I must go on. I can't stop myself, you know, I really can't. It's the moonlight; must be. It's hypnotized me. All these black and white lines; they're driving right through me. Won't go away until I've made things balance. That moon out there, it looks like an eye. (Why did he have to come back? Why?) I'm thinking of eyes even as I stand over him with the knife raised, but it's straight for the belly that I strike.*

Twisting, tearing; quick ruin. Up, beneath the ribs, though flesh and muscle, scraping bone. I feel it. I feel it. He gasps and his eyes flick open. He grabs my wrist; my hands are still around the knife-hilt protruding from his flesh, but his hold just slips away. I am already greasy with his blood. The blade has gone all the way in. I rip it out. He says nothing, just looks at me, his face bleached white, his hair, eyes and mouth deepest black. Maybe I should have obliterated his face; I couldn't. I just keep on stabbing, ripping into his belly until there is nothing left to stab. He never even tries to defend himself. Why? No, I don't care why. He could have warned us; he didn't. If we'd known, maybe Pell would be alive now. With me. A life for a life. That is the law. Nothing unfair about that, is there?

I am warm with his blood and drag him from the house. Take him home. The temple, the Nayati. A fine surprise for the next blind worshippers. I hang him from the rafters by his own guts. My mind is blank; no feeling. It doesn't hurt me to do this, doesn't sicken me; nothing. There is a red film of blood over his dead eyes; he will watch the moonlight through the long windows forever. Let him remember. Let him rue the day he kept silent.

That's it. Nothing else. I steal a horse and leave, galloping north. By daylight, the lunatic remembers nothing.

* * *

It is surprising how quickly you get to know people, travelling together on the road. I found Kruin mostly easy-going, although he does like to take control, which Panthera doesn't like at times. Panthera himself is an enigma to me. In Piristil, I'd categorized him to be someone very much like Cobweb; proud, vain and veering sharply towards the feminine. Out here in the wilds, he seems completely different; competent, sharp and helpful. He has also shown, in sometimes hair-raising circumstances, that he has no fear whatsoever. He is frightened of nothing. Sometimes, this kind of thing can prove to be a disadvantage, like not being able to feel pain. It's convenient most of the time, but just occasionally it is extremely useful to feel the burn as you walk across hot coals; it preserves the flesh and bone of the feet! Sometimes, it is best to feel afraid. I've never been ashamed to admit when I've been frightened gutless.

We often wonder whether Jafit has worked out which way we've come yet. None of us has dared to think he's given up the chase. It is deathly quiet in this landscape of snow; all the land is sleeping. We are following the river canyon east, climbing all the time. Our supplies are running low. Kruin urged the need for haste. We rest the horses as little as possible.

Yesterday, we passed a small, snow-covered shrine nestling in a shallow hole in the rock face. There was a spring there, a wide, stone bowl, but the water was frozen. Kruin and I broke the ice and melted some of it in a saucepan over the fire. Our horses nosed dispiritedly through the snow, looking for something to eat. We'd had to be mean with their rations for some days now. One of them chewed bark off a tree.

Panthera said, 'Well, well, this is a shrine dedicated to the Aghama. I wonder what it's doing here, in the middle of nowhere?'

An icy shudder, that was not caused by the weather, passed right through me.

'Gelaming use this road sometimes,' Kruin said. I couldn't help glancing nervously behind me, down river. Panthera must have noticed.

'I doubt if they pass this way in winter,' he said. 'I expect they'll all stay comfortably in the sublime land of Almagabra, and I don't blame them!'

'Not if someone is due for relief in one of the stations they occupy along the Natawni/Maudrah border,' Kruin argued mildly.

'They don't travel overland very often,' I said.

'This must be a stopping point then,' Panthera decided, stroking the stone of the shrine.

I shuddered again, not being able to imagine anything worse than a troupe of Gelaming materializing out of thin air at any time. Even Jafit and a horde of Mojags would be preferable. I was anxious to move on. Kruin and Panthera wanted to camp there for the night, as it was so sheltered. The rock wall on this side of the river was quite high and overhung with trees. I tried to argue with them but could give no good reason for my aversion. The rock protected us from the wind and it was doubtful anyone could sneak up on us unseen. It was eerily silent in that place; the river was frozen, its life hidden deep beneath the ice. As darkness fell, I wrapped myself in a blanket and climbed up the rock to survey the countryside. It was difficult to see anything.

Presently, Panthera joined me. 'You're afraid of the Gelaming, aren't you,' he said.

'Hmm. To them I carry the mark of Cain,' I answered.

'And what's that?'

'It's something that tells me to keep away from them at all cost, if I value my sanity and my freedom.'

'Oh.' He thought about this, not sure if he was supposed to have understood my answer. Panthera was much younger than I, of course. He was born of another world, born Har.

'There are stories, other legends, from a long time ago,' I said, but then could not continue. The tale was too bleak. Wind sliced my skin; cold to the heart.

'The past *is* interesting,' Panthera agreed, knowing he'd get no more out of me. He clambered back down the rock, leaving me to stare out at the endless landscape of grey and white and snow-covered pines, poking rock.

Several mornings later, we passed through the gateway into

Jaddayoth. Totems along the path proclaimed that this was Hadassah territory. Kruin told me that the Hadassah are perhaps the most gregarious tribe of Jaddayoth, and never discourage travellers. 'Smell the air!' Panthera cried joyfully, filling his lungs with it. Only seconds before, we had been in Fereng. The air smelt no different to me. I must admit that having Jaddayoth soil beneath our feet did make us feel safer. Slightly. Would Jafit risk pursuing us this far? Was Panthera worth that much to him? How mad was Jafit, how deep his thirst for revenge?

'I think we should head south immediately,' Kruin said. 'We can pass through Gimrah. The land is flatter there and we'll be able to travel faster.'

'Elhmen might be safer,' Panthera said.

'Hmm, perhaps, but I still don't feel happy about the Fallsend trackers,' Kruin confessed. 'We got away too easily. Only reaching Jael by the quickest possible route will make me feel safe!'

We didn't argue with him.

'Strange, in a way, I hope they *do* find us,' Panthera said, after a while. Neither Kruin nor myself deigned to comment. It was clear from Panthera's tone that he still thought Jafit had a debt to pay.

The following day, about mid-morning, we rode into a Hadassah town, Caraway. It was quite a busy place, though not large, and had been constructed recently (during the last twenty years or so). Many — too many — Harish towns are those claimed from humans. There was something curiously fresh about this little place that was not. Hara looked at us with interest as we rode by, but no-one stopped us and asked our business. I commented on the number of inns. Kruin laughed and pointed out that he'd already told me the Hadassah welcome travellers. Because of our severe lack of funds, it was decided, rather glumly, that we couldn't really afford the luxury of a decent meal at an inn, which was a shame because we were all starving. Our meals along the road had necessarily to be frugal, but we did agree to partake in one small measure of ale each, which was cheap.

The inn we chose was warm and cosy inside and, because of the early hour, nearly empty. We stood around the roaring fire and put our drinks on the mantelpiece, holding our stiff, unmittened hands to the blaze.

'We're going to have to find more funds,' Panthera said.

Kruin agreed with him without argument for once. 'We might have to sell one of the horses,' he said.

'Won't that slow us down too much?' I asked, still the nervous one.

'Not as much as slowly starving to death,' Panthera said wearily. 'Why the hell does it have to be winter!'

Presently, the pot-Har came from behind the bar to talk with us. He was dressed in brightly-coloured clothes and wore heavy brass jewellery. He commiserated with us over the bitter cold and told us that he, personally, would hate to have to travel at this time of year. We agreed earnestly.

'Will you be ordering a meal?' he asked. 'We serve lunches from mid-day, but I could get you something from the kitchen if you're hungry now.'

'No, thank you,' Kruin said politely. 'I'm afraid we are travelling with light purses. One glass of ale each is as far as we can stretch, and a free warming in front of your splendid fire of course.'

The Hadassah smiled, and gestured towards the highly polished tables beneath the back windows of the inn. 'Please sit down,' he said. I looked in puzzlement at Kruin, who ushered me to the nearest table. Panthera followed. We sat, and the Hadassah disappeared through the door behind the bar.

. 'Ah, Hadassah hospitality!' Kruin beamed. I asked him to explain. 'We'll be given a free meal, that's all,' Panthera said. 'The Hadassah are famed for their generosity. The pot-Har pities us.'

'I get the feeling that you anticipated something like this when you mentioned we had no money,' I said, wagging an uncontrollably contented finger at Kruin.

He smiled and made a non-commital gesture. 'A small gamble,' he said. 'We had nothing to lose.'

I was quite impressed.

Hadassah fare was offered to us in the form of thick, vegetable soup, hunks of warm bread and sour winter fruit, softened with sugar and cream. The pot-Har watched us devour the food with satisfaction. He refilled our glasses and sat down with us. 'You've come down from Fereng?' he asked, Kruin nodded, assuming leadership, as usual.

'Hmm. We hardly get any travellers from out of country passing through at this time of year,' the pot-Har said casually. 'Strange we should entertain two parties within two days.'

Panthera, Kruin and I swapped uneasy glances.

'Another party from Thaine?' I asked.

'Well, to be honest, they were a little uncommunicative, in fact, quite rude. Because of that, I took the liberty of charging them more than usual for their meals. They were asking if we'd seen any other strangers recently.'

'Which road did they arrive on?' Kruin asked, with enviable calm.

'The south road, I believe. Don't envy whoever it is they're after; they had killer eyes.'

'They intimated they were *after* someone then?' I enquired.

The Hadassah shrugged. 'It was reasonable to assume so. Certain questions were asked. Had I seen any other outlanders recently? I hadn't. They seemed satisfied with my answers.'

'And where are they now, this other party?' I asked, as carelessly as I could.

'I'm afraid I'm not sure. They weren't staying here. They may have left Caraway.'

'Thank you,' Kruin said, and the pot-Har inclined his head and left us.

We resumed our meal in silence.

'Jafit's trackers?' Panthera asked after a while. An obvious remark which we'd all been contemplating, I'm sure.

'Seems likely,' I said, convinced of the fact. 'But from the south? How could they have followed our trail?'

'Maybe they didn't!' Panthera said. 'There are few clear roads into Jaddayoth at this time of year. It wouldn't take a genius to work out which way we'd have to come.'

'They probably went south into Elhmen from Fallsend,' Kruin continued, 'and when they realized we hadn't gone that way, simply circled round, knowing full well they'd have a good chance

of intercepting us once we turned south. That Jael is our destination is unfortunately obvious. As Panthera said, clear roads are few
and far between.'

'It was luck, just luck, on their side!' Panthera interrupted
bitterly.

'Well, they don't know we're here yet, hopefully,' I said.
'Perhaps we'd better move on as soon as possible.'

Outside the inn, the friendly town of Caraway suddenly seemed
threatening and hostile. Perhaps there were unseen eyes watching
us, spies reporting back, even a Sensitive poised somewhere with
probing mind. We set off at a brisk pace and were cantering down
the south road out of the town within minutes. Our silence was
only breath steaming on the air, panting breath. We did not look
back. It is an ill-omen to look back. At noon we entered a dense
forest, veering off from the main road, where the snow was packed
and hard, into a desolate place of wind-sculpted drifts and stark
pines. Kruin was vaguely familiar with the path, but it was difficult
to follow under these conditions.

'This track should come out of the forest near the town of
Jasminia,' he said, shaking his compass.

We slowed to a walk and the only sounds were the muffled
tread of our horses' hooves in the snow and the occasional, startled
rattle of a bird spiralling up through the trees. There was no
outward sign of anyone following us, but we were all plagued by
the horrible feeling of being observed. As the sun began to sink and
the trees cast gloomy shadows over the snow, we were still deep in
the forest. There were no clouds; it was bitterly cold. Kruin
annoyed Panthera and myself by continually muttering, 'We *should*
be out of the trees, we *should* be.' We weren't. A painfully definite
fact that was not going to change in a short time. And we didn't
need reminding of that. Panthera said that the way things were
going, we would just have to try and find work in Jasminia — if we
ever got there. 'There's no way we'll reach Jael on the supplies we
have, and the horses are beginning to lose condition.'

'Want to risk hanging around then?' Kruin asked tetchily.

'We have no choice! Anyway, we have no proof that it was Jafit's
people who were seen in Caraway.'

'Don't be stupid!'

'I'm not. Why don't *you* stop being paranoid! We have to face this problem. There's no way it's going to just vanish. I haven't broken out of Piristil just to freeze to death in Hadassah!'

They continued to snipe at each other, but not with any great feeling. Their eyes and their minds were kept mainly on the gaps in the trees. I rode along behind in a kind of idiot daze. Perhaps it was just the cold, but I'd felt strange ever since leaving the road, picking up memories like bad visualizations. Pictures kept surfacing in my mind like murder victims in a mud patch. Unfortunate simile. Feelings, smells, tastes, a snatch of words. It all just drifted over me. I should have known it was a warning that power was near. Before Fallsend, I'd have put spur to flank and ridden the horse to death to escape that feeling.

At sundown, we crawled beneath a fallen pine and curled up together among the roots, in our blankets. We did not light a fire and I, for one, was thankful for the hot meal the Hadassah had given us that morning. I could not sleep, discomforted by Kruin's elbow in my chest, the sound of breathing all around me, that distanced any sounds beyond the branches. I stared up through the black, root fingers hanging over us, that were dripping with frozen soil. After several cheerless hours, I must have drifted off to sleep, only to awake soon after with an excruciating urge to urinate. I was reluctant to leave our bony nest of shared body warmth, but the need was too pressing to ignore. Fumbling through the branches, I stretched into the icy air.

All around me the forest lay white and black and silent, the snow sparkling in the light of a white, round moon that sailed above the treetops. My nerves were still raw and itching, but I roughly tried to suppress such sensations. 'Paranoia, Cal!' I chastized myself, which was foolish. I deserved what happened. There I was, in mid-stream, for want of a better term, when someone said softly, 'Calanthe.' It was not the best time to be surprised by an unwelcome visitor. I looked, squinted, into the trees and a figure materialized out of the gloom. My first thought was 'Gelaming!' and I froze, helpless in blind panic. If I'd realized who it really was I might have reacted differently. A knife blade kissed my throat with its sharpest point. I could not turn my head without risking injury, but I knew it was Jafit standing beside me. He grabbed my hair as I modestly rearranged my clothing, his thickly-gloved hand yanking my face close to his own. He shook his head as if in sadness. 'I'm disappointed in you, my dear,' he said.

'Then you were a fool to trust me,' I replied, finding my voice. 'Get your hands off me, Jafit. You have the position of advantage here, I think.'

'Haven't I just!' he agreed affably. 'Where's my Panthera?'

'Not *yours*, Jafit.'

'Be quiet. You are surrounded. You have no chance. Just hand him over, Calanthe, and I might, just might, let you off with a thorough beating.'

'What, and then let me go free?' I laughed in his face. 'You can drop dead, pimp! Both Panthera and myself will die before you take him back to Piristil!'

'Oh, how touching,' Jafit said, nastily.

I realized that, by this time, Panthera and Kruin must be awake, but were obviously lying low, waiting to see what would happen. I was not entirely sure how I felt about that. Support would have been most welcome at that point. Jafit, barely able to suppress his nauseating, triumphant leer, clicked his fingers and five Hara emerged fully from the cover of the trees, to stand menacingly beside him and around me. Three of them were Mojags, one of these was Outher. Outher stared at me blankly, obviously still raw from my betrayal. I had hoped never to see him again, mainly because he was not a bad sort, and I knew I must have hurt him.

'Search the area!' Jafit ordered, with a tasty mouthful of satisfaction.

'That won't be necessary, Jafit.' The voice was cool, and there was Panthera with his back to the fallen pine, looking as mean and deadly as a she-cat about to defend her young. He held a slim-barrelled gun in his hands, which was pointed directly at Jafit's head. Jafit looked thunder-struck with surprise. Was he really so stupid that he thought Panthera couldn't defend himself away from his chains? The Mojags scorned firearms, but the other two (who were deducably trackers) quivered to draw their own. 'Tell them to be sensible,' Panthera said, still clear, still calm. He must have felt wonderful in those moments. Jafit didn't respond, but the trackers lowered their hands anyway. 'Kruin!' Panthera called. 'Get the weapons.' Like a shadow, forest-creature that he is, Kruin slipped past us. Jafit's Hara made several disgruntled protests as he took their knives and guns. The Mojags also had axes and slim, whip-like swords, which must look rather incongruous in their large paws. Kruin looked up and smiled at me.

Too late, out of the corner of my eye, I saw the quick gesture that Jafit made, and that was when Outher, obeying some subtle command, decided to become a hero. With a roar, he jumped Kruin from behind, his large, lithe body covering several yards in one leap. Panthera should have shot him immediately. He didn't. I don't know why. He'd kept his head until that moment. Outher was much taller than Kruin; an easy target. Instead, incensed by whatever inner rages were motivating him, Panthera decided to empty the contents of the gun into Jafit's brain. Jafit fell to the ground, grunting in surprise. One shot would have been enough at that range.

'What the fuck are you doing?' I screamed. 'Stop it! There are *five* of them!'

Panthera remained staring at the twitching body of Jafit. The gun smoked in the chill air. Behind us, Outher and Kruin grappled noisily, though Kruin's cries were from pain and frustration, Outher's from glee. The others were advancing warily, perhaps unsure whether Panthera, in his new role of mad, indiscriminate killer, had any more weapons on him.

'Panthera!' I cried again. He seemed to shake himself, wake up. 'The others!' I said, gesturing wildly.

'Oh, the others,' he said and raised the gun, but of course, the barrel was empty and all the spare ammunition was beneath the tree. Outher threw Kruin, coughing, to the ground, where he lay groaning, knees to stomach. Outher appeared to have assumed leadership of his fellows.

'Bring Calanthe to me,' he said and stood back grimly, with folded arms, to let the others take us. We fought as best we could but, in our defence, I can only say that three super-fit Hara of any tribe are no match for a single Mojag. They really are a mutated strain of the Wraeththu type. Panthera kicked up and out viciously, and was nearly always on target, but free from the influence of Diamanda, they could shrug off his assault as if it was merely the brush of an insect's wing. I can remember clearly a pretty array of stars exploding inside my head as a Mojag fist (it felt three feet wide) smacked me heartily in the face. After that, things get a bit muzzy for a while.

Jafit's party must have made camp further away from the road. When I came to my senses again, I found myself lyig in a heap on the floor of a large, leather tent. It was quite warm and pungent in there. For a moment or two, I couldn't remember what had happened to me, then I became aware of the lumbering presence of Outher as he squatted beside me. The light inside the tent was dim and brownish, but I knew it was him. He was indistinct, but there was no mistaking the hostility of his manner. I pulled my aching bones into a sitting position. 'Any chance of a drink?' It was difficult to speak. My face felt several sizes too large for my head. Outher did not answer me. It was clear that, as far as he was concerned, I was merely a wayward whore who had stepped above his station, fit only for the dubious practices of pelcia and chaitra. I could see he was regretting ever having offered me a way out. He'd misjudged me and that had made him angry with himself and me. He'd treated me with honour, which had been wasted. I was only a thing to be used. Never speaking, he lunged towards me, throwing me backwards, ripping at my bruised body with steel, wounding paws. I struggled gamely, calling on every forgotten god I could think of and screaming out withering curses, but it was all to no avail. Tense against his brutality, I felt my flesh tear. I don't know whether he intended to kill me or not, but it was one of the vilest experiences I have ever lived through. In the back of my mind lurked the horrid, saintly thought that this was something I'd deserved for a long time. As a Uigenna warrior, I'd thought nothing of violating those weaker than myself. Self-loathing, pain, and fear of death do not make a palatable cocktail.

When Outher threw me away from him like a used rag, I was weeping uncontrollably, blood and snot and tears hanging from my face in strings. It was the absolute depths of the abyss. He threw a cupful of water over my head, which brought me to my senses a little. It was too painful to wipe my face. I sat up, knees to chest, dazed, yet aware that something terrible was over. Outher was fastidiously rearranging his clothing.

'Where are the uvvers?' I croaked. He did not answer. 'Outher?'

He turned and looked at me, perhaps surprised to see that I was not as beautiful as he'd once thought. He had no words for me though.

'C'n you really blame me for what I did?' I said. 'If you'd 'ad any sense you'd 've done the same thing, years ago. Panthera's fam'ly'll pay 'ighly for'is return.'

Outher stared at me stonily. 'Panthera will be returned to Piristil now,' he said.

I made an exasperated noise, which had me wincing in agony. It was becoming more and more difficult to speak as my face swelled with every second. 'What for?' I asked, in a muffled voice. ''Afit 's dead. Surely, 'n mos' people's eyes Piristil 's no more.'

'In most people's eyes, Piristil is now Astarth's,' Outher said, 'and I have no doubt that he will continue to pay my wages just as Jafit did. Panthera earns a damn sight more for Piristil than his family will ever pay for his return, I can assure you.'

''Ot abow moral obligation?' I managed to gobble out. It was surprising Outher understood me, but he did.

'Oh, and what can you tell me about that, Calanthe?' he asked meaningfully. The silence was tense.

''Ot're goin' t'do wi' me?' I mumbled at last. ''Ot abow Kruin?'

Outher finished lacing his shirt. He paused to consider before answering. 'You will be bled to death. Both of you.'

'What!' Despite the pain, I couldn't help bubbling out an uncontrollable laugh. 'Bled t'death? You serious?' I couldn't believe it.

'You want reasons, Calanthe? Shall I jog your memory? First,' he held up one finger, 'you have abducted a slave. Two,' another finger, 'you have murdered your employer …'

'No, Thea 'id dat,' I interrupted.

'Two, *conspired* to murder your employer.'

'Bullshit Outher!' I exclaimed, with remarkable clarity, but still emitting a spray of red-mottled saliva. 'You're goin' t'kill me 'n yer own c'lourful way 'cause I … I … you …*hurt*!' My garbled speech, (which was probably even less coherent than I have related) dissolved completely. Before I could utter further painful truths (in both senses), Outher knocked me backwards with his foot.

'Quiet, Calanthe. If you annoy me again, I'll just have you tied to a tree and leave you to starve to death, if the cold doesn't finish you off first, of course.'

'Kruin …' I said. 'Why? 'Ot's 'e …?'

'I just don't like him,' Outher said, as if that was a grand and flamboyant thing to say. He put his booted foot on my chest.

'The Aghama has given you a fine body, Calanthe,' he said. 'It is almost a pity to take its life, but then it will serve as a splendid sacrifice!' He snarled and walked out of the tent.

I longed to throw some smart remark out behind him like, 'You're lousy in bed, Outher!' but it was too much effort. I heard him laughing as he ducked beneath the door-flap. Obviously, his friends were waiting outside. I lay on the floor for a long time, until I started to feel really cold. All the adrenalin had gone. I tried to sit up and my head protested with a furious swipe of pain. Squinting, I looked for my clothes. They were nowhere to be seen. The tent was virtually empty. I wrapped myself in the rough blanket of Outher's bed and staggered, nearly bent double, to the door-flap. All I did was lift the leather curtain a little before some over-conscientious guard outside slammed a gun butt down on my wrist. Cursing unintelligably, I retreated like a beaten animal to the bed and eased myself down. Where were the others? Had they suffered similar abuses to my own? I desperately needed a drink and there was no more water. Outher had made sure of that. I needed to rest but my mind was too hectic. When was our execution scheduled to take place? How much time had we got? What, in God's name, could I do about it?

I fretted alone for what seemed hours, but which was probably just minutes, before the door-flap was lifted again and Outher's statuesque frame was silhouetted against the light.

'Right you; outside!' he ordered.

'Don't you mean "outside *please*"?' I managed to enquire with quite a steady voice, whilst lurching to a swaying stand. 'Where are your manners, Outher?'

In reply, he grabbed hold of my arm and hauled me out of the tent behind him, blanket trailing. He took me a short way to a small clearing in the trees, where the snow beneath our feet was muddied. My legs could not work; I let him drag me. In the clearing, looking embarrassed, and blue with cold, a defiant Kruin stood naked facing the Mojags and the trackers. One of the Mojags was restraining a bound Panthera by holding onto his luxuriant hair. Outher threw me into the clearing and Kruin broke my fall. he bent to help me up. 'My God, Cal, you're ...' He waved a fist at Outher. 'Bastard!' he screamed, following that with a colourful string of profanity. The Mojags laughed. Outher sauntered over to Panthera and grabbed his gagged chin in his huge hand.

'Now, little cat,' he said, 'we're going to have an entertainment. Hope you're not squeamish; it's especially for you. In your honour. Now make sure you watch it.'

Panthera moaned and writhed, helpless. A tracker and a Mojag hauled Kruin and myself over to a large tree. Our hands were tied and the rope nailed to the trunk, so our arms were above our heads. As they secured the nails, Kruin said, 'I've heard of this; it's a popular method of execution in Mojag.'

'Does knowin' that help us?' I burbled weakly.

'No.' Kruin's voice was tight. I think he was afraid, although, strange as it sounds, I was not. Perhaps I was numbed by pain and wanted only to be released from it, or perhaps it was because I have never been afraid of Death. There are far worse things in this world to fear. I was prepared for unpleasantness, the sensation of slipping away, even more pain, and wished we were being dispatched by a quicker method, but my mind was uncommonly calm. My life did not flash before my mind's eye, but I did think of Pell. I wondered if he was still watching me, whether he was writhing in anxiety because we were so far apart. Could he have done anything to help us? Perhaps these thoughts were what saved us; I don't know. A shining thought of Pell. But of course, I'd had intimations of Gelaming proximity in the forest the day before, which I'd ignored.

Outher came towards us, showing us the razor-sharp knife with which he hoped to take our lives. It was all very solemn. No more laughter. I could see Panthera, dimly, struggling against his bonds. From far away, I could hear his muffled cries.

'Well, here we go then,' Kruin said in a shaking voice. 'See you on the other side, Cal. Better luck next time.'

'Not till I've haunted these fuckers to death,' I murmured. The blade touched my throat, forcing my head up. I closed my eyes. 'Now,' I thought. 'This is it. Now. Everything for nothing. I've been such a fool ... Oh God ...'

But the incisive kiss never got deeper. It was as if everything around me seemed suddenly to stop; no, not suddenly, it was more like a winding down, a film slowing down. I couldn't open my eyes. I couldn't even breathe. I couldn't move anything, but it did not matter. There was no discomfort. It was not like being frozen, but like being utterly incorporeal and numb. My soul should be roaming free but it was trapped within my flesh. Astral travelling within my own body? An odd sensation. Is this death, I wondered. Was it that quick? And then I became aware of people around me; movement and voices. I became aware of the cold blade still pressed against my skin and then it was taken away. Breath shuddered painfully through my lungs, sucked in powerfully as if into a vacuum. A few seconds later and I could move again. I opened my eyes and then shut them again quickly. There was a raw shout that cried, '*No!*' Mine.

'Oh, yes,' another voice answered softly. 'We meet again, Calanthe. Please, look at me.' It would have been petty and futile to resist, even ungrateful; I presumed I'd just been rescued. I opened my eyes and looked at him.

'In the nick o' time, Arahal,' I mumbled. 'S'pose I shou' thank ...'

He inclined his head, an outlandish vision of silver and waving black feathers. Tall as a Mojag, twice as handsome, three times as intelligent. I knew him as the Gelaming Arahal, a commanding officer in one of Pell's armies, and one of the most highly respected members of Immanion society. Through fate or chance or purpose, he had materialized here, in order to save my miserable skin. Gelaming do that sort of thing. It is not unusual. It is the kind of display of power that appeals to their naturally — aggressively — peaceful natures. Had they been watching me again? How long? Arahal took a dainty, ornate knife from his belt and cut my bonds. I fell into his arms and he breathed healing, anaesthetic Gelaming breath all over my face. I could not help but welcome it, no matter how much I wanted to deny it. Effortlessly, almost without thinking, he drew the pain from my body, and fed me with his limitless strength. 'Made a mess of your face, haven't they,' he said conversationally.

'Why are you here?' I asked. He sat me on the floor, with my back to the tree and continued to explore my injuries with the light from his slender fingers.

'Hmm? Oh, we had a message.' He threw this remark out lightly, hardly concerned with what he was saying. 'Cal, you'll have to rest.'

'Watching me …? Have you …?'

He smiled and stroked my cheek. 'Now then, don't worry yourself about such things.' He wrapped me in the fallen blanket. 'Now, I'd better see about sorting out your friends, hadn't I?' He stood up and gestured towards the edge of the clearing. About half a dozen Gelaming were shimmering there, all mounted on the fabulous, white horses of their tribe, that do not just gallop over land, but through space and time and dreams. At Arahal's beckoning, the Gelaming dismounted and spread out through the clearing. Arahal twisted his fingers high in the air, cried out, and there were the Mojags, who had been immobilized, lurching to life again, just as I had. I smiled inside at their bewilderment. They staggered a little. Then Outher saw Arahal and pulled himself up straight, clenching his fists at his sides. Gelaming are unmistakable. Anyone recognizes a Gelaming when they see one, even a Mojag.

'Before you say anything,' Arahal said to him mildly, 'I must point out that under the ruling of the Confederation of Tribes, the cold-blooded taking of life is a gross offence.'

Outher spluttered for a moment, before crying indignantly, '*They* are the murderers!' pointing a rigid finger at me. I could not turn my head to look at Kruin, but I could hear him gasping heavily, obviously still disorientated.

131

Arahal made an irritated gesture. 'It is not for you to take justice into your own hands, tiahaar, no matter how aggrieved you might feel.'

'But ... I ... we ...' Outher was lost for words.

'Be quiet. Now, you have a fire; bring hot water. Learn humility. See to these Hara's wounds.' Arahal shivered. 'By the Aghama, it's cold out here! Zaniel, free the other two.'

Once unbound, Kruin huddled up against me. 'What's happening?' he asked. 'What's happening? God, I *ache*!'

I shook my head. Presently, Panthera joined us, bringing a blanket for Kruin. Neither of them seemed to have been knocked about too badly; I felt crippled.

'They're Gelaming, aren't they,' Panthera said to me, staring curiously at my battered, multi-hued face. 'Why did they come? How did they know? They *did* know, didn't they?'

'No questions,' I said. 'Not yet.'

'I'm sorry,' Panthera said, lightly touching my blanketed arm. 'Here, I'll help you to one of the tents. Come on, lean on me.' Clutching each other, Panthera, Kruin and I shuffled past the dumbfounded group of Fallsend trackers and Mojags. They eyed us stonily. I could hear Arahal lightly issuing orders.

Arahal let me sleep for nearly a day. Early the next morning, he came into our tent and politely asked Panthera and Kruin if he could speak with me alone. He had brought me some hot coffee liberally spiced with fragrant shrake, a Gelaming liqueur. Gelaming always carry such luxuries with them.

He watched me drink, shaking his head. 'You are a puzzle to me, Cal,' he said. 'When are you going to learn?'

'Learn what?'

He stood up, sighed. 'Do you really need me to tell you? Are your senses that dull? I remember that, at one time, Calanthe would have had no trouble outwitting Jafit and his kind.'

'I've been through Hell, Arahal,' I said. 'When you're living from day to day like a sewer rat, it's hard to remember you were anything but a low form of life.'

'Rats have instincts, surely!'

I lay down and put my arms over my face. 'I don't want to argue about this, Arahal. You know as well as I do that I can either live like this or as the Tigron's little pet. I can't say either of those choices are good ones, but what else can I do?'

'Are you going to keep on running forever then? Let me remind you, Cal, that no-one has estimated a Harish life-span; you might be running for a lot longer than you'd like.'

'Did *he* send you?' I asked bitterly. Arahal didn't answer. 'How do you think I feel, knowing he watches me all the time?'

'You don't know that.'

I laughed without mirth. 'Don't I? How come you arrived so quickly then? Why wasn't I left to die? If Pell hasn't enough guts to face me, he should let me die! He won't come himself; he sends you! The Pell I loved is dead. Maybe I should be too!' I didn't mean that.

'Lord Tigron, to you,' Arahal said, out of habit.

'When we thought we were about to die, Kruin said, "Better luck next time". He's right, Arahal. Maybe it would have been the best thing. This life of mine is a mess. I'm involved in things I don't want to be involved in. I have a conscience that watches me do the wrong things just so it can make my life a misery afterwards. Why are you smiling? I'm desperately unhappy!'

'I don't think so!' he said, offering me another measure of shrake from a silver bottle he untucked from his belt. 'Enjoy Jaddayoth, Cal. It is a colourful country.'

'You mean I'm free to go?'

'Of course! We are not gaolers. I, as much as anyone in Immanion, want to see you well again.'

Meaning what precisely? I wondered. 'This is a blood sport. You'll hunt me again!'

'We've never hunted you. Don't be absurd!'

'After Megalithica …'

'After Megalithica what?' he snapped brusquely. 'You were given a choice, Cal, but we bear no malice against your decision, just regret.'

'You've always hunted me,' I continued self-pityingly. 'I've always been followed.'

'You're deceiving yourself, Cal. We never have.'

I turned my face away from him. I did not believe it. 'You're lying.'

Arahal sighed and rubbed his face. 'There is a limit to what I can say to you.'

'Oh, run out of the lines he fed you, have you?'

He smiled sadly. 'I will not comment on that, because I can understand your pain. As soon as you're strong enough, we shall escort you and your companions to the next Hadassah town. The Mojags too. You can all take penance there for your crimes. You would do well to remember a certain unfortunate Har who now lies poisoned in the mud of the Fallsend canal, I think.'

I snorted. 'Oh, you know me, Arahal. Life means nothing to me!'

'Certainly not your own, it seems!' He ducked out of the tent and left me alone with a sour taste in my mouth.

Kruin and Panthera respected my desire to remain silent over the subject of the Gelaming, although I know that they discussed it thoroughly together when they weren't with me. Perhaps they even asked the Gelaming questions, but I doubt that they were answered. Only a privileged few know of the peculiar set of circumstances that link me to the Tigron and Immanion, and it's not something that the Gelaming would want to make public. They buried Jafit in the forest and brought our horses back to us. In two days, I felt well enough to leave.

CHAPTER

10

The Huyana and the Vision
'My body was the house,
And everything he'd touched an exposed
nerve'

Stephen Spender, An empty house

Jasminia is a much larger town than Caraway, and only a few miles away from where we were camped in the forest. So close to safety, yet so far! The Gelaming escorted us so that, as they tactfully put it, the Mojags would not be tempted to explore further transgressions along the way. It was evening by the time we rode through the carved, wooden gates of Jasminia, but the town appeared to be as busy and full of Hara as it would have been at mid-day. Snow had been cleared from the narrow streets, crackling torches threw sulphurous light across the rooftops. Most of the buildings in Jasminia are single-storied, but sprawling.

Arahal had already mentioned that we would all have to pay a penance here and, along the road, Kruin had enlightened me as to what he meant. The Hadassah have a strict custom concerning the penalty for violence and murder. If anyone should commit either offence, it is required by law that he present himself at the nearest temple of the Aghama, to confess to the priests (or huyana as they are known in Hadassah), and be given absolution. The soul is cleansed of negative impulses by partaking in ritual aruna with the huyana. All Hadassah abhor the taking of life, but they are a boisterous tribe, fond of their alcohol and not unknown to be consumed by fits of temper when drunk. The huyana must always receive gifts for their services, whether money, food or other goods.

A good impression of the nature of Hadassah may be gained by examining the fact that the temples (and their huyana) are incredibly rich. I thought that the temples must be rather like musendas, but whose kanene have divine administrative powers and higher status.

The temple of Jasminia was concealed behind a high, wooden fence in the middle of the town. Arahal handed me a fat purse of money. 'Now, don't think about sloping off to the nearest inn until you come out of the temple,' he said, with a grin. As if I would! The Mojags had been firmly instructed to return to Fallsend without us. Outher could do nothing but agree to this. He was sensibly wary of the Gelaming and had realized we fell under their protection. This did not stop him hating us though; we would all feel more comfortable once Outher and his party were far away from us.

'So, it's goodbye again is it?' I said.

Arahal would not be coming inside the temple with us. He smiled down at me from his horse. 'For now, Calanthe, although I feel sure we shall meet again, don't you? Perhaps when you finally come to us in Immanion.'

'You think I want a home there?'

Arahal shrugged. 'Only you can answer that, of course. Do you ever tell yourself the truth, I wonder?'

'It's my life,' I said. 'Tell the Tigron that!'

'Any other message?' he enquired bleakly.

'No, no other message.'

'Until next time then ...'

'Sorry, but I don't want there to be a next time.'

Arahal merely smiled. He raised his arm and the Gelaming trotted behind him, down the road away from us, increasing their speed as they went, until, in a blinding yet invisible flash, they were gone from this earth, and the road was empty. Everyone stared at the place where they had vanished. I pushed past them and knocked on the temple gate.

'Who seeks ingress?' The voice was polite and business-like, anonymous behind the thick, wooden panels of the door. I was tempted to answer, 'Miserable sinners, of course. Open up!' but before I could speak, Kruin had shouldered up to me and said,

'Travellers, tiahaar, seeking penance.'

There was no further word from beyond the door, only the sound of wood sliding back as bars were removed. The door opened easily, without creaking, to reveal a veiled figure standing just inside. I was instantly reminded of the holy dancers of the Froia, the marsh people of Megalithica. The dancers (or theruna) always appear veiled, and they too are adept in the art of aruna magic. The Har before us wore a thick, fur cloak around his shoulders and the veil over his face was so diaphanous and sheer, we could see the kohl around his eyes. He bid us all enter and stood aside. Before us stretched a wide yard, snow-covered except for a pathway through the middle which had been swept clear to reveal coloured tiles beneath. Two Hara muffled in woollen cloaks came to lead our horses away. Kruin made plaintive noises about the baggage to which the huyana raised his hand.

'No need to worry,' he said. 'Thievery is unknown within the temple walls. Come, I will escort you all to the fane.'

I kept my bag of notes well tucked under my arm. I had come to hate being parted from them. The huyana glided ahead of us up the cleared path. In spite of what Arahal had impressed upon Outher, I was still not happy about being so close to the Mojags. They wanted our blood and here in Jasminia would only have to pay a further penance if they spilt it. Now that the Gelaming had left us, I had no doubt that Outher would soon forget his fear of their word. Moonlight cast long shadows across the yard. It was getting colder as the dusk became deeper; another cloudless night. Behind me, I could feel Outher's eyes boring into my back, causing the flesh between my shoulder-blades to itch. Two immense statues of stone guarded the door to the fane itself. One held out the silken cloth of forgiveness, the other a broken sword. I was not sure of the symbolism implied in that; it could be taken many ways. The emblems of the Aghama were scored into the door-lintel; the double-headed axe, the winged beetle, the prescient eye of our god. Beyond the doorway, all was in smoky darkness. None of us made a sound. Intoxicating perfumes — chypre, mimosa, green sandalwood — floated and merged in the icy air; twisted grey fumes that writhed like spirits. After passing along a high-ceilinged, columned passage, we were shown into a small chamber, where several other Hara were clustered around a cheerful fire, murmuring softly together.

'Please wait here,' instructed our veiled guide. 'The hour approaches, but you are free to refresh yourself before the time.' He gestured towards flagons of wine standing on a broad shelf near the fire; already well explored by the other Hara in the room, I suspected. Outher and his cronies went directly to help themselves and our guide left the room, closing the door behind him. Kruin, Panthera and myself sat down on a bench by the wall.

'Well Kruin, you're the expert on Hadassah customs; what's going to happen next?' I asked, hoping it was not going to be some dull, spiritual flaying. I'd had more than enough of that kind of thing.

Kruin smiled, showing nearly all his teeth. 'Ah, you'll have to wait and see,' he said smugly. 'I won't spoil the surprise by telling you!' He slapped his thighs, smacked his lips together and went to fetch us some of the wine, which was red and tart, but warming. Panthera grimaced and put his cup down on the floor, where it remained untouched. Across the room, Outher kept on delivering hostile glances. It is not pleasant to look into the eyes of someone who wants to take your life. All your instincts cry, 'Flee! For fuck's sake, flee!' I sat there uncomfortably and tried to ignore him.

In a short while, the chime of a bell echoed through the room. What light there was began to dim; unnerving because the lamps were powered by burning oil, not electricity. Everyone stopped whispering and stood up, put down their wine-cups, straightened their clothes and their spines. I could almost sense every Har in that room holding his breath; the atmosphere was full of suspense. The bell sounded again and I turned towards the direction it came from. The wall on that side of the room was curtained from ceiling to floor, and now that curtain was wrinkling back and upwards, revealing another room beyond suffused by an orange glow. Veiled figures stood in the gloom. 'What now?' I hissed at Kruin. He laughed softly, put a finger to his lips and pushed me forward. One by one, as if bewitched, the Hara in our side of the room began to walk slowly forward, towards the vacillating forms of the huyana.

Slim arms emerged from floating robes to draw them further into the chambers beyond. I couldn't remember moving, but suddenly I found myself across the room and face to face with a creature, whose face was unseen, but whose overpowering scent of wood-musk made me feel light-headed. He put his hand on my arm to draw me away. I glanced behind me, looking for Kruin and Panthera, but they had disappeared. I did not like the idea of us being split up.

'Have no fear,' my chosen huyana murmured. 'Within these walls, you are safe. You are all safe.'

That sent a little shiver through my skin. The huyana seemed to speak with more than casual knowledge. I narrowed my eyes at him, but I could not see through the veil. I could not see whether he was smiling. We drifted away from the other Hara and he took me into a simple chamber, deep in the heart of the temple. Glowing glass globes on the floor provided light. A large wall painting of the Aghama's axe symbol was the only decoration. There was no bed, but a number of animal skins were scattered around the floor, some stuffed to form cushions. Against the far wall was a low, wooden stool. The huyana sat me down on it and knelt before me with lowered head. 'I am Lucastril,' he said.

Totally ignorant of what was required of me, I answered, 'Hello Lucastril. I'm Calanthe.'

'You are Cal,' he said and put up his hands to remove his veil. I was half afraid there'd be a face I recognized beneath. His cheek-bones and eyelids were painted with gold, the forehead tattooed, his hair drawn up into a coil. Only the strength of his throat and jaw betrayed his Harness. It could have been a human female kneeling there. In some Hara, the female is very strong. My heart was hammering in my chest. It wasn't fear exactly, just a kind of presentiment. I had an awful feeling that the reins of control had just been snatched from my hands again. It is the sort of feeling that makes you want to look up at the sky and shudder; deeply.

Lucastril took my hands in his own. 'We had been told of your coming,' he said earnestly, leaning forward.

I snatched my hands away, roughly. 'Gelaming!' I hissed and it was in me to reach for his throat. I didn't. 'You know nothing about me!' Both outbursts (as my inner desires, no doubt) were met with amused patience.

'It is beyond my powers to absolve you, Cal,' Lucastril said, with some regret.

I stood up and went for the door. 'It's my life!' I shouted. 'Mine! You can all keep your meddling, psionic hands off me! Good-day to you, Lucastril!'

He stood up and pulled me back, with strength that shouldn't have surprised me at all, but which did. 'Don't go,' he said. 'You are here for a purpose. This is just the beginning and, because of that, important. Important, do you hear?' This slim, little creature shook me by the shoulders.

'What do you mean?' I asked. He would not let go of me, perhaps afraid I'd make another run for it and succeed.

'Listen. Listen and learn. We've been told you record everything, all that happens to you. Learn from that.'

Another icy shudder, suppressed. Who gave these Hara their information? Arahal? The Tigron? 'And what am I here to learn, Lucastril? Who told you I was coming? What do you know?'

He shut his eyes, lowered his head, shook it. 'I can't tell you.'

'Can't? Surely that should be "won't", tiahaar!'

He shook his head again. 'No. Just let me do what I'm instructed to do. It is for your benefit.'

'I doubt that.' I let him take me to the cushions however. I let him push me down. 'What am I to learn then?'

'The first thing,' he said. 'The first of many.'

'Will it take long?'

'That is up to you.'

'Well?'

'My art,' he said. 'Allow me to demonstrate.' He stood away from me and sinuously cast off his robes. Then he knelt at my feet and began to unlace my boots.

'One moment,' I said and he looked up.

'You will not leave here until we have taken aruna together; that is the law.'

I shrugged. 'Very well. I don't know what results you're expecting though.'

He smiled, knelt against me and took my face in his hands. We shared breath until he broke away.

'You have taught yourself well how to guard your mind,' he said.

'Even from interfering little mystics like yourself,' I agreed.

'There is much darkness.'

'Not really. I don't think so.'

'You are lying or you are wrong; no matter. This is the first step on a great and golden staircase. Who knows what lies at the top? Let me lead you a little of the way up.'

I thought that Lucastril's job was simply to needle my mind during the ecstasy of aruna; either to extract information or implant feelings there. Now I'm not so sure. I knew he was doing *something*, but I was helpless to resist, physically, thinking that knowledge was resistance enough. For a moment, I remembered Terzian, and what Gelaming mercy had done to him, how his body and mind had been shattered by the strength of their will alone. Was that to be my fate too if I did not comply with them? Terzian had resisted them with all his might, and he had died for it. Not a warrior's death, as he deserved, but a slow, lingering, quenching of the flame, terminal illness. I couldn't stand that. I'd rather die ... or comply? So, I let Lucastril happily invade my mind under the cover of invading my body. I could feel a strange sensation of stretching, flickering currents scraping my spine. I'm convinced that Lucastril was the first link in a chain of events destined to change my life. I also believe he was truly unaware of what part his small service would perform in the whole. My mind was a rusty, neglected machine. It had to be cleaned and oiled. Soon it would be reachable in every way. There was only one possible end to all this preparation. Only one. My life is not my own. Am I strengthening *his* power by repeating that?

After our bodies had parted and Lucastril was curled up against my side, I lay awake in the darkness. There was a high-pitched whistle in my head. My whole being was thrumming; an instrument plucked by an invisible, yet potent, hand. I could trust no-one. How was I to know that Panthera, or even Kruin, was not part of some huge, elaborate Gelaming scheme? Lying there in the musky, hairy darkness, it seemed like the whole world was closing in on me. I was floundering in a shoreless sea, trying to find ground beneath my feet, searching the horizon for land, finding none. My friends could not help me; I was alone. Even if Panthera and Kruin were not part of some immense Gelaming scheme, I could not risk involving them. I did not want to involve them; I could not speak of my past to anyone. It hurt too much. It made me feel ashamed. Was I afraid, that if I opened up, my confessions would be met with revulsion? Then a hot, sour tide turned my uncomfortable shame to anger. Yes, I had done all those things, but hadn't it really been Pell's fault? It had! Surely, *he* had made me what I was now. You see, in the depths of my self-indulgent wallowing, I had managed conveniently to blot out the entire time I'd lived with the Uigenna. Why do I still love him? I thought. Why? There's nothing left to even *like* anymore. He is Thiede's lapdog; arrogant, egotistical, condescending. It was because of knowing Pell that I'd risen from being just an average kind of Har to being a huge kind of scapegoat villain. Just from knowing him. It all seemed so long ago. I could see his face before me, as I'd first known him, laughing, shining with innocence, utterly enchanting. Not a king; just Pell. How I wished that he'd stayed dead to me. Why had I ever had to find out? Now there is a monster clothed in Pell's flesh that follows me like a curse. Does some remnant of the old Pell still exist, yearning for the past? Is that it? Pell has the vast power of the Gelaming empire behind him now. He can have anything he wants, yet he still cannot face me in the flesh. Perhaps, like me, he is afraid of being consumed. I feel that should I ever let the gates of Immanion close behind me, I will be as good as dead. Pellaz would wither me. He could not be the same, yet too similar not to affect me. We would be unable to speak. It would be Hell. It is something that, deep inside, in spite of everything, I still want more than anything.

In the morning, Lucastril woke me up from a disturbing dream of caves and ghost-lights. He stroked my face as I twisted and whimpered like a child, half-asleep in his arms.

'The first message will come soon,' he said. 'I have cleared the way as best I can. Wait for it.'

'I don't want to hear it,' I said. 'Can't you understand that? I'm a prisoner. The world is vast and I wander in it like a gypsy, yet I'm a prisoner. Of the past.' Tears spilled from my eyes; I couldn't stop them. They were hot with anger, not sadness; the culmination of my confused agonising in the night. Soon I must go out there again, scurry haphazardly around, go where they pushed me. Perhaps I would have been wiser to stay in Piristil. At least there I'd owned a spurious kind of safety. Lucastril helped me dress. I felt dizzy; weak yet, at the same time, full of untapped strength. My head was whirling.

'You may eat here with your friends before you leave,' Lucastril said. I took some of the money Arahal had given me and threw it on the floor. Lucastril picked it up and handed it back to me. 'There's no need for this,' he said. 'We have already been paid.'

'Keep it!' I said that more savagely than was necessary.

Lucastril took the purse from my hand and put the money back inside. 'Don't be stupid. You may need it.'

I stuffed the purse into my trouser pocket and followed him to the dining-hall. Some of the previous night's sinners, cheerfully cleansed, were still there, eating and talking, but I was relieved to see that Outher's party appeared to have gone. Panthera and Kruin were sitting alone at a table in the corner. I stood in the doorway watching them, not quite sure if I wanted to go over. Perhaps I should just leave Jasminia on my own. After all, I was in Jaddayoth now. I had Arahal's money and could find work for myself in somewhere like Gimrah for a while. Perhaps I should just go where Fate led me. It looked to me as if Kruin and Panthera would not welcome my presence anyway. Their heads were close together; they were talking earnestly. I could guess the subject of their conversation. Hesitating, I was just about to turn and leave the place, when Panthera looked up and saw me. He smiled and waved and all my plans disappeared in a puff of weakness. I went over to them.

'Are you OK?' Panthera asked. 'Your face is still a bit of a mess.'

I sat down. 'I'm fine, just fine!' There was a pot of coffee on the table, nearly empty. I took Kruin's drained cup and half-filled it.

143

Kruin handed me a roll of bread and some cured meat, inspecting me silently.

'So, where to now then?' I asked. It hurt to eat, but my stomach was aching from hunger.

'You sure you're up to travelling?' Kruin enquired. 'You look terrible. It should be safe now to stay here in Jasminia for a day or two if you like.'

I looked quickly at Panthera who appeared to be carrying no external signs of our struggle with Mojags. 'I told you, I'm fine! For God's sake, let's get moving. I'm sure Panthera is anxious to get home.'

Panthera smiled wanly. 'Anxious yes, but a couple of days won't make much difference. It'll only slow us down if you're not up to it.'

'Oh, please! It's just a few bruises. It's nothing!'

Kruin shrugged. 'Very well, if you're sure ...' He brightened up, his responsibilities absolved. 'Anyway, how did you two get on last night? Civilized method of punishment, isn't it? No wonder the Hadassah are so fond of fighting!'

Panthera's face had gone a deep crimson colour. He fidgetted uncomfortably. 'Personally, I prefer to answer to nobody for any crimes I might commit,' he said.

'And I'm naturally suspicious of mystics,' I said. Kruin rolled his eyes.

'Oh, I see! Well, I enjoyed myself thoroughly!'

Panthera and I did not comment. I had no intention of revealing what was happening to me and Panthera obviously still harboured deep misgivings concerning aruna. We let Kruin ramble on, lewdly and happily. We let it wash over our heads. Panthera smiled at me.

'Let's get you home,' I said.

The Message
*What we call the beginning is often the
    end
And to make an end is to make a
    beginning.
The end is where we start from'*

T.S. Eliot, Little Gidding

We left Jasminia round about mid-day, taking the south road
into Gimrah. The sun was shining, making the snow on the
ground and trees sparkle like crystal. There were quite a few other
travellers on the road; mostly Hadassah. There was a great sense of
camaraderie. We joined a group of a dozen or so Hara who were
travelling to a town on the border. They shared their liquor and
biscuits with us. We sang songs to pass the time. I can remember
clearly that I was filled with happiness. On such a beautiful
afternoon, it was impossible to believe that the world was anything
but the way it seemed at that moment; untainted. I felt free. Surely
my fears about Pell were just the product of a paranoic mind. That
still didn't explain Arahal's timely appearance of course, or
Lucastril's meaning-laden words, but that day I was desperate to
convince myself I was leading a simple, ordinary life; no part of
anything great. Panthera was a joy to watch. I found myself
thinking that over the past couple of weeks, I really hadn't noticed
him properly, or maybe it was just that the air of his home country
made him bloom and had blown away the cobwebs of his confinement in Fallsend. If, I thought, just *if*, I could act utterly independently, I could think about wooing Panthera. Then we could live
together forever in a high castle in Ferike. I would write stories to
pass the time; he would paint exquisite masterpieces. We would

exist together sublimely, riding nervous, pale horses through the mountain forests every morning. In the evenings, if we should want company, we could invite lofty Hara of neighbouring castles to dine with us, drink wine from long-stemmed glasses and converse intellectually about the outside world which we would never see. Ah, such would be a life! Who could yearn for more? I have travelled too long. Perhaps my ghosts have worn themselves out. Living with Panthera, perhaps my dreams could only be those of the sweetest kind.

'You look pensive, Cal,' Panthera said, breaking my reverie.

'Mmm,' I agreed. 'I was just thinking about the sort of life I would like to have.'

'Then live it!'

'Too many factors are beyond my control, I'm afraid.'

'It is never impossible to take control of one's own life, I believe,' he answered. 'That's what my father says and he never speaks unless he's sure of the facts.'

'I wish I could agree.'

Panthera brought his horse more closely up against mine. I could see Kruin watching us, perhaps straining to hear what we were saying. 'Is it ... it is *power*?' Panthera asked tentatively.

I looked at him steadily. Could I? Could I? 'Some Hara are very powerful, yes,' I replied carefully. 'Some seek to control the lives of others.'

'Cal, the Gelaming ... What is it you're mixed up in with them?'

This was the first question of the many that I'd been expecting from my companions. So far they'd had the discretion to remain silent, keeping their observations to themselves, between themselves. It must be driving Kruin mad, because he's naturally a gossip. 'Don't probe too deeply,' I said. 'I'm not being close out of stubbornness, Panthera. It may be dangerous for you. If I tell you, I automatically involve you, and then whatever is out there may decide to organize your life for you as well. I don't want that on my conscience.'

'Cal, I'm not afraid of that! If you tell us, or even just me, I can add my strength to yours. You'd have an ally. Surely that would make things easier.'

'For me perhaps, but what about you? You have a life waiting for you, Thea. What about cousin Namir? I don't want you to ask me again. Is that clear?'

Panthera's eyes went cold. He does not like being spoken to sharply and is also convinced that his wishes should be granted at every turn. 'I think you're being very foolish,' he said stiffly. 'And your excuses are pathetic. What I do with your life is my choice. I'm insulted that you won't accept my assistance! Anyway, cousin Namir has probably taken another consort by now. Can't you see, that life you talk about, the one that was waiting for me, has gone? It went the minute I set foot in Piristil. You're not the only one with problems, Cal.'

'Maybe not, but I'm the only one with my problems!'

This argument could have continued in similar vein for some time, but at that point, Kruin's curiosity overwhelmed him and he trotted over to join us, only to encounter a tight-lipped silence. I had no doubt that later Panthera would tell him everything I'd said.

It would take us at least two days to reach Gimrah, and then a further couple of weeks to get to Ferike. Now that we had money, we would be able to stay in inns rather than camp out in the open, which was a definite improvement! Whenever he had the opportunity, Kruin kept on praising our good fortune over the incident with Arahal, in the hope that I'd say something enlightening about it, which I wouldn't.

'Gelaming have lots of money,' I said. 'This is nothing to them. Now, if they'd really wanted to be generous, they'd have given us three of their horses. We'd have reached Ferike in a matter of hours then.'

'Is that Arahal a friend of yours?' Kruin asked bravely.

'No.'

'Is …' Kruin began again, but Panthera interrupted him.

'Don't bother, Kruin. He won't tell you.' They exchanged a meaningful glance, which meant they thought I was enjoying needling their curiosity.

That evening, we decided to spend the night in a roadside inn; all that was left of an old human town. We were all in dire need of a good night's sleep. Our Hadassah travelling companions were all set for a serious evening's drinking first and Kruin elected to join them. Panthera and I went up to separate rooms. I locked my door and went to bed with a bottle of betica, which was locally brewed and a much finer concoction than that experienced in Fallsend. I lay staring into the darkness of the room, trying to get so drunk my sleep would be free of dreams. I must have drifted off, for suddenly I was wide awake as if I'd been shaken. I was bitterly cold, lying face down, and my bed was unbelievably uncomfortable, as if strewn with broken glass. I opened my eyes and for a second thought, 'Oh, I am dreaming', yet the sensations were incredibly real. I was lying face-down on the road outside the inn, half-clothed; an icy wind ripping at my exposed flesh with serrated fingers. I pulled myself up on my knees, looked around. To my right the inn was in darkness, the only light coming from the sky, where a round moon bobbed on breakers of cloud. To my left, a pine forest steadfastly worked its way across a landscape of concrete and fallen buildings. The waving shadows might conceal anything. Through the wind, I could hear an insistent sound; rhythmic, pounding, getting closer. 'Why, it is horses' hooves,' I thought sagely. 'I'd better move off the road.' Whoever was travelling at that late hour, was travelling very fast indeed. Sluggishly, numbed by cold, slow as the urgency of nightmare, I tried to stagger towards the inn, but my limbs refused to co-operate. Sleep-walking was not a thing I could remember having done before. I fell to my knees again with the image of the inn receding as if being drawn away. Perspective became acute. The moon cast stark shadows; everything looked two dimensional. I was aware of time passing and it was a speed I was unfamiliar with. Squinting, I tried to peer down the road, towards the south, where the sound of hooves seemed to be coming from. A vague blackness was moving there, rolling like a ball of smoke, but approaching at speed. I told myself, 'This is not real … *surely*', and out of the distance, between a tall, shadowy avenue of snow-stippled pines and humped rubble, a pair of horses pounded along the road, their powerful limbs surging with unnatural slowness, the ripple of muscle, the swing of silken hair, all slowed down, shards of ice flying with the grace of birds off the hard surface of the road. I did not move. I did not try to. Mesmerized, I could only watch. The riders of those horses were swathed in black, their faces covered. They sat straight, not bending with the animals' pace at all. From their shoulders black spikes rose up behind their heads. I could see shining black gems upon their gauntletted hands. Riding close together as they were, I did not notice their burden until they were really close. Whatever they carried was slung into a white sheet, lolling with horrible suggestiveness, between them. I knew they carried a Harish body. It was as if I could *see* it. They came to a halt some feet away from me. I could still see nothing of their faces. The horses blew plumes of steam into the cold air, tossing their heads. Their bridles jangled, their feet stamped. I looked up and the riders hurled their burden down before me. It landed on the road with a dull thump and rolled slightly before lying still. The sheet had fallen partly away. I could see the face of what it had concealed; eyes staring wide, the flesh white as bone and bleached even further by the light of the moon. I realized with an odd, analytical calm, I was afraid, no, more than afraid — stricken with terror. The body lying at my feet, the face so familiar, of course I knew it. It was mine! Me lying there as dead and cold as the landscape. I looked up helplessly at the riders. They must be Gelaming; they could be no other. Covering their faces could not deceive me; no. Then, a movement from the road attracted my attention. I didn't want to look, but a sick fascination swivelled my eyes downwards. Even as I looked, the dead lips cracked and worked. (Oh God, it's trying to *speak*!) I must have made a noise of horror, must have. The eyes rolled. The thing that looked like me wriggled foully from its confinement of cloth. I could see the body was not marked by injury at all. It rolled onto its stomach and lifted the upper half of its body like a rearing snake, not using its arms for support. The face was inches from my own. I could smell nothing. It spoke; a ghastly, rasping sound. It said, 'Beneath ... beneath the mountains of Jaddayoth,' followed by a gulping sigh. That was when I screamed. I can remember that sound shattering the stillness of the night air. The wind had dropped, completely. There was no answering movement from the inn, no lights switched on, no windows thrown wide. The thing that was myself lurched forward as if to touch me. I covered my face with my hands, powerless to

149

move and fell ...

When I opened my eyes, I was lying face down on my bed in the inn. Wholly awake, I threw myself over the edge and hurried to the window, throwing it wide, wide. I leaned out, feeling the ice press against my naked stomach. The road beneath was empty, the new snow unmarked, gentle flakes still falling. The road towards the south stretched unblemished as virgin skin. Stunned, I sank to the floor and leaned with my back against the wall, my head resting on the wet sill. My mind seemed empty. I looked at my bed, which was rumpled, disordered. I made a sound, small, not frightened, not amused, but something of both. My blankets, my pillow, the floor around the bed, were sprinkled with snow and it was melting fast.

I slept for the rest of the night on the floor, covering myself with a blanket. Beneath the mountains of Jaddayoth ... Had I dreamed it? Was that vision merely a sick manifestation spewed forth by my own sicker mind? But if it was true ... *What* beneath Jaddayoth? What? Was death waiting for me there, or merely submission? My room was cold. In the morning, Panthera came in and eyed my position with suspicion. Snow had blown in through the window and there was a thin covering of it on my blanket.

'Drunk again were you?' Panthera enquired with derision. He snorted when I didn't answer and went downstairs. My limbs were stiff. I dressed myself slowly. Clearly Panthera considered me a drunkard. I looked at myself in the mirror. It was a far from pleasant experience, for my face still bore the yellowing marks of Outher's attentions, accompanied by bleary, bloodshot eyes. I looked, in a word, terrible. For a moment, I leaned on stiff arms, my forehead against the glass. 'Pellaz', I thought, and then aloud, 'Pellaz.'

His name is a curse, a prayer.

In Gimrah
*'You dozed, and watched the night
        revealing
The thousand sordid images
Of which your soul was constituted'*

T.S. Eliot, Preludes

I did not mention my nightmare (experience?) to my companions, but the feeling of it lingered like a sour taste in my mouth. I
had locked my door before going to bed yet Panthera had walked
right in unhindered in the morning. It didn't bear thinking about. I
could deceive myself no longer; whatever I thought I'd escaped in
Fallsend had found me again, but even so, nothing like last night
had ever happened to me before. Goodbye castle in Ferike.
Goodbye pleasant dreams. I felt I had no future; only the past,
which stretched behind me raw and bleeding for examination.
That day I could barely speak. Kruin and Panthera thought I'd got
a hangover; I got no pity from them.

The road became quieter. There were fewer travellers.
Townships we passed were prevalently areas reclaimed from
nature that man had abandoned to rot. As the silence of the White
— as Hadassah call it — became more intense, Kruin told us we
were now near the border. One grey, overcast afternoon, our horses
waded thigh-deep through a drift of snow from which reared the
black, horse-hair-fringed totem of the Gimrah. Two more steps
and Hadassah was behind us. A valley swept down before us; a
carpet of pristine white. Kruin was worried. He said that this could
be treacherous. The snow had drifted; we had no idea how deep it
was down there. A slight, cold wind worried the edge of our furs,

our horses' manes, carrying small, dancing motes of snow. Night creeps up on you quickly in the winter glow. Slightly behind the others, I experienced a sudden, sharp, bitter-sweet pang of déjà vu. If I narrowed my eyes, could it not be Saltrock down there; not snow-plains but caustic shores of soda? Just a hint of its bitter scent. Now I am back there, riding in. Drunk and wretched. I am thinking: how can I tell them? What can I tell them? My water bottles are empty. My knees and arms are scabbed, my lips cracked by desert scour. I am alone. Alone. Alone. How much it echoed then. How much it echoes now through the overgrown cavities of my heart. I can remember being in love, remember happiness, but it was short-lived. (*A scream; a horse's scream.*) No! Kruin urged his horse down the slope. It skidded, bunching its hind-quarters, head up, ears back. He becomes a moving thought through the vacuosity of a dead mind. He turns round. 'Come on!' he shouts and Panthera and myself follow him down.

The sky was black by the time we saw lights shining in the distance. Kruin said he'd known there was a settlement near here. Lemarath, it was called. All Gimrah settlements are a combination of large farm and small town, proudly independent of each other, savagely competitive concerning their live-stock. As we rode through the snow towards the light, to keep our minds off the numbing cold attacking all extremities, Kruin and Panthera told me about the Gimrah. Originally of Gelaming stock, they had split off from the main tribe to pursue their own breeding programmes for their horses. The founding Hara had all been employed in Gelaming livery establishments and had constructed for themselves a whole way of life about the animals they nurtured; a whole religion in fact. Almost unique amongst Harish kind, who generally worship aspects of the Aghama under various guises and aliases, the Gimrah worship a goddess. This is unusual in that while rejecting all human trappings of sexual division most Hara can only countenance revering a super-being of dual sexuality like themselves, or the life-force of the Earth itself, which is predominantly female, but mated to the male aspect of the sun. The Goddess of the Gimrah is naturally equine in form. In worship, all Gimrah Hara subvert their masculinity. To the Goddess, they are soume; all procreation must take place by sunlight. On top of this rather eccentric custom, the Gimrah are the only tribe in Jaddayoth who share their territory, even their homes, with humans. When staking their claim on the land, they offered aid, employment and support against less tolerant Hara, to the ailing human population. As conservationists, the Gimrah have decreed that all human males must conceive a child or two with females of their own kind at an early age, whereafter they are incepted to Wraeththu. A strangely civilized arrangement. All adult humans in Gimrah are female. The two races exist together in perfect harmony, with the humans content to let the superior race take the upper hand. To the women of Gimrah, Hara are not hermaphroditic, but merely other women who have absorbed the male; thus negating the need for them. It was unsettling to live with at first. There are no walls around Gimrah estembles, as their farms are called.

Frozen nearly to death, we threw caution to the winds and knocked on the first door we could find in Lemarath. A medium-sized wooden and stone house that had several larger outbuildings at the back; a barn, stables possibly. A lantern swung, creaking in the wind over the door. All the windows were curtained tight, but we could see light beyond them. The door was opened to us by a human girl-child who had wrapped herself in a thick, woollen shawl. She squinted against the nipping snow-flakes. 'Yes, what is it?' she asked, quite impertinently I thought. I was used to surviving humans being subservient. Warmth swirled out into the night from behind her, a tantalizing hint of the comfort to be found within.

'We are travellers from Hadassah,' Kruin explained. 'We need lodgings for the night. We were hoping you could suggest where we could find some.'

The girl looked up the road behind us, wrinkled her nose, pulled her shawl closer around her body and stepped towards us. She extended a thin hand to the nearest horse. 'Have you any money, tiahaara? It is a cold, fierce night is it not!'

'We have money,' Kruin answered carefully.

'One moment then. You may be able to stay here; I'd better check.' She went back into the house and shut the door in our faces.

We all exchanged a glance of surprise but Kruin waved his hand briefly and shook his head.

'It is a strange land and we are strangers,' he said. It was explanation enough. After only a few moments, the door opened once more.

The girl came out to us, taking all our horses' reins in one hand. 'You can go in,' she said. 'I'll see to your animals. My mother charges three spinners for a night's lodging and a hot meal — each.'

Kruin sucked air through his teeth. 'Expensive for country fare, isn't it?'

The girl shrugged, leading our horses behind the house. 'It is a hard season, tiahaar!'

We went inside the house and found ourselves in a spacious, low-ceilinged kitchen, typical of any well-to-do farmhouse. Kruin went straight over to the roaring fire. Several cats and dogs raised their heads from sleep to look at us suspiciously. Panthera, carrying most of our luggage, threw it onto the floor and slumped in a chair.

'God, this is so welcome!' he said, in a dazed, chilled-from-the-cold voice.

'No more welcome than your money'll be at this cruel time of year!' A woman had come into the room through a door at the farthest end of it. We all turned quickly. She was drying her hands on her apron; a tall, bony creature, with rather a sour face. She wore thick, woollen trousers and shirt, her hair concealed by a patterned scarf. She took off the apron and hung it over the back of a chair, stretching, rubbing her neck and grimacing. 'Not the weather for travelling, tiahaara! Please, sit down. All of you.' She gestured towards the table. 'Excuse me — we had an emergency down the road. An untimely birth you might say! I'm just about done for, but I think Jasca should have got my meal ready. You're welcome to share it with me.' She sauntered over to a huge cooking range and lifted lids off pots. Tempting smells wafted towards our straining noses. 'Ah, beef stew is all it is! Travellers are few at this time of year, tiahaara. I've nothing fancier.' She continued to chatter as she set plates and food down before us. 'More snow they say, up at the House. More! We spent the last two days digging a road to the south pasture where my neighbour Lizzieman nearly lost her yearlings! Then Clariez has to drop a child on us! By the Goddess she'll give us no rest till spring, I'll wager! Still, new faces are welcome, tiahaara, most welcome.'

We learned that, during the summer, the woman (whose name was Cora) earned a substantial part of her living providing lodgings for travellers. Many Hara travel south from Hadassah and Natawni for the horse-fairs. The stew was excellent. Cora offered us wine, which she boasted that she had fermented herself from rose petals and tree-sap. It was sparkling and delightfully delicate; I found my eyelids drooping. Cora must have noticed. 'How many rooms will you be wanting?' she asked, in a straight-forward manner. There was a moment's silence.

'Can we get back to you on that?' Kruin enquired smoothly.

Cora shrugged, finished her wine and stood up. 'Of course. Shout if you need me; I won't be far,' she answered and disappeared into another room, shutting the door behind her. A tactful, perceptive creature.

After she'd been gone a few moments, Kruin cleared his throat and said, 'Are we all comfortable?' I shrugged and Panthera didn't answer. 'I think,' Kruin began again, hesitantly, 'I think that tonight ... we should be together.'

'I think not!' Panthera protested with rather too much venom and volume.

Kruin winced. 'Suit yourself,' he said drily. 'Two rooms then, Cal?'

I sighed. 'If you like. I'm afraid of dreams when I sleep indoors anyway.'

Kruin reached for my hand. 'Since Fallsend, I have longed to suggest this many times,' he said.

Panthera made a derisive sound and rolled his eyes. 'Oh, *please*!' he cried sarcastically. He is a rigourously unromantic creature.

I must admit it was a pleasure, almost a relief, to experience once more the langourous delights of aruna. Kruin's body had always pleased me, even when he'd been paying Jafit through the nose for the privilege of enjoying mine. Recently my libido had become subdued, which was an alien condition for me. Unlike Kruin, thoughts of closeness had not really crossed my mind since leaving Fallsend; the cold hadn't helped much, of course. Though perhaps the disgusting, debasing humiliations I'd had to endure (and initiate) in Piristil were more to blame, coupled with the violation by Outher. Such things do not exactly quicken the sexual appetite. The time with Lucastril in Jasmina had not been exactly inspiring either. Maybe it also had something to do with the fact that I feared Pell was watching me all the time, but in Cora's house, I felt safe, and curled into Kruin's arms I felt even safer. Now that we were nearer his home country, Kruin was adamant about sticking to his tribal code, which suited me utterly because I was feeling too pathetic and drained to be ouana. Even though we were dog-tired and further exhausted by aruna, neither Kruin or myself felt much like sleeping. We spent some time gossiping about Panthera, which I felt was a timely change from them talking about me. I was surprised to learn that Kruin was really quite offended that Panthera didn't want to be with us. Knowing Harish nature not to be as straightforward as it's believed to be, I hadn't been offended at all, even quite understanding. I tried to explain to Kruin that Panthera would have to put Piristil a long way behind him before he could think about forming relationships with other Hara. Kruin, naturally, did not agree.

'Such wounds should be healed, and healed quickly,' he said earnestly. 'You know that any Har's life is incomplete without aruna; it's our lifeblood.'

'Not all the time, Kruin,' I replied. 'In a perfect world, maybe, but occasionally circumstances intrude upon the well-being of our juices, so to speak. Panthera's young. He only needs time. Once he gets home, I'm sure he'll be alright. Someone will fall in love with him and coax him out of his shell.'

Kruin was in the mood for debate, but I was too tired to argue further. Tired of the subject probably. Kruin rabbited on happily about the necessity of aruna (warm to the subject because he'd just had a good time) and then realized I wasn't really listening. 'Cal, what *is* wrong with you?' he asked, stroking my face in such a way that it was impossible for me to turn away. 'I know you try to hide it, but there is something wrong isn't there. It's to do with the Gelaming, isn't it?'

'You're too inquisitive,' I said lightly, closing my eyes.

'It's not just that! I'm concerned for you. You're difficult to like at times, Cal. I don't know why, but I do care, no matter how much you might wish I didn't. Why don't you trust me?'

I looked at him. 'It's not a question of that, Kruin. I think I'd trust you and Thea with my life now; we've helped each other. We're friends, aren't we? That's why I can't open up to either of you. You're my friends.'

'Can't we help you then? Maybe you're wrong about whatever it is; maybe we can help you.'

I didn't answer. I couldn't. He may well have been right. It was as if there was a valve on my throat that wouldn't let the words out. Kruin sighed. 'Alright, alright, I'll be quiet. But please remember, it's not that I'm being nosy, OK? If you ever want to talk, well, you know …'

I smiled at him and touched his sharp, elegant jaw. 'Yes I know, Kruin. Thanks.'

He took my hand and kissed it gently. A small gesture of affection that reached my heart. There was a lump in my throat. Kruin gathered me close and I held onto him tightly. 'Oh Cal, Cal, don't be scared, don't be miserable,' he said, helplessly, not knowing what I needed reassuring about. For a moment, I felt as if I could tell him everything, but the moment was brief. Kruin was not destined to be part of it.

I woke up lying in hay; crying out. Threshing, hysterical, for a second or two, I thought: this is a dream. I'm dreaming again. I was in a high barn and, this time, my movements were unrestricted. I clambered down from the loose bales beneath me, across the dusty hay-strewn floor, to the tall, slightly open door. A heavy wooden bar lay across the threshold. Outside, across a snow blanketed yard, I could see the back of Cora's house; to the left and right of me were shuttered sheds and loose-boxes. It didn't feel like a dream; not at all. I was freezing, my clothes unfastened as if donned quickly, my feet bare. No lights showed from the house. Glancing behind me into the darkness of the barn, which was bare of everything except shadows and hay, I eased through the door. I must be sleep walking, I decided; an uncomfortable thought, but not as distressing as another hallucination. Above me, the sky was brilliant with stars, the air crystal hard. Snow had drifted up against the back door of the house. It must have started falling again in the night, although the yard was thickly covered; too thickly. Surely Cora and her household must clear it every day? I began to run, but the house never came any closer. I felt sick. Panic spumed through me on a crest of nausea. I was straining against an invisible wall. Choking on dry breath, I fell onto hands and knees, shaking my head, willing myself to wake up, but it was real. 'Cal!' My head jerked up. The silence was stunning. What had I heard? My name? Where had it come from? 'No,' I answered sensibly and then quietly pleading, 'no, no, no.' Only stillness all around. I curled my arms around my head, kneeling in the snow, waiting, waiting. A faint, icy breeze lifted my hair. The stillness was pressing in, full of energy. 'Show yourself!' My cry was oddly muffled; no echo. Still nothing. I scrambled to my feet which were now burning with the cold. I must cope with this rationally. I must focus my will. I must walk towards the house. I took one step and then another and then a hand grabbed my hair from behind, a strong arm was around my neck, pulling me backwards. There was a body; a person clad in leather and musty fur. 'Always useless in times of crisis, Cal, always!' This voice against my ear, which I recognized at once. I could feel his clouded breath, warm and damp upon my skin. This could not be a dream.

'No, you're not here,' I said empathically. And then, to convince myself further, 'You *can't* be!'

He laughed gently, politely. 'Oh, forgive me, but I *am*, Cal. Aren't I always with you? I feel I should be, if only for the sake of memory.'

He turned me round to face him. His head was covered by a thick, tasselled scarf, only the eyes showing. His eyes haven't changed, but I remember that once he never had a deep, white scar through the left brow, a permanent frown. He unwound the cloth from his face with one hand. 'My faithful one,' he said. 'Aren't you going to greet me? It's been so long. In meetings hearts beat closer ... don't they?' Of course, he looked older, leaner and his natural wildness was somehow *contained*.

I had once known him, intimately, as Zackala; now I had no idea what or who he was.

He examined my thoughts. 'I am not an illusion,' he said, 'don't ever think that. You must not deceive yourself, not even in daylight, my Cal. Admire my restraint. I could have made myself known to you a long time ago.'

He was the hound on my trail. I should have known this. Perhaps, deep inside, I had. Perhaps that was why I'd been nervous of leaving Piristil, coming out into the open. My finer senses have become as dulled as those whom I had mocked in the musenda. It was my own fault; Arahal had been right, but it was too late to do anything about it now.

'Pellaz brought you back, didn't he,' I said.

Zack laughed in my face. 'Brought me back? From where? For God's sake, Cal! Did you really think I was dead? Did you see me die? No, as I recall, you didn't hang around long enough to see what happened. No, my dear, Pellaz didn't bring me back; I found *him*.' An expression convulsed his face, which I suppose was disgust. He pushed me away from him.

'What do you want with me?' I asked, still not convinced he was really there.

'Don't you know? Oh Cal!' He laughed and pulled the scarf away from his neck. 'See my scars? Thankfully not fatal; but nearly, very nearly.' He is naturally dark-skinned; the scars glowed very white. 'Someone dumped me on a good healer. Lucky, eh? It took a long, long time to get well though. The world's changed, hasn't it.'

'Are you with *them*?' I asked.

'I'm with you, Cal,' he answered silkily. There was an eerie glitter in his eyes; red fire. He reached for me. I backed away. 'Oh come on, my dear; share breath with me, if just for old times' sake. Come on, let's remember ...'

I put my arms up in defence, but too late. His breath was a roar, his lips peeled back, pouring himself into my silently screaming mouth. There was an immediate darkness in my head, a pounding, the slice of a knife, a silver scream. I was lost, losing ground, in a hurricane of feeling; hatred, bitterness, frustration, pain. I could

159

feel his hands on my back, claws scoring flesh, his teeth grinding against mine, but such physical things were not reality. What was real was the poison of betrayal, the yellow, sweet perfume of the guilty. We were clashing, not like swords, but like oily liquids; colours blending and repelling. I could feel myself sinking, too weak, vitality atrophied, strengths withered. He was ink in my soul; I was drowning in it. Slipping, sinking, I fell … And awoke with a start next to Kruin, a cry in my mouth and a taste of sourness. Kruin was alert in an instant, frightened to wakefulness, leaning over me, pushing me back, saying in a scared, quick voice. 'What, Cal, what?' I wanted to scream. I needed that release, but could make no sound. My body was cold.

We have been in Lemarath for over a week now, because the south road is blocked. Cora is confident that it will be cleared soon, but everyone is very busy at the moment coping with other emergencies caused by the weather. The amount of snow falling is frightening, too fast for it to be cleared away. I can feel myself slipping into a comfortable decline. Lethargy caused by the cold, I tell myself, but I have been writing almost non-stop for two days now. I'm alone quite a lot of the time. Kruin and Panthera are helping the Gimrah. The kitchen is very quiet. Because of the thickly clouded sky, it seems to be dusk all day. I quite like this place; the people are cheerful and strong. Cora shares her house with three others; her daughter, Jasca, her six-year-old son, Natty, and a young woman named Elveny. They all work together every day, shoulder to shoulder, shovelling snow, humping bales of straw and hay, mixing feeds; never a cross word between them.

Last night, after dinner, Elveny read my palm and told me seriously, that I must let the woman in me bleed.

'And just what do you mean by that?' I asked her sweetly.

She had dropped my hand and was gazing into my eyes. 'Beauty alone is not enough,' she said.

Perhaps she thought I understood her, which of course I did, but I pretended not to. I picked up a kitchen knife. 'See this?' I said, waving it. 'This is the moon.' I cut my wrist (on the back naturally).

Elveny pulled a face. 'Oh don't!' she said. I let the blood run

160

down my arm, but the scratch congealed before it could drip on the table. There is probably a moral in that.

Jubilee Hafener was here yesterday. The Hafeners are the Gimrah family who own Lemarath, who run it and sustain it. Jubilee is the son of Gasteau and Lanareeve who rule the roost. Natty told me the Hafener's house is called Heartstone, but we can't see it from here because of the snow. I was sitting at the kitchen table as usual, paper and pens before me, wine to the left, scrounged cigarettes to the right, when I heard a commotion in the yard. I went to take a look. The Hafener rode a tall and stocky horse which was clothed in fleeces. He was accompanied by two armed women and a young Har who appeared to me to be newly incepted. Cora came hurrying out of the barn, pulling the scarf off her hair, which is thick and attractively streaked with grey over the left ear. Jubilee Hafener wore a heavy coat; his straight black hair was plaited to his waist. His skin was very white. I took a good look and went back indoors. More snow talk. The Hafener's women and the young Har came into the kitchen. I thought I'd better be polite and said hello. 'How about a hot drink?' one of the females asked. She looked as if she could skin an adult lion with her teeth. Smiling, I went to the range and poured the coffee.

'Travellers, Cora says,' the woman said.

I presumed she meant my companions and myself. 'Yes,' I answered. 'Dreadful weather isn't it.'

She sat down with a grunt, in my seat, and took one of my cigarettes, offering the packet to her companions. This is, of course, normal behaviour in Gimrah where everyone shares everything. They have no petty rules of etiquette. I sat down with the others and we ended up talking about Fallsend. Ghoulish curiosity on their part, but they were neither censurious nor shocked. I like these people. After a while, Cora brought the Hafener in. I half expected his people to stand up, but they didn't. He's not tall, but appears to be; the mark of true nobility.

'Are you ill?' he asked me. 'You're not working with the others.'

Because of that, I found myself offering to help with the feeds that evening, but my heart wasn't in it. I'm working on half-power, half of my brain is trying to sleep because it's too afraid to be awake. On the morning after my dream about Zack (I won't admit it was anything but a dream), I looked out of the bedroom window and found the yard utterly cleared of snow. I was the first up too. Explain that. Kruin is worried about me, as if he's afraid I'll damage myself. Panthera is aloof. I think he's decided I must be some kind of criminal, and a drunken one at that. I know I do drink too much, but who cares! Anyway, I need it and I deserve it. Yes, I know I'm letting myself go. This is a defiance. Perhaps Pell will leave me alone if I'm no longer desirable. As Elveny said, beauty alone is not enough. If that's all I've got, let's see what happens without it. It's frightening that I'm thinking like this. I always used to be so strong, so impermeable. Have *they* done something to me? I can't help thinking of Terzian again. Am I suffering the same fate? Time for another drink. Cora has been feeding me all kinds of concoctions in a desperate attempt to improve my health. She thinks I picked up some kind of infection on the road. She has also started watering the wine, I notice. If I look out of the window now, I can see Panthera playing with Cora's children in the snow. He has been created to torment me, I'm sure. He is dressed in furs and his mane of dark hair is laced with snow. Now I am aching to hold him close, because he reminds me of Pell, the real Pell. When these thoughts come to me, I must write them down, because it is cleansing. Today I am confused. How much longer can I continue in this way? What is going to happen next? Oh dear, stop it Cal, you're becoming a dreadful bore!

Out of curiosity, I think, the Hafeners invited us up to Heartstone. We all went, Cora's family as well. The women treated it like a real occasion, dressing up in long, soft woollen skirts and painting their faces. Panthera borrowed some of Elveny's clothes and brushed his hair for half an hour. I watched them get ready with cynicism for a while, until my vanity got the better of me and I joined in. I dressed in white, washed my hair and painted my lips bright red. 'That bloody enough for you?' I asked Elveny, grimacing at her.

She smiled weakly. 'Made to kiss, I think,' she said. 'There's little power in that.'

'You're wrong,' I answered. 'Continents can rise and fall on the strength of a kiss.'

'Kiss me then,' she said. Elveny is truly lovely. I've never kissed a woman in my whole life, not even when I was human.

'Aren't I poisonous to you?' I asked.

'No, of course not. Your semen is deadly of course, but I'm only talking about a kiss.'

We were not alone, but no-one else was listening. I took her in my arms and kissed her. Her female body was naturally softer than a Har's. It was interesting. I've never felt like that about a woman before, but then, the women here are virtually Har anyway. Inside, they are just as male as we should be. Male and female. Kissing Elveny made me think about what it used to be like being a half creature. As soon as I'd recovered from my inception I realized what a dull, unexplored existence it had been. Gimrah humans seem to have overcome that. 'I've always hated women,' I said to Elveny.

She smiled. 'Of course. When you were male you used to love men, didn't you?'

That floored me. I'd got too used to Wraeththu superiority. 'You've found the Way here, haven't you,' I said.

'We surely have,' she answered.

'I'm glad that men have gone.'

'Me too.' She poured us wine and we drank to it. I was in a comfortable daze by the time we got to Heartstone.

The house was not as big as I imagined. Two-storied, roofed with tile, its windows quite small because of the bad winters they have in Gimrah. Gasteau Hafener is Tirtha of Lemarath; a tribe leader. A servant met us at the door to Heartstone and took away our wet furs and boots. Soft felt slippers were provided for the comfort of the Tirtha's guests. The house was warm, the ceilings low and beamed. We were shown into a dark, fire-lit salon, where the Hafeners were gathered together, drinking mulled wine and conversing politely with their other guests. We were introduced. One of the Hara was a Natawni; he and Kruin began to gossip. I sat down with Panthera and Elveny and glasses of warm liquor were thrust into our hands. Panthera had been eyeing me very suspiciously since he had seen me embracing the woman. That he thought me rather strange already was a foregone conclusion, but now I felt he considered my strangeness to be a sort of madness; best not to be discussed. I didn't really care. Whatever motives my companions might want to read into it, both Elveny and myself understood the reasons for our brief contact and were not deluding ourselves in any way. Panthera lacked confidence in my judgement. As I said; I did not care. I drank my wine and looked around.

'Oh look!' Elveny hissed. 'Here is Jubilee.'

I would have known without looking across the room; first because I became aware of being watched, and second because Cora, standing near to us suddenly straightened up and became alert, like a hound desperate to show us how capable, trustworthy and handsome it is. I glanced at Elveny, raised a brow.

'Mmm,' she said meaningfully. 'Jubilee Hafener is as yet unbonded to another. As far as I know Lanareeve has more or less promised Cora that Natty shall be taken as Jubilee's consort once he has been incepted.'

'Is that politics or choice?'

Elveny pulled a wry face. 'A little of both, I think. Cora is a pillar of the human community; her words carry great weight. She is also a good friend of Gasteau and Lanareeve and it is no secret that she is very fond of Jubilee.'

'Ah, I see; she will live out her desires through her son.'

'You are cruel, Cal,' Elveny scolded, shaking her head, although her smile did not waver. 'And too critical. In actual fact, she has known Jubilee since he was a Harling; don't misinterpret her feelings.'

I laughed, unconvinced.

We were shown into another room to dine. The Hafeners are a handsome family. Both Gasteau and Lanareeve are tall, both pale-skinned and dark-haired, a trait that has been passed onto their sons. As well as Jubilee, there was Danyelle, his consort Onaly Doontree and an older Har, who though unrelated in blood, had taken the Hafener name; this was Wilder. As we sat down to eat, Jubilee Hafener asked if he could sit beside me. This was not unexpected. 'How long are you staying in Lemarath?' he asked me.

'Oh, as soon as the south road's clear, we'll leave,' I answered.

'Where are you heading?'

'Jael, in Ferike.'

He smiled. 'Well, I doubt if you'll be here much longer then. This snow fall will have stopped by the end of the week. The road can be cleared after then. What a shame. I had hoped to spend the rest of this bitter season wooing you into a wild affair.'

'How direct of you!'

'Brief affairs are always the most poignant, don't you think?'

I shrugged. 'If you say so. I've had more pressing matters on my mind recently.'

'Are you chesna with the Natawni?'

'No. Don't flirt with me, Jubilee Hafener; you are distressing the mother of your future consort.'

He ignored this. 'You don't have to go back to Cora's house tonight.'

'I don't have to do anything, do I!' I replied awkwardly. He left it at that. The meal was excellent, the company sparkling. Across the table, Panthera watched me blandly, constantly. The robe he wore left his shoulders bare, where he made the bones glide and slide beneath his pale skin. Sultry in the lamplight he was, lovely as a white lily wreathed in vines. The most beautiful thing in the room, and so unattainable. The Hafeners flattered him. Only Jubilee had the sense to realize his barriers were unassailable, which was presumably why he decided to have a go at me. Hara in these rural communities must get so bored being cut off nearly all winter. We left the house late, singing in the snow as we tramped back to Cora's. Panthera walked beside me.

'Well,' he said, 'now we have fine new horses to ride back to Jael on. What did you get?'

I was surprised. 'Nothing,' I said. 'Who gave you the horses?'

'Gasteau,' he replied with a charmingly wicked grin. 'you think I'm such a prig, don't you. I think I should be insulted that you're shocked.'

'I'm not shocked. What did you have to do to get them?'

'Don't be coarse, Calanthe! All I had to do was smile.' He laughed.

'You do things the wrong way, obviously.'

'And left Jubilee Hafener's side empty-handed. Clearly you are right, my pantherine!'

On the last night in Lemarath, I stood in my bedroom window and stared into the snow, in the direction of Heartstone.

Kruin came into the room. He said, 'Oh, for God's sake, why don't you go over, Cal? We're leaving tomorrow. More days of comfortless travel! Why don't you go?'

We had discussed the Hafener heir's interest in me. I had a bottle of strong wine on the table. That was enough. 'What's the point, Kruin?' I asked. 'Why settle for something less than I want?'

'I don't know what you mean,' he said angrily.

He didn't. I couldn't really explain myself. I sat at the table and drank the wine. Tomorrow we leave. Another long, dull, painfully cold journey. Panthera came and put his head round my door.

'Can you possibly remain sober tonight?' he requested wearily. 'We want to make an early start tomorrow.'

'Panthera,' I said, 'don't judge me!'

He twisted his mouth a little and raised one eyebrow. 'I don't judge you Cal. How can I? I don't know anything about you. You wanted your privacy. Do you want me to beg for confidences?'

I could not answer. This conversation was not going in the direction I'd intended. 'Wait until we get to Jael,' Panthera said, in a softer tone.

I looked up at him then, unsure of what I wanted to see in his face. 'Why?' I asked sharply.

He leaned against the door and folded his arms. He smiled, and the room lit up. 'It is a safe place,' he said. 'You will be able to rest properly.'

I laughed grimly and reached for the wine bottle.

'You've changed so much,' Panthera observed pensively. 'Do you have to do this to yourself, Cal? I get the feeling you're falling apart inside. Whatever's bothering you, don't let it beat you like this.'

'You have such clear sight, my pantherine,' I said.

He shook his head. 'Alright, I know what you're thinking. I'm much younger than you; I know that, but I'm not completely ignorant. You are in trouble, obviously, and I can see that you are making things worse for yourself. Don't say anything, Cal; I know I'm right.' He turned away, began to close the door behind him. 'Please think about what I've said,' he told me.

I stared at the door after he'd gone. Panthera can be such a pompous little beast at times.

The House of Jael

'... (the) richly glowing
Gold of frames and opulent wells of
    mingling
Dim colours gathered in darkened mirrors'

Martin Armstrong, In lamplight

We left Lemarath early in the morning, as Panthera had desired. We had three new horses from the Tirtha, plus a mule for carriage, which would speed things up a little. Cora and her family bid us farewell, exacting promises from us that one day, in the summer, we would return. I would really like to. My promise at least, was heartfelt. New furs, new supplies, new horses. We began at a fast pace, our animals clad in fleeces because the Gimrah keep their best stock shorn of winter coats. We travelled across the country much quicker than we'd expected. The roads were not as bad as we'd feared. Each settlement we visited was hospitable and friendly, but none as welcoming as Lemarath. Every estemble has a governing Harish family, although several families may be under their control. Every estemble has a Tirtha, who in turn is just one delegate of the Gimrah council of estembles. This council meets six times a year to discuss the problems and policies of the tribe as a whole, and to show off their prize stock, of course. In fact, these meetings are generally nothing other than glorified horse-fairs.

Now we are in Ferike, although the country has been changing for quite some time; more hilly, more forests. I've not written anything down for a long time, mainly because I haven't felt the need to quite so much. My sleep has been mercifully free of dreams. Perhaps I am being allowed to 'recover'. Maybe *they* knew they were driving me too far. I do feel slightly better; less harried. Looking back over all that has happened recently, I find myself wondering if Zack is really still alive. Of course, I had once thought Pell was dead, and I'd seen him die with my own eyes, so anything in this world is possible. I should be prepared for anything.

At the moment, we are staying at an inn in the town of Clereness, which is about twenty miles north west of Jael. Tomorrow, there is no foreseeable reason why Panthera will not see his home once more. Kruin, in his head, has already started spending his reward money. His plans are becoming rather tiresome. Me, I have no idea what I'm going to do with the money. Perhaps I could return to Lemarath. Ah, thereby hangs the tail. I have asked myself a hundred times; why didn't I? It would not have been beyond me to wheedle myself into Jubilee Hafener's affections to the extent that he would have taken me as his consort. I'm an old hand at that sort of thing, as Terzian's family will be able to tell you. Why didn't I? It would have effectively ruined whatever plans the Gelaming have in mind, wouldn't it! I don't know what I want; I can't even think about it properly. Places to go, to run to, to hide in; just excuses really. If I don't go to Lemarath, I could go back to Megalithica perhaps. Forever's the nearest I've ever had to a home, after all. But then, Terzian's son is now the consort of Seel Griselming, and Seel, I know, would prefer never to set eyes on me again. He has seen me kill. This is sad, because Forever is very close to my heart.

Sitting here now, I am thinking, if it is winter in Galhea now all the long gardens of the house will be covered in snow, the lake frozen, the summer-house dark within because of snow on the windows. I can see Cobweb, walking through the white gardens, wearing a long, flowing coat, his hair loose around him like smoke. There will be dogs bounding in front of him, probably Harlings behind … Harlings. Yes. Have I forgotten that so completely? I feel uncomfortable thinking about it, because I know it is just another example of my skill at betrayal. Forever holds more than just the secrets of my past. It hold a secret that flowered within myself; not thought, but flesh. My son. Terzian's son. His name is Tyson, and he would have become an adult a long, long time ago. I did not abandon him because I did not care (which I still do when I remember to), but because of what I am. I do not want my badness to taint him more than is necessary. One day, perhaps ... Oh, useless sentiment, but I would like to go back there. If I thought that Seel could find it within his heart to forget all that has happened, I would go tomorrow. Terzian went back there too, at the end. Oh God, I must get off this downward, melancholy spiral! Panthera is right; I must start fighting. If I concentrate hard enough, I can draw my scattered strength back into myself. The past is done. I spend too much time wallowing about in it. I have a future, even if it is destined only to be a short one. I must seek my destiny. What pompous crap! I sound like Pell. It seems more than likely I shall spend my reward money seeking the answer to those riddles that have been set me. Trying to see beneath the mountains of Jaddayoth.

Ferike is an exhausting place; so many steep hills. Your neck is forever craned backwards, trying to see over trees. There are long avenues of pines, where the roads are in darkness, for no sunlight could ever reach them. There are many tiny villages, many abandoned, larger towns, almost unrecognizable under their winter, white blankets. Wild dogs haunt the ruins of Mankind's dwellings, but they are cowardly and would never attack unless they came upon someone alone and unawares. Some of the villages are built deep into the rock face. Clereness itself stands on the edge of a vast, still lake. Across it, rising directly from the water, are gaunt, grey cliffs, which Panthera tells me are named Fortress Shield. Birds have built their nests there. In the morning, I can throw open the window and see them swooping down, to glide above the surface of the lake. I don't want to be unhappy here, for, even in the depth of the season, I can smell the promise of spring. The Ferike are a contained people, quite unlike the gregarious folk of Hadassah and Gimrah, but they are not uncivil. This is a land of peace and healing. There is quiet here. I am no longer afraid of visitations, hallucinations and nightmares. A respite; probably brief, but I must enjoy it while it lasts.

Last night, I sat in Panthera's room, here at the inn, and watched him comb out his hair. We were feeling tranquil and relaxed. Panthera laughed and said that Kruin's hair was still full of the moss and leaves of Natawni; he would never get a brush through it. 'But then, I suppose you know that,' he added in rather a sharp tone.

'Thea, you were not excluded at any time; you know that.'

He put his comb down quickly on the table, staring at his hands. 'Cal, do you really think I can bear to let anyone touch me now?' I gave a non-committal shrug. 'In Jasminia, I paid the huyana to let me off the penance,' he continued. His face was flushed. He was ashamed of admitting that, even to me, whom he looked upon as a friend.

'In time, you might come to feel ... differently,' I said, which I knew was not much help.

'No feybraiha garlands for me,' Panthera said wistfully, looking at himself in the mirror, as if trying to see the virgin thing he had once been. 'No, you are not the only one with problems, Cal.'

I sat on his bed, knowing that once I would have tried desperately hard to seduce him; I would have relished this ideal opportunity. Perhaps he was hoping I would. But I could only watch him and remember that. Panthera gave himself a shake, sniffed, and picked up the brush once more, raking his hair vigorously. He looked at me in the mirror.

'You are tired, Cal,' he said. 'You are always tired. It shows. Once we get to Jael, you must rest properly. Stay with us until the spring.'

I smiled at him, unwilling to commit myself. I didn't want to appear ungrateful, but I was nervous of the Jaels being unwittingly drawn into something they might not want. I was not so stupid as to believe it was all over; this was just a lull, a freeze, like the season. Come spring, I felt sure the whips would be out, attempting to drive me in the direction of Immanion once more.

As if reading my mind, Panthera said, 'Are they watching you now?'

The evening light was red when we started upon the upward road that led to Jael; a road that hugs the side of a tree-covered hill. Jael is at the top. It is a beautiful place, and very old. Panthera started to get nervous as soon as we could see the turrets of the castle above the trees.

'Cal, shall I have to tell them everything?' he asked me, and his voice was very young. The child who had grown up here was not far away, I thought.

'What do you think their reaction will be?'

He shrugged. 'I'm not ... I'm not sure.' He did not want to put his fears into words, those fears that this parents would be ashamed of him, angry, would wish him dead rather than an ex-kanene.

Kruin had to say his piece. 'They will naturally be surprised and pleased to have you home again,' he said. 'I should save any explicit details until you are settled.'

'I'm not sure I'll be able to hide it,' Panthera said dismally. 'I feel as if it's written all over me.'

'It's not,' I said.

The castle has a thick outer wall, with a drawbridge over a dry moat. Panthera said that the bridge is never raised. We rode over it and Panthera pulled the bell-chain attached to the huge, wooden gates. I could almost smell his fear. After only a moment, the gates were opened and a servant came out to ask our business.

'Tell the castlethane that his son is here,' Panthera said with a shade of the old, familiar arrogance.

The servant looked at us all suspiciously and then told us to wait. Panthera explained that this was a Har he'd never seen before, obviously someone employed since his disappearance. 'Time waits for no-one,' he said. 'I wonder how many other new faces there'll be inside?' His hands were shaking, his face white.

I reached out to touch his arm, but then we could hear a great commotion beyond the gates. Panthera's father had obviously lost no time in answering this summons. Dogs came barking under the stone arch and the gates were thrown wide. We all looked within, at the tall Har striding towards us, several yards in front of those that followed him. We all looked into the face of a Har who dared not believe that his wildest hope had become truth.

'Ferminfex; my father,' Panthera told us weakly and dismounted from his horse.

Ferminfex, like many Hara, was very tall. Looking at him, it was not difficult to see how Panthera had been born so lovely, I reached this opinion even before I'd met Lahela, who is something of a legend himself. Ferminfex came to a stop a few feet away from us. He said, 'Panthera', and Panthera walked towards him. They embraced each other in silence and then Ferminfex led his son into the yard. Hara respectfully backed away from them, staring. Neither Kruin nor myself had been acknowledged and we shared bewildered glances, unsure of what to do. 'Oh come on,' I said, 'we might as well follow.' A stable-Har had come and taken hold of Panthera's horse. Kruin and I handed him the reins to ours and went after Panthera into the main house.

We stood in the hall and gawped around us. The sight was most impressive; marble, tapestry, stone, and dark, polished wood. It was also surprisingly warm. A servant came to intercept us as we made to investigate one of the passages that led into the heart of Jael. 'The Castlethane would like you to refresh yourselves,' he said politely. 'Please come with me.'

We followed him up a red-carpeted corridor and were shown into a parlour, quite a large room, though probably small by Jael standards. Long, pointed arch windows curtained with floor-length, heavy velvet, offered a view of the gardens. The servant, an imperious creature, told us to make ourselves at home, refreshment would be brought to us shortly. He backed softly from the room and closed the door. Kruin, as he always does, went straight for the fire.

'Wonder when we get to talk business,' he said, in rather a mercenary manner.

'Just look at this place!' I exclaimed, throwing myself down in a plump, well-cushioned chair. 'The Jaels are clearly more than just comfortably off, by anybody's standards!'

'If that's the case, then they'll probably skimp on the reward money. That's how most rich people become rich.'

I thought Kruin was being a little too hard. The walls of that room were virtually covered with oil paintings of various size and style, although most of them were portraits. From all around us the sultry, yet austere, arrogance of the Jaels looked down straight and imperious painted noses into the room. I recognized one picture as being of Panthera as a Harling. He hadn't changed all that much. In the picture, he was leaning against the knees of a seated Har who could only be his hostling. They shared the same deep, green eyes and haughty beauty.

Kruin broke my reverie. 'Do you think we'll be given rooms in the servants' quarters?' he said.

Presently, our refreshment was brought to us. It took two Hara laden with trays to bring it in. My appetite hadn't been that good for a while now, so despite the tempting smells, I only took a bowl of soup and a tankard of ale. Kruin fell upon the meal with gusto. One of the Hara told us that the Castlethane would be along to see us very shortly.

When Ferminfex came into that room, Kruin and I stood up immediately. It was done without thinking, although I must admit I felt rather foolish when I realized I'd done it. Ferminfex has a regal air that commands that sort of behaviour. He waved us back into our seats. Many Wraeththu Hara take to autocracy like a duck takes to water. I was reminded of Terzian yet again. Once, long ago, I'd been in a very similar situation to this in Galhea. It was not Terzian's son that Pell and I returned to him, but his very sick consort. Unlike Terzian, however Ferminfex is not a person to be feared. I could see that straightaway. With Terzian you could see the steel inside him that lifted him above (or below) morality; Ferminfex has a similar steel but its blade is tempered — there's no savagery in it. He thanked us warmly for helping Panthera to get home and then mentioned that, in the morning, his secretary would speak to us about our 'expenses'. It was all very civilized. The word 'reward' was not mentioned once.

'You are welcome to stay here in Jael for as long as you wish,' he said, and then to Kruin, 'You are Natawni? In view of the season and the exceptionally heavy snowfall in the north, I think you'd be wise to remain here until the spring. I also think it would help Panthera considerably if you, his friends, stayed with him for a while. He'll need some time to readjust.' He sighed and rubbed his hands together. 'Now, you must be tired. I think we should all meet again at breakfast tomorrow and discuss your plans. I'll have someone show you to your rooms. Excuse me.' He inclined his head and left us.

'Rooms!' Kruin exploded once the door had closed behind him. 'The cheek of it! No question of us being together, was there!'

'Oh, stop being so pernickety!' I answered, irritated. 'This isn't Cora's, Kruin. That was politeness, he was avoiding being indelicate.'

'You love this sort of thing, don't you!' Kruin said accusingly.

I could only shrug. 'Yes I do. It reminds me of home.' It was the truth.

I would have welcomed the chance to be alone that night, but Kruin insisted on sharing my room with me, which he claimed was more comfortable than his anyway. My bones were aching; that was always a bad sign, but I hoped that it was simple exhaustion in this case and not a presentiment of something worse. Panthera came to see us before we went to sleep. He looked very different; clean and well-dressed, his hair pinned up. Obviously he'd just attended a family reunion. He looked tired.

'How's it going?' I asked him.

'Oh, OK' he answered wearily. 'I think Ferminfex has decided that I've picked up some dreadful habits in the outside world. If only they knew!'

'What have you told them?' Kruin asked.

'I haven't lied,' Panthera answered. 'I told them nearly everything. I told them I was a slave, but not what kind. So far, I've been asked no awkward questions; but that'll just come later. Once they start thinking about how I came of age away from home. Lahela will start worrying about my sex education; that's when it'll all start getting unpleasant. I won't be able to lie about that. I know I won't.' He looked so down-hearted.

'Perhaps you should tell them before then,' I said. He looked at the floor and shook his head. Rather him than me.

In the morning, Kruin and I were woken up by a servant bringing us cups of hot, herbal tea. We were told, as the curtains were flung wide to let pale, winter sunlight into the room, that breakfast would be served in half an hour. An explanation was given on how to find the breakfast-room and would we care to have our bath run for us? We said we would.

Kruin, despite his reservations about the Jaels, was enjoying this immensely. 'Some servants' quarters eh?' I teased him. Our room was round, on the third floor of a turret. I went to open one of the arched windows, leaning out to gaze down the smooth, stone walls. Kruin complained of the cold. It was a lovely morning; crisp and hard and bright. There was a smell of cooking, sounds of activity in the yard below. I felt warm and secure. If I closed my eyes, it could be Forever around me. Panthera had sent us some clean clothes, plain and dark, in the Ferike style, but eminently flattering and stylish.

In spite of the directions we'd been given, it still took Kruin and myself several tries to find the breakfast room. By the time we found it, the rest of the family were already seated. There were over a dozen of them, and that wasn't counting the Harlings. The room was airy and light, carpeted in a pale colour with matching drapes. The table was of highly polished black wood with all the Jaels sitting around it, poised in the act of politely inviting us to join them. Spaces has been left on either side of Panthera. We sat down. Panthera forked slivers of ham onto my plate. He looked very serious, his hair still pinned up, revealing the longest neck I'd ever seen.

'You smell wonderful,' I said.

He smiled without looking up. 'It's only the food,' he answered.

'No, it's not. Don't you think I'd recognized the perfume of your soul if I smelled it?' He looked at me then, right at me, light off the cutlery high-lighting his skin; his eyes were luminous. He was thinking. I felt the breath catch in my throat. I smiled and he smiled back at me. It was our first shared moment.

Lahela made a splendid entrance when we were all half-way through our meal. He was dressed only in a bathrobe, his hair knotted untidily on top of his head, though most of it was dangling down his back. The art of stylish scruffiness. He looked marvellous. Ferminfex lit up when Lahela walked in the room and I don't blame him. Lahela yawned and slumped down in a chair at the opposite end of the table to Ferminfex. A servant skidded to his side and offered to heap his plate with food. Lahela groaned. 'Coffee please!' he said, 'And a lightly grilled piece of toast.' Like Ferminfex, he thanked us for bringing Panthera home, except his gratitude was delivered in a far warmer manner. He drank his coffee without using the delicate handle of his cup, and smoked three cigarettes. I could see the other Jeals exchanging long-suffering glances. Lahela seemed oblivious, but because of what Panthera had told me, I knew that this was a staged ritual of Jael irritation that Lahela must perform fairly regularly.

'Has 'Fex has his little talk with you yet?' Lahela asked me.

'No, he hasn't!' Ferminfex answered stonily before I could speak.

Lahela smiled. 'Don't look like that, Cal. He won't bite you, will you my dear?'

Ferminfex rolled his eyes, shaking his head, smiling.

CHAPTER

14

Reliving the Past

'Take this white robe. It is costly. See, my blood

has stained it but a little. I did wrong:
I know it, and repent me. If there come
a time when he grows cold — for all the race
of heros wander, nor can any love
fix theirs for long —
take it and wrap him in it,
and he shall love again'

Louis Morris

After the meal, Ferminex took me to his study. 'I would have left this until later, but as Lahela mentioned it, I thought we might as well get it over with.'

'That sounds ominous,' I said lightly. He didn't answer that.

'Please, sit down,' he said. It was a pleasant, dark and cosy room. A fire roared in the grate and there was a heady smell of pine. The desk was enormous. We faced each other across it.

'I want to come straight to the point,' Ferminfex said, and then watched me carefully for a second or two. 'We knew, were informed, of your coming here.' He offered me a cigarette, which I took automatically.

My body had gone numb with the familiar cold. The room was closing in. I wanted to get out. I couldn't breathe. Panic. *They'd* been here before me then. Nowhere was safe. Everyone was in on it.

'Now listen, Cal. I can imagine what you're thinking. I was only concerned about Panthera; that he was still alive and coming back to us, but someone is concerned for you too, Cal ...' (*Don't I know it!*)

'No,' I said eventually. 'No, look I'm sorry, Castlethane; I don't want to involve you or your family in ... whatever. I'm sorry they've ... contacted you. I ...'

'Shut up,' Ferminfex interrupted mildly. 'There is nothing to apologize for. All that happened was that I was ... requested ... enjoined perhaps, to offer my assistance to you if I thought it was needed. I didn't have to tell you this, Cal. You do see that, don't you?'

I nodded, carefully.

He smiled. 'Good. Now that's understood, perhaps we can go on. I am supposed to talk to you, impartially, but I don't like deception. I thought it only fair to tell you the score. If you don't want my help, then fine, we'll leave it at that. Panthera is concerned about you though. He spoke a little last night about what has happened.'

'Did he!' (Fine to reveal my secrets then, if not his own).

'Yes, he did, and with the best possible motive, Cal. Now, I don't now what you're mixed up in with the Gelaming, and I don't particularly care; whatever it is can't offend me. We all owe you a lot, Cal. I want to help you. What do you say?'

'You've been honest with me?' I asked.

'I have. I cannot ask you to trust me, because I can see you don't trust people easily, but I'm sure you'd be able to tell if I was deceiving you.'

'You flatter me,' I said. 'I'm not sure of my own senses anymore. Anyway, I really don't know how, or where, to begin.'

Ferminfex nodded in understanding, chewing his cheek thoughtfully. He took a long draw off his cigarette and spoke through a plume of smoke. 'You could try starting with why the Gelaming have such an interest in you.'

'I could, yes. I'm not sure if I want to.'

'Hmm, of course, it's not really my business, but I feel you gain nothing from bottling all this up. How can it possibly affect me, or even you, if you let it all out?'

'I don't know. I've always felt it should be something I keep to myself. If I tell you, you're implicated, Ferminfex. Remember, you don't know what it is yet.'

'If you're afraid you may cause suffering by telling me, forget it. The Jaels have a very secure position; excellent positions in the esteem of both Almagabra and Maudrah. That is unassailable. Do you really think you'd have been allowed to come here if they didn't want me to know?'

'Your arguments seem sound,' I said, still reluctant to speak.

'Well?'

'Well. It's not the Gelaming exactly that have the interest in me. It is their Tigron.'

'Ah, Pellaz-har-Aralis,' Ferminfex said softly, looking beyond me. It was strange to hear that name quoted with such respect.

'Yes,' I agreed, 'it is he.' I wished I didn't have to go on. It was like ripping out my own heart, to put it on the desk before us, and watch it bleed. Why, after all this time? Why should it still hurt? Am I just crazy? Is that it? I'd always sort of *known* that one day I'd have to tell someone, but it was still hard.

'So,' Ferminfex prompted, 'and what interest does the Tigron have in you?'

'It's hard to explain.'

'Is it? Then try.' Ferminfex leaned forward on his desk, his chin resting on his clenched fists.

I took a deep breath. I closed my eyes. 'A long time ago, long before Pellaz became Tigron, he and I travelled together. We were ... close. Of course, it had been mapped out for him from the moment of his inception what he was to become, but we didn't know, you see. We were aware of the fact that Thiede had his eye on Pell, and for that reason, Pell tried to progress in caste as quickly as possible. Looking back, I can see we were so stupid — blind. To Thiede, I started off being an admirable bodyguard, someone who could teach Pell how to survive, but eventually, I became rather an inconvenience. There was no place for me in Pell's grand future, as far as Thiede was concerned. He hadn't counted on our feelings for each other. It was because of my heritage, you see, which, I'm afraid to admit, is Uigenna.'

Ferminfex sucked in his breath at that. 'Ah, I *do* see! Now there's something Phaonica would rather keep quiet, I'd bet! The Tigron was once chesna with a Har of the Uigenna; hardly a savoury background. How embarrassing!' He laughed out loud.

'I'm glad you understand,' I said drily.

Ferminfex waved his hand at me. 'Sorry, it's just that the Gelaming are such a pompous lot, so sanctimonious. I find your relationship with the Tigron is simply poetic justice, which they well deserve. The Gelaming would do well to remember their own origins at times!'

'I agree.'

Looking back, it becomes obvious that Thiede had planned to get rid of me from the start. He bided his time and then ... smack; it came. I couldn't look at Ferminfex's face as I told him about it. Oh no; I didn't want to watch any pain mirrored there. I looked out of the window, speaking to the sky. I still feel that Thiede's plans were far too ornate and fanciful. Why kill Pell at all? Was it just to fool me, having him murdered under my nose? Did Thiede think I'd just forget about him then? Probably. Uigenna are not famed for the depth of their passions. It was only later that Thiede understood the extent of my grief, the madness that it inflicted on me. I'm still not sure if I've recovered my sanity. For years I believed Pell to be dead. I'd burned his body myself. I knew I had to try and forget, but deep inside, something must have told me. I don't know. It was as if I *knew*, because whatever I did, whoever I was with, I couldn't stop thinking about that hare-brained, idiot, lovely child; my Pellaz. It was totally uncharacteristic of me, and still is. As far as Thiede was concerned, as soon as he'd grabbed Pell from my clutches, I was simply past history. But there was something he hadn't accounted for; Pell had a heart and a mind of his own. True, he was still Thiede's creature, through and through, but as long as I lived, Pell would look for me, and if I was dead, Thiede was afraid Pell might still look for me. Dangerous. An unhinged and bizarre state of mind. A messy wound that Thiede just could not suture. What a dilemma. Eventually, I meandered my way back to Galhea; not intentionally. Terzian's people took me in and when Terzian's son Swift went in search of the Gelaming looking for his father, I went with him. Oh, I was petrified of meeting them, sure enough, but at the same time ... An exciting, but terrifying, thrill. I wanted it. Why? When I reached them, I still knew nothing about what Pell had become; nothing. I went to them unarmed, in every sense. Perhaps that was a big mistake, perhaps it wasn't. It was certainly inevitable. Seel was there with them, utterly Gelaming by then. He ignored me.

I stopped speaking; clouds had covered the sun outside.

Ferminfex shifted in his seat, leaning forward. 'Did they tell you then about the Tigron?' he asked.

This story was delighting him. I put my head in my hands, the taste of Imbrilim in my throat, the memory of so many faces filled with contempt. I had dredged these thoughts up from a deep, dark dungeon of my mind. Difficult. It had taken years to suppress them. Now I felt dazed, swamped, unsafe.

'Tell me? I don't … It's …' The room was electric around me, Ferminfex's fire crackling, popping like a pyre. Outside, black birds were lamenting, voices echoing.

'Please try, Cal.' Now my host was blatantly eager. It was foul. When I looked up from the darkness the day was bleached and stretched. 'You must let it out, Cal. Relax. Come on, it can't hurt you now.' (*It can! It can!*)

I gulped air through a throat that was squeezing itself shut. Ferminfex squatted beside me. I'd literally collapsed. I was on the floor. He put his hand on the back of my neck, hauled me into a sitting position, pushed my head between my knees. 'Are you alright?' Now his eyes were filled with concerned not morbid hunger. Had they ever been otherwise? I don't remember. I nodded weakly at him. He stood up to fetch me a glass of wine, which I had to hold with both hands.

'I'm sorry,' I said, clambering back onto the chair. 'I don't know what happened to …' And then the glass fell from my fingers to shatter on the floor. My body arched, all the muscles flexed to agony. The sound of my mindless, almost divine, grief was the cry of a huge, tortured beast. The room was full of it, more noise than my frame would allow. Ferminfex was white, unsure of what to do. I hurt so much, every fibre of my being vibrating with a real yet imagined pain. After a while, like a spirit wind dying down, the feeling began to recede, back into me. I sobbed, sucking air into my lungs, wiping tears from my nose and finding that it was blood. A subdued Ferminfex offered me a soft cloth to wipe my face. I don't think he knew what to say. We'd touched on something forbidden. We both knew that, without even mentioning it. But it had to be faced; that was another shared certainty. I felt raw, opened up, ready to be examined. That was an accurate analogy, but we'd have to work fast before the wounds healed.

'Can you continue now?' Ferminfex asked me.

'Yes,' I said. 'I want to.'

'Can you remember everything?'

'Not yet; but I will. I have to begin.'

'Then take your time.' He gave me another glass and sat down.

I remembered that day in Imbrilim so clearly. Strange that before now I hadn't really been aware of forgetting it. Habit; must be. We'd just been waiting around, Swift and I, waiting for something to happen. Swift was quite ill with it all. Me, I felt as if there was one hell of a big stone hanging over my head by one fragile thread. It was vile. Why couldn't they just get on with whatever they wanted to do with us? One day, when Swift was out of the way, they sent a guard to take me to Arahal. One of Thiede's top dogs is Arahal. Then they made me wait in his pavilion; more agony. When he came in, he was very brusque with me. I remember saying, 'OK, do your worst', having no idea just how bad that could be. He handed me a photograph. It was of a splendid Har, obviously Gelaming, robed in feathers, crowned in feathers and silver filigree.

'Do you know this Har?' Arahal asked. 'Do you ... *remember* him?'

I must have looked at him stupidly.

'Why?' I looked at the picture again.

'Just answer. Do you?' He took it off me, leaving my hand in the air, holding nothing.

'Well, it looks a bit like someone I knew once, yes, but he's dead now. It looks like someone called Pellaz.'

'Yes, it is,' Arahal said coldly. 'I was afraid you'd say that.' It was then that the cold dread started creeping in from the diaphanous walls of the pavilion, invading my flesh, penetrating deep. With it came a vivid recollection. A scream. A horse's scream. Flying blood and bone. The rain. Cold. Cold. Cold. I thought I'd learned to control it. My heart was going mad. Panic. It hadn't happened for a long time. With that memory came the feeling of death; my death. My brain exploding, my soul being sucked away. I was frozen; an imbecile. 'Calanthe!' Arahal said. After a moment, I'd mustered enough self-control to look at him. He smiled then and the smile was almost gentle. 'I'm afraid I'm going to have to ask you to go to Immanion,' he said.

'Why?' A husky little question.

'Because Thiede is anxious to talk with you.' He waved the photograph at me. 'You've caused no end of trouble in Pell's name, haven't you. Cal, that's bad for us. Very bad. For the simple reason that the Har you thought was dead lives on. He is Pellaz-har-Aralis, Tigron of Immanion.'

It was a shock. It was a great shock. What more can I say?

Another slice of the past removed from my heart. There was silence in Ferminfex's room. He lit another cigarette. Outside, it had begun to rain; the day was dismal.

'There's more isn't there?' he asked.

'Oh yes, there's more. But I don't think I'm supposed to remember it. What's happened? How come I can speak of it now?'

Ferminfex shrugged. 'I don't know. Have you really tried to tell someone before?'

'I think so. I can't remember. This is scary, isn't it?'

Ferminfex nodded. 'I'm afraid I must agree with you.'

'It's not just my sick mind is it?'

He smiled. 'No, it's not just your sick mind. I'd like to flatter myself that I was the key needed to turn those locks in your head, but if I am then someone else is turning it, not me. Are you ready to go on?'

I shivered. 'I'm afraid. I don't feel safe.'

'We have all day, no need to rush. Come with me.' He took my arm and helped me to rise. My legs were like jelly. Why did I feel like this? What happened had been years ago. I'm not a weak person. Memories, however harrowing, should not affect me like this. I thought I'd got over all that in Galhea.

There was a couch at the other end of the room, next to the fire. Ferminfex told me to lie down on it. He wrapped me in the woollen, fringed blanket draped over the cushions. My fingers were freezing. He took my hand. 'Let's make this a little easier,' he said. 'Relax, Cal. Let me take you back.'

Simple hypnosis. His voice washed over me and talked me back. It *was* easier that way. Living the past, I could not experience the pain of the present. I found myself sitting in a small room. I'd been there for some time. The building was the administration office in a town some miles north of Immanion. I hadn't slept for several nights. Neither had I eaten anything. They kept bringing me food which I wouldn't touch and talked in whispers behind my back. I was sitting on the edge of a narrow bed with my eyes closed, thinking of nothing. Then someone came and touched me on the shoulder. They said, 'Calanthe, Lord Thiede wishes to see you now.' They had to help me walk. My mind was a blank. If I tried to think at all, I was flooded with images of Pell's blood. I could feel the sting on my cheek where a shard of flying bone had cut me. I could smell the hot, sweet perfume of fresh blood, I could smell burning. They led me into another room. The rooms were all the same there. Tasteful, functional, soothing. Elegant plants and comfortable furniture. A Har sat behind a desk, his feet crossed at the ankles on the glossy surface. A Har with flaming red hair and an unmistakable aura of immense power; Thiede.

'Ah Cal,' he said sociably. 'Oh dear, you don't look at all well. Come on, come in, sit down. Here.' He clicked his fingers and someone swooped in with the inevitable hot coffee. Thiede heaped sugar into my cup and pushed it into my hands. He shook his head. 'My, what a state you're in!' He laughed. I couldn't speak. Leaning across the desk, he took my face in his hand. I spilled coffee over my lap. 'Now, you're really going to have to pull yourself together, aren't you my dear. We've got to have a little chat and I can't speak to a gibbering idiot, can I now?' He put his fingers over my eyes and blasted me with white, searing strength that nearly knocked me backwards. When my vision had cleared, all feeling had come back to me. One of those feelings was rage. I remember swearing at him, which he listened to indulgently. When my invective had run out, he said, 'Finished? Good. Now listen to me, Calanthe, you really are proving to be rather a thorn in my side.'

'Good!' I said. 'I hope the pain kills you.'

He laughed. 'Oh, no chance of that! Very sorry.'

'Why did you do it?' I asked. 'Why? Just tell me that.'

'Do what?'

I shook my head, unable to speak it.

He sighed. 'Oh Cal, it really is all a bit beyond you, I'm afraid. Just live out your little life and let Hara like me deal with the important issues. Pell's like you, you know. He won't let go either.'

'Of the past?' I had visions of Pell flinging himself around, reliving his own death every day.

Thiede shook his head. 'Oh no, not exactly. He is everything I'd hoped he'd be. He rules for me, Cal, and one day, his authority shall be over the entire world. He was a good choice. No, what he won't let go of is you. I'm afraid I'm finding it hard to see why, looking at you now, but I suppose you have been through a lot. Every creature in the world has an ideal partner, a soul mate. Only a few are lucky to find each other. You and Pellaz did, but then, that was unlucky because you had to be torn apart. It damaged you both more than I thought it would. You are nothing Cal, you don't matter, but Pell can't afford such scars.'

'So, what are you going to do? Kill me?'

Thiede pulled a careful, disgusted face. 'Oh, please! We are not barbarians. We are not Uigenna. No, there is a much more palatable solution. Of course, as you are now, you're wholly unsuitable for Pellaz to be associated with. It would cause a terrible scandal. He holds a position higher than any other Har in Wraeththudom. But he's had to pay the price for that privilege. He's had to learn to live without privacy, to be as spotless a creature as he can. He's an example to our race, Cal. He has to be perfect. Do you understand this?'

Oh, I understood it all right. 'So, what's your solution then?' I asked bitterly, still thinking of death or banishment.

'Well, in a perfect world, you would be taken to Immanion to undertake a course of ritual purification, so that, eventually, you would be fit to take your place at Pell's side, and could be brought forth for this end as yet another example to the people of how even the most base creature can aspire to perfection.'

I made an explosive sound, which Thiede raised his hand to silence. 'But,' he continued, 'this is not a perfect world — yet. Pellaz already has a consort, which I, admittedly, did rather bully him into taking. They are bonded in blood, which is insoluble. I'm afraid the liaison has not been a happy one, but there you are! Even I can make mistakes. So you see, whatever vows you and Pell made before cannot stand up against a bloodbonding. You cannot be his consort; there is no way around that, unless Caeru the Tigrina was to die. Unfortunately for you, he is young and healthy and, although not entirely popular with the Hegemony (which I regret is probably Pell's doing), he is well-loved by the people. Although his relationship with Pell may be barren, Caeru has carved a niche for himself in Wraeththu's heart. He does his job very well. No-one outside of Phaonica would ever know they are not perfectly matched.'

I felt sick. 'What are you trying to tell me?' I asked.

'Merely this. You must take the course of Cleansing. There is a position in Immanion for you, Cal, in the royal household. I know I could use your talents, and what you and Pell decide to do between yourselves, behind closed doors, is nobody else's business. Naturally, you'll both have to be very careful. Can't afford to let anyone know what's going on. I'm sure you understand that. It will help if I can find you a consort of your own. Arahal can employ you in his staff. You are untrained, so he won't be able to offer you much at first. You'll have to work your way up, but I'm sure you won't find that difficult. Now, what do you say?'

What I said was, 'How dare you! You think I can be brought to heel, trained like a dog, to wag my tail and fawn at your Tigron's feet? You must be insane! You say that Pell still feels strongly about me? Well, let me tell you, Thiede, I may be the lowest of the low in your eyes, but there is no way, even now, that I'd ever be bonded in blood to anyone else but Pell. I respect what we had before, even if he doesn't. No, I'm not a toy, Thiede. Not like he is!' At that moment, perhaps for the first time, I hated Pell.

'Now just calm down!' Thiede said, still grinning. I wouldn't. My anger got hotter and hotter. In the end, he had me taken away and locked in my room. 'Obviously, we shall have to talk later,' he said, and there wasn't even a hint of irritation in his voice. It was almost as if he was pleased with my reaction. As if it was a *relief*. We did talk later. We talked many times. I was moved from place to place, probably (or so I thought) to prevent Pell finding out Thiede had me in confinement. Strange things happened to my sense of time. Sometimes I'd wake up from a winter night's sleep and find that it was high summer outside my window. I began to lose time. This always happened after one of my intimate chats with Thiede. I tried to rationalize, thinking of it as an hallucination Thiede had created purposely to keep me disorientated. I was treated very well, given everything except my freedom. Gelaming are rarely physically cruel, of course. They have more subtle methods of torture. At the beginning, they even let me out to visit Terzian when he was dying. I was followed just to make sure I kept in line, but it was still a sweet touch. I suppose Thiede tried everything to get round me. I slept with a silver-haired har who never spoke, whose eyes were completely black, who loved me in a silent, distant way. I never even knew his name. Thiede would sometimes come to see me three times a week, and then I wouldn't hear from him for a couple of months. Every time we talked it got round to the same subject. My character was undesirable. I would have to change. I must publicly speak out against my own past and praise the way that Thiede had made me see the light. And no, there was no chance of my going free. I must recognize my duty to Wraeththu and to the Tigron in particular. Had I no sense of responsibility? In public, I would be allowed to be Pell's colleague, albeit a low-ranking one. I would have to bow to him and call him Lord. In private, well, how could there ever be such a thing. I wouldn't even let myself think about it. In case some small part of me said, Yes, yes, this is what I want! No, no, it was against my nature; impossible! Thiede enjoyed our wrangling; I know he did. Afterwards, my black-eyed companion would try to comfort me, ease the stress from the back of my neck. Maybe I did forget for a little while then. I could see no end to it. I'd wake up and it'd seem like years had passed.

Eventually, I came to be confined within a tower. I'd had enough. I didn't know how long I'd been locked up. One day, Thiede came to see me and he seemed different, just a little tense, watching me carefully. We drank iced wine on the high balcony and I said, 'Just let me go, Thiede.' I hadn't said that for quite some time, knowing how fruitless it was to bother. I'd made up my mind to throw myself from the tower if things didn't change soon. How long I'd have gone on promising myself that, I cannot guess. Thiede tapped his fingers against his lips, looking down into his wine.

'You really want to turn your back on Pell?' he asked casually.

Hope leapt in my chest like a crazy bird. 'Look, if you let me go, I'll disappear, go away as far as you like,' I babbled. 'Tell Pell I'm dead; anything! I won't be an embarrassment to you, I promise! No-one will ever know about Pell and me, I swear it! I'll never breathe a word to anyone. You have my word. Take my life if I break it.'

Thiede just threw up his hands. 'Impossible, I'm afraid! Pell won't ever stop wanting you, looking for you. I have ... er ... *spoken* to him, Cal. He does know I'm in contact with you. Naturally, he is distressed by some of the things you've done. The incident in Saltrock springs to mind. But it is beyond me to dissuade him from caring about you. The problem is, I *do* understand it. Though he and Caeru may be bonded in blood, I am convinced that you and Pell are bonded in soul. I must stress that your only course of action is to do as I suggest; take the Cleansing. Come to Immanion.'

'And be there for Pell to play with whenever he feels the need to?' I butted in angrily. 'How many times do I have to tell you, Thiede? The answer is no. It will always be no. I couldn't live that life. I need my freedom. I need my self-respect. More than I need Pell. Anyway, I know we could never be happy living like that. It would be nothing like we had before. I'd hate it and so would he, I'm sure. It's better for us to suffer being apart than learning to loathe each other together. I'm right, Thiede, we've both changed. The Pell and Cal that loved each other are both dead. And even the memory of it must die. You can't argue with me; you know I'm right.'

He was silent for a moment. 'Hmm. Now listen, Cal, I don't think you've quite grasped the extent of Pell's power here,' he said wearily. 'His word is law. He is your Tigron too, Cal. If he wants you, then I'm afraid he's going to have you. It's against my wishes, I've done all I can to prevent it, but there's nothing I can do to change his mind. I've tried! All I can do now, is nudge events along in the most civilized manner.'

'Thiede, it's disgusting and you know it!'

'Oh, I agree, entirely. But Pell has more important things to worry about than this. For God's sake, realize how small you are in comparison and make things easier by doing what I suggest.'

'Sacrifice my life for the good of Wraeththu? Forget it! Let me go, Thiede!'

'You will merely delay the inevitable by that.'

'I can go far away. I've told you!'

'Nowhere will be far enough.'

'I'll hide!'

'You can try — certainly.' He smiled at me. 'You're a problem, Cal. A bull-headed wild child, if ever there was one. No wonder he loves you! Please think about what I've said though.'

'Oh, I do. Every time you say it!'

'I admire you. I really do.'

'Yet you want to change me.'

He shook his head. 'I can see your side too, you know. You have my sympathy.'

'Oh, sure I do. Look what a help it's been!'

He shrugged, stood up. I remained seated, staring at my hands. Thiede took a deep breath, stared out over the countryside.

'You have a good view here, don't you.' I didn't answer. I felt him staring at me. 'It's your choice,' he said, in a silky voice.

'I've had enough, Thiede.'

'Yes. I know.' And then he left me.

I sat there for a while, finished my drink and then went inside. Everywhere felt strange, deserted. I couldn't find my companion anywhere. I ran down the winding steps to the door that was always locked from outside. The hall looked different that day. No wonder. I'd always seen it in gloom, now it was full of sunlight. The great door was wide open. The tower was empty. Outside, a white horse lazily cropped grass, loaded with supplies. I sat down on the front step and stared at the outside world for several hours. I did a lot of thinking. Pell is my life, but I also knew that what I loved most about him was his innocence, his freedom, his simplicity. I couldn't believe that had survived along with his soul. It was impossible. He was Tigron. It took some time, and even some guts, but in the end I just walked out of that tower and never looked back. I mounted the horse that Thiede had left for me and galloped it towards the north. Funny how the people you most hate can surprise you with sensitive gestures occasionally. Oh, Thiede understood me, alright. I kept heading north. There was money in the saddle-bags; plenty of it to start with. In a week, I was in Thaine, shying at shadows, numbing my sleep with alcohol. I'd been in confinement for many years. Now I was free. No-one had won. There was no victory.

That was when Ferminfex brought me back. I was shaking as if terribly cold, yet my skin was hot. I drank wine and took the cigarette he offered me. 'What can I do?' I asked.

Ferminfex knelt down beside me. 'I want you to rest now,' he said. 'Panthera tells me you've been keeping a sort of diary of what's happened since. Fallsend. I'd like to read it while you're resting. Tell me where it is.'

I hesitated, but then, hadn't he witnessed my soul already? I told him where it was, and he left me alone, hurrying to fetch it. I lay there feeling like I'd come round after an incredibly serious operation, which could have killed me, but hadn't.

Pages turning. I lay on the couch, watching Ferminfex reading my notes. I could almost tell which parts he was reading by the exclamations he made. A guilty thought stole through me. All of Panthera's secrets were in there too. 'Ferminfex,' I said, worried, 'about your son. He ... well, I wouldn't like him to know I've showed you that.'

'Don't think I haven't realized some of what Thea's been through, Cal,' he replied. 'I'm not stupid. This manuscript might be painful for both of us, but I do want to read it; as much to learn Panthera's troubles as help you.'

'That's sneaky, Ferminfex!'

'Don't worry. Panthera will never know I've seen this, I promise you.' He looked up. 'I hope that one day he will want to tell me himself what happened. If he does, I'll tell him how I feel about it, that I'm just glad he got out of there alive. Nothing else matters. I don't think he realizes that.'

'He's a proud creature,' I said.

'Yes, that's Lahela's blood for you,' Ferminfex commented bleakly, although I thought that Ferike austerity was more to blame than Kalamah vanity. No matter what Ferminfex said, I could tell that it still shocked him deeply to learn of his son's humiliations in Piristil. At one point, he looked up at me and said, 'I know the taking of life is the worst of crimes, and I wish Panthera hadn't shot Jafit, but for simply one reason: I'd like to have done it myself!' He rubbed his eyes with his hands. 'Lahela must never see this,' he said. At the end of it, he put his head in his hands.

It was late afternoon. We sat together in silence, me on the sofa, he behind his desk. A knock came on the door. Lahela had sent one of the househara with a tray of food. I was hungry, and went to sit at the desk once more. Ferminfex stared at me for a moment and then tapped the sheaf of papers with his fingers, smiling wrily. 'I must say your feelings for Panthera cause me some concern!'

I squirmed in mortification. 'Oh, I wasn't myself when I wrote that,' I replied lightly.

'Now don't take that the wrong way! I don't think your blood is tainted. Let's face it, any one of us who was incepted to Wraeththu rather than born to it has shady areas in our past histories. It was just the time for it. You don't strike me as evil, Cal, far from it. Tormented, maybe. What I should have said was, does Panthera return your feelings? I don't want him to be hurt more than he already has been.'

'Oh no,' I said. 'Panthera has no idea I was lusting after him on the journey south. Anyway, I'm sure you'll agree, he's in no condition to return anyone's feelings at present.'

'Yes, he needs time, that's true. But anyway, we're here to talk about your situation, not Thea's. Let's just analyze what we know. Since leaving Thiede's tower, you have been plagued by dreams which lately have culminated in two very frightening experiences. You have been aware of being followed, perhaps by this shadow figure from your past ...'

'I don't understand where Zack fits into all this,' I said.

'No, neither do I. Perhaps it is to make you all the more keen to recant your past, I don't know. I think the main question you've got to ask yourself is, who is behind all this? And what is its purpose?'

'Well, that's obvious, isn't it? Pell and Thiede. The purpose; to drag me to Immanion, make life unbearable for me anywhere else.'

Ferminfex shook his head. 'I wouldn't be too sure of that if I were you. There is something you aren't aware of yet. The message that came over our thought transference unit was very carefully guarded; no visuals whatsoever. But there was no mistaking the fact that whoever sent it wasn't Wraeththu.'

'What do you mean?'

'Just this; it was female. Must have been human, of course, but a terribly advanced human.'

'Then it's obvious!' I cried, leaning forward, eager to explain. 'Maybe I'm not being paranoid about feeling everyone I meet is in on this. The woman must have been Cora. She was the link in the chain before you. I'm being manipulated, nudged in the direction of Immanion.'

Ferminfex shook his head. 'Oh think, Cal! It can't be Cora. From what you've told me, it's obvious she, or even the girl who lives with her, isn't that far advanced. I'm talking about an incredibly powerful human mind. No, you're wrong about the Gimrah. They have no part in this.'

'Then who has?'

He shrugged helplessly. 'I can't tell you that. What we've got to remember is that there are powers in this universe stronger than Wraeththu, stronger even than Thiede. Cal, there is more to this than meets the eye. You've got to learn the real reason why it's so important for you and Pell to be reunited. I don't think Thiede revealed more than he had to. I'm only acting on hunches, but ...'

'If I don't black out and lose all this information again!'

'That won't happen.'

'Don't be so sure. It's happened before, in Galhea. My mind blotted out crimes I'd committed, Pell's death, everything. It took a blast of power to clear the blocks. Seems I did the same over my imprisonment; I can't trust myself. My machinery is faulty, somewhere.'

Ferminfex didn't agree. 'Have you ever thought that is precisely what you're supposed to think. It's obvious why you couldn't tell people; you were prevented from doing so. Hypno-suggestion, mind coercion, any number of ways.'

'Then why could I tell you?'

'If Thiede put the block on you, but somebody or something else is behind all this, nudging you to Jael, then maybe the time was right for ... God, I don't know! It's beyond me!'

'What is all the secrecy for then? Why can't I be told? Surely it's just wasting time.'

'Mmm.' Ferminfex leaned back in his chair and screwed up his eyes in thought. 'You're on a journey,' he said. 'Self discovery? Maybe. Or something more? I agree that you are being driven in certain directions ...' He sat up. 'The message you had, what was it again?'

'Beneath the mountains of Jaddayoth. Is that referring to caves or a grave do you think?'

'Neither. I believe it's referring to Eulalee, an underground kingdom, home of the tribe of Sahale. Clearly, you've got to go there.'

'And if I don't?'

Ferminfex made an exasperated noise. 'Look, how can you fight when you don't even know who the enemy is? Don't be ridiculous. Go along with this for a while with your ears and eyes open. The huyana in Jasminia spoke of preparing you for something. He spoke of messages. You've got to face it, don't you see? And look at things another way too. How about Pell? He must know that a relationship with you is impossible at the moment, except under the most excruciating terms. What Thiede says he's demanding is like the demands of a child, and Pellaz-har-Aralis is far from a child, I can tell you! Perhaps Pellaz is being manipulated too. Think about it.'

I let myself slump over the table, sighing. 'I don't want this. I don't want any of this!'

'Of course you don't,' Ferminfex soothed. 'You want to make a life in Ferike with my son, don't you? Shall I give my permission for that? Will you do it if I ask you to?' We stared at each other. I shook my head and smiled. 'Wait until the spring,' Ferminfex continued. 'You have plenty of time. We'll talk about this again.'

* * *

So, it was settled. Come the thaw I would ride into the Elhmen; the only known route to Eulalee. I didn't know what I would find there. Coming out of Ferminfex's study that day, I felt ravished, but renewed. The boil had been lanced at last. That night, I dreamed of Pell, but he was far away.

What He Learned From The Water

'Though lovers be lost, love shall not'
　　Dylan Thomas, And death shall have no
　　dominion

Life in Jael is conducted at a leisurely, sedate pace. Every morning, the family gathers together for breakfast, and in the evening for dinner. There are two separate rooms for this. Panthera now has two brothers, one hosted by Lahela, one by Ferminfex. There are also uncles and cousins, and cousins' cousins. Everyone carries the refined, attenuated features of the family Jael. Only Panthera, his hostling and his brothers have more of a sensual, languid Kalamah caste to them. Lahela told me he suspects Panthera and I have some kind of *relationship* (Lahela's italics!) Tactfully put, I suppose. Lahela still knows nothing about what happened to his son in Piristil. Because of this, I don't let on either way if his suspicions are true or not. The sun always seems to shine in Ferike. Every morning, we wake to another frosting of snow upon the trees and in the yard, but all day the sun reflects with hard, crystal brilliance off the land.

One evening, hara from a neighbouring castle came to dine with the Jaels. It was an elegant affair. After the meal, we all sat and listened to some of Panthera's relatives play music in one of the large drawing-rooms. Hara conversed with me in hushed, intellectual tones. I heard one or two disparaging remarks about the Gelaming, which pleased me. Gelaming artists were accused of plagiarising Ferike works. Someone said to me, 'The Gelaming strive for originality, wishing to shine at everything, and hoping, I would think, to attract the interest of the royal houses of Maudrah and Garridan, who will pay highly for works of art.' The Har sniffed eloquently.

I sensed an opportunity to pry. 'Ah yes, the Maudrah! I have heard much about Ariaric, their archon.'

'Hmm, a charismatic character.'

'Was he born in Jaddayoth?'

The Har smiled. 'Born here? Do you know nothing? I doubt that any of the Maudrah were born here, and let me tell you, they aren't too keen to tell people just where they were born either!'

'Would the word Uigenna have anything to do with that?' I enquired delicately, but it is impossible to be delicate using that particular word. My companion winced, drew back, and I realized I'd blown it; no more information would be forthcoming.

And so the weeks passed. I drifted into a womblike contentment; everything outside of Jael had taken on a dreamlike, insubstantial quality. The Ferike spend their time perfecting their artistic talents; painting, literature, music. I used those weeks to rewrite my notes neatly, but Kruin rapidly became bored, being more a creature of action. He was chafing to return home to Natawni. Panthera had closeted himself away in his studio, intent on making up for lost time. I saw him only at meal-times, and often, not even then. One morning, when I awoke, the snow was sliding from the trees and the long icicles hanging from all the windows were dripping into the yard. At breakfast, Ferminfex commented that the thaw had begun. Lahela spoke spiritedly about venturing once more into Clereness and beyond, to restock supplies.

I learned that very soon, representatives from other tribes would begin arriving at Jael to purchase items from all that the family had produced through the long winter incarceration. When I'd first arrived in Jael, I'd often been woken up at night by what sounded like a rhythmic thumping coming from under the ground. I'd been told that this was the printing press in the cellars of the castle. What was conceived in the high, airy rooms above was committed to paper down in the cellars. Pictures were also framed there. It was the workplace of the screen-printers, the potters, the sculptors. It wasn't just the family who were craftsmen in Jael. Panthera had painted me a picture of a dark forest, which I'd hung on my bedroom wall. Before falling asleep, I liked to stare into its haunting depths where the suggestion of secret life seemed to rustle. I would have liked to give him something in return, but I have never been much of an artist.

The thaw continued. A clear stream ran down the road from the castle; the bare branches of the trees were sprouting sticky buds. One day, Panthera suggested that now all the snow had gone, we should take a walk into the woods together. Kruin was too busy packing his things to accompany us; he was leaving soon. Panthera said he'd teach me how to draw. I didn't like to tell him he'd be wasting his time. We set off early in the morning, on horseback, which was my idea. Spring seemed to be creeping quickly over the land. The ground was damp and lush with new grass. Small, spring flowers were blooming around the trees, and sunlight came down through the high branches as we rode away from Jael. After a mile or so, we veered off the road and cantered up a steep bank of bracken-strewn peat. The colours were marvellous; so vibrant, as if they could only have come from an artist's palette. Panthera led me deep into the trees; these woods were like a second home to him. We dismounted and led our horses through clustering trees that ached with the most acid of greens.

'Let's stop here,' Panthera said.

We had come to a fast-running brook, that cut a deep, chuckling channel between banks of mossy sand-stone. Branches dipped longing fingers into the water and the grassy ground seemed wreathed in a faint mist as the sun gently dried it out. We sat upon the bank and our horses began to crop the grass, tearing mouthfuls out by the roots, so sweet it was, so eager their desire for its taste. Panthera gave me a sheet of paper to draw on, but I lacked inspiration.

'Do you think that Astarth really does run Piristil now?' he asked me. It was the first time he had spoken of Fallsend to me since reaching Jael.

'Who knows?' I answered, because I wasn't really bothered.

'Why did he let us get away like that?'

'I don't know. Why do you care, Thea? It's over. Forget it.'

'It'll never be over for me.'

'O.K, I'm sorry. You want a theory? Astarth wanted us to get away, he wanted us to be followed by Jafit, he wanted us to kill Jafit.'

'Of course! You must be right, how stupid of me. With Jafit out of the way, Astarth becomes house-owner not whore.'

'Seems likely, doesn't it. Although, in Fallsend Astarth could easily have bumped Jafit off and nobody would have raised an eyebrow.'

'Don't count on that,' Panthera said. 'The musenda owners are all pretty close. Honour amongst thieves and all that. I don't think Astarth could have got away with anything too blatant.'

'Oh well, so what! I hope he's happier now.'

'I wonder if the others are though?' Panthera was concentrating very hard on whatever it was he was drawing. I'd thrown my paper and pencil down onto the grass.

'Look,' Panthera said and handed me his sketches. Of course, they were of me.

'Am I really that emaciated?' I asked, rather appalled.

'Not on the outside, no,' he replied, taking them back again. He looked thoughtful, put down his pen, and lay back on the soft ground, staring up through the branches above. 'Cal, I've decided to accompany you into Elhmen,' he said.

At first I made no response, but his look of enquiry was difficult to ignore. 'There's no need,' I said at length. 'I've travelled alone most of the time.'

'You don't know the country around here though.'

'True, but I can follow instructions. It may be dangerous, Thea; I don't know. I've no idea what's waiting for me there. And I'm sure Ferminfex will not thank me if I take you away from home again so soon. He's worried about you. I don't think he'd like you to get involved with me any further.'

'You're wrong!' Panthera argued hotly. 'My father would expect me to go with you. After what you did for me, it's the only honour-able thing to do.'

199

'Honour!' I laughed aloud. 'That outmoded concept? Men used to die for honour, didn't they? We must live our own lives, Thea, make our own values. I don't want to endanger you.'

'A more sensitive person than I might suspect you were insulting their courage, or indeed ability,' Panthera said carefully. 'Are you afraid I'll be a hindrance to you?'

'Don't be silly! You don't mean that! I just don't want to involve anyone else in ... well, whatever.'

'In what?'

I didn't answer. Panthera sighed and sat up, resting his chin on his knees. 'Don't you think it's about time you told me? You've spoken to my father about it, I know.' I looked at him for a long time; the light patterns rippling off his face and neck, reflections from the water, his shaded green eyes. Oh Panthera, what I would give to have met you years ago! 'Well?' he said.

And I began. It didn't hurt any more. I could speak freely without fear. Of course, I didn't give him all the details, as I'd done with his father. The forest around us seemed utterly silent, the sunlight was very hot. I got a creepy feeling of being watched, but still I told him. When I finished speaking, he rested his chin on his knees once more and gazed at the water. There was a silence I could not break.

Eventually he said, 'I didn't think it would be anything like that. I thought you'd committed some kind of crime. I ...' He shook his head.

'I have committed crimes, Thea; that's part of the problem.'

'No more than any Har in Jaddayoth, I should think.'

'Yes, maybe so, but Immanion isn't in Jaddayoth is it? It's different in Almagabra; very civilized.'

'That's not what it sounds like to me. Why can't the Tigron accept it's over? Any normal person would. He must be power mad!' Panthera's ferocity surprised me.

'Stop it!' I said. 'You've no right to say that! You don't know anything!'

'It's not over for you either, is it? Look at you defending him. You're both stupid! Oh, what do I care anyway! It's your life!' he picked up his pen and drawing pad once more and scribbled furiously. I took several deep breaths. The silence was electric. I lay back again with my arms above my head and gazed with slitted eyes through the leaves. Trees clung precariously to the stream banks, leaning out over the water. Eventually they will have to fall in. I must have fallen asleep. When Panthera shook me awake, my head was throbbing because I'd been lying face up in the sun for too long. We'd brought food and wine with us, which Panthera was now unpacking from a saddle-bag.

'Are you hungry?' he asked stiffly.

'A bit.'

He cleared his throat. 'I want to apologize,' he said. 'No, don't say anything. I suppose you just told your story so well; I got too involved. You're right; it's none of my business, but I still want to come to Elhmen with you. Can I?'

As if anyone could refuse those eyes! 'OK.'

He smiled. 'Good. We'll start making preparations then.'

We drank wine from the bottle. I reflected that I'd be happy remaining in any of the Jaddayoth countries I'd passed through. Ferike would be no exception. Panthera must have been wondering what I was thinking about.

'Look, there's a waterfall upstream,' he said. 'It's very beautiful. You must see it before we go back.'

I stood up and peered through the tunnel of overhanging trees. 'Alright; are you coming?'

'No, there are a few more sketches I want to make.'

'Another forest painting?'

Panthera wrinkled his nose. 'I hope so. I want to make this one really *live.*'

Laughing, I ducked between the low branches and began to walk upstream. At that moment, I could not remember a time during the last few years when I'd felt more contented. A shame I would have to leave. In Ferike, there were no pressures of any kind. Not even, if I thought about it, those delightful, most welcome pressures of desire. My mind was utterly at rest. Perhaps that's what brought it on; what happened next. After a while, I could hear the rushing sound that presaged the waterfall. I took off my boots and stepped down into the stream. It rushed round my legs; icy, breathtakingly cold. I stopped to take a drink, and it was like a light, heady wine in my mouth. As I stooped, a blinding light reflected off the water, like sunlight on glass. I looked up quickly.

Ahead of me, through a tunnel of overhanging greenery, shining steadily, a white, powerful radiance reflected off the water. I waded forward, against the strengthening flow. The branches parted before me and I stepped out into an arena of light. The waterfall cascaded into what seemed like a roofless cavern, spilling over a lichened lip of rock. Sunlight fell right into the bowl and the water of the pool bubbled like sparkling wine. I could see glittering droplets hanging in the air, bursting in the air, rainbows of light shimmering around me like insubstantial, ethereal beings. Riotous ferns sprouted from the green, rock walls. A cluster of brightly coloured lizards were curled together on a flat stone, taking the sun. Dragonflies skimmed the surface of the water. I was awe-struck. Nothing is so stunning as natural, pure, untainted beauty — beauty such as Pell's once was. I knelt down in the spuming water and let the spray soak me thoroughly. My chest was heavy with an emotion I could put no name to. This place was sacred. It was the home of a god, but the god was not at home. Such moments bring enlightenment. For a brief flash of time, it is possible to understand everything in the world, and in the wake of that realization comes a swelling, bittersweet sadness, that is also the most poignant joy. In that moment, I knew that I could go forward without fear, and face whatever lay in store for me. I thought, 'No-one else can direct my life. I am important, but only to myself and, for that reason, shall take control.' It was strength, pure strength. If a time should come when I finally do have to face Pellaz-har-Aralis, Tigron of Immanion, then I will do so without tremor, with clear mind. I'll tell him that, yes, we had once loved — the memory of it will last forever — but time goes on and life goes on; now I must live my own, which is different from his and always shall be. The scars must be covered with new flesh, comprised of sense and reason, and clear sight. I decided that my future lay in Jaddayoth; nowhere else. Pell will have to listen to me. If some vestige of his former self still remains, he will agree that I am right. I'd convinced myself Pell had become some grim, egocentric tyrant; power-hungry, grasping.

Had it been Thiede who'd made that happen? Can't my own heart tell me the truth? Old wounds had to be cleaned before they could heal.

I stood up in the water, looked one last time at the shining cataract, and thought of returning, back the way I'd come, to Panthera, who was lovely and young, who needed healing as much as I did. I should have realized this before.

I turned to follow the flow of the water and fell ... On my knees with glistening spinnerets of light flashing in my face. The sound of the water had become a roar, the roar of battle, of crowds shouting. 'Oh no,' I thought; just that. My skin was prickling with the presence of power, my bones aching. The air smelt of ozone and the magical strength of the place was increased a hundred fold. Then I thought, 'Remember; you are strong', and stood up again. There was no-one there, only the unearthly crescendo of light and sound. 'What do you want?' I cried, without fear. If it was Zack, I could handle it. If it was Gelaming phantoms, I could handle it. Even if it was a vision of myself, dead and shrouded, I could handle it. It was none of those. I heard a sound, another sound, above the crash of the water. It was like a single note, a voiceless voice. It hurt my eyes, that sound. A glowing bubble of misty light detached itself from the waterfall. It drifted towards me, turning slowly, enveloping my head, my shoulders, my body. I couldn't breathe, but there was no discomfort. I was filled with gold, a golden feeling seeping through the pores of my flesh, my open mouth, my staring eyes. And oh, that feeling, it was the warmest thing on Earth. It was love itself, nurturing, selfless, supportive love. I smiled, held rigid in the arms of that bodiless emotion. There was a voice in my head. It said, 'You are my soul'; softly, chiding. What it did not say was, 'Would you forget me, deny me?' but I knew those words were there. I gasped. 'I love you', and the light contracted about me, squeezing the breath from my lungs. I could smell him, taste him, all around me. A cold wind hit my skin. I opened my eyes and a pulsing ball of light was spinning away from me, up into the white sky. I called him, but it was too late. I could hear birds singing, the water chuckling; he was gone.

In a daze, I splashed back downstream. Panthera looked

astounded when I emerged, soaked to the skin, bootless, crawling up over the bank to lie gasping at his feet.

'Cal?' he said.

'Thea, it was him,' I gabbled. 'Pell was there. He spoke to me. I *felt* him!'

Panthera gritted his teeth and dragged me further onto the grass. He gazed up the stream towards the hidden waterfall, hands on hip; an aggressive stance.

'He's no fool, is he,' Panthera murmured softly. He squatted down beside me and pulled a twig from my wet hair. 'He'll not let you go easily. Is it a fight he wants?'

I was still panting painfully. I could not speak, but whatever Panthera saw in my eyes turned his own to flint.

'A fight it is then!' he decided.

It was not until later that I realized what he meant.

The Land of Elhmen

*'Nothing of him that doth fade
But doth suffer a sea-change
Into something rich and strange.'*

William Shakespeare, Full fathom five
(from The Tempest)

16

Kruin left Jael just as the deep purple flowers were unfurling along the castle walls. Our farewell was unsentimental. He wished me well and told me not to forget to look him up if I ever found myself in Orligia. He left Jael a comparatively rich Har. On top of the reward Ferminfex had given him, he also took several Ferike paintings home with him which were probably worth more than the money.

The night before Panthera and I planned to begin our journey, we had a small, private gathering with Lahela, Ferminfex and Panthera's brothers. Ferminfex wrote a letter of introduction that we could use throughout the journey. Obviously, this would only be effective with Hara to whom the family Jael were known, but at least it was some protection.

'It should get you an audience with the Lyris, leader of the Sahale,' Ferminfex said. 'Although I have never met him personally, Jael has conducted some business with the royal house of Sahen.'

'Straight to the top, eh!' I joked.

'Why bother with anything less?' Ferminfex shrugged. 'The Lyris is Nahir-Nuri; he, if anybody, should be able to enlighten you.'

After the meal, Panthera and his father spread sheets of paper over the table to draw maps and decide which would be the quickest route to Eulalee. Only one gateway was known to Hara of other tribes; Kar Tatang, some miles north of the Elhmen capital of Shappa. Lahela watched them introspectively.

'I did try to dissuade Thea from coming with me,' I said, in apology.

Lahela smiled at me. 'He's doing what he thinks is right. Panthera is a tough little brute, he always has been, but please, don't hurt him, Cal.'

'I have no intention ...' I began, blustering.

Lahela raised his hand, shook his head. 'I know. Just think; that's all I ask.'

We travelled light. The weather was warmer, so there was no need to carry heavy furs. We had been travelling for over a week and now, ahead of us, the sheer mountains of Elhmen soared into a pale, blue sky, their summits mantled with late spring snow, girdled with cloud. Panthera rode ahead of me, his hair flying back, clad in black leather, patterns burnt into the hide. He rode with a grim kind of determination as if it was his destiny we were following, not mine. Perhaps it was. Looking back, I know that I was afraid, although at the time, I just thought it was excitement. I was filled with a sense of 'approach', which increased as the mountains loomed nearer. My sleep had become fitful; I was so full of energy. I thought it was some kind of climax building up. Perhaps, on the other side of it, I could find some peace, and if that peace meant death itself, I was not afraid to meet and fight it. It is a strange thing, and perhaps common only to Wraeththu-kind, that we expect death whenever we are gripped by spasms of presentiment. From experience, I already knew that this was rarely the case (well, obviously so, otherwise I wouldn't be here to write this!), but it is still something we all seem to dread. I suppose it is some vestige of guilt, left over from the dark times of our arrival in the world. We fear the heavy tread of the dark giant because we have thrown stones at him from afar for so long. Perhaps too it is the curse of the near-immortals; can death be cheated so easily?

By mid-day, the gently swelling hills had sharpened to younger, spikier ridges and valleys. Water ran swiftly, coming down from the mountains, where the thaw was not yet complete. Rocks had enclosed us; the land of Ferike seemed far behind. We had dismounted, leading our horses to give them a break. Predatory birds whirled lazily on the air over our heads, screaming fiercely.

'Don't you feel it?' Panthera asked softly. He had stopped walking, tilting his head to the side as if listening.

'Feel what?' I doubted that we could feel quite the same things.

'Power,' he answered.

I looked at his face, his clear, luminous skin, the dreamy yet concentrating expression in his eyes. 'Yes,' I said, 'there is certainly power here.'

Panthera glanced at me archly, alerted by my tone of voice and caught me staring at him. His neck bloomed with colour. 'I don't think you understand,' he said drily. 'Or you do and are merely being facetious, as usual!'

'Sorry. What kind of power?'

'Elhmen. They must be watching us now. I can sense it.'

'Friends or foes?'

'It is never possible to tell with Elhmen!'

We carried on walking and came into a deep canyon. Moss grew like alien flowers from the stones above our heads.

'Where are the Elhmen hiding then?' I asked in a loud whisper. Panthera shot me another derisive glance.

'Elhmen do not always tolerate strangers,' he said, 'not even from as near to home as Ferike. We are not known to them; we shall need their consent to pass through to Eulalee. It is unfortunate we have to pass through these territories; once we reach the city of Shappa it should be easier. My father is known there.'

'Panthera?'

'What?'

'Tell me what you think I'll find in Eulalee.'

He shook his head. 'No-one can tell you that. You'll speak to the Lyris, leader of the Sahale, as my father suggested, but after that, who knows? I'm not even going to try to guess.'

'It would help if we knew, wouldn't it.'

'Naturally, that's probably why we don't.'

Naturally.

By late afternoon, we had come to be riding alongside a cataracting stream between high, rugged walls of rock that sprouted acid green clumps of grass and was stained with dark red and gold lichens. Panthera was still edgy, alert for signs of Elhmen proximity, although I could sense nothing. Because we were out in the open, I hadn't been feeling safe since we'd left Jael. We made camp as the sun went down, planning to set off once more at dawn, and hobbled the horses. I made a small fire and Panthera went to fill our metal cups from the clear, cold water. 'This is like old times,' he said.

'Very much,' I replied and I was thinking back, way back. Panthera sensed this and I could almost feel his inner wince at what he thought was his tactless remark. He rarely spoke of Pell (neither did I), but I could always tell when he was thinking about him. I suppose the same was true in reverse. Perhaps that's why we never spoke about it. I had no doubt that, for my sake, Panthera hated Pell bitterly. I ought to have told him not to, but I remained silent. Perhaps I was afraid of what might come out of such a conversation.

Once we had wrapped ourselves up in separate blankets, I heard Panthera say, 'Are you afraid of the dark, Cal?' I could not think of a witty reply. I shivered.

'Sometimes I'm afraid of everything,' I said.

He reached for me in the darkness and squeezed my shoulder. I could feel his claws graze my skin. When I touched his hand, he withdrew it quickly, as if scalded.

In the dead of night, I woke up, opened my eyes. Silence. Too quiet. I raised my head, conscious of the humped form of the sleeping Panthera. Our horses stamped and snorted somewhere in the darkness behind us. And then there was a ghost before me. This ghost wore a shimmering veil made entirely from silver-white hair that covered its frail, luminous body. Its eyes were slanting, dark in the marmoreal pallor of its face. Its mouth was smiling. I tried to rise, spring up, reach for a weapon, but I could not move. I tried to call Panthera's name but could force no sound from my throat. The ghost raised its arms. 'Travellers,' it said and lowered its arms again, gracefully. My body shuddered, and then, with a jerk, lifted itself off the ground. The ghost drew me towards it with the power of its eyes, and such power! Nahir-Nuri must be ...! I could not turn my head, but became aware of Panthera suspended beside me. We bumped together; logs on a stream. His flesh felt rigid. In front of us, the white figure turned and began to climb up the rock face on the other side of the stream. As if on invisible tethers, Panthera and I floated eerily behind him. In pleasanter circumstances, I expect it would have been a wonderful feeling, like flying. Then it was merely imprisonment; frightening. Gathering my senses, I put out a mental call to Panthera. At least my mind was unaffected by whatever occult paralysis gripped our bodies.

'What is this?' I asked, and Panther answered, 'Elhmen.'

'Does he mean to harm us?'

'Who can tell?'

Ahead of us, the enchanter did not even look back, although he had probably overheard our thoughts. He was confident enough in his magic to know we would follow him helplessly. We drifted through a tangled forest that sloped downwards into a pine-ringed glade. The Elhmen flickered through the trees, pausing only when we came to the mouth of a cave, set in a huge, mossy wall of sandstone. We followed him inside, down a winding, natural passage, lit by torches, and at length into a rosy-lit chamber, where we could see several other Elhmen seated on the floor around a strange fire that did not smoke and whose light was blue-white. With a shiver of the Elhmen's hand, our enchantment was broken, and Panthera and myself tumbled to the floor in an ungainly sprawl.

'These people *are* powerful,' I said to Panthera, rubbing my bruised arms.

He ignored this rhetorical remark. Psychokinesis itself is only a low-caste talent, but it is most unusual to find any Har with an ability to sustain it, especially so over living beings.

'All Elhmen are the same,' Panthera said. Five heads turned to look at us, all smiling gently, probably at Panthera's remark.

'Not powerful, Ferike,' the one who had found us said quietly, 'but simply dedicated. Hara such as yourselves spend too much time examining the mundane. Here in Elhmen, we devote

209

ourselves to cultivating our innate talents.' His smile broadened. 'We do not like to have our soil disturbed, our waters contaminated, by alien disruptive auras...'

'Such as our own, I suppose,' I said.

The Elhmen spread his hands. 'As you like,' he said.

'We are travelling to Eulalee,' Panthera said. 'We have business there. We cannot help passing through your territory, but if you wish us to pay a toll, we shall do so gladly.'

'A toll!' All the Elhmen laughed gleefully. 'Money has little value in Elhmen. You'll find yourselves handicapped if you wish to *buy* your way into Eulalee.'

I had the distinct impression that we were being played with. Our chances of getting into Eulalee at that point seemed depressingly slim.

'I am Arawn,' our captor told us, 'and these are my brothers. Enjoy, if you will, the hospitality of Elhmen!' They all laughed sweetly and in a flash, Panthera and I found ourselves smack against the carved, ragged ceiling of the chamber, along with rather gamey legs of meat and strings of vegetables.

'They have devoted themselves to their talents, yes,' Panthera said, in a strangled voice beside me, struggling, 'but it is rumoured that some of them have strayed far from the Path. Some Elhmen, if the mood takes them, have been known to be cannibal.'

'Why didn't you tell me!' I cried. 'You are a fool, Thea! We should have made proper preparations for contacting them.'

'Waste of time,' Panthera replied. 'There is no proper way to meet the Elhmen. This is probably the only way.'

'Then how ...?'

'Shut up,' Panthera said mildly. 'I know what I'm doing.'

'Like mentioning money, I suppose.'

Panthera gave me a hard look. 'Sometimes they will take it. It all depends on their mood. Now, be quiet; I need to concentrate.'

The Elhmen appeared to have forgotten about us. They were whispering to each other across the flameless fire. Like Arawn, they were all clothed only in their hair, which came to their ankles. Exquisite creatures, attenuated and elfin. Beside me, arms outstretched along the uneven roof, Panthera began to hum. His eyes were closed, his brow furrowed in concentration. At first, he hummed one long, monotonous note, which gradually began to rise and fall in pitch. Now the sound was steady, and quite powerful. I would have liked to have put my hands over my ears. Shortly, one of Arawn's brothers looked up at us, touching those on either side of him quickly, lightly, on the arm. They watched us as if listening deeply. Whatever Panthera was communicating to them, I could not penetrate. My senses were too rusty from lack of use, the thought too deep. But Panthera obviously implied the correct message, for in a second we were plummeting floorwards again, landing awkwardly, missing the fire by inches.

'So then,' Arawn said cheerfully, 'you are offering us something without the implication of insult?'

'You must forgive my earlier solecism,' Panthera replied gravely. He delivered this obsequious remark with admirable dignity. 'We need to get to Eulalee. We have to pass through your territories and, for this privilege, feel honour bound to offer something in return. I will present you with a tale. It is a story of magic, whose beginning was in the childhood of our race. This story has no end ... as yet.'

'Please, be seated,' Arawn said generously, gesturing to a space by his side next to the fire. He raised his hand carelessly and a flagon of ale and two metal cups disappeared from a shelf in the corner of the room to materialize at our feet. We sat down and Panthera poured us each a cup of ale before settling to begin his tale. Different Wraeththu tribes never cease to amaze me. Imagine paying the Varrs, the Uigenna, or even the Gelaming for that matter, with nothing but a story.

Panthera cleared his throat and leaned forward. 'Many years ago,' he said in a hushed voice, 'and far, far away from this land, in a place of darkness and savagery, a city of grey ruins and blood flames, there lived a tribe feared above all others. This story begins with them, and with a young Har stepping onto the Path for the very first time. He was beautiful, his hair was yellow, but his heart was grey. His name?' Panthera looked at me and smiled. 'Ah, that I cannot tell you, but his eyes were the colour of a stormy sky and indeed could flash with lightning sometimes ...' He paused, glanced once more at me, then closed his eyes to continue. 'One day, I met this Har upon the bank of a stream and he told me this ...'

Heard from someone else's lips, I must admit that my history does sound rather unbelievable. In fact, it's surprising anyone ever does believe it! Perhaps that's one of the reasons why I rarely talk about it. Of course, in a story, all the exciting bits happen together, which is far removed from real life. For every escapade with Pell, there were weeks and weeks of tedious riding around, being uncomfortable and hungry. But Panthera had a way of telling it, that made even the most trivial events sound magical and startling. The Elhmen appeared entranced by it. I wonder if they guessed that, even though all the names were changed, the story was based on fact. By the time he'd finished telling it, Panthera's voice was hoarse and the flagon of ale at our feet was empty. My legs were numb. I shifted uneasily to another position.

'Well!' Arawn said, putting his hands upon his crossed knees. 'The mouth of Eulalee, Kar Tatang, lies just beyond Shappa, a city northeast of here. It is only a few days' travelling, not far. But now, it is nearly dawn and you must rest. There is a pallet over there which I suggest you make use of.'

I presumed we'd won our passage through his territory. The pallet was nearly invisible in the shadows beyond the fire. The white heat had dwindled to a sullen violet. All the Elhmen, except for Arawn and one other, stood up and filed from the room. Panthera and I exchanged an amused glance. The pallet was strewn with blankets of fur. We took off our boots and lay down, Panthera wrinkling his nose in distaste as he covered himself with a blanket. Personally, I found the heavy, musky smell quite comforting. With my back to Panthera, I lay there watching Arawn and his remaining brother. They had a certain, furtive air about them. For a moment, they both turned their heads towards me, staring, then away, faces close together; the echo of whispering. Arawn stood up. 'Nanine ...' he hissed softly.

'It is I,' his brother answered, and fluidly fell back beside the fire.

It looked as if he lay upon a silk-tasselled rug; but this was his hair, transparent, catching the light of the fire, turning lilac. I could see the bones of his hips protruding sharply, the concave sweep of his belly, the down, curling mane of fur that grew up from his groin. Arawn sprinkled herbs on the prostrate body, kneeling beside it, staring up at the ceiling. He spoke several arcane words and I heard my name mentioned. Ah, I thought, probably some ritual to guarantee our protection. It wasn't that exactly, however. Arawn took up a curious knife, curved and barbed, which he drew lightly over his brother's chest. Beads of blood burst from the skin, gleaming like jewels, each one perfectly formed. Arawn drew his right forefinger along the line and the jewels became smeared liquid. He looked at me, and I shut my eyes guiltily. 'Calanthe, approach the fire,' he said. Up on my elbows, I glanced behind at Panthera. Whether that was for reassurance or advice, I can't be sure, but he was flat out anyway (so quickly?), snoring gently in an impenetrable sleep. 'Come,' Arawn encouraged quietly, one arm extended from the robe of his hair to beckon me. Curiosity alone had me slipping from under the furs and creeping across the floor. 'Look,' Arawn said softly, and I followed the line of his pointing finger. Nanine's head was turned to the side. I could see a single tear upon his exposed cheek. 'In olden times,' Arawn said, 'It was almost a custom for heroes to be offered gifts from the gods. A sword, perhaps, or a shield, a magic helmet. The concept of the Quest is an old one indeed, Calanthe. True heroes have always been watched over by intelligences of higher form.'

'And what has that to do with me?' I asked suspiciously, sure I would not like the answer.

Arawn smiled. 'Oh, come now, you don't need me to tell you that you follow a quest of your own. In times to come, your adventures may well be related as the exploits of a Harish paladin.'

'I've never thought of myself as a hero,' I said drily, feeling that Arawn had drastically misconstrued my purpose in life. It was quite embarrassing. 'I don't believe there's any such thing, except in fairy-tales.'

Arawn inclined his head slightly. 'What is a word, a term? Nothing. It is the deeds behind the words that are important.'

'If you say so.' I was impatient with what I considered to be his esoteric twaddle. Leave that to the Gelaming and other similar creatures, whose hedonistic, leisurely lives gave them the time to waffle on in such ways, to believe in heroes. To ordinary Hara, this was out of the question. I have always found it exasperating.

Arawn shook his head. 'You are bitter,' he said, 'which is understandable, I suppose. Have you heard the legends concerning our tribe?'

I shook my head. 'Not really. I'm only just beginning to learn about Jaddayoth.'

Arawn nodded thoughtfully. 'Well, some people say that to take aruna with an Elhmen will raise your caste automatically by one level ...'

I rolled my eyes and laughed. 'Really! That good is it?' In recent times, my caste, which was Pyralissit (second level Acantha), had ceased to have meaning for me, coupled with the fact that my abilities had atrophied somewhat through neglect. Arawn was not offended by my laughter.

'You are right to scoff,' he said. 'Such legends are a wild exaggeration of the actual truth. Only the Har himself has the ability to raise his caste; no-one else can do it for him. I'm sure you're aware of this.'

'Yes. So?'

In reply, Arawn once again gestured to the recumbent form of Nanine. 'Drink,' he said, and began to walk away.

'Wait!' I cried, but he did not pause. A door at the back of the room closed quietly behind him. Panthera was still fast asleep. 'Wait,' I said again, uselessly, slumping. Now what was I supposed to do? I thought that Nanine was unconscious, but now Arawn had gone, he turned his head and opened his eyes. The scratch down his chest had dried already to a crust.

'You must open this up again,' he said, running his fingers lightly over the scar.

'What!' Visions of blood-drinking rose uncomfortably to mind.

'Are you afraid?' He reared up like a snake, took my hand and pulled me forward. 'Don't be.' He put the knife in my hand. 'Quickly!' I could tell this was not a part of the ritual he enjoyed. What ritual?

I knelt beside him. 'Must I?' He did not answer. Sighing, I put the hooked end of the blade against the flesh, hardly aware of what I was doing. Experience had taught me that once adepts get it into their heads to assist you, it is always better to indulge their generosity and get on with it. I wasn't sure what the Elhmen thought they were doing for me, but it was less hassle to comply.

Nanine arched his body. 'Not ... so deep,' he said.

'Sorry.' Shortly, my irreverence would start to annoy him, but of course patience in another virtue that Hara of high caste always wave liked a goddamned flag. Blood began to flow.

Nanine put his hands in it. 'Disrobe,' he said, in a choked voice.

After a pause, I turned my back and self-consciously pulled off my clothes. I could hear Nanine breathing deeply, changing the atmosphere of the room, summoning power. 'So, what is it I must do?' I asked. Must I kneel to drink? I turned around. Nanine had adopted a position of submission, his male organs drawn in.

'Drink,' he said, and then I realized this was not a literal request. Soume is water; it had nothing to do with blood. As I've intimated before, my libido was not exactly a frisky young thing, galloping through fields of desire at the time. I felt exposed, pale and unhealthy — and not in the least bit ouana-active. Nanine called to me. He said, 'My brother spoke of legends, and beauty such as yours is indeed legendary.'

'Is that supposed to encourage me or what?' I asked and he shook his head.

'Not at all. Come.' Still sighing heavily, I lay down beside him. His flesh was unexpectedly cool, but, as they say, the touch of Elhmen is always cold. I did not find it unpleasant. I bent my head to his own to share breath, thinking that this was as good a way as any to begin, but he put his fingers on my lips.

'No,' he murmured softly, 'not yet.' His arms came around me, pulling me close until I could feel the dampness of his blood against my skin. Far from repelling me, I felt a strange and insidious stirring within me. Nanine pushed me onto my back, leaning over me, showering me with hair. He took my wary, but not totally complacent, ouana-lim in his bloody hands, painting it with his blood, blessing me in the name of fire. The beast flexed its muscles and flowered beautifully. So fire and water must meet; to what effect I was unaware as yet. Bodies always take over when they get the chance, shouldering the intellect roughly aside. Mine has never been an exception. Sluggish maybe, but Nanine's touch gave it a whack on the back of the neck which woke it up. Consumed by a strengthening fire, I pushed him back and he offered himself passively. Without hesitation, I plunged deeper into the pool of his body, his soul, and drank deeply. Primary urgency subsided to a gentler tide; time was unimportant. Nanine could control his internal muscles; they felt as dextrous as fingers, regulating effortlessly the heights and calms of our communion. If I'd thought to be a fire to make steam in his water, I was wrong. I was merely a small, plunging ship cleaving a great and powerful ocean. One storm too vigorous and I'd be lost forever. The climax of this elemental fight was a roaring crack like thunder-bolts and lashing streams of ice. Panting upon Nanine's heaving body, I could feel that my hair and flesh were wet, not with sweat, but as if I'd been out naked in a heavy shower. I was cold. Nanine pushed me closer to the fire. I was trembling in every part of my brain and body. He whispered softly into my ear, small comforts one would give to an animal and, as I shuddered there, he bent his head to my own. We shared breath for the first time, and the warmth came back into my skin. In his mind, I could see a shining path, upon which I must walk. Terrors to right and left, but the path was strong. I sighed lay back, and Nanine wrapped me in his hair.

'The legends are right,' I said, 'and Elhmen must have immeasurable power.'   .

Nanine just smiled. 'Look to your soul,' he said, 'then, only then, speak of my power.'

I was far too tired to think about souls or power. I fell asleep.

Concurrent with such events, you might expect that I woke up on the pallet, next to Panthera, trying to remember a weird and realistic dream; but no. It was Panthera who shook me awake, yes, but I was still curled up with Nanine next to the fire. Sunlight was falling in shafts from cracks in the cave's roof, illuminating all the darkest corners. Panthera curled his lip at me disdainfully and ordered me to get dressed.

'We must get moving,' he said sharply. 'I don't want to be away from Jael for longer than necessary. I have work to do.'

'I didn't ask you to come!' I pointed out, just as sharply. I could see that it was in Panthera's mind to say, 'That may be so, but you need me,' but he was looking at the drowsy, sinuous form of Nanine and said nothing. I could hear him slamming around unnecessarily, pulling on his boots.

'Will our horses and provisions still be safe?' I asked, wriggling into my shirt.

'Of course, we are not thieves!' Nanine replied, but without rancour. 'Now we must eat and refresh ourselves. Afterwards, I will take you to Shappa.'

'You!' Panthera snarled. 'That won't be necessary. We can find our own way.'

Nanine shook his head. 'Perhaps you can, but it will take you much longer. Control your hard feelings, son of Jael!' He smiled and Panthera coloured vigorously. Nanine and I shared a conspiratorial glance. I thought it was Panthera's repugnance towards aruna that was causing the short temper.

Arawn and the others began to drift in, bearing plates of food, greeting us politely. Nanine dressed himself in a robe of white muslin and let me plait his hair for him. Bound, it felt like rope. 'Once,' I said, 'I was travelling in the southern desert of Megalithica. In that place lives a tribe named the Kakkahaar. It was there that we met a young Har of the Colurastes; a venomous witchling if ever there was one. He had hair like yours. Occasionally, he would use it to throttle people.'

Nanine laughed. 'You must be speaking of Ulaume, the consort of the Kakkahaar Lianvis.'

'Oh, you've heard of them?' I asked, surprised.

'Well, of course; hasn't everybody? Lianvis attained quite a high position in the Council of Tribes in Immanion, once the Gelaming took control of Megalithica.'

'You're joking!' I exclaimed. The Kakkahaar, as far as I knew, were devout followers of rather dubious, dark practices. I couldn't imagine the saintly Gelaming tolerating any of it.

'No, it's true,' Nanine continued. 'More than a few Hara questioned the Gelaming's judgement, or motives, for it, but

Thiede and the Tigron must know what they're doing, mustn't they?'

'So we all suppose,' I said drily, 'or are led to believe.'

'Double standards!' Panthera snapped, throwing me a meaning-ful glance, which I wasn't sure how to interpret exactly. Naturally, all references to actual tribes and places had been disguised in Panthera's story the previous night. I wondered how much the Elhmen knew. Something, obviously, but what? Had they guessed Panthera's story was about me? As we walked to where our horses still stood, hobbled under the trees, I attempted to draw Nanine out on this. I could get nothing out of him. Was it possible that the Elhmen too had had some forewarning of our arrival?

The horses' harness was wet with dew, our bags lying untouched beside our blankets. Nanine did not intend to ride, which Panthera complained would slow us down.

'I know the quickest routes,' Nanine said, 'and most of the way, it will be impossible for you to ride anyway.'

We set off once more, following the course of the stream, up into the mountains. Panthera maintained a profound and sullen silence, which I decided was best to ignore. Round about mid-day, we approached a huge, natural arch of rock. It was possible to pass right under it, into a stone-choked gully which sloped briskly downwards, but Nanine pointed out an opening in the rock which appeared to lead right down into the ground on the left side of the arch. It was nearly hidden by bushes and tall, dead grass. Being on horseback was now out of the question; we were going under-ground. Nanine carried a carved, wooden staff which I thought was to help him scramble through the rocks, but as we entered the stone passage, he held it aloft and its farthest end began to glow with a soft, but penetrating light. We could see for about six feet all around, which was very fortunate, for once the passage turned a corner we would have been plunged into absolute blackness. The ground underfoot was packed hard, as if travelled by many feet, but Nanine explained that the passage was rarely used during the winter. Come spring, Elhmen Hara started wandering about a little more. By summer, he said, the entrance would be clearly visible, even to those not looking for it. Occasionally, sections of the wall would be smoothed off and carved with patterns that were rather runic in design. The horses were awkward and nervous at first; the darkness worried them, the feeling of pressure, but Nanine crooned softly beneath his breath and it seemed to comfort them.

'Is this part of Eulalee?' I asked.

Nanine, ahead of me, looked back. 'No, it is merely a place where we can travel as the crow flies. Eulalee is deep, much deeper, beneath the mountains.'

'How far does it extend? Just the width and breadth of Elhmen?'

'I can't tell you that,' he answered. 'Only the Sahale, the people of Eulalee know that. Elhmen only supervise the main thoroughfare, north of Shappa. Doubtless, there are countless entrances to Eulalee that no-one but the Sahale are aware of.'

'I see. Are the Sahale as hospitable to strangers as the Elhmen?' I enquired rather drily.

'Oh, was our hospitality that lacking then?' Nanine replied with amusement.

'Well, without Panthera's tale, perhaps...' It seemed impolite to continue.

'You are wrong,' Nanine replied. 'Arawn was only playing with you. We knew who you were.'

Rather belatedly, a dull, cold shock coursed through me. I stopped walking and Panthera cursed softly as he bumped into me. 'What do you mean?' I demanded, and the echo of it sailed past us down the passage. Nanine turned around again. 'Was it the Gelaming that told you? Was it?' Panthera was exuding a weird kind of satisfaction behind me; I could sense it clearly.

'Not the Gelaming,' Nanine said.

'Then who?'

'I cannot answer that. I'm sorry.' He turned his back on me and continued to walk along the passage. 'I can't believe you're surprised by this after what occurred last night, but if you are, then all I can say is, you must accept and learn. It is the only way for you.'

I made an exclamation of disgust.

Panthera put his hand on my shoulder. 'Let's keep moving,' he said.

We passed through vaulted caverns, natural cathedrals of rock, whose roofs were open to the sky. We passed underground lakes, complete with solitary, stone isles that rose like petrified monsters from the black water. We rested only when we were tired, for underground, there was no precise way of telling whether it was day or night outside, on the surface. Panthera and I would spread out our rugs in smooth, sandy hollows in the rock, whilst Nanine sat apart, cross-legged, meditating on the high, secret things that Elhmen ponder upon. The first time we rested, Panthera lay with his back to me, rigid and sulky. Was this unusual? No, not really, but I still said, 'OK, spit it out; what have I done now?'

'Nothing.' His answer was muffled, but sharp.

'That's funny. I thought you were angry because I took aruna with Nanine.'

'Oh, shut up!' he said, out loud and with disdain. The sound echoed clearly. Below us, Nanine did not stir.

'OK,' I said. 'I won't say another word.' Panthera did not answer. More to soothe him than anything else, I lifted the hair from his back and kissed his neck. He was still silent. I lay back and put my arms behind my head, staring up into the blackness above. 'I don't need this,' I thought. 'Leave well alone.'

I dreamed.

It is a hot, hot day. The sunlight is almost too bright to bear. I am standing alone at the edge of what seems to be a great battlefield; it is scattered with the debris of conflict. I can smell a hot, sweet yet sour aroma and the air is full of small, desperate sounds. Ragged birds investigate the flesh of the fallen. I cannot tell which tribes have been involved, or whether the fight has been between Hara and humans instead. The Gelaming are in black leather and silver, their hair like haloes of steam, turning bodies, looking for survivors. I decide to follow them because I know they cannot see me. As I walk, the smell of carrion becomes stronger, a taste of sweet metal. A pavilion appears on the horizon and suddenly I am standing right in front of it. Two Hara of obviously high rank are seated beneath a tasselled canopy, one on each side of a wooden table. Attendants stand silently behind them in the shadows of the tent. The seated Hara are drinking sparkling wine from tall, stemmed glasses. The battlefield stretches all around them; a testament of carnage. I recognize one of them. The recognition comes slowly, but soon I am sure it is Zackala sitting there. The other has fair hair and the confident aura of someone who knows fame and power. He has a nasty wound above the left eye, blood in his hair, which is tied behind his head. There is another stitched wound on his shoulder. I can hear them talking, but not the words. Then, Zackala lifts his glass; sunlight makes it come alive with bubbling fire. He smiles. 'To Cal,' he says, 'wherever you are . . .'

I awoke with a start, jerking back, and the darkness above me was spinning, writhing. There was an echo of a cry in my throat. Panthera leaned over me. 'What is it?'

'A dream,' I answered. 'Gelaming.' There was a foul taste in my mouth, stale and sour.

'Forget them!' Panthera hissed wildly. 'Don't let them frighten you.'

'I'm not afraid,' I said, and I could feel Panthera's breath above me in the darkness, but it was not the time. 'Thanks,' I said.

'That's alright.' He lay down again and I reached for his hand. Contact of fingers in the dark. He did not move away.

Sahale
'For they are creatures of dark air,
Unsubstantial tossing forms . . .
In mid-whirl of mental storms.'

Robert Graves, Mermaid, dragon, fiend

From a distance, Shappa is virtually indistinguishable from the surrounding mountains. It is built entirely from grey stone; built into the rock itself, in fact. Nanine pointed out a curl of smoke rising above the city. That's how we knew where it lay. We came to a paved road, and here the Elhmen consented to ride doubled with me to save time. As we drew nearer to Shappa, other travellers joined us on the road, appearing from other tracks that converged onto the main route. Panthera and myself were regarded suspiciously but Hara spoke to Nanine without reserve. The gates of Shappa loomed up before us, casting a long, black shadow on the road. There was a lot of activity, but the guards on the gate were still sharp-eyed enough to order Panthera and I to halt, so that they could examine our luggage. I can't imagine what they were looking for.

Eventually, their curiosity satisfied, we were waved on into the streets of the city. As Shappa is built into the side of a mountain, one would expect the streets to be rather steep, but some of them are virtually impassable. All the ground is cobbled; mainly so that Hara can have footholds as they climb. It is a very clean city; the buildings high and narrow. Shop-fronts are unobtrusive and not many of the inns provide tables outside; presumably, so that their customers don't go sliding down to the city gates after a few drinks!

A lot of the buildings go way back into the rock, so that Shappa is a great deal larger than it appears from outside. Elhmen Hara in Shappa seemed more sophisticated than Nanine and his brothers; they were primly dressed in long robes, their long hair woven, bound and confined in a variety of styles.

'Well, first we find an inn,' Nanine decided, 'then try and hire you a decent guide to take you to Eulalee.'

'What do we need a guide for?' Panthera asked in a voice that implied he thought Nanine was spending our money for us unnecessarily.

'Ask that again after you've been there,' Nanine replied.

It was late afternoon. Nanine led us to a hostelry he knew to be comfortable and cheap, leaving us alone while we scoured the streets for a guide. Panthera and I decided to sample some of the local food in the inn's dining-room. We sat near the back window, which overlooked a yard whose floor was unlevelled rock. Bright flowers bloomed in cracks; a chained, black dog stared contemplatively into space, head on paws. I could not help feeling that Shappa had almost a holiday atmosphere about it, as if it catered mainly for tourists.

'It is the only stopping place before Kar Tatang,' Panthera said. 'And of course a lot of Hara come here from other districts to take the air and mineral waters. There is a meditation centre in Shappa, quite reknowned further east. Many rich Hara send their sons here for caste education.'

'You haven't been here before though.'

Panthera shook his head. 'No, although my father has, many times. The Jaels trade with Elhmen here; we have regular customers. One of my father's paintings hangs on the wall in the foyer of the Meditation Centre. Elhmen might be careful about which strangers are wandering about the countryside, but once you are known to them, visits are encouraged. If they feel they'll gain something from your presence, of course! You must remember, they have little to trade but their knowledge.'

About an hour later, Nanine turned up again with a young Elhmen Har named Kachina, who was looking for work. He told us he'd already made fifteen trips to Sahen.

'None of my clients ever complained,' he said, earnestly. 'I get them to Sahen by the quickest possible route.'

Nanine assured us that we would be in safe hands if we agreed to hire Kachina, and in pocket because his services were cheap. We saw no reason not to trust his judgement, even though Kachina did look rather young. We took our leave of the city early the next morning. Nanine embraced me and wished us luck. As in Gimrah, an invitation to return some day for a social visit was extended. Panthera waited grumpily. I had spent the night with Nanine in a separate room and Panthera's foul silence because of that was almost unbearable. We followed Kachina to the east gate of Shappa, where we took a northern path, cut through the rock. Kachina told us that, at Kar Tatang, the gate to Eulalee, we would be able to stable our horses at livery for a reasonable price.

'The keepers of the stables at least must be confident that travellers will re-emerge from Eulalee,' I said.

Kar Tatang was merely an hour's ride from Shappa. The gate itself was an awesome sight; a gigantic, gaping face carved into the rock, whose heavy-lipped mouth formed the entrance to the land below. The blind, stone eyes were turned skywards, as if each mouthful of travellers was exceedingly difficult to swallow. The village of Kar Tatang itself, clustered around the chin of the gate, comprised inns and stables and very little else. I had imagined that the doorway to this eerie, underground kingdom would be silent and lonely, but was surprised to find it a bustling, crowded place. There was much to-ing and fro-ing; that was clear. We found lodgings for our horses and paused to take a meal in one of the inns before venturing through the gate. I was beginning to feel a little nervous; anything could be waiting for me down there, but I was comforted by the thought that many other travellers would be following the same route as ourselves.

Elhmen guards, hooded and dressed in black, questioned all travellers as they passed through the gate. We were asked our business, whereupon Panthera produced our letter of introduction from Ferminfex. It was studied with insulting thoroughness before one of the guards thrust it back growling 'Pass!' and waving us through. Beyond the gate, we came upon a vast cave. Stalls selling provisions (and, oh dear, talismans of protection) were set up precariously on galleries around the walls.

'From now on, it's downwards all the way,' Kachina said. At first, the road was wide and gently sloping. We had time to admire the surroundings, which were impressive to say the least. In some places water ran down the walls, into clear pools where travellers could pause and drink. Great, white, gnarled stalactites depended ponderously from the roof. After an hour or so, Kachina pointed to a dark opening to our left.

'This is a short cut,' he said. 'Not as comfortable as the main ways, but it will save a lot of time.' He looked at us hopefully. Panthera shrugged.

'Lead on,' I said. 'Whatever's down there, I might as well get it over with as quickly as possible.'

The new path was so steep in places that it made me dizzy, as if I could pitch forward at any moment and fall and fall. We walked sideways. Sometimes, the passage would level out, and the ceiling would be lower so that we couldn't stand upright. I wondered whether the main routes became half as treacherous as this one. Presumably not, for how could the Sahale transport goods below if they did? Kachina informed us that the journey would take about a day and a half. This was a blow to me, who had estimated a figure of several hours at the most. Oppressed by the heavy weight of the mountain above us, I was already twitchy with claustrophobia, something I'd not experienced before. The air was stale, smelling oily and sour. Dim illumination was provided by strangely glowing bulbs of orangey-red light. I could not work out how they were powered, but there didn't appear to be any wires. It couldn't have been electricity. Kachina led us onwards effortlessly, knowing instinctively which branch of the road to take when it forked. I was curious as to where the other passages led. Kachina told us about other Sahale settlements; temples and havens of retreat. There were no signs to mark the way.

Inconvenience struck. Half-way along a twisting, narrow passage, the lights went out. Kachina swore mildly.

'What now?' Panthera asked nervously. 'Can we continue?' He had reached for me in the dark; now we clung to each other's arms.

225

I'm quite sure that, if it hadn't been for Kachina's calm, we would have panicked like animals.

'Yes, we can continue,' Kachina answered. 'We won't be in utter darkness. I have this.' It was a kind of emergency light-cell, similar in many respects to Nanine's glowing staff, powered by psycho-kinesis alone. It only gave off a dull glow, but this was enough to stave off hysteria.

When we were tired, we lay down in resting places cut into the rock. Our water tasted sour and neither Panthera or myself felt like eating anything. Panthera confided that he too did not enjoy being so far underground.

'I don't like feeling trapped,' he said. 'We'd be helpless if anything should attack us, or if the roof fell in. I hate not being able to get myself out. Let's face it, we'd wander about until we starved to death or went mad if we got lost down here. My sense of direction has gone completely.'

So had mine. Even Kachina's spirits had dampened since the lights went out. As we lay in the darkness, resting our protesting muscles, I thought, 'Why am I doing this? Someone is going to pay, I swear it!' Then I slept . . .

. . . And dreamed. I am in Phaonica, the palace of the Tigron in Immanion. The rooms are all of dark, Etruscan colours; red and brown and gold. Bizarrely patterned curtains fold to the floor, pooling on the lustrous tiles. Amongst the drapes, I see the glint of metal, the lustre of jet. The floor is black and red, black and red. I walk across it. Here is the doorway to the Tigron's bedchamber. It is empty and I pass right through, past the canopied bed, whose hangings are waving in a gentle breeze from the open window. The room is dark. Beyond this room, I can see light, hear the sound of water. I follow it. This is a white and green place. The bath is really a pool set into the floor, approached by marble steps, the water gently spuming. Lilies ride the wavelets, cut petals and scattered ferns. There is a sharp, herby scent in the air. Oh, there he is: Pellaz, rising from the water like a young god; a goddess. His body looks harder than I remember it, but of course, he is much older now and this is a different body. He has bound up his hair for the bath, and now he is pulling out the pins. Hair tumbles down to stick to his wet flesh. He shakes his head. He is still beautiful. He is still dreaming. There is a small,

*private smile on his face. He senses movement and calls to the other room,
'Who's there?' Does he sense me? No.*

*'Only I, your humble servant!' a voice replies, and then a tall, scruffy-
looking Har is leaning on the door-frame between the rooms. His hair is grey
from road-dust. He has a dried wound above his left eye and his face is still
stained by old blood. This is a warrior; I have encountered many of his kind.
His clothes are grey. He looks weary. Pellaz calls him Ashmael and, of
course, I have heard of him. Who hasn't? Another of Immanion's immortal
stars. Pellaz has wrapped himself in a towel. These two are close friends, I
can tell, but not that close.*

'You look a little unkempt,' Pellaz mocks him.

Ashmael shrugs. 'I just got back.'

*'Ah, you've completed the task of single-handedly subduing Megalithica
then, have you?'*

*Ashamel raises an eyebrow. He says nothing. Pellaz flicks a towel fringe
over his shoulder, pulls his hair from under it. He gestures at the water. 'Take
a bath, Ash; be my guest.' He begins to call for servants, but Ashmael takes
the Tigron's wrist, shakes his head.*

*'No, just let me soak alone,' he says, and Pellaz pulls away fastidiously,
somewhat affronted. I watch him wander through to his bedroom, but I do
not follow. Maybe I can't. I watch Ashmael pull off his clothes instead. There
is a dark, sulky bruise all along one side of him. His shoulder has been
stitched together. I sympathise with his deadened weariness. He stretches and
winces, testing the water with a grimed, tentative toe. He shudders, glancing
around him, as if sensing unseen eyes. Mine? I don't suppose he has ever been
watched before. He is one of the privileged. It is he, and his kind, who usually
do the watching, the spying. He eases himself carefully into the water,
grimacing. Bubbles swirl around him. He sighs and smiles, leaning his head
back, against the side of the bath. After a while, Pellaz comes back, carrying
two goblets of wine. Ashmael is dozing, and the Tigron watches him for a
moment. Then he kneels down on the marble tiles. He puts the cups down
beside him and reaches to touch the stitched wound on Ashmael's shoulder.
Ashmael yelps in surprise and sinks, floundering, beneath the water. Pellaz
is laughing. 'Jumpy!' he says.*

*'Well, I expect to be safe in these rooms,' Ashmael replies, shaking his
hair from his eyes. Of course, he is safe, and so at home there; I hate him.
Pellaz offers him a goblet and they drink together.*

227

'Only the best,' Ashmael says.

'Naturally.'

I get the impression they are mocking their positions. Pellaz takes up a slim decanter and pours fragrant, liquid soap onto Ashmael's head.

'You shouldn't do this,' Ashmael says, enjoying it immensely. He lies back and revels in the attention. I am familiar with that touch. I can only envy him. That should be me there, surely. This is my dream. Pell rubs the grime, the blood, the weariness away. His touch is magic. I know that look upon his face; he is considering, thinking. Just a whim. Rinsing the soap from his hands, he stands up and throws off the towel. He dives into the water and, for a moment, the stunned expression on Ashmael's face is unmistakable.

'Pell?' he says.

'Here!' And Pellaz explodes from the water, rising up, shimmering jewels of water flying everywhere. Now they look at each other and I am trapped. This is where I should wake up. It is a dream, isn't it? Why can't I make it end? I am in the water, dizzy, and I can feel Ashmael's arms around me, his mouth on my mouth, his breath in my chest. I want to devour him. I have wanted to do this for a long time. Come with me. Follow me. I lead him from the water. Dripping, we go into the next room. I lock the door. There is no-one else there. I draw the drapes across the long, open windows that lead to the balcony beyond. The room is now in sun-stained, afternoon dimness. I have not submitted to soume for a long, long time. This is because of ... someone, someone who seems so part of me, I can hardly ... feel myself anymore. We dispense with preliminaries because we are both so hungry, Ashmael and I. He spears me swiftly, mercilessly, and I cry out in pain, shuddering beneath his strength, which I cannot throw off. There is no way I could get out of this now; no way. Who am I? The visions come and I am deep beneath the dark earth. Against my lips, the taste of Ashmael's wound. I pull one of the stitches with my teeth and he laughs fiercely. A bead of blood seeps into my mouth. Who am I? Is this some kind of betrayal? But against whom?

I woke up twitching and snarling. Panthera shook me to my senses. The dark body of the earth was pressing against us, bringing dreams. I forced my eyes hard into Panthera's shoulder and he held me tightly.

As soon as Kachina was awake, we continued downwards. Still

no lights. How could it have happened?

'Oh, it does sometimes,' Kachina said. 'You see, the Sahale do not need the lights to know the way and very few travellers follow this route. It might be days before they're fixed.'

'All the other Hara at Kar Tatang,' I said, 'where were they going? To Sahen?'

'Some of them, but a lot more head east to Pir Lagadre. That's a temple settlement, not so far underground. It is where the Sahale conduct most of their trade with the outside world.'

We continued to walk. This was a fairly level stretch and we could stand upright. Sometimes, though, I was convinced I could hear noises ahead of us, rather chilling ones at that. Scrabbling, muttering.

'Kachina, is this journey dangerous?' I asked: 'By that, I don't mean because of the dark, but ... other things?'

Our guide didn't answer for a moment. 'I've made this trip fifteen times,' he said at last. 'I've never come across anything dangerous, but I have *sensed* it at times. I believe the lights act as a deterrent to anything unpleasant.'

Perhaps it was the morbid humour of Fate that made me bring it up, but it seemed best not to continue that conversation. Maybe half an hour later, Kachina stiffened and hissed us to silence. We all stood still, tense and listening. I could hear nothing.

'Sense life,' Kachina whispered, and that slight sound echoed around us. Nothing happened. 'Keep moving,' Kachina said, 'it's not far now ...'

And then his words were cut off as something *large* rumbled swiftly from a side passage just ahead of us. I was dimly aware of teeth, eyes and hair and a miasmal stench. Kachina, in the lead, cried out and raised his staff, but it was too late. Before he could throw whatever power he possessed at the attacking beast, it clipped him with some gigantic, furred appendage and the staff fell to the ground, followed quickly by a stunned Kachina. For a second, the beast, whatever it was — and surely not sprung from this earth — hung between spidery legs, staring malevolently yet without expression at Panthera and myself. I could hear a whistling sound that may have been its breath or its voice.

'What is it?' I squeaked.

Panthera did not care about such details. 'Quick, Cal,' he hissed, 'combine force. Acantha level. We must. Pyro — killing strength!'

'What!' I had entertained no doubts that Panthera's occult training had been more refined than my own, but this was something completely out of my field. Pyrokinesis is the ability to make heat, intense heat, even fire, by the power of the mind alone. Panthera groped for my hand to strengthen the bond.

'Open up!' he ordered and I automatically slipped into mind touch.

'Panthera, I'm not really sure whether I ...'

'Shut up! We have no time! Follow my signal!' It happened swiftly. A fireball was igniting, swelling, between us. I didn't have much to do with its construction other than lending Panthera my strength. It was he who pointed the commanding finger, he who released a bolt of white-hot radiance from his taut body. With a thin screech, the beast scuttled backwards, but not in time. Within seconds, it was ablaze, moaning and screaming terribly. Fortunately for us, it decided to back blindly into the tunnel from whence it had come, instead of charging forwards. We could hear it squealing and creaking until it died away into the distance. Panthera leaned forward, hands braced on knees. He wiped sweat from his face. He was shaking and so was I. 'Oh God; Kachina!' Panthera went to kneel beside the motionless form. 'Oh God,' he repeated and his disgust and horror could not be contained. Whether the beast had killed him or not, we shall never know. Unfortunately, Kachina had been in the line of fire of our heat blast. Very little remained that was recognizable as Elhmen. 'Oh Cal!' In the light of Kachina's rapidly dimming light-cell, I could see Panthera's chalk-white face looking anxiously up at me. He wanted me to reassure him that we had not just committed murder. I would not comment, but picked up the light cell.

'Can you operate this?' I waved it under his nose.

Panthera took it and examined it carefully, too carefully. Clearly, his mind was in a whirl. 'Yes,' he said at length. 'Yes. I can.' Sparing Panthera any further unpleasantness, I dragged the body of Kachina into the beast's tunnel, going back for the bits that dropped off as I dragged it. Panthera and I then walked on into the darkness, grimly.

'You are more accomplished than I realized, Thea,' I said. 'How come you didn't use these talents to break out of Piristil, or to confound Outher and his cohorts? It would have saved us a lot of time and bother!'

'You don't understand,' Panthera replied, in a bitter tone.

'Try me.'

'Alright. It is something to do with aruna.' He spoke as if his mouth was full of something noxious. 'When I was captured and taken to Fallsend, I was only third level Kaimana and incapable of mustering my powers alone. As I aged, I did try to improve myself in secret, but as you probably know, Hara are such sexual creatures; we need aruna to progress. All that happened to me only served to hold me back. My powers were minimal and unreliable …'

'And what has happened since you returned to Jael then?' I asked sharply. 'I wasn't aware that the situation had changed!'

'It hasn't! Not exactly. I've been purified, of course. My father raised my level to Acantha to purge the contamination of pelcia and chaitra away …'

'That still doesn't explain how you managed it without aruna … or didn't you?'

'No, I didn't. If you *must* know, I've been taught some exercise in auto-eroticism. It's intended that such practices will rid me of my distaste for physical contact. But now I've learned a way to get on without it, I don't see why I should ever seek it, if you know what I mean. I don't want anyone to touch me again. It revolts me.'

'Thank you for being so frank,' I said, rather taken aback.

'You're welcome.' He sighed deeply. 'Oh come on, Cal, you're my friend. Let's get the hell out of here. One wrong turning and neither of us will have the chance to worry about such things again anyway!'

We hoped the road would not branch again, but since our encounter with the beast, Panthera felt that his powers were completely trustworthy. 'If necessary, I shall *smell* which is the right way to go,' he said. 'I'm not afraid.'

'Are you ever?' I enquired drily.

'Not really, no.'

We kept walking. Sometimes, we could hear strange groanings from tunnels, that led off the main passage, causing us to increase our pace, but nothing else actually attacked us. I'm not sure what kind of beings stalk the tunnels of Eulalee, whether they have always lurked there unseen or whether they are the children of powerful and malefic thoughtforms, but it appeared they had been discouraged from molesting us by the fate of their fellow.

'I wouldn't like to have to explain to the Elhmen what happened to Kachina,' Panthera said, meaning he was having trouble explaining it to himself.

'He was killed by the beast,' I replied. 'Believe it Thea! Don't think anything else; there's no point.'

Eventually, a red haze became stronger in the passage before us, which was widening considerably. Statues of naked Hara wreathed in flaming hair stood in alcoves along the way, where offerings of fruit and bread had been left at their feet. Ahead, we could see the glow of an intense radiance, and within minutes, reached the end of the path, emerging onto a lip of stone. Below us stretched a vast, underground valley, lit by a thousand, thousand points of fire. Gases and multi-coloured bursts of flame jetted from cavities in the rocks and valley floor. The air was richly perfumed; very sweet and smoky. Sahen; uncomfortably like a vision of hell.

CHAPTER

18

Encounter With the Lyris

'All shall be well …
When the tongues of flame are in-folded
Into the crowned knot of fire
And the fire and the rose are one.'

T.S. Eliot, Four Quartets

'So, how do we get down?' I asked, peering over the edge. There was no apparent way from where we were standing.

'Look above you,' Panthera said smugly, pointing.

'What is it?'

'Cables. My father talked to me of this. It's a kind of public transport here in Sahen. We'll have to wait.' He reached up and pulled a white flaglet out from the wall, which would be clearly visible below. Shortly, a cable-car shaped like a vast, wing-furled bird swept gracefully up to us, and paused at the brink of the ledge. 'Passage to Sahen?' Panthera said politely and the pilot answered, 'That'll be three fillarets.'

We didn't have anything smaller than a spinner, so Panthera was magnanimous and told him to keep the change.

'And where is your intended destination, tiahaara?'

'The residence of the Lyris,' I replied, grandly, and without a remark, the pilot released the brakes and we were sweeping, as if in flight, down to the city of Sahen. The buildings were incredible; a forest of stalagmites, precarious walkways linking the gnarled towers, spider strands of cable sweeping between them. All the Sahale have ferociously scarlet or crimson hair (variation in hue depending upon cast). As we swooped along, the pilot's hair (far from all-enveloping as an Elhmen's, but still impressive) billowed out behind him like flames. Panthera and I huddled together on the floor, both of us rather concerned about our safety, for the car rocked dangerously at times, and we were given terrifying visions of the city beneath us. Tall spires seemed to graze the car's wooden floor, often rising right above it, as it weaved and skimmed its way between them. It was a rollercoaster ride to end all rollercoaster rides. Panthera, of course, had never heard of such things, and looked at me blankly when I mentioned it.

The car glided to a halt upon a large plaza in the centre of the city. In front of us rose a magnificent confection; the palace of the Lyris. It resembled a crown of stone, spiked and starred, bridges swaying from spire to spire, where small figures could be seen mincing along them. Our pilot lowered the side of the car and we stepped out, none too sure of our feet. 'Over there,' he said, unnecessarily, pointing. 'Go to the outer gate. If the guards consider your business worthwhile, you may be granted entrance. If not, allow me the liberty of recommending the inn on Ash Row. It is owned by my uncle, true, but good and cheap fare are to be found within, nonetheless. Good-day to you, tiahaara.'

Panthera and I glanced at each other quizzically and advanced towards the palace.

'A strangely hospitable and amenable race considering their habitat,' I commented.

'Well, I doubt that they ever encounter *unwelcome* visitors,' Panthera replied. 'No-one who was unwelcome would ever get this close, I'm sure!'

Thinking back on the oppressive darkness, snaking tunnels and unspecified, mannerless monsters, I was inclined to agree.

The guardians of the Lyris rival the palace itself in magnificence. Two of them stood to attention at the outer gate, their spears crossed. Helmets of spectacular design adorned their heads. From beneath, braids of flaming hair fell to their waists. Their armour was moulded to their bodies as if sprayed there. Long skirts of pleated silk hung from waist to ankle. They gazed at us mildly as we stood before them, but did not smile. Panthera produced the letter of introduction from Ferminfex, which he offered for their scrutiny. One of them took it, alternately peering at the page and glancing at us. Panthera shifted the weight of his bag on his shoulder and sighed.

'You seek an audience with Lyris,' the guard said smoothly. We nodded mutely, wary of saying the wrong thing. 'Well,' he continued, 'I cannot guarantee you satisfaction, but you are welcome to wait in the Hall of Hearkening with all the others who desire the same. Here, you better take this with you.' He returned the letter to Panthera.

We thanked him profusely and passed through the gate. Within, the palace was like a town within a town. We came out into a vast, tiled courtyard, plunged into a bustle of activity. Hara milled around noisily, shouting to each other, pausing to examine merchandise for sale on the gaily coloured stalls set up around the edge of the square. Nobody spared us a glance as we wandered wide-eyed and rather aimlessly towards the other side. Eventually, I stopped a passing Har and asked him the way to the Hall of Hearkening. He rolled his eyes. 'Ah, simple! Through the Red Gate over there, down the left corridor, take the third right, across the Fountain Plaza, then second right. The Hall's down that passage; you can't miss it!' He smiled at us and passed on.

'Can't miss it,' I said, bleakly. Panthera sighed and took my arm. We walked on.

After several abortive attempts and further questioning of passersby, we finally found ourselves at the grand, open doors of the Hall of Hearkening. A Registrar sat in a booth outside playing chess across the counter with a soldier. 'What's your business?' he asked us in a bored voice, not looking up from the chequered board. We explained, Panthera waving the letter, which the Registrar did not bother to examine. He wrote our names disinterestedly in a ledger and gave us a numbered ticket. It was stamped with a date (presumably) which neither Panthera or myself understood: '23 Blue Foresummer — 12:05'. It was also numbered 217.

'Are these issued from nought daily?' I enquired. The Registrar looked at me properly for the first time; answering that question was obviously one of the few pleasures of the job.

'Yes, tiahaar. Don't look so glum. This is a fair society.

Therefore anyone may speak to the Lyris. But, needless to say, all the fairness in the world won't make more hours in the day.'

'Does the Lyris spend *all* his time speaking to his people?' Panthera asked coldly.

'No. Two hours in the morning, two early evenings. Some matters are cleared quickly or passed to his clerks. You may have a chance ... sometime this week.' He went back to his study of the chess board. I had noticed the soldier moving men furtively around whilst we'd been speaking.

'Come on, let's go in,' I said.

'Seems a waste of time. Perhaps we should come back tomorrow,' Panthera replied. The Hall beyond was packed full of Hara, all talking loudly. Panthera groaned. 'You see? We could be waiting here for days!' He dropped his bag grumpily onto the floor. I couldn't disagree. Several Hara were sitting huddled in blankets around the edge of the room among rows of black pillars. I had the sick impression that they'd been there for several days themselves. I threw my bag down as well. Perhaps I'd been wrong to complain about the Gelaming (or whoever it was) announcing our arrival in the right ears before we got anywhere. We could certainly do with that kind of help in Sahen.

After a while, a Har selling provisions came over and offered to show us his wares. I enquired about the queueing arrangements to see the Lyris. He answered the query easily. 'Keep your ticket,' he said. 'Let me see it. Ah, 217. The Lyris has enough time to see maybe 50 hara a day, if their business is quick. Tomorrow you may move up the queue, cash in your ticket for another one. It's all done fairly, no-one can steal your place, but don't lose the ticket, otherwise you'll be at the back again.'

'In my estimation, that means we'll be here at least four days,' Panthera said, none too cheerfully.

The vendor shrugged. 'My brother is a coffee-vendor,' he said, 'I could send him over if you like. You look as if you need refreshment.' To get rid of him, we agreed to this.

'Family ties are important to the Sahale, it would seem,' I said.

'Mmm,' Panthera assented, still sour.

'Now, I wonder if a brother, cousin or uncle of the Lyris is selling anything around here — like a few minutes' of the Lyris' time, for example?'

'Don't be stupid,' my charming companion replied.

'Actually, I'm not. Neither am I joking. Think about it! How much money have we got left?'

Panthera moodily examined our joint purse. 'Not that much really. Just fifty spinners. Is the Lyris' time that cheap, do you think?'

I let this sarcasm wash over me. 'No, I expect his time is priceless or at least beyond our bargaining power, but perhaps someone who can help us could be bought for less.'

'Fifty spinners won't buy much,' Panthera argued. 'A floor scrubber in the royal apartment, maybe …'

'I was thinking more along the lines of one of the more upwardly mobile household staff, if you don't mind! They could show the Lyris your father's letter.'

Panthera considered this. 'Hmm,' he admitted grudgingly. 'If the Lyris *has* been given advance warning of our arrival, it may work. If he's never heard of you, he may use the letter to light his next cigarette. But you never know.'

'If the Lyris has never heard of me, then I suspect we've come to the wrong place anyway,' I said. Panthera gave me a hard look. 'That's not conceit talking,' I continued, 'just logic.' He shrugged. We sat down against the wall, and presently, as had been promised, the coffee-vendor weaved his way through the crowd towards us. We bought two coffees and he gave us a handful of change. I put this back on his tray meaningfully.

'Could you point out to us a member of the Lyris' staff?' I asked. 'Maybe someone fairly high up in the royal household?'

The coffee-vendor laughed. No doubt our plan was a common one, he'd heard many times before. 'Nobody that high-ranking ever shows their face around here,' he said, 'this is the pleb's Hall, but I am acquainted with Zhatsin, who's an under-valet of the Lyris. For a price …' He smiled.

'Would two spinners induce you to bring him here?' I asked sweetly.

'As it happens, it would, tiahaara,' the coffee-vendor replied, 'but I feel honour-bound to point out to you that just about everyone who comes here tries to buy their way into the Lyris' presence. Quite often, it's suspected that those who are hired to facilitate this need simply throw away whatever notes or letters they've been given and pocket their money with a smile ...'

'Thank you — we'll take that risk,' I said.

'Very well. Wait here. I'll be back as soon as I can.' He held out his hand hopefully.

'You'll be paid when you return,' I said, and he shrugged, disappearing back into the crowd.

'That's the last we'll see of him!' Panthera complained. 'I doubt he knows anyone in the Lyris' household.'

Thankfully, Panthera was wrong. Presently, the coffee-vendor returned accompanied by a startling, blood-haired Har who smelled strongly of patchouli and looked down an aristocratic nose at us. He would not speak to us directly at first. His friend, the coffee-vendor, told us that Zhatsin would be happy to accept thirty spinners to deliver our letter of introduction to the Lyris. Like the coffee-vendor, he silently held out his hand for the money. Panthera was going to hand it over straightaway (he had learned nothing), but I stopped him in time.

'No,' I said, 'you get the money when we get to see the Lyris.'

The Sahale looked indignant. He spoke for the first time. 'That seems a little unfair. My delivering this letter does not automatically guarantee that he will see you, does it! What if I complete my side of the bargain and he throws your letter away? How do I get my money then?'

'Let's just say that I'm confident the Lyris will not disregard the letter,' I said. 'How about if we up the price to thirty-five spinners?'

'Forty.'

'Thirty-seven?'

'Tell them I'll do it,' Zhatsin said to the coffee-vendor, who duly told us and took the letter from Panthera's outstretched hand. Zhatsin snatched it away and whisked off in a boiling cloud of crimson hair and muslin.

'Beautiful, but haughty,' the coffee-vendor said, as if in apology.

'As is often the case,' I said, smiling benignly at Panthera, who snorted angrily, folded his arms and stared into the crowd.

After about an hour, I noticed two splendid palace guards asking questions of the crowd. Eventually, they sauntered over to us. 'You from Jael in Ferike?' one of them asked. His arms were sheathed in beaten silver to the elbow and a fern-like silver chain hung from his left ear to join a sparkling stud in his nose. We introduced ourselves. The guard nodded. 'Come with us. The Lyris wishes to convey that he is impressed by your letter of introduction and will grant you a few minutes of his time, even though the evening Audience is some hours away yet.'

Just a few minutes of his time? I knew better but I still said, 'We are grateful' and ducked a slight bow, to show we understood this honour.

We were taken through a side-door of the Hall of Hearkening and through a number of low-lit corridors, where the air became smokier and more pungent. A double row of fat, polished pillars led to an enormous pair of doors framed by snarling dragons painted crimson and gold with black tongues and white tusks. Here, our hireling Zhatsin was waiting smugly with outstretched palm. The guards waited patiently as Panthera completed the rather sordid task of counting out the thirty-seven spinners. I thanked Zhatsin for his help and he smiled at me narrowly before stalking away from us, jangling his bounty in his hand.

'Are you ready?' one of the guards asked. Were we? I nodded, and he rapped upon the impressive doors three times. After a moment, both swung silently inward and we were ushered inside.

'Good God!' I exclaimed, under my breath.

'By the Aghama!' Panthera echoed, illustrating for a moment our difference in age. We were both surprised by the opulence. The room within seemed to be have been constructed entirely from gaudy, flashing gold, the brightness only softened by diaphanous curtains that swathed the walls and tented the ceiling. Censers swung on chains, exuding thick drifts of sweet smoke and globes of light hung in clusters shedding ruby, violet and lemon vapours. In the centre of the room lay a wide, round hearth, where a smokeless fire bloomed with heatless light. Round this, an oiled and naked Har danced to the racing pound of hand-drums, held by shaved and painted Hara dangling from the roof in jewelled cages. At the end of the room, directly opposite where we stood gawping, the Lyris reclined in a magnificent throne on a raised dais, his favourites draped sinuously across the steps. He watched the dancer with unflinching concentration. His hair was many different shades of red and gold, his chest and feet bare, his body glistering with jewels and precious metals. But more than this, he had the aura of power that proclaimed him king; a radiance that jewels and finery had no part in. Panthera and I were obliged to wait until the dance had finished. Then one of the guards indicated that we must follow him across the room.

'This is how royal households are supposed to conduct themselves,' I said to Panthera. 'Remember this when we return to Jael.'

Panthera smiled thinly. Every eye in that room was turned upon us; not a comfortable feeling. Neither was the curious silence. I'd expected the Sahale to be very similar in their habits to the Elhmen. Not so. The Lyris looked up at us lazily as we approached, waited until we were within ear shot, and raised his hand. The guard halted our progress by slamming the butt of his spear across our chests.

'Which of you is Calanthe?' This came from a pinched-faced Har, robed in blue, standing next to the throne. I pushed aside the spear and took a step forward.

'I am.' It seemed best to bow. The Lyris bent his head to speak to his aide, who then addressed me once more. He beckoned me closer until I stood with my toes nearly touching the bottom step of the dais. The Lyris' favourites fixed me with eyes that were not hostile, but not without contempt either. I could feel them taking in my appearance, my shabby clothes and unwashed hair, my lack of jewels and perfume. Perhaps they thought nothing of it, but I certainly felt horribly conscious of my appearance.

'You are quite famous, it would appear,' the pinch-faced Har remarked, to which it was impossible to reply. I shrugged. 'We have had notice of your visit,' he continued. (Surprise, surprise.) Thanks for the welcoming committee, people of Sahen. 'If you would be so good as to come with me, the Lyris has asked me to inform you he will speak with you later.' Ignoring whatever my reaction to this might be, he looked over my head at Panthera. 'Take this son of Jael to one of our guest-suites, see to his comforts!' I could hear Panthera's vague protests as he was efficiently whisked away. Pinch-face flicked his hard eyes back to me. 'Come,' he said, extending a clawed hand. I looked at the face of the Lyris. He looked back, but did not smile or even register that he could see me at all. His aide descended the dais and took hold of my arm. 'This way,' he said, pulling me.

'My luggage ...' I said, looking back.

'... will be taken care of. Come along!'

He led me through a door behind the dais into more corridors of dim lit and smouldering opulence.

I shook my arm free of his hold. 'Do you speak for the Lyris all the time?'

He looked puzzled. 'No. Forgive me; I haven't introduced myself. I am Iygandil, First Shriever of the Lyris. His second pair of hands and eyes, his second voice, if you like.'

'Hello, Iygandil, and will the Lyris speak with me himself, or have you been delegated that honour?' The First Shriever saw no slight in this. 'The Lyris himself will speak with you. And remember, it is *you* who is honoured!' He smiled, baring his teeth. 'In here, if you will.' Another clawed gesture.

The room beyond was nearly in darkness until Iygandil raised his hand and ruby light blossomed from the walls. A sultan's den, fit for a clutch of concubines, I thought.

'I wait here?' I asked, flopping down with passable elegance onto a plump cushion.

Iygandil shook his head, looking worried in case I'd soiled the satin beneath me. 'Not yet.' He clapped his hands and two Hara came into the room, ducking beneath a fringed curtain. Iygandil turned to me. 'Get up,' he said, flapping an impatient hand. I did so. 'This is Tatigha and Loolumada, attendants of the Lyris. If you would go with them, Calanthe ...'

'What for?'

The First Shriever rolled his eyes. '*Please*,' he stressed. 'Am I forced to broach such indelicate matters? Through there is the bathroom. Need I say more?'

'You mean I need a good wash, is that it?'

'Please co-operate. The Lyris will be here shortly.'

Sighing, I followed the attendants from the room. Without speaking, they led me past an enormous green pool, which was gently steaming, a wooden tub of bubbling, scented water and ultimately into a white-tiled room with a slatted wooden floor and benches around its rim.

'What's this?' I asked, standing there, but my words were swept away from me. Standing back, to avoid being splashed, the one named Tatigha turned a handle in the wall and hot, spitting water gushed from a dozen concealed outlets, soaking me in seconds. I spluttered, arms cartwheeling and tried to get out. The Sahale were laughing.

'We'll give you ten minutes. You'll find soap in that green jug over there.' No sensuous massaging then. I rubbed my face. Steam rolled around me. My clothes had gone grey, brownish streams were pooling round my feet. I hopped around, and pulled off my clothes. The water in Sahen is incredibly soft, which I realized only after I'd doused myself with the liquid soap. Cursing, I was still trying to rinse it off when Loolumada and Tatigha returned. One of them promptly turned the shower to icy cold, so I was obliged to emerge half-slippery. I stood there shivering as they towelled me down. After this, I was conducted to a hand-basin and presented with a tooth-brush and gritty paste, designed to remove mouth slime. Perfumed powder was provided to blot the last traces of dampness from my skin.

'Much better,' Tatigha pronounced, forcing my arms into a long robe. 'This way please.' I was taken to a room of mirrors where they dried my hair and painted my eyes with black kohl. The image in the mirror reminded me painfully of the Har who'd lived and worked in Piristil; I don't think I'll ever be that comfortable wearing cosmetics again. The sweet smell of the powders and colours will always bring a vision of that place back to me. Now I was fit for a king. Water: fire. It was not a difficult deduction. I had a disturbing vision of Iygandil standing there to whisper the sweet nothings into my ear as the body of his lord plunged into me. Was this what I should expect? The Sahale are a strange people.

The Lyris was already waiting for me when his attendants took me back to the luxurious salon. He was reclining on a pile of cushions, sipping from a crystal goblet and smiling at the wall.

Loolumada cleared his throat. 'My lord, may I present Calanthe, from the house of Jael, in Ferike.'

The Lyris looked at me. He actually spoke. 'Thank you Looma, you may go.' He looked much younger now than I'd thought him to be; olive-skinned too, which seemed odd for someone who lived underground.

'Won't you sit down?' he said. I perched on the edge of an ornamental chair. He appraised me. I appraised him. No way would I be the first to speak.

'Well,' he said, turning away from me to pour himself more wine. 'So you have been sent to me.'

'Not exactly,' I replied. 'Let's just say that I had a message that told me "beneath the mountains of Jaddayoth". Ferminfex of Jael interpreted it as meaning I should come here to Eulalee. For what purpose ... I really don't know ... fully.'

'How unfortunate for you.'

'Do you know why?' The question was perhaps a little bold.

He shrugged theatrically. 'Do I know why ... Only that I have to complete a process that was begun in Elhmen and thereafter that you should be allowed to descend to the deepest caverns, which are my personal domain and known in Sahen as Shere Zaghara. Does that mean anything to you?'

Being coy would waste time. 'The first part, yes. I take it I'm supposed to take aruna with you. It happened that way in Elhmen. Yes, I'd worked that much out; why else would you want me so clean? Purged by water, seared by fire. Symbolic. Why? I want answers and if the only way of getting them is to play along with this charade for a while, I will.'

The Lyris nodded thoughtfully, unabashed. 'The purpose of ritualistic communion is to recondition wasted souls, minds, whatever term you want to use. Whatever abilities you possess have been neglected, we are informed, and useless for what you have to do.'

'Which is?'

He sat up and rested his elbows on his knees, caressing the wine-cup. 'We were told only what we needed to know. Elhmen and Sahale are often called upon for this procedure. Yours is far from an isolated case, believe me. Rich fathers from Maudrah, Garridan, even Hadassah, often send their sons here for this refining treatment. It's an education into what can be achieved through concentrating the force of aruna. But clearly, you are not here because your father sent you! Who did?'

'I don't know. Who told you about me?'

His eyes didn't waver from mine. A convincing actor or an honest Har. Did it really matter which? 'I received word from Elhmen. Arawn communicated with me. He told me little but did seem to stress that the matter was important. Oh, forgive me! Most remiss of me; here, take a cup of wine.'

I did so, although I found it a little too sweet for my taste. 'Perhaps you'll find the answers you seek in Shere Zaghara,' the Lyris continued.

'Maybe. It seems too easy.'

'You'll find an oracle there. However, it won't speak to you until you're ready, until I've *made* you ready.'

I pulled a face. 'Fire,' I said, mulling that over towards unpleasant inferences.

'Not trial by it, but refining.' The Lyris raised his glass and smiled.

The answer. Was it this close? Was it here in Sahen that I'd learn how to escape the clutches of the Gelaming, their Tigron in particular? (Yes, seems too easy. Scary.) If I was honest, did I really want them, those elusive, provocative, teasing answers? I'd chased them across a continent, and I wasn't convinced I'd cornered them yet. Even if I had, it might be that I'd be happier not getting acquainted with them. It was Ferminfex's pet theory that there was much more to all this than we could guess, and it would take an utter half-wit not to be somewhat frightened of that. In grand schemes small people are often expendable; especially after they've trotted off dutifully and completed their allotted quests. After all, it was not inconceivable that the aruna bit with Nanine and the promise of it with the Lyris was, in actual fact, the Cleansing (fanfare, fanfare) that Thiede had tried to force on me. He'd asked me outright; I'd said no. Was I now being tricked into going through with it? I'd had my own thoughts on what Cleansing would be; nothing like this. Was that a mistake? How could I find out? Visions, messages, proddings and pullings, signs and omens; a clever, intricate game, and here was I, a pawn, puffed up with his own importance, scurrying hither and thither, in the name of seeking answers. How could I be sure there wasn't a cold-blooded intelligence behind all that had happened to me saying, "Yes, this is the moment, soon he'll be ready"? I couldn't. I had the cards in my hand, but I couldn't read them. Throw down the hand on a gamble and I might find myself whisked off to Immanion on a pink cloud, grinning like an idiot, brain dead, scoured, sculpted and garnished, to be served to the Tigron on a silver platter. Powerless. If I still possessed a mind, my power could never equal his. In Pell's presence, my blood would be turned to powder, my brain to stone. Dilemma. Should I stand up now and walk out of Sahen? Would that be foolishness or just a way to save myself? OK, more-superior-than-human brain, work that one out, and let me know the result pretty damn fast.

The Lyris stood up, sauntered to my side. He sighed, crouched down and took my shoulders in his hands. I flinched. I didn't want him that close until I was sure what I wanted to do. 'Why are you afraid?' he said. 'Are you worried I'll hurt you?'

That simple? No. If only. The Har thinks I'm an imbecile. Join the world consciousness, Lyris! 'Hurt me?' I laughed, trying to get his hands off me. 'No. At least, not in the way you're thinking of.'

He didn't stand up, squatting there with his hands resting on his knees. 'I'm not sure I understand you, Calanthe.'

'OK I'll explain. Will you answer my questions truthfully?'

'If I can.' He was wary though.

'Fine. What I want to know is this. If I go through the *process* you were talking about, could anyone take advantage of me because of it?'

'What do you mean?'

'It's a kind of Cleansing, isn't it?'

He shrugged, pulled a face, then nodded. 'In a way, I suppose so.'

'Ah. And if I were Cleansed, might it be possible for Hara of great power to impose their will over me?'

'Is that what you're afraid of?' The Lyris stood up, his knees cracking as he did so. 'I don't know your circumstances,' he said.

'No, you don't, but that shouldn't prevent you answering the question, should it?'

'In my opinion, you should gain strength from the Rituals, not suffer weakness. It is not a process completed for "power over", but for "power from within". I must say, there's no way I'd be a part of this if I thought it was being used for the wrong reasons.'

'I wasn't saying you would, but as you pointed out, you're only told what you need to know.'

He nodded, 'True, but remember, I know the result of this communion. I've seen it, many times. You haven't. Unfortunately, I have no way of convincing you its effects are entirely beneficial until it's done. A risk you'll have to take ... or avoid. It's up to you.'

I stared at him hard. He didn't look like a liar. I know I'm too suspicious but who can blame me? I smiled, drank some sweet wine. 'Take me, I'm yours,' I said. He smiled too and put down his wine-cup.

'I'm glad you trust me! Now, I have to go to the Hall of Hearkening for a couple of hours. Are you hungry? Wait for me here, I'll get someone to bring some food for you.'

'Thanks. Can I see Panthera Jael?'

'Not yet, no. He's been taken care of, and there's no sinister meaning behind that! Just relax. Completely. Understand?'

I nodded, happy to cause him no further nuisance. After he'd gone, I sat there and thought of Nanine. I'd treated his part in this with a kind of irreverence. I didn't feel like that now. An insidious sense of solemnity was creeping over me. I was looking forward to the next stage. Perhaps I was just feeling horny.

Tatigha and Loolumada brought me food, but I didn't really have much of an appetite. I just needed soothing. The Sahale were sensitive to that. Tatigha began to sing to me, unrecognizable words, the ruby light casting violet shadows in his coiled hair. Loolumada came to kneel behind me, humming the tune beneath his breath. He stroked my neck and shoulders with accomplished fingers. Wallowing in this pampering, I began to feel drowsy, so they led me from the cushions and laid me down upon the floor, still singing, sometimes chuckling, an eerie sound. The light seemed barely light at all, just a slight, steady glow where figures moved as black shadows. I thought I'd been drugged, even while I knew that thought to be false. My body flowed into the carpeted floor. Now I was naked although I couldn't remember being undressed. I was clean and vibrant; floating free, like lying on the deck of a ship sailing on a calm sea. Sun beating down. Hot wood, the creak of hot wood and the breeze is warm. My eyes were closed. A bitter perfume crept into my lungs so I looked about me, too comfortable to move, eyes sliding this way and that. There was Loolumada, holding a candle in a long, pewter stick. I could see his skin, his solemn face. He knelt, putting the candlestick upon the floor, his spine casting shadows across the flesh of his back. Something was coming back to me; a memory. A feeling. Tatigha was at my shoulders, laying down the flame. I could hear him whispering beneath his breath and I thought clearly, 'This is a caste elevation. Of course.' A long time since I'd thought of such things. I'd been second level Pyralis ever since I'd left the Unneah, and had allowed my abilities to sink into decline. Most of what I'd learned then was half-forgotten now, mainly because I'd considered it irrelevant to my existence. The huyana Lucastril had started something in Hadassah. I had a feeling this was the end result.

I was still drifting in a stupor when the Lyris came towards me from the dark. He stood at my feet and, with that immense vocal power only Nahir-Nuri possess, by words alone made me female. My body could not disregard the potency of what he said. He did not have to touch me to do it. He said, to my female form, 'We deceive ourselves in so many ways. We are not perfect, not new, nor absolved from the laws of this planet. What we are about to do is as old as civilization itself. Think of the past. Honour it, for we are closer to Mankind now than at any time since the Destruction, when we were born. Man burned himself out from within. He had no balance; without it he perished. We have our own balance; it is flexible. Calanthe, for this time you are woman, an incarnation of the Goddess and I am man, incarnation of the God. Our communion is sacred and must be honoured in love.' When he spoke again, it was to pray and I closed my eyes. He knelt to kiss me and said, 'There is a danger in the world. You must go to the source, the source!'

I tried to lift my head. 'What? How? But ...'

'But nothing! Have you learned only how to carry a burden of guilt?' He stood at my feet once more, his attendants on either side, looking up at him. 'Submission shall be praised as welcome. As you trust me not to burn, so I trust you not to engulf. Maiden and boy, guardians of the threshhold; open the gates unto me.'

And at these words, his attendents each took hold of one of my ankles. Lowering their gaze to the floor, they gently parted my legs; sea-gates. I felt completely submissive, yet with the strength of a lioness. The Lyris lay upon me and his attendants did not raise their eyes again. In Elhmen, the experience of water had been wild and untramelled, elemental female. Here in Sahen, the experience of fire was governed, controlled, the elemental male, the emperor. When the heat came, it burned me inside from what felt like stomach to throat, but it was not a terrible pain. I had an intimation of what we were really doing, and how aruna is probably wasted a million times a day by two million Hara. Most of the time we cannot see. Sometimes we can; this was one of those moments.

CHAPTER

19

The Oracle of Shere Zaghara
'Though art slave to fate, chance,
Kings and desperate men.'

John Donne, Death be not proud

Panthera was shown into the Lyris' apartments early the following morning. I suppose it's strange that, away from the light of the sun and the moon, the Sahale should regulate their days as normal, but they do. Panthera studied me carefully, aware of a certain change about me, but not quite sure what it was. I was dressed and ready to begin the next stage of our journey; not a long one, thankfully. The Lyris had gone some hours before. I had slept alone.

'And what happened last night?' Panthera asked me tentatively, as if speaking to an invalid sensitive about the accident that had maimed him. He felt obliged to say something.

'Thea; I am now Algomalid!' This seemed the safest answer.

His eyes widened, then narrowed. 'You've had no training!' he accused.

'Haven't I?' For a moment, I felt bitter. 'Oh, I've had my training, don't you worry. Years and years and years of it! A lesson learned; or dozens of them!'

'So, you know the *answer* then, do you?' Why that note of sadness?

'No, not yet,' I answered defensively. 'Not *the* answer.'

He wanted me to say more. 'How many are there then?'

'Who knows? I have to go to Shere Zaghara, deep carverns,

north of Sahen. Of course, you don't *have* to come with me ...'

Panthera stood up. 'I never have,' he said. 'When do we leave?'

The Lyris had granted us passage through his private conduit to the deepest grottoes of Sahale. 'It is not a difficult or treacherous route,' he told me, 'so you may go there alone, or just with your companion, as you prefer. Go to the burrow of the fire-saucer. It is the chamber of greatest light and unmistakable. Your answers may come to you there.'

May. We went down through the palace and at first the stairs had plastered, painted walls on either side. Eventually this changed to gnarled rock. Feverish cavern-lights cast eerie shadows in corners and across our faces. At first we travelled downwards in silence. I was thinking deeply and eventually had to tell someone.

'Panthera.'

'What?' He sounded disinterested, but I carried on.

'I can see the end now, I think.'

'Of these steps?'

'No! Of everything. Of trouble. I can see it all through.'

'Have you only just decided that?' he asked wearily, perhaps doubting my sincerity. I didn't blame him.

'Perhaps it's been decided for me, but I don't want to be wishy-washy about it any more. The best form of defence is attack.'

'Or a mirror.' That could have meant many things, some of them not quite flattering. 'So you've admitted to taking up the quest then, have you?'

'I'm not as weak as you think.'

He glanced at me quickly then and I could see that he thought I was deceiving myself, wondering how on earth I could be third level Acantha when I was such a fool.

'Listen, Thea, you didn't know me before Piristil, did you, when I was in Megalithica, before Pell ...'

'And during, and after!' He did not hide the bitter sarcasm. 'It's all him, isn't it? The God figure!'

I ignored this. 'Let's just say that after Pell died, I let go of the reins, lost control. That has got to end.'

'Oh? And how do you plan to regain control of reins that curb the bits of other people's horses?'

'They were my horses once.'

'Who rides them now, though?'

'This conversation is getting out of hand!' I laughed.

Panthera wouldn't even smile. 'Maybe. Perhaps everything is getting out of hand.'

'What do you mean?'

He would not say.

The steps beneath our feet were becoming warmer, the rocks glassier and the air held a hint of sulphur. We could hear strange booming sounds coming from a long way below us. 'Are we on our way to Hell?' Panthera asked, too wistfully for it to be a joke. Now the passage was levelling out, widening and heightening. Landings swept away from us to either side, offering glimpses of swooping galleries and dark or flaming caverns. Ahead of us, a smooth sweep of glossy, black stone led to a narrow slit in the rock wall. From here a sliver of intense brightness shone like a ray of sunlight into the passage. It was stronger than sunlight. 'This is it,' I said. Bulbs of spectral, red light clung to the arching, throated walls like clusters of bubbles, but they were hardly needed. My heart had begun to pound about twenty steps up from here, half with fear, half with excitement. As we approached the entrance, I could see that the gap was just wide enough for me to squeeze through. We paused at the threshold. Panthera put his hand upon the wall, running his fingers over the undulating grooves.

'Should you go in there alone, Cal?' he asked. For a moment, I thought he was afraid. There was a fine lacing of sweat along his upper lip, but then I looked at his eyes; they were dark and tranquil.

'Perhaps I should.'

'I'll wait for you here then.' He turned away and then, impulsively, wheeled around to embrace me. 'Take care.'

'Don't worry.'

'And don't change too much.' He smiled and put his cheek, briefly, against mine.

As soon as I wriggled through the gap in the wall, it was as if a heavy, impenetrable curtain of time and distance had fallen between us. I was alone. Beyond me, I could see the glistering walls of a huge and camerated natural vault. There were veins of micra, taut tendons of mineral splatterings, and a thousand, thousand eyes of warm, living gems, glowing from the walls, sullen in the light of a slowly licking fire. The saucer itself was maybe only six feet across and of simple rough stone, broken in places as if it had lain there unseen for millenia. I could not decide whether the flames rose from a cavity in the saucer's centre, coming up from the earth itself, or if it simply existed upon the stone; a fire without fuel. I approached the light. A pottery cup and a flagon of liquid sat in the sand, attached to the stone bowl by a thin, metal chain. I had been instructed by the Lyris to take up the flagon, pour some of the liquid into the cup and drink it. Sitting cross-legged on the floor, I did so. It tasted like stale, warm water; a strong, mineral flavour. For a moment, I calmed myself, controlling my breathing as I'd been taught so long ago. Then, making the genuflections of entreaty, I addressed the genius loci of the cavern, and opened up my mind for the reception of thought. The entity that lived within the flame, as if used to such encounters with Harish kind, introduced itself without preamble and asked my business. As instructed, I opened up the part of my mind that was like an illustrated book of my life. The entity read it slowly, thoroughly, and took pleasure in it. My small life, entertaining at the best of times, apparently captured its interest; it read with relish.

'You seek answers to questions you cannot form,' it decided. 'If you knew the questions you would know the answers.'

'May I ask one of you?'

'You may.'

'Why am I important?'

'You are important only as all natural things are important,' it answered obliquely, and then added, 'If time is a tapestry, then you are one thread, whose colour improves the whole, and without which some threads may become unravelled or cease to have been at all.'

'This much was known to me,' I said. 'You must agree that it is a circumstance that could be applied equally to every living being on this planet.'

'Precisely.'

'I'm not asking the right question am I?'

It did not answer this, but instead honoured me with a physical manifestation of itself, which appeared as a slim, rangy hound with glowing eyes, whose fur was brindled and short, and who had a crest of copper-coloured fronds growing from its neck. It lay down some feet in front of me and licked its paws fastidiously with a blue tongue. The fronds all pointed towards me like eye-stalks.

'Must I go to Immanion?'

'Yes. Is that an answer you did not already know?'

I rubbed my eyes. The words were bitter in my mouth, but I had to say it. 'Is my destiny to be the Tigron's concubine?'

The hound looked up at that and pricked its ears at my indiscretion. 'If that were the case,' it said indignantly, 'then you would not be here now asking questions of me! Don't waste my time!'

'Sorry. No insult meant by that. Tell me then, what must I know?'

'One thing. What you are. Another thing; what must be done. The tying of loose threads. Finish what has been started, and in the right way. Make it smoooth.'

'I still don't understand.'

'What is most important to you?'

I pretended to think. It took some time to force the words out. 'Pellaz and myself ... Are we destined to be ... together again?'

'You will meet in Immanion.'

'As lovers?'

I could hear the flames cracking, spitting in the fire-saucer. The fire hound looked at the flames. 'You cannot do this alone. Help is needed. Go to the Dream People and join with them in the saltation of vision. They are to be found in the east, and are known in this land as the Roselane. All nears completion. A great cycle draws to a close and heralds the morning of a new age. Among the Roselane, you shall see yourself, and the mirror shall be clear. That is all.'

I could feel the creature drawing away from me.

'That is not all!' I cried desperately as its image wavered upon the sand. 'You did not answer my question!'

'I have answered as I can, and as I must. Do not believe everything you are led to believe. That, too, is part of it.'

'But the visions ... what are they? Is it real? The dreams? Are they?'

'You do not need me to answer that!'

'And Zack, what has he to ...'

'No!' I was interrupted firmly. 'That is not part of what I have to tell you. I've delivered my part. Remember it well. That is all. Now, leave quietly!'

The flames in the saucer suddenly jetted skywards and then abated to a dull, crimson glow. The pottery cup fell over at my feet. I did not bother to right it again. I walked straight out.

Panthera was sitting where I'd left him, his back to the wall. When he saw me scrambling through the rock, he got to his feet. 'Well?' he demanded, searching my eyes for the answers I'd not received.

'Riddles! Just riddles!' I snapped and strode right past him, heading blindly for the stairs.

Panthera hurried after me. 'What do you mean?' He grabbed my arm.

'There are no answers!' I turned on him viciously. 'Can't you understand? There are no answers. Just another place to go, another move in the game!'

'Didn't you expect that?'

I couldn't answer.

'What happened, Cal. What did it say?'

'You really want to know? OK, I'll tell you. I had a cosy little talk with a supernatural beast. What it told me was nonsense. I'm no wiser. Go to Roselane, it said. Can you believe it? We came all this way, Kachina was killed, for *that*! If it's somebody's idea of a joke, then I'm not playing anymore. It's ridiculous!' I started running, not bothered whether Panthera was following or not. Near the top of the stairs, my chest began to ache. I could not continue. I had to stop; leaning down, shoving my head between my knees, I gasped for breath.

Panthera watched me for a while before coming out with the inevitable, 'Cal?' and touching me warily on the shoulder.

'Don't touch me!' I yelled, shrugging him off. Oh, that felt good! I struggled onwards, one hand on the wall, feeling like about the biggest martyr in the whole of history. Panthera did not speak again. He walked behind me.

We returned to the palace of the Lyris, to pick up our luggage and see about finding our way back to Elhmen. The Lyris had just finished his evening audience in the Hall of Hearkening. More time peculiarities courtesy of fire-saucer beast-hound. There was no way the trip could have lasted a whole day. He told Iygandil to bring us a meal. Panthera was now touchy about being in the Lyris' presence, probably because he suspected something of what had happened the previous night. We were both anxious to get on our way, I suppose. The Lyris had good news for us about that. It would not be necessary to struggle all the way back to Kar Tatang and from there to Ferike. As Nanine had intimated, there were hundreds of secret entrances to Eulalee. Conveniently, one of them was just a few miles from Clereness. It would be much quicker to travel underground, especially as we'd be going by boat. Eulalee has an extensive canal system. Panthera asked the Lyris if he could arrange for our horses stabled at Kar Tatang to be given to Kachina's family or closest friends. I knew it could not appease Panthera's guilt over the Kachina episode, but I think it at least made him feel a little better. There was a cold and unfriendly politeness between us all the way back to Jael.

Coming of Age
'We have given our hearts away; a sordid boon!'

William Wordsworth, The world

We've been back in Jael a week now. Over the last couple of days, I've sat up here in my room and read and re-read everything I've written. Piristil is no longer real to me. A blessing, perhaps. Sometimes I'm scared that I'm getting dangerously close to being the sort of Cal that Thiede wanted to drag back to Immanion. (See, I'm still not sure about the Cleansing.) Occasionally, I allow myself the luxury of thinking about Pell and about the type of reunion I'd like us to have. The destruction of Almagabran society predominates in these fantasies and it would be me pulling the sole survivor from the wreckage; the Tigron. Then we could resume our wanderings together, ride off into a glorious sunset. I know it's impossible. The chances are, that once in Roselane, I shall merely be given yet another clue to the puzzle, shoved off into the unknown on another journey. Bearing in mind everything else, this seems distinctly plausible. How can I believe, sitting here, that my life has great purpose? I look at my hands; they are scratched from rock clambering, yellow around the first and second fingers on the left hand through chain-smoking. They are not the hands of a hero; no. To be fair to myself, I have started working again; you know, the *real* work of Wraeththu, flexing the muscles of my strange abilities. Every evening, I've taken to sitting in meditation wih Ferminfex. The visualization's OK, but I can't say I've learned anything dramatic from this battered head of mine. Most of it's memory, but I know that has to be relived until the stings have worked themselves out before I can get on with the heavy stuff. Self-examination. I've never really liked it. Demons with my face. I don't want to be faced with the gravity of existence, because it forces me to become obsessed with the concept of time, aware of how much of it I've wasted. Each moment is terrifying in its brevity, never to be relived again, for better or worse. Perhaps I'll be two hundred years old by the time I see Pell again and we'll both last long enough to say hello before death steps in to say, 'That's long enough, you two!' It wouldn't surprise me. Not at all.

The family Jael celebrated themselves silly when we returned. It was all supposed to be nice and friendly, but nothing could breach Panthera's ass-stupid silence, which even caused his doting parents to look askance at him. I've not been alone with him since Sahen. It would seem that our friendship, which was never very close at the best of times, is doomed to wither. For some reason (unspoken) he has decided to take offence at something I've done or said. All of Panthera's actions (and reactions) are premeditated; I've learned that much. He is doubtless furious that I haven't worked out what I've done wrong yet. Ferminfex wants me to stay here in Jael for a couple more weeks before I set off for Roselane. (You see, I *am* going there.) By then the weather should have warmed up a bit. I haven't yet worked out my route, but it seems fairly certain that either by coincidence or design, it'll pass close to Oomadrah. After all, didn't the fire-hound tell me to tie off all my loose ends? Well, if the Archon of Maudrah is who I think he is, that is definitely a loose end I want snipped off, if not tied. Perhaps it is all circumstantial, just coincidence. The law of averages dictates that Wraxilan should have been killed a hundred times over back in Megalithica; he certainly deserved it. Wraxilan. We all go back to the beginning sometimes, don't we. For Pell, it would be me, but for me it is always the Lion of Oomar. Like a glamorous, brutal father, he influenced my Wraeththu shaping, is perhaps responsible for what I am now. I feared him, I supplicated at his feet. OK I was sixteen, for God's sake! That's forgivable, isn't it? I want to see him again so he'll know I made it alright (comparatively) without him. It might not be part of the plan — it might be the ultimate self-indulgence — but it's something I have to do. Anyway, it's not going to happen yet. I have Jael to enjoy for a while longer. Now it is evening, and Jael is a magical place of soft shadows and fading spring sunlight. I can smell the dinner cooking; vension in wine. Yes, I feel good at the moment; about myself, about everything. This is probably transitory, and because of that, dangerous, but who cares! Soon, I shall go downstairs. Another evening of routine comforts.

Panthera was late for dinner. Lahela had to send a servant to fetch him from his studio high up in the castle. He came in smeared with paint, indignant at having been disturbed.

'Immerse yourself in work if you want to,' his hostling reprimanded him politely, 'but one custom I wish to uphold in this house is that we eat together in the evenings. It would be pleasant if you could avoid looking on this as an inconvenience!'

Panthera mumbled an apology and helped himself to food; small portions. He was sitting next to me, but I might as well have been a stranger. I wondered whether he was angry with me or disappointed, or had just decided he did not particularly like me.

'Panthera,' I said, 'I would like to talk with you after dinner.'

'I'm busy. Can't it wait?'

'No.'

He looked up from his food wih cold eyes. My first instinct was to wince away, but I managed to hold his gaze. He snorted and pushed food around his plate with his fork. 'Very well then, but not for long!'

The evenings were still cool in the high towers of Jael. Fires were still lit in the deep grates. Panthera and I went to sit in a comfortable, private sitting-room on the third floor. Panthera stalked restlessly around. He found a pack of cards and suggestd we play some game or another. I'd had more than enough of games, of any kind.

'Are you joking?' I asked, with preténded horror. 'Do you know what those cards are?'

Panthera riffled impatiently through the pack. 'Of course. They are divining cards. Nobody has used them for ages. Shall we gamble?'

'You lack respect for the unseen, my pantherine,' I said gravely, still joking.

Panthera threw down the cards angrily. 'You've changed so much!' he accused me bitterly. 'You never used to be such a prig! What's happened to you? I almost prefer the seedy drunkard of our journey from Thaine!'

'You will never be satisfied, obviously. Here is a lesson from life, little cat. You can never alter people's characters to suit yourself.'

'Oh, shut up!' He sank moodily to the floor, his back against the sofa arm, staring sulkily into the fire. Spellbound by his loveliness, I experienced those familiar feelings of longing to touch his untidy, black hair, coax desire from his sensual yet passionless mouth, and ease the frown from his autocratic brow. I watched him. He knew it. I picked up the deck of cards and shuffled them. Laying them down on the floor, I cut the pack. 'Oh look! How appropriate!'

Panthera could not resist a look, bristling visibly when he saw what lay there. 'Ace of Cups, of course. This clearly indicates the next drinking binge you'll embark upon once your shallow mind becomes bored of hidden knowledge,' he said, pleased with himself.

'Cut them,' I suggested.

He shook his head. 'No need. Obviously, I will draw a reversed king and possibly the Devil.'

'Is that how you see yourself?'

Panthera raised a sardonic brow. He said nothing. I cut the cards again. 'What a coincidence! Two of cups,' I said.

'Very clever! The cards have not been used for years. Possibly, the last owner died and left a binding of untruth over the pack. What are you implying anyway?'

I shrugged. 'Nothing. It was you that wanted to play a game.'

'You're insufferable!' he cried angrily. 'No wonder Thiede let you out of the tower! There was a moment's hideous, electric silence during which, I should imagine, Panthera dearly wished he'd kept his mouth shut. Then he felt he had to go on. 'You look down on everybody, don't you!'

'Well, I am quite tall.'

'Oh, you make me sick! You know what I mean.'

'In that case, so do you. I'm surprised you're not cross-eyed!'

Panthera ignored that. 'Everyone tries to make you seem so special, don't they! It must have gone to your head over the years. The truth is, you're a selfish and deceitful charlatan. I've always been able to see right through you.'

'Oh, I'm flattered! Panthera has spoken and the words of the mighty ones are levelled to dust!'

'Mighty ones!' he spat. 'And who do you mean by that? No, don't tell me, it's the Gelaming, isn't it! Those honourable, smarmy trendsetters of our wondrous, blossoming culture. Don't make me laugh!'

'Why ever not? That was the intention of my last few remarks, after all!' I smiled at him engagingly.

Panthera ruminated on this, unsure of whether to laugh with me or not. He was afraid of looking foolish. 'I'm not wrong, Cal,' he said.

'Why did you come to Sahen with me then?'

'I told you; honour.'

'Ah, so at least I'm worthy of that then.'

He sniffed and stared at the fire. 'This is getting us nowhere, Cal. I have work to do. What was it you wanted to say to me?'

Not the best of cues, but clearly the only one I'd get that evening. 'Just that I'm sorry we've grown so apart.'

'Why? We've never been close.'

'No, not really, but I don't want things to get any worse. At one time, I thought we got on quite well. Can't we go back to that? What have I done? Have I really changed that much?'

He turned and looked at me thoughtfully. 'I wish I could tell you the truth,' he said. 'I thought you'd guess, but you haven't. Too wrapped up in your own affairs, I suppose. We're really not that much alike, are we?'

'No. I don't suppose we are,' I agreed. 'but I've learned not to avoid the truth, so tell me.'

He bowed his head. 'I can't. It's no use. You must go from here and complete whatever quest it is you've involved yourself in. I know where it'll end, we both do. I've accepted that …'

'Panthera …' It was obvious what he meant. How could I have been so stupid? But what could I have done about it anyway?

'No,' he said. 'Don't say anything. I've told you; you've got your reason. Don't say anythng; it's best that way. I'm sorry. If you hadn't asked, I'd never have told you.' He scrambled up and struggled from the room. I didn't stop him. I was dazed. Panthera had frozen me out because, dare I say it, he *wanted* me?

After a while, I went along to my room and lay down fully clothed on the bed. All the curtains were open and I could see a pale, round moon beyond the windows. I was lying there thinking of bodies, all the ones I'd touched, some of them now faceless to me. I'd always relished challenges, the slow, sinuous winding towards seduction of the glacial, beautiful creature who denied me. And there'd been more than a few. With Panthera I had made the decision not to bother, primarily because I respected him. Other reasons would include my obsession with the Tigron and, let's be honest, myself, my apathy, the certainty that seduction of Panthera would inevitably harm him in some way. He was right, wise beyond his years, not to pursue it. Most young Hara would have done. It's what they grow up with after all. But Panthera knew I would leave soon; it wasn't just aruna he wanted. I must leave him alone so he could forget me without pain. And yet, much as I tried to dismiss the thought, I wanted to be close to him because nobody ever had been, and he stirred my soul. Between us lurked the spectre of Pellaz and, perhaps eventually, the reality. I tried to sleep, but my body ached. I wanted to give my pantherine some of what Nanine and the Lyris had given to me; magic. Real magic, the kind that when it's over you know the world is just the wonderful place your dreams were always telling you. All the shit doesn't matter because your head has just exploded into somebody else with a thousand stars, and they felt so good; like fur, like ice, like flames, like silk, like feathers and, by Aghama, you want to experience that again. That's magic. I couldn't stop thinking about it; so maudlin and most unlike me really. After about an hour of this useless longing, I threw off my clothes and lay in bed, smoking a cigarette. Perhaps I should leave here sooner than Ferminfex suggested.

Stubbing out my cigarette in the saucer I'd used that morning, I pulled the covers over my head and furiously tried to get to sleep again.

And eventually I slept. I know this because, when I sensed somebody come into the room, I thought I was dreaming. Then I realized I wasn't and I was reaching for a knife or a gun beneath my pillow which could not possibly be there. I held my breath, waiting. Someone crept towards me, my back was turned to the door. In a moment, I would turn and have somebody's throat between my hands. But first I wait. Weight on my bed, the covers lifted. I almost laughed. This was not threatening, oh no. I let my saved breath out in one, long hiss. He slithered into my bed, cold and shivering. He curled his arms around me and pressed himself hesitantly against my back.

'Cal, Cal, don't be asleep. Talk to me.'

I recognized his smell, his slenderness and took one of his hands in my own. He gripped it hard. We didn't say anything at all. For a while, we lay like that, and it wasn't calculated when I turned to face him. I just did it. In the moonlight, I could see he was weeping silently, his face all wet, like he didn't really want to be there, but couldn't help himself. I understood that. Our first kiss was fumbling, like children, breath visions fleeting and undecipherable. He had never been touched before except in violation. He had never given love. His skin, perfumed with the earth smell of cinnamon, was like cat-skin, furred yet smooth. I wanted to pounce, plunder that lithe pliancy; only some vestige of good sense held me back. I had to speak, because they were necessary words; even though he knew I was thinking them anyway.

'Thea, I understand what you're giving me. I really do. Don't get hurt because of this, will you. Promise me that, you won't get all churned-up and grieving. In the future ...'

'Hush,' he said. 'I'm not a child. I know what I'm doing; all of it.' Nearly all of it. He smiled. 'I don't want you to show me anything. It must be done my way.'

No, he was not a child, but he *was* afraid. I knew that because the caressing went on for far too long. I was starting to think he wouldn't dare and I'd have to indulge in my original desire of conquest. I held him close, burying my nose in his wonderful hair, trying so desperately to feel passive to him, not frightening, not engulfing, just receptive, yearning. He stroked my skin, fascinated by it, because it was not a skin covering cruel desires to break and tear.

'You are scarred,' he said. 'Your flesh is soft yet you are hard beneath, I know it, like iron under moss in the forest. I thought you used bleach on your hair because your eyes and brows are so dark. You have cynical eyebrows, Cal. They always look so disdainful; they know everything and they love it when all the other poor fools don't.'

'Just my eyebrows, Thea?'

He laughed. 'Started off that way. I got side-tracked into the rest of you. I've wanted to touch you for a long time, you know. And so many people were doing it, all so experienced. I couldn't get near you. So many people have touched you, haven't they.'

'My body, yes, but not often my mind.'

He nestled against me, his head on my chest. 'If we could just hold each other forever, the bad things will go away,' he said. 'I think I must love you, Cal, even though it's senseless and sort of self-destructive too. You belong to *him*, you always will.' He sighed.

'We don't know what's going to happen,' I said, rather untruthfully.

'No, we don't.' There was strength in those words.

We shared breath again; I let him move against me. Clearly, his responses weren't damaged at all. I wriggled us around until I was under him, wondering what else I could do to help without being obvious. There was no need. Suddenly, unexpectedly, he just found his way inside me and let nature do the rest. The time was right. Everything was fine. He was nothing like I'd anticipated, not timourous, but powerful, vigourous, dominant. I'd have to sort that out later. At the moment of orgasm, he screeched like a wild beast in pain right in my ear, drowning any responding cry I might have made myself. I thought he'd hurt himself, but he only laughed at my concern. Could I have met my match? Calanthe is renowned across Megalithica and beyond for his savage, skilful aruna. Usually, it was me doing the gouging and chewing. I was quite alarmed.

Panthera said to me 'Cal, I want to see Roselane,' and lying there in his arms, feeling battered but lazy, it seemed like the only course of action.

That night it was decided. We may have been wrong, but if we were, it was because our hearts were taking control of our minds. Panthera would accompany me to Roselane, and beyond. We would take responsibility for the consequences, whatever they were.

Morla

'If I think of a King at nightfall.'

T.S. Eliot, Little Gidding

In spring, the steppelands of Maudrah are a glistening, undulating ocean of waving, feathered grasses. This can even be seen from the sea, as a faint and distant glimmering, like sheets of silk hung across the horizon. We'd had to choose the quickest route to Roselane, which was over water from the Ferike port of Saphrax, east across the Sea of Shadows, grazing the southernmost tip of the Thwean region of Jaddayoth. From there it was north into the Sea of Arel, passing the summer ports of Gaspard and Oriole, to Chane. After that, the journey would be continued over land, through Garridan to Roselane. At no point would our travels take us even within spitting distance of Oomadrah. I could not bear to leave my notes behind me in Jael, perhaps because I feared I would never go back there. Many times, I've sat upon the deck of this Ferike vessel, with my back to the coast of Maudrah and read through them. So many pages, and yet so little said really. I have spoken of my first client in Piristil, but to read what I wrote of it does not convey the disgust I felt or — no matter how hard I fought it — the shame. Neither can Elhmen and Sahen live as brilliantly, as vibrantly on paper as I experienced them in reality, nor does the time I first held Panthera in my arms convey the actuality of that moment. I suppose it is impossible. It happened. I lived it. Here the grass is glowing with light across a shard of sparkling sea. Can you picture it? Panthera and I are not blind to the possible consequences of our relationship. It may be doomed to ephemerality; it may not. We have no way of knowing. Because he does not read this, I can say that I do not love him — not in the same way as I did (do?) Pell. It is different, but no less genuine a feeling because of that. What we have we shall enjoy.

Ferminfex has no contacts in the land of Roselane, but has given us another letter of introduction all the same. This ship is named the *Auric Wing*, a merchant vessel, heading for the Emunah ports now that the ice has melted. The sea of Arel is impassable in winter. Yesterday, we stopped at the Maudrah port of Pelagrie on the tip of Thwean and I had my first glimpse of Maudrah society. Glimpse it was as well. Our Captain, Asvak, advised us not to go ashore, although the other two passengers ignored this. We are not sure whether they are Maudrah themselves or not, as they are surly and don't seem willing to make conversation with us. Panthera and I take our meals with Asvak, while they dine in their cabin alone. We were carrying several paintings which were to be picked up by some Maudrah family in Pelagrie, so the pause in our journey was only short. Panthera and I stood leaning upon the rails of the ship, gazing at the town. On the docks, black-haired Hara, stripped to the waist, were heaving barrels and crates on board other vessels, taciturn as our fellow passengers. Asvak came to join us, smoking a long, curiously curled pipe. He gestured at the Maudrah with it. 'Happy souls, aren't they!'

I looked beyond the docks towards the gaunt, grey buildings of the town itself. 'Is the paw of the Lion that heavy then?' I asked lightly.

Our Captain made a disparaging noise. 'Not heavy, perhaps, but it has an eye on the end of each pad! See them?' He pointed towards a group of Hara dressed in black, watching the workers. They were standing back from the proceedings, but clearly had a supervisory role. 'They are the Aditi,' Asvak continued. 'The eyes and hands of the Niz.'

'Niz?' I queried. 'is that *another* name for the Lion?'

Asvak laughed drily, taking another draw on his pipe. Panthera squinted in distaste through a cloud of acrid smoke.

'No, far from it, or perhaps ... well, judge for yourself. The Niz are the priest figures in Maudrah and to be honest no-one can say whether Lord Ariaric controls them, or vice versa. If you take my advice, you'll take great pains to keep out of their way.'

'We don't intend to spend much time in Maudrah,' Panthera said, looking hard at me.

'Is Oomadrah far from here?' I asked casually.

Asvak narrowed his eyes so that he could think better. 'Quite some way, although once we reach the Sea of Arel, we'll be closer.'

'Have you ever been there?'

Here, Asvak pulled a forlorn face. 'Yes. Can't say I enjoyed that visit too much either. Luckily, I was with a Har of Maudrah origin who prevented me from making any *noticeable* mistakes.'

'What do you mean, mistakes?'

Asvak laughed and patted me on the shoulder. 'Don't ask! Believe me, even drawing breath in the wrong way is a mistake in Maudrah. Now, if you'll excuse me, tiahaara ...'

Asvak's footsteps hadn't even died away before Panthera launched into the attack. 'We can't go there, Cal!'

'Go where?' I asked lightly. Panthera is sometimes annoyingly perceptive. I'd told him about Wraxilan some time ago, and had wondered then whether I'd regret it later.

'To Oomadrah, of course! Do you think I'm stupid? I think *you* are! Not only is it dangerous, but a waste of time! Are you trying to delay reaching Roselane on purpose?' (That was snide.)

'Oh, be quiet!' I said impatiently. 'I've got my own voice of conscience, thank you! Just remember, I was told in Sahen to tie up all loose ends.'

'I can't see how Ariaric or Wraxilan or whatever he calls himself can be one of them, Cal,' Panthera said with dogged determination. 'It's just your curiosity. You should let well alone. Haven't you enough on your plate already?'

'Oh,' I replied drily, ignoring most of what he'd said, 'and don't I get a say in what I consider to be my own loose ends?' Panthera pulled an exasperated face. 'Look Thea,' I continued bravely, 'Wraxilan was my beginning; he's never let me forget that.' Have I ever let myself forget it? 'Perhaps I want to see where his destiny led him. It may be that I can learn from it.' (How I'd come to dread those times when Panthera looked at me as if I was stupid.)

'OK, let's just imagine we *do* go there,' he said, as if seriously considering such a suggestion. 'Would you care to explain to me how we'd get to actually see him. He is Archon, remember; not just anyone can walk in and demand an audience.'

'Don't be silly, Thea! We carry a letter of introduction from your father headed "To whom it may concern" …'

'You are foolish beyond words or indeed comprehension!' Panthera declared as if it was written in stone. 'We wouldn't survive five minutes in Oomadrah. We don't know the customs, we don't know the law. This ship can take us straight to Chane. We could be in Roselane within two weeks. Why can't you chase phantoms in Oomadrah after that?'

I could not say that, after Roselane, there was always the possibility I'd no longer be able to take independent action. For if I did, Panthera would first accuse me of acute pessimism and then chew it over privately and worry. I opted for an easier way out. 'Because I trust my instincts and my instincts want me to go there now, that's why. There must be Hara who can be hired as guides, interpreters, whatever, to take us there. I'll ask Asvak about it.'

Panthera nodded sourly. 'Oh yes, and supposing we are successful in meeting the Lion. What are you going to say to him, Cal? Have you thought of that? Do you think he'll be pleased to see you? Will he even recognize you after all this time?'

'Oh, he'll recognize me, I have no doubts about that! As for the other questions, I really don't know, but I'll have worked something out by the time we get there.'

'It's decided then, is it? We're going to Oomadrah?'

I reached to touch his face. 'Panthera, I must be honest with you; I decided that quite some time ago. Of course, you don't *have* to come with me …'

My sultry Panthera smiled then, and the sourness dropped from his eyes in an instant. 'Oh Cal, as you said, I'm just an extension of the voice of your conscience. You must be asked these things. I'm not afraid of Maudrah. As a matter of fact, though I was loath to admit it, there is a distant relative of mine there, on my hostling's

268

side. I believe he is employed in the royal house itself. Even if he agrees to see us, we'll need our wits about us though, and an efficient guide.'

This was more than I could have hoped for, but I wasn't going to let my feelings show. 'Can Asvak drop us off somewhere convenient do you think?' I asked coolly.

'Well, we can ask him to take us to Morla, although this ship would probably have called there anyway. We'll need the luck of the Aghama on our side for that; let's hope he's listening.'

'Quite,' I said.

Late afternoon, as the tide was turning, we set sail once more. It was a glorious day and the ensuing sunset was breath-taking. Asvak had a couple of his crew members set out a table on deck for the evening meal and brought out a bottle of his finest wine. A gentle breeze carried a smell of grass from the distant shore, which complemented the exquisite aroma of spiced meat, if not Asvak's rather overpowering perfume. Half-way through the main course, I mentioned that Panthera and I had decided to go to Morla instead of Chane. This was met with silence. Asvak was obviously suspicious of our motives. It was not an unreasonable misgiving. After all, he had to trade in Maudrah and didn't want to risk incurring the displeasure of the Niz. It was not inconceivable that ferrying dissidents of any kind to Maudrah would be regarded unfavourably. Luckily, Panthera managed to persuade him otherwise (his charm, when he deigns to use it, is humbling, to say the least). He told Asvak about the relative in Oomadrah.

'Our original plan was to pay him a visit on our way back from Roselane,' he said, 'but we've changed our plans in that we now intend to carry on to Kalamah instead, so Maudrah must come first. Roselane will have to wait a little while.'

'Very well,' Asvak assented, after another of his grinding thinks, 'but if you should run foul of the Niz, you did not reach Maudrah through me.'

'Naturally,' I said. 'Can you recommend a guide to take us to Oomadrah, and who might be able to keep us out of trouble?'

Asvak was still wary. 'There are one or two in Morla,' he said. 'I may be able to affect an introduction for you. You realize I take a considerable risk in helping you.'

'My purse realized that before I even thought of it,' I said, and Asvak managed a weak smile.

Dawn was just breaking when the gaunt spires of Morla appeared against the sky to our left. It had taken us about three and a half days to reach it. Panthera and I were up on deck, bags packed and ready, to watch the approach. Behind us, Asvak's sailors called to each other eerily from the rigging. Wide-winged birds hung in the sky investigating our presence. In the town, a bell was tolling, and light flashed off the tallest spire, which was crowned with metal. Ahead of the *Auric Wing*, the sky was opalescent and hazy; all the sea was shining like oil.

Asvak offered to take us to a guide he was acquainted with, and who was best suited to Hara unfamiliar with the country. 'It would be best if you wore dark clothes, cloaks if you have them, to go ashore,' he said.

The streets of Morla are narrow and murky. It was strange and disorientating to walk upon solid ground once more and disappointing that we could not go into the nearest inn for a meal and tankard of ale. It is not that there are no inns in Maudrah, but because of the rigours of the local customs, it is inadvisable for strangers to go into them. We soon gathered that the best mode of behaviour was one of steady inconspicuousness, which was difficult, for a Har can be recognized as alien even by his stance. 'You may come to regret this,' was all Asvak would say. We descended a narrow flight of steps, leading to a gloomy lane, overhung by cramped, leaning buildings. Here, Asvak pressed us back against the damp wall to allow a single file of chanting, dark-robed figures to pass.

'They are novitiate Niz, combing the streets with the hems of their robes,' Asvak told us. 'It is a ritual performed every morning, whatever the weather.'

Half-way up the lane, he knocked softly upon a low, heavily-lintelled door. A code. Three knocks, pause, one knock, pause, three again. After a while, a window was opened with difficulty on the upper floor and a pale face looked out. 'Dawn blessings,' Asvak said, touching his brow and his lips with two fingers. The window closed and presently we could hear a series of bolts and locks being drawn and turned behind the door. It was opened by a Har with white face and hair, dressed in dark brown and grey.

'Dawn blessings, Asvak of the Ferike,' he said. 'You are welcome in peace over this threshold.' Asvak kissed this Har upon each cheek and led the way inside. The house was dark and smelt damp. Our host lit a lamp to reveal a wide, sparsely-furnished kitchen. 'May I light the fire?' he asked Asvak.

'The hour is early,' the Captain replied. 'I will lend you my hands also.'

Panthera and I were left standing there, exchanging confused glances, while they made the fire and lit it. A much longer process than the task merited, I felt. Once this was done, Asvak deigned to introduce us.

'Lourana, this is Calanthe and Panthera of the house of Jael in Ferike. They would honour you with a request.'

'Which is?'

'A guide to Oomadrah,' I said, 'if you would help us …'

Here, Asvak screwed up his face in mortification. Lourana had assumed a stony expression and slid his eyes to Asvak. Offence had been given. I assumed.

'You must forgive them,' Asvak said. 'They have not set foot in Maudrah before.'

Lourana gave us an icy smile. 'It is plain to me. If I can lapse into the common tongue here, Asvak, and address your companions?'

Asvak waved an arm. 'You may.'

'Please, sit down.' Lourana gestured towards the table, where wooden benches were set along either side. We did so, and he took his place at the head, folding his hands on the worn surface. We were appraised, very slowly, one after the other. Then Lourana spoke. 'This is a danger-frought situation, if ever there was one! Friends of Asvak, I must tell you that for the transgression you just unwittingly committed by speaking out of turn, you could have been taken into custody by the Aditi and asked any number of awkward questions. You look confused. Well, remember this: as an outlander, you must never speak directly to a native of Maudrah

271

unless they have spoken first. If you wish to attract somebody's attention, you must speak your request out loud, to the Aghama, so that he may speak for you.' (I dared not look at Panthera. Lourana was serious.) 'If you really are ignorant of all Maudrah customs, you must remain silent and stooped at all times when other Hara are present. Leave all communication to me. Now you must offer me payment.'

I looked at Asvak and he nodded discretely. 'How much do you require?' I asked.

Lourana shook his head. 'No, that is not the way.' He sighed. 'Make me an offer, an offer way too high. Then it is for me to suggest a fair figure.'

'A hundred spinners?'

'Thirty will be plenty.' The Maudrah were cheaper to hire than the Sahale then. I shudder to think, how much Zhatsin would have charged for taking us on such a journey.

'Would it be possible for me to pay you now, plus any extra for the purchase of horses and supplies?'

'Payment in advance will be welcome,' Lourana answered, 'but horses will not be necessary. I have a vehicle.'

'A vehicle? What kind?' Panthera asked, clearly unconcerned with whether that was a permissible question. Lourana had the courtesy to ignore any transgression.

'A crystal powered car, such as are used by the Garridan and the Gelaming, and, of course,' he smiled slightly, 'the Maudrah.'

'The journey will be quite swift then,' I said.

Lourana inclined his head. 'Very swift. I've found that this is the safest way with strangers. There are too many hazards upon the roads, too many encounters I'd rather avoid. The sooner you leave Morla the better. Oomadrah is more tolerant of outlanders. This is a small town. Everybody knows each other here.' A strangely ominous remark.

Asvak stood up, as if suddenly remembering where he was. 'Yes, I'd better be back on the *Auric Wing* before too many people are abroad in the streets,' he said and held out his hand to us. 'Good luck to you, tiahaara, may you reach your destination in safety.'

I put some coins into his hand, to which he made no comment.

He was eager to be gone. I experienced my first pangs of misgiving. Once the *Auric Wing* had set sail we were stuck here.

'You must have good reason for visiting Oomadrah,' Lourana said, prying.

I waited until Asvak had closed the door behind him before replying. 'I do. I want to speak with Ariaric.'

Lourana did not flinch. '*The* Ariaric?'

I nodded and Lourana stared at me very closely. He reminded me a great deal of Flounah (which was not very comforting) even though his hair was white where Flounah's was black. They shared the same ascetic appearance however, and the same piercing grey eyes.

'You are a brave Har,' he said evenly. 'I am not here to question your requirements, merely to do the job I'm paid for. It may be that you wish to harm the person of the Archon, in which case, by assisting you, I run the risk of displeasing the Niz — never a wise course of action — but, as I have accepted this contract, I must abide by my decision.'

'I can assure you,' I said, 'I'm not an assassin.'

Lourana held up his hands and closed his eyes. 'Please, no more,' he said emphatically. 'I do not want to know what you are or what your business is. It's safer that way.'

It was decided that, as anonymity was such a vital factor, we would wait until dusk to leave Lourana's house. He lived alone, in the dark and the cold, like a wraith-light. In fact, Lourana was the only touch of brightness in the place. From outside, he must look like a lonely ghost flitting from window to window, wandering the rooms, looking for life. He drew the curtains (dingy things) across the kitchen window and gave us bread and meat to eat, accompanied by large mugs of bitter, lavishly-sugared tea. Every time we heard footsteps pass the house, Lourana winced and glanced at the curtains. I could not help wondering why he stayed in Morla; he seemed far from content there. Perhaps it was for love, though somehow, that explanation didn't ring true. It was a dismal day we spent there, Panthera restless and pacing, Lourana tense as wire, wide-eyed, and infecting both Panthera and myself with taut nerves. We spoke little, only learning that once in Oomadrah, we

273

should submit our letter to the city's administrators and hope for the best. Clearly, Lourana thought his responsibilities ended there. I could not resist enquiring; I asked. 'Lourana, if a native of Morla wanted you to take them in your crystal-powered car to Oomadrah, how much would you get off them?'

'Three spinners, maybe,' he answered. 'Now do you see why I have to risk taking strangers there?' Yes, very clearly.

As the light began to fade, Lourana set about gathering the things we would need for the journey. I helped him carry bags and boxes out to a shed at the back of the house. Here, the sleek grey car lay like a prize cat, waiting to be aroused to purring life. I can't say I understand the way such vehicles work but they run without wheels and are not hampered by weight. The yard was greasy and black. Lourana opened the double doors to the shed onto another high walled lane at the back of the house. There did not appear to be any sign of life in the other dwellings in the row, but of course, quiet behaviour is standard in Maudrah, so this was not really surprising.

'Now, get in the back,' Lourana instructed, lifting up the transparent dome of the car. 'Hurry up, get that luggage in. Noise will attract attention.'

He jumped nimbly into the front and breathed upon an oily-looking panel beneath the control sticks. With a yawning whine, the vehicle shivered, sighed and levitated gracefully three feet off the ground. Spots of light bloomed around the controls, which Lourana touched lightly, in sequence, with the tips of his fingers. The car edged warily forward into the lane, slanting slightly as it turned. There was no-one around.

'Strap yourselves in,' Lourana commanded, still fingering the light panels. 'Please make sure the canvas over the baggage is secure.'

Once satisfied that passengers and luggage were in place, Lourana increased the speed to normal walking pace. We emerged from the dank, dark lane into a wider thoroughfare, where other sombrely clothed Hara could be seen shuffling, head-down, along the pavement. I heard a metallic swish and looked up. Another car flashed overhead, leaving a luminous trail behind it which quickly dispersed. Even though Morla was lit by street lamps, the feeling of darkness was not alleviated. We passed inns, but no sound of revelry, or even conversation, drifted outside. Sour-faced Hara clutched glasses of ale in the doorways, looking at the ground. Lourana pulled the hood of his cloak over his glowing hair.

'Keep your eyes lowered,' he murmured over his shoulder, 'and your hoods up.'

I was beginning to feel apprehensive. The appalling, oppressive atmosphere of the town was getting to me. Danger seemed to lurk in every shadow. We drifted onwards at the same sedate pace. Occasionally other vehicles would pass us, causing us to shrink back in our seats. Our direction was north. It took us a good half hour to reach the outskirts of the town, and Morla is not a large place either. Now the streets were wider and the houses spaced more widely apart; clearly a residential area. Perhaps this was where the Niz lived. Lourana increased our speed a fraction and the buildings fell away to reveal the grassy plains of Hool Glasting stretching away before us into the night. Lourana stopped the car, letting it hover a few inches off the ground.

He slumped forward, emitting a long, shuddering sigh. 'The Aditi are very vigilant in Morla,' he said. 'You don't know how lucky we are to have passed through without them stopping us to ask questions.' He straightened up. 'Are you ready, tiahaara of Jael? Now, we may really *travel*.'

We were ready. Lourana savoured this moment. He lifted the car to a height of six feet or so, before quickly touching the light panel. I had once owned a horse, who, at a command, could jump straight into a gallop from a standstill. Lourana's car had a very similar response. It seemed to bunch itself up, take a step backwards and then shoot forwards at sickening speed. Panthera and I were pushed hard against our seats, the wind of our flight whipping our hoods back, lifting Lourana's hair like a white flag. He touched the light panel and the dome of the car slid silently over our heads, sealing us from the wind. We shot like a comet over the land. Looking back, I could see the ghostly shimmery trail of our passage, dissolving and floating to earth. The car rose in the air until the ground was some thirty feet below us. Lourana told us he was setting the course. Now he could sit back and relax. I asked him if we could smoke. He said yes, so I offered him one.

As he took it, he said, 'This is sinful,' and then laughed as I offered him a light. Now that we were out of Morla, our guide seemed much more inclined to talk. He told us that he liked being with outlanders, because then it didn't seem to matter what he said or did. 'Sometimes, I must admit, the strictures of my life do sit rather heavily upon my shoulders,' he said.

'Then why live it?' Panthera asked. 'Couldn't you find work in Hadassah or Gimrah?'

Lourana shook his head. 'You don't understand. The way we live is the right way. I am weak to yearn occasional respite from it, and shall no doubt have to pay for it some day. We cannot live like men; look what happened to them! We need order so that we may develop ...'

'Oh come on!' I couldn't help interrupting. 'No-one I saw in Morla could be described as a particularly enlightened soul!'

'The individual may only learn through suffering. We carry a great blood-debt on our hands ...'

'You do?' I couldn't hide the cynicism; I didn't want to.

'But yes,' Lourana insisted with furrowed brow. 'From the old times, the Destruction, the Agony of Birth. Wraeththu squandered their abilities; now they are undeserved. It will take many generations to appease the guilt. I can see the sense of it all, but sometimes it's hard to live. That's part of it, I suppose.'

Doors were beginning to swing open in my head. If Wraxilan had fled east, banished from Megalithica because of his evil, it was not impossible that he'd suffered some kind of warped revelation. He may be assuaging his own guilt by passing it onto his people. Curious. I couldn't wait to see what had become of the Har I'd so admired and feared in the past. Ariaric seemed the exact opposite of everything Wraxilan had stood for; which was riotous excess in everything and having a bloody good time while doing it as well. Perhaps I'd been wrong. Perhaps Ariaric wasn't Wraxilan; then we'd be in trouble. But then, hadn't Liss-am-Caar known what I'd meant back in Fallsend? I'd have to be patient. Soon I would know for sure.

Our flight was swift; by late afternoon the next day, Lourana was circling his car high above the outskirts of Oomadrah herself. To the north was the pale track of the caravan route, that looped around the farthest end of the gunmetal lake Syker Sade with its fringe of Har-height reeds, its screeching birds. From there, the trail stretched south-west to Strabaloth (the second largest Maudrah settlement) and the plains of Wrake Tamyd. The flat grasslands roll from east to west unremittingly, unbroken by tree or hill. Herds of Maudrah horses graze unmolested, rubbing shoulders with cattle and deer, and beyond them rise the sheer, black walls of Oomadrah herself; female if ever a city is. Her walls are polished obsidian, soaring so high as to cast a perpetual shadow over the edge of the city within. Such protectiveness. Only the Rique Spire of the Lion's palace Sykernesse rises above them. Many gates stud the walls, but even as I was worrying about how we'd get past the guards, Lourana had dipped the car over the south wall of the city, which spread out her secrets before us.

'How come they let you pass so easily?' Panthera asked suspiciously.

'Because my car is known to them,' Lourana answered. 'I make this journey several times a week; I have to. To live.'

We drifted down towards the black and silver streets below. To see it is to believe it. The predominant colours in Maudrah's streets, are silver, black, grey or darkest violet. Sometimes, high-ranking citizens can be glimpsed wearing clothes the colour of dried blood red, indigo or brown, but for the lesser Hara it's always unremitting grey or black. Maudrah Hara have hair of deepest black or silver white. They are generally a tribe of striking appearance and their austere mode of attire somehow complements this. Outlanders — there are quite a few, which surprised me — can usually be recognized by their hair. Most people from outside affect Maudrah style of dress pretty quickly, but is never possible to blend in completely. This is because, more than a difference in appearance, Maudrah really do have a serene kind of inner quiet, which marks them, and is inimitable. It is said that they can kill and maim without a tremor in the name of progression, without even glancing away. They can love you and destroy you in the same instant; that is the legacy of the Lion.

Oomadrah
'*A bloody arrogant power
Rose out of the race
Uttering, mastering it.*'

W.B. Yeats, Blood and the moon

Lourana brought his car to a swooping halt upon a grey plaza. The stone beneath us was as polished as glass. Other cars were clustered there, beads of black and silver. Hara walking sedately among them; no-one hurries in Oomadrah. Although Panthera and myself had stayed awake for most of the night talking to Lourana, we'd managed to catch up on some sleep during the remainder of the journey in the morning. Now we had to suffer stiff limbs and a lurking sleepiness.

Lourana suggested that he took us to an inn that catered for outlanders. 'They are more lenient there, but it would still be best if you kept your mouths shut. I'll be staying overnight; I haven't slept for two days.'

We were more than happy to let him take control of us. Lourana left his vehicle unprotected because stealing is unknown in Maudrah. This is because the inhabitants nurse a healthy fear of the all-seeing Niz. Lourana told us to keep our heads lowered as we walked, but I couldn't resist the odd sly peep. What I saw amazed me. Nobody turned their backs on a Har of higher rank than themselves; peers must also pass each other frontways. So, whatever strictures are placed upon merrymaking in that part of Jaddayoth, the people of Maudrah certainly dance. They whirl and bob and glide amongst each other like the cranes nesting on the grasslands beyond the city. Everywhere the swish of robes, the tap of feet as the correct steps are made. Lourana made genuflections to indicate that Panthera and I were foreigners and thus absolved, to a certain degree, from the rules of their society. As long as visitors are seen and not heard, all seems to be well, but we were aware of the steely eyes of the Aditi vigilant on every street corner, alert for serious transgressions. Lourana had warned us what forms these could take; a sneeze in the street, an unfortunate raising of eyes should a high-caste Har be passing by, an increase in walking pace when it was not warranted. I wondered what would happen were someone clumsy enough to fall over in the street. A hundred conventions would be broken in one stroke; a cry, an incorrect wobble, a flailing of naked hands. And yet, it must be said, the Maudrah are actually comfortable within the cage of their laws; they thrive. A perfectly executed walk through town, observing every nuance of custom and tradition, can provide untold satisfaction. Whatever outlanders may think of Maudrah, it would appear that the natives themselves are far from discontent.

Lourana took us to what he considered a commercial inn named the Grain and Bowl — no brimming tankards in Oomadrah! It was a plain but reasonably comfortable establishment. He signed the register for us and then announced that we must present ourselves to the Office of the Niz right away. Panthera complained of hunger. I would have welcomed a chance to freshen up.

Lourana shook his head at our complaints. 'No. Take your luggage to your rooms. Don't do anything else. If you fail to identify yourselves with the Niz, you may find your next meal less than welcome — your toes for example. There'll be plenty of time for eating and washing later on. You need a Pass to come and go in Oomadrah; your letter of introduction should provide you with one. You are lucky that the name of Jael is fairly well-known in the city. I've heard that the palace is full of Jael artifacts, so the Niz should be willing to let you remain here. It's more than I'm being paid for, but I'll show you the way, if you like.'

Panthera took a couple of spinners from his pocket and put them in Lourana's hand, staring at him owlishly. Lourana sniffed, put the money in his purse and led the way outside.

As we walked along the clean streets of Oomadrah, Lourana advised us on how to behave in the office of the Niz. 'You would be wise to tell them that Panthera's father wishes him to make a tour of all the major cities of Jaddayoth as part of his education; that will appeal to their sense of pride. Mention that you are seeking out remote branches of your family and would like to be presented to your distant cousin who can be found in Sykernesse.' This caused a moment's confusion because Panthera realized he couldn't even remember the name of his relative in the Royal House. This would not look very convincing. Lourana was outraged, his pale face actually flushed pink and he would not take a step further. 'Are you out of your mind?' he hissed. 'If you wander into the Office so ill-prepared, so casually, the Niz will have you flayed, and me too very likely!'

'Don't upset yourself,' Panthera replied airily. 'There can't be that many Kalamah in Sykernesse. From what I recall, he is employed in the service of the Lion's consort Elisyin, quite high-ranking too.'

Lourana looked annoyed, mainly because that meant he had to say, 'Oh, in that case, you probably mean Lalasa.'

'In that case I probably do,' Panthera replied, 'the name does ring a bell.'

'Let's hope it's the right one otherwise the Niz may wring our necks,' I said; a weak joke, but still enough to start Panthera laughing. Lourana hurried us along, looking in every direction at once in case someone heard us.

The Administration Office of the Niz was a grim, imposing building, set in a square of its own, unadorned save for the main entrance. Here, polished columns reared sombrely to an arch where squealing birds squabbled among pendulous, tatty nests. The reception hall inside was enormous, the only sounds being those of brisk footsteps and hushed voices. The floor was so polished it was like looking into a black mirror. Lourana approached the low, unfussy desk to our left, which was staffed only by a single Har. As we waited, black-robed Hara drifted past us, heads bent together, never lifting their eyes.

'Panthera, this place is *spooky*,' I murmured. Panthera pulled a forlorn face of agreement. He didn't want to risk speaking out loud. After a moment, Lourana came back to us, ushering us further away from the desk.

'You are to be interviewed by the Niz's Prefect,' he said confidentially. This did not sound like good news to me. 'Have you got your letter with you?'

'Safe in my pocket,' Panthera said. 'I never go out without it.'

Lourana did not smile. Presently we were approached by a young Har dressed in tight-fitting grey, who requested us to follow him to the Prefect's office. His hands were gloved, his eyebrows plucked bare. Lourana insisted on accompanying us, although the Prefect's underling made it clear that he was far from happy about it. I presumed we were being honoured in a way that Lourana was unworthy of sharing. I said, 'This Har is employed by us; he is our guide, our teacher in the lore of Maudrahness. His vocation was outlined personally by the Aghama, I believe.'

The underling gave me a hard look, but nodded his head briefly at Lourana.

'Remember,' Lourana said as we were taken away, 'do not speak unless you are spoken to. Better still, do not speak at all. Let me do the talking.'

The Prefect's office was on the third floor. We climbed a wide, shallow staircase carpeted in dark blue. The office itself was immense, ridiculously so. White, marble floor, ten foot drapes of dark purple velvet, windows all along one wall offering a view of the square and one large, gleaming desk. A gigantic portrait of a Har I presumed to be Ariaric hung on the wall behind it, so stylised it was impossible to tell if he looked anything like Wraxilan. The Prefect stood up as we entered and dismissed his minion with an imperious wave of his hand. Aware that we were outlanders, he addressed himself directly to Lourana. This was a complicated procedure, involving a lot of words, but where very little was actually *said*. The Prefect seemed satisfied by it, however. He nodded and sat down, scanning the papers that Lourana had brought with him from the reception hall.

'Panthera Jael,' the Prefect said. Lourana shot Panthera a quick glance, nodded. 'That is I, tiahaar,' Panthera replied in his best clear, regal voice.

'Your letter of introduction, if you would be so kind ...' The Prefect held out his hand. To me, he was an unimpressive Har, medium stature, unremarkable in feature or style; soft yet mean. Panthera stonily handed him the letter. The Prefect looked up, caught my eye, sniffed disdainfully, shook the letter and began to read. Gripped by a spasm of annoyance, I wanted to stare at this insignificant creature, perhaps wither him to dust. It shouldn't be difficult. He examined the letter for far too long; maybe he was a pathetically slow reader, but I took it as measured insult. Really, the letter was nothing to do with him at all. Such things were for the eyes of Sykernesse staff alone. Lacking in glory, the Prefect made the most of his brief moment of power over us.

'Lalasa, I understand, a courtier of the third tier and a valet of the Archon's consort ...' We all made various noises of assent. 'Hmm, well, your application will be passed on. Perhaps in a week or so ...' Here the Prefect sniffed again in an insulting and derogatory manner. 'You must appreciate we are plagued by outlanders' petitions constantly. Many claim to have relatives in the Royal House. You must wait your turn, I'm afraid.'

That was when I decided I'd had enough. I've suffered most insults in my time, but never have I had it implied that I was a parasite. Fighting with a red mist before my eyes, I found I had the Prefect by his collar, and had half-dragged him over his desk. Clearly, he was unused to such behaviour. His eyes were so round, I could see the whites all about them. 'Excuse *me*, tiahaar,' I said, 'but I feel you have misconstrued the urgency of our request. We expect to be presented at the palace tomorrow at the latest, and would be grateful if you could see to it immediately. Not only is my companion a close relative of Lalasa, but I am an old friend of the Lion himself. I feel he might be upset if I am forced to wait ...'

For a moment or two the Prefect actually considered whether I was telling the truth or not. He looked once at the door, but decided not to summon help. I was Algomalid; I doubt if the Prefect was even Acantha. His will was like butter. He extracted himself from my hold, took great care to avoid my eyes, and wriggled back into his seat. His neck was red. He coughed to hide his embarrassment.

'You must forgive me, tiahaara; an oversight. Return to this office first thing in the morning and I will arrange for you to be accompanied to Sykernesse.' He handed me Ferminfex's letter. 'Here, take good care of this; it is precious.'

Lourana led the way stiffly from the room. Once outside in the corridor he allowed himself the luxury of one or two repressed outbursts.

'You are both insane!' he decided. 'Tomorrow, the Niz will be waiting for you! You have blown your chances of entering Sykernesse. By Aghama, to assault the very person of the Prefect! I can't believe it!' He shook his head sadly.

'You worry unnecessarily,' I said, thumping him on the back. 'That wimp in there won't risk his neck. His mind is empty; no match for mine.'

'You are confident,' Lourana remarked drily.

I shrugged. 'Tomorrow the Prefect will have taken us to Sykernesse. The only disadvantage is that Ariaric may have been informed of my presence, thus ruining my surprise.'

'Shock,' Panthera corrected.

Lourana had us back there virtually at daybreak. Perhaps he had developed a fondness for us; we could not persuade him to accept any more money than he had originally asked for. 'Not even a couple of spinners for your nerves?' I asked. We were early. The Prefect had not yet arrived at work. A bland receptionist told us he was due at eight o'clock and, lo and behold, just as the clock above the stairs shuddered to the hour, the Prefect came bustling in through the door. He came over to us as soon as he saw us, smiling unctuously. I presumed he had already been in touch with Sykernesse about us.

'I myself shall take you to the palace,' he said, grinning horribly, 'but not until ten. May I suggest we offer you a light refreshment until then?'

Two hours. I doubted whether any refreshment in Maudrah could be termed as light.

We were taken to a small reception room, tucked away in the back of the building. Lourana tagged along behind, now more curious than loyal, I was sure. The room was pleasant enough, if featureless. The only decoration was another stern portrait of Ariaric that stared beadily into the room. I went to look up at it.

'Ferike work,' Panthera said, taking my arm. 'This style is formal, but far superior to that we saw in the Prefect's office.'

The face was nearly the same as I remembered it (which was a relief, because I'd still had doubts about the Archon's identity), but the mane of the Lion had been shorn. He wore a close-fitting hat which covered all of his hair, if indeed any remained.

'I hope you know what you're taking on,' Panthera said, squinting at the portrait critically. 'I'm afraid I'm finding it hard to place any resemblance between the Har you described to me and the face I'm looking at now.'

I didn't answer that, mainly because I agreed with him. Had I been wrong to come here? Would my caste elevation be enough for me to cope with what might follow? I was going to meet a stranger without arming myself with weapons or foreknowledge. Beside me, I could sense Panthera's echo of my mood; fear and resignation, plus a certain relief that he had a relative in Sykernesse.

After a brief, but uncomfortable wait, a servant knocked on the door, bringing us a tray of cinnamon-milk served in cups of white china and a plate of hard, sweet biscuits. The drink was too sweet, but its aftertaste was pleasant, a hint of earth and bitterness. Presently, another door opened behind us to admit a pair of scantily-adorned entertainers. They bowed to us silently and then proceeded to enact a rather lurid drama, which involved too much scourging and suffering to be classed as entertainment. Panthera and I exchanged quizzical glances. Was this normal practice in Maudrah? It was certainly a place of weird contrasts. A reputation of brutality, yet a society that appeared pious and humble. A ballet of bureaucracy followed by a performance of bestiality. I asked Lourana to explain.

He looked surprised. 'I can't understand why you ask this. Surely, one of the first things you learned after Inception was that without pain, pleasure cannot exist. Beauty is worthless without

284

the contrast of ugliness. An honest society must learn to balance these things. Justice and outrage. Strength and meekness, aggression and humility …'

'In other words, a society of ridiculous extremes,' I said, rather pompously. 'On the journey here you spoke of blood debts, a need to make amends for the past and yet Maudrah is regarded as one of the most power-hungry, blood-thirsty tribes of Jaddayoth. You must admit, these two facets do not really make sense.'

'A diamond is multi-faceted, surely,' Lourana answered, just as pompously, before popping a biscuit into his mouth, munching in relish, while staring with shining eyes at the performance.

I couldn't watch it. There were too many unpleasant reminders of Piristil within it. Panthera looked positively green. His sickly drink was untouched, developing a thick skin on its surface. Those two hours passed with agonising slowness.

The Prefect returned at ten minutes to ten. By that time, the bizarre entertainers had gone. 'It is my pleasure to escort you to the palace,' he said, savouring the words. An honour for him as well then.

Sykernesse has three spires. One, it is said, to celebrate the birth of each of Ariaric's sons. The Prefect took us there by public conveyance, a car very similar to Lourana's. We'd left our guide behind us. There was no way the Prefect would let him follow us into the Palace. In a way, I was sorry to say goodbye to him. His knowledge of Maudrah had made us feel safe; now we felt alone. Sykernesse is surrounded by a high, impenetrable wall. Cages upon the wall contain the remains of condemned traitors, or perhaps Hara who had accidentally fallen over in the street. I shuddered. What in Aghama's name was I doing here? Madness. We were the cause of some minor fuss at the Main Gate as we sought entrance. The Prefect argued unintelligibly with the guards. Administration assistants were summoned to indulge in more earnest discussion, scanning forms and lists carried on clipboards. Panthera and I took the liberty of reclining back in the car to smoke. We'd had two cigarettes each by the time the problems were smoothed out. Then the car lifted itself with a sigh and swept grandly inside the shadow of the gates. The Formal Entrance to Sykernesse revealed itself in morning splendour. Wide, white steps, rows of columns, carved doors, heavy banners lifting sluggishly in a faint breeze. Braceleted ravens stalked and flapped and grumbled along marble terraces and velvet lawns. A groom, leading two glossy, enormous horses, excused himself as he crossed our path. The Prefect directed the car's driver to veer towards a smaller side door. The grandness of the front entrance was intended for the Archon and visiting lords alone. The side entrance was still fairly impressive though. We were ushered into a wide, dark passage by a grave and gracious servant and conducted across a polished hall. The Prefect followed us into a formal salon, furnished in deep crimson. I was beginning to doubt whether we would ever get to see the Archon himself. It was doubtful whether Ariaric, or even his staff, ever ventured onto the ground floor other than to leave the palace. The Prefect asked us to sign a document. Rather carelessly, I just scrawled my name without reading it. Panthera spent some minutes trying to scan the text, but just signed it and tossed it back at the Prefect in disgust after being unable to decipher the official jargon.

'Just a formality,' the Prefect insisted sweetly, folding it tidily into an oblong. 'We like to keep a record of all foreign visitors to Oomadrah. Now, if you would care to take a seat, someone should be along shortly to see to you.' He backed from the room, bowing and smiling.

Panthera made an eloquent sign at the door with his fingers; a rare gesture for him. 'Now what?' he asked accusingly. 'Cal, we could be well on our way to Roselane now.'

'Don't remind me,' I said.

'Ah, prepared to admit you made a mistake then?' He smiled smugly.

I shook my head. 'No. Let's wait and see, shall we.'

He laughed. 'Yes, let's see. You know, I never thought Oomadrah would be like this, did you?'

'No. I didn't think *anywhere* would be like this nowadays.'

'What do you mean?'

'Only that life before Wraeththu would have held little pleasure for you, my pantherine.' He raised his brows, but we were interrupted. The door burst open and a tawny-haired Har, dressed in white, virtually exploded into the room. He looked around quickly, raking a hand through his hair when he saw us sitting apprehensively on the nearest sofa. He smiled, rushed forward.

'Greetings cousin,' he said. 'Whichever one of you *is* my cousin.'

'Lalasa?' Panthera enquired hopefully. He extended his hand which the Har took in his own.

'Ah, Lahela's son; I should have known. Yes, I'm Lalasa. Now, what godforsaken reason brought you to this little nest of vipers?'

'Of course, the rigours of Maudrah society are somewhat relaxed in Sykernesse,' Lalasa told us, as he poured us coffee. Servants hovered in the background, anxious to be at hand should he need them. I admired the way he was so convincingly oblivious of them. He was a typical Kalamah, I suppose. It was easy to see that he shared Lahela's blood. 'We get quite a lot of outlanders here,' he continued, 'many visitors, many Hara presented at court. Elisyin won't have Maudrah restrictions anywhere near his apartments. Even the Niz aren't welcome there, except for Wrark Fortuny, but he's a friend of Ariaric's, so that's different. How long are you planning on staying here? What the hell do you want? I can't believe you've just come to see me.'

'Well, we haven't,' I agreed bluntly. 'I want to meet Ariaric.'

Lalasa did not gasp, or even change his expression. 'That figures,' he said, rather enigmatically. 'If you're from Megalithica, you can expect to be sent on to Garridan rather swiftly. Our beloved Archon does little to encourage faces from the past to remain here. I guess it embarrasses him or something ... I doubt if he'll kick you out straight away though, and he'll certainly secure a good place for you in Garridan before he does ...'

'I don't think you understand,' I said. 'I'm not looking for a permanent position.'

'Aren't you? Forgive this indiscretion, you know, mentioning the terrible word, but a lot of Uigenna have headed this way, thinking that now Ariaric has his own little kingdom, they'll be able to sponge off his good fortune and hard work. We have to be careful.'

'Ah, so it's no secret he was once with the Uigenna then?'

Lalasa pulled a face. 'Oh, *please*! He never was! You'd best remember that, my friend. Ariaric only left Megalithica because things got a little out of hand over there. He didn't like it.'

'That's the official version?'

'It is.'

'Do any of the visitors from back home ever get to meet him in the flesh?'

'Are you kidding?' Lalasa pulled yet another expressive face.

'No, I'm serious.'

'Well, what do you think? I'm with Elisyin. I get to hear things. No-one with Uigenna blood gets past the first floor, believe me. They might get sent on with a full purse, but he won't see them, not even for old time's sake. If you knew Ariaric before, best not mention it. Understand?'

'Yes. Unfortunately, I was rather indiscreet with the Prefect. I mentioned I was an old friend of the Lion.'

Lalasa shrugged. 'I wouldn't worry too much about that. The fool's an insect, a pen-pusher. He has no influence and no contacts of importance here.'

'If I write a letter to the Archon, will you see that he gets it?'

'No, not on your life. Write to Elisyin. I'll probably be able to get you onto his floor. He likes having pretty Hara about the place and you'll certainly suit requirements there. Just don't mention past alliances. Say Ferminfex sent you to tout for business amongst the idle rich or something. Panthera, can you paint portraits?'

'I can paint anything,' he answered sourly.

'Good, that's the way in then. All of Elisyin's court are extraordinarily vain. Let's get cracking.' He called for paper and a pen. Servants were driven into a panic of activity. Whatever I might have said about Kalamah indolence before, forget it. We were installed in a suite on the second floor within an hour.

The opulence was exquisitely understated. We had two rooms, plus a bathroom, which was modest by Sykernesse standards, but probably more than we deserved. After all, we were far from official envoys from Ferike. The apartment had an air of impermanence about it, as if all of its previous occupants had never stayed there very long. All the furnishings were terracotta red and brown and cream. Panthera examined an object hung on the wall.

'What's this?' he asked, pressing various buttons.

Lalasa snatched it from his hands. 'A telephone,' he said. 'Be careful.'

'A what?' Panthera was only used to thought-transference units; even I was slightly surprised.

'A primitive form of communication device once used by men,' I explained to him. 'Well, it looks as if we might be back in the twentieth century, doesn't it!'

'We're not that far out of it yet,' Lalasa remarked. He told us that Elisyin would receive us later in the afternoon. I wasn't convinced that the Lion's consort had any interest in us at all really, but obviously Lalasa had no small degree of influence with him. No doubt he had dropped heavy hints about how grateful he'd be to have his relative from Jael received at court.

'I don't feel safe here,' Panthera decided once Lalasa had left us alone. 'It all seems so genteel on the surface, but I feel that it is just on the surface, don't you? I feel as if it would be very easy to, you know, fall out of favour.'

'Ah Thea,' I replied, pulling the rank of my experience on him, 'when you've been in as many royal houses as I have, you'll realize they're all the same. Even Jael to a degree. A code of etiquette must be maintained, an elegance supposed to transcend the grubbings of humanity. As a race, you'll find that Wraeththu are suckers for pomp and circumstance; they love playing Olympians. You just have to know how to play the game to survive. It's not that difficult.'

'Hmm, as I recall, when we first met, you were working as a kanene after having "grubbed" around the country for some time. Did you forget the rules, Cal, or was it a voluntary choice to opt out?'

'I always underestimate you,' I said.

'Perhaps you look on me as a child,' he replied. 'I've found that first generation Hara always do have a slightly condescending attitude to those of us who are pure-born, as if we haven't "lived". That's not fair, is it? Can you really say I haven't experienced anything?'

'I wouldn't dream of it, my dear. All I'm saying is, I've lived with Varrs, I've lived with Gelaming — even if it was under restraint. I know this scenario. Take away the grand buildings, the luxuries, the clothes and you have the leader's clique of the Uigenna. It's not that different.'

'I hope you're right.'

'So do I.'

Sykernesse
'I must be satisfied with my heart ...'
W.B. Yeats, The circus animals' desertion

23

I always expect the consorts of Wraeththu leaders to be effeminate, gentle creatures, whose sole purpose is usually for the generation of heirs. Elisyin was an exception to this rule. His hair was hacked short, consciously unkempt, his attitude restless and self-willed. From the moment I first set eyes on him, I could see why he wouldn't have anything to do with the petty restrictions of Maudrah society. First, it would bore him to distraction; second, it would get in the way of more important things. Elisyin liked to be direct. Form and ceremony held no interest, no comfort for him. Ariaric probably adored and slightly feared him. Terzian had once felt that way for Cobweb; perhaps I was being too subjective about Elisyin because of that. Elisyin was not tall, but as graceful and aesthetic as you'd expect from a well-bred Ferike. He did not wear cosmetics except for painting his fingernails deepest indigo. His ears were pierced at least a dozen times by earrings of all shapes and sizes, but he wore no other jewellery. His suite of rooms was sumptuous, but untidy; it did not feel particularly royal.

Lalasa led us through a gossiping cluster of courtiers to the couch where Elisyin was presiding over a game of cards. Nobody seemed to be taking it very seriously. The consort of the Archon smiled politely at us when were introduced, but it was clear that he had little real interest. Many people, seeking positions in

Sykernesse, must be presented to him in this way, so that two more new faces were just too unremarkable for words. Elisyin didn't ask us why we were there; he didn't care. I have to confess that it pricked my pride badly. I wanted to show him how different we were to the sycophants that surrounded him. It angered me that we should appear as such. It would have been madness to consider attempting mind-touch with this elevated Har, but consider it I did. Only the desire to remain 'faceless' for a while prevented it. Vanity was still something I had to get under control. Lalasa went to great pains to impress on us how privileged we were, being introduced into such august company. He showed us off to a few of Elisyin's cronies, some of whom actually stirred themselves to take an interest in us. One or two Hara mentioned they would like to have their portrait painted. Panthera gritted his teeth, smiled and talked about making preliminary sketches. He considered such things beneath his art, but hid it well. After an eternity of endless chit-chat he came and whispered in my ear; 'Roselane!'

'Soon,' I promised. It shut him up but we both knew that wasn't exactly truthful.

For three days we played the game. For three days, we rose late in the morning, dined like kings, went on tours of Oomadrah with Lalasa, said the right things to the right people. In the evenings, we visited the theatre, the horse-races, the art galleries, all within Sykernesse itself. All so civilized.

Panthera was going crazy. 'You're wasting time, Cal,' he said. 'What the hell are you doing here? This is madness. Have you forgotten Elhmen and Sahen so quickly?'

Oh, I knew he was right. Elhmen seemed a million miles away, Immanion but a dream. The way things were going, it seemed unlikely we would ever get to see Ariaric. Elisyin's people rarely interacted with those of the third floor. We didn't even know if the Archon was in residence or not. On the evening of the third day, I was prepared to admit I'd been wrong about diverting our journey. What had I been expecting? A fiery confrontation with the Lion to show him how much I'd achieved despite having been kicked out of the Uigenna? You see, I couldn't even be sure of my motives any more. Perhaps it was simply pride. I said to Panthera, 'Tomorrow we leave', and he had the grace not to say anything. 'I told you so' would have been just too obvious. We began to pack our bags and there was a knock at the door. Panthera looked up at me dismayed; presentiment. It was Lalasa. He didn't even notice we were packing.

'You've got an hour to get ready,' he said. 'Look your best. Ariaric has returned from the Natawni border and there's going to be a celebration in his honour. Elisyin asked if you'd like to come.' (I bet!) 'It may be the only chance you'll get, Cal. Make a move — now.' He swept out before we could say anything.

Panthera did not look exactly elated. He stared at me meaningfully, no doubt wishing he'd bullied me into leaving the day before. 'Be careful,' he said.

The bulk of Sykerness is four-storied. The ground floor is the domain of the servants and staff, offices and reception rooms for visitors, kitchens and store-rooms. The first floor houses the offices of state, suites for visitors worth more than the ground floor but not high-ranking enough to qualify for a suite on the second or third, conference room, libraries and the living quarters of those Hara who administrate that floor. The second floor, as I've already intimated, is the territory of Elisyin, his friends and staff. The third is Ariaric's and the province of the Niz. They alone have access to the towers and spires of Sykernesse, the observatories and private temples. Most of the court, including the Lion's family, reside on the second floor. And it was there that the celebration to welcome the Archon home was held.

Lalasa took charge of us, ushering us into the right corridors, 'Stay by me,' he said. 'Whatever you do, Cal, don't attempt to speak with Ariaric. He may notice you. He may not. You are in the hands of Fate. Tomorrow you may be requested to continue your journey east at once. We shall have to see.'

The gathering was surprisingly informal, held in a large, but low-ceilinged room, where the colours of palest dove grey and darkest indigo melded to a refined and tasteful effect and the lights were discrete, flattering Hara who passed beneath them. Tables were set out at one end of the room, laden with food, but there were few seats. Servants glided silently among the guests, supplying glasses of dry, iced wine. Hara mingled, conversing softly, but all eyes kept flicking to the doors. Panthera and I accepted a glass of wine each and then secreted ourselves in a corner to watch the proceedings. My heart was racing. Lalasa hovered close by, keeping an eye on us. Presently, Elisyin made a grand entrance, and we were witness to a mind-boggling display of sycophancy; the court virtually fell to their knees as he passed among them. Elisyin appeared not to notice this. He had an autocratic young Har on each arm, whom Lalasa told us were his sons. At his heels came a tall, robed figure, who kept his hands hidden in his sleeves. That, we were informed, was Wrark Fortuny, High Priest of the Niz. It was the first Niz we had seen since entering Sykernesse. Panthera and I quickly became bored by it all. We were too insignificant for anyone to come and speak to us and we couldn't help scorning everyone's fawning behaviour towards Elisyin.

After half an hour or so, the elite of Ariaric's army made their entrance. More swooning and grovelling on behalf of the court. Panthera rolled his eyes at me. But the best was yet to come.

Presently, Wrark Fortuny took his place on a raised dais at the far end of the room. The music which had been playing so softly I'd barely noticed it ceased immediately, and there was an audible sibilance from the room, which quickly lapsed to silence. Fortuny raised his hands, his head, and closed his eyes. He took a deep, deep breath. Exhaled.

'As you are gathered here,' he intoned in a ringing voice, 'so shield your eyes from the Light as it falls upon you. Keen your welcome for the Son of Brightness, the Breather of Life, the Stern Deliverer of Justice, Semblence of the Aghama on this Blighted Earth; Ariaric, Archon of Oomadrah, known also as the Lion for the Intentness of His Gaze, the Soft Walker of the Deserts, whose Eyes are the Twin Lights of Destiny and have looked upon the Mysteries. As the Spirit of the Aghama resides in Him, so do we recognize the Goddua within the Har, and avert our eyes until he gives us leave to see ...'

Within the room, every chin sank towards every breast. Breath was held as a single breath. Panthera and I exchanged a nervous glance. 'Avert your eyes!' Lalasa hissed at us desperately. For the time being, I looked at the floor. Out of the corner of my eye, I saw the wide doors onto the corridor outside thrown open. A clarion was sounded; five, sweet, clear notes. Fortuny spoke a blessing and Ariaric, accompanied by his closest friends, came into the room. I had to look up. Had to. It was a vital moment to me, a sweeping clean of the path of time so that two points could meet and blossom in understanding. I did not raise my head; I strained my eyes to see. I was the only one. Ariaric turned and smiled at his friends, who smiled back. He approached his consort Elisyin, whose head was bowed as everyone elses, and kissed him on the cheek. Elisyin raised his head, nodded. He was saying, 'I am fine, beloved'. I'd known that language myself once. Fortuny, inhaled deeply, as if he could smell their contact. He opened his eyes and Ariaric raised his hand. 'Look now upon the Light!' Fortuny cried exhuberantly, and everyone sank as one to their knees. A few outlanders like Panthera and myself were standing rather self-consciously around the edge of the room. The Archon took a quick look at us. Perhaps he was always afraid of seeing old faces there. He looked me right in the eye, but gave no flicker of recognition. Even so, I knew he had recognized me. I felt his blood run momentarily cold, his heart miss a beat. For a second, we were both back there in the past, knees touching as we squatted in an old warehouse store-room, he with a cut palm, me with a crazy fear. He had been so strong then, but I'd faced my fear. I'd lived it through. I had a son now; somewhere. What of Ariaric? Had he grown too? I was Algomalid, but to his people, the Lion was a god. An incarnation of the Aghama. Impossible. But I could not dispute it … yet. I had been mistaken about his hair, he had not cut it off. Whatever austerities his new role demanded, he was too fond of his mane to lose it. It was braided tight against his head, down his back, showing off the bones of his face and neck, and darker in colour than before. Obviously, he'd been working on his inner balance. The aggressive masculinity had been tempered by serenity and grace. I expected his voice would be softer. He said, 'Rise, my people,' and they did so. His voice *was* softer, but it carried far. I could feel his power, which may just have been confidence. As Lalasa had said, we would have to see. Every face in that room was shining with pleasure; how they loved him. I just watched. He kept looking at Elisyin and Elisyin would grimace back and I wondered about what jokes they made about these fawning Hara when they were alone together. Perhaps they didn't joke at all. For a moment, I was intensely envious. The thought, 'That could have been me' sprang instantly to mind, but it was not as potential consort to the Lion that I thought it. No. For perhaps the first time, I found myself thinking, 'If I had accepted Thiede's offer, if I had gone with him to Immanion, would there have come a time when I would have met Pell's eyes across a room like this? Would we have smiled together, sharing our secret, savouring it?' It was a far more complicated feeling than that, but difficult to put into words. Panthera put his hand on my arm and brought me back. Perhaps he had guessed what I'd been thinking.

'Is he as you remember him?' he asked me.

I shook my head. 'No. Greatly changed ... maybe.'

I knew he would speak to me soon.

The evening wore on, swirling around us. The music became louder, voices higher as more wine was consumed. I kept thinking about the difference between this and life in the city below, and commented upon it to Lalasa.

He smiled. 'Not really double standards,' he said. 'In ancient times, men did not expect to live like gods, neither would they have dared to criticize the way in which their gods conducted themselves. Ariaric is Divinity in Maudrah; his behaviour is beyond reproach, similarly the behaviour of his court.'

'And what exactly is Goddua?' Panthera asked.

'Simple,' Lalasa answered. 'It is the God and Goddess combined; as are all of us.'

Panthera was ready to argue. 'God and Goddess cannot be termed as 'he' surely,' he said.

'You think it should be changed then?' Lalasa asked. 'Should a new term be thought of that is as androgynous as we are?'

I sighed, and let my attention wander. It bored me too much to point out that theirs was a subject that had been argued dry about thirty years ago. Who cares whether we call ourselves he, she or it? Not me. I scanned the faces in the room, but could not see the Lion anywhere. Many Hara had drifted outside, spreading themselves throughout Elisyin's apartments. I decided to leave Panthera to it and sidled away. I wanted to explore, and yes, I was looking for Ariaric. Who wouldn't have?

I wandered around the second floor, drink in hand, looking in every room I came across. Nobody spared me a second glance. I passed a mirror, looked into it and thought, 'Yes, OK, that'll do.' I was rehearsing what I would say to him when I found him. It was all very dramatic. Almost surreal, but absorbing. Eventually, I found myself in empty corridors, without even a servant around. Walking mechanically, I found myself at the foot of a great staircase, that disappeared into a velvet gloom. I walked right up it. Darkness fell about me like a veil and the sounds of merriment seemed very far away. Miles away. Before me, tall, gleaming pillars stood sentinel to a cathedral calm. The ceiling was lost in shadow high above me. This was Ariaric's floor. I shouldn't be here. Perhaps I shouldn't continue, but turn around and go back to Panthera. If I was found here, it could mean unpleasantness, but even as I thought this, I was walking, walking, and the staircase was soon far behind me. Was Phaonica like this, noble, grand and silent? I could sense melancholy, but probably only because I wanted to. Something was leading me, of that I was sure. I let it happen. How could I have known which turnings to take, which stairs to climb? How could I have found my way to the studded door that opened upon the base of a spire? Almost in a trance, I closed the door behind me and began to climb. Round and round and up and up. I could hear the wind whistling its single, mournful note and feel the air become colder. Up and up. Panthera was far, far away from me and I climbed a finger of stone, distanced from all that I knew.

At the top of the curling steps, I came out, breathless, into a room with a black and white tiled floor. Black pillars and curtains; the smell of incense. This was a temple. Before me, I could see an altar supporting only a white, tasselled cloth and a drawn sword. Beyond this, was a statue. Bland of face, one hand raised, the other palm upwards in its lap. The face was a face I knew, a face etched indelibly on my brain; Thiede's. Perfumed smoke blew across its features as it smiled at the room. And kneeling before this altar was a figure robed in crimson. Ariaric, Wraxilan, Lion of Oomar or Oomadrah, what did it matter? I had found him. That was all. He appeared to be deep in meditation, his hair unbound, but ropy with oil. I crept up behind him, cat-footed, unsure of what I would say or do. He raised his head, but did not turn around.

'I did not think you would come,' he said. 'I hoped you wouldn't.'

So these were the first words. Disappointing? What had I expected? Surprise for one thing.

Ariaric sighed and got to his feet, his knees cracking. He faced me, rubbing his eyes. 'Cold in the marshes,' he said, smiling. 'I've seen too many battles, I think. Perhaps I've outgrown them, or is that a euphemism for saying I fear I'm growing older?'

'No-one will know that until some poor Har dies of old age,' I answered. 'All the Hara I've know who have died have met, shall we say, untimely ends?' (Flying bone, blood, a scream, a horse's scream. No! I deny this image.)

The Lion of Oomadrah nodded and chuckled to himself. He did not hear my thoughts. 'A point well taken, my friend.' We looked at each other. He shook his head. 'Ah, Cal, we cannot meet as strangers.' He held out his arms to me and we embraced as brothers. I felt like weeping. This was not happening at all how I'd planned it. Ariaric grunted affectionately and then held me away from him. 'In meetings hearts beat closer,' he said.

'In blood,' I responded.

'In blood,' he added quietly. His hands dropped to his sides. Now he could think of nothing to say.

'Do I take it you were expecting me then?' I asked. Why on earth I hadn't anticipated that, I cannot understand.

'It was a ... possibility,' he said guardedly. 'Look, we cannot speak here. We'll go somewhere more comfortable. Please.' He indicated the door.

'One thing,' I said, facing the altar once more. 'Why is it that the Archon of Maudrah pays homage to the image of Thiede the Gelaming?'

Ariaric stared at me for a moment. 'Ah, he didn't tell you *that* then!'

'Tell me what?'

'Cal, all Hara worship the Aghama don't they? Thiede *is* the Aghama.'

A long time ago, a mutant runaway came alive into the city … Thiede? Frightened, and dangerous in his fear … (Thiede?!) Wretched, helpless, abused mutant freak. Our progenitor. Thiede. Reviled as vermin, revered as a god, full of hate and bitterness at his condition; it had flowered into an insatiable appetite for power. And he had succeeded. He had taken it, bleeding, with his bare hands from the under-nourished, pigeon-chest of mankind. Thiede. Yes, it made sense. By any god that still lived, the megalomaniac that styled himself our deity earned my respect in those moments. Whatever his faults, he had fought against incredible odds and won. Now, presumably, he was laughing. I don't blame him. It's a good joke. I could feel things beginning to tilt into place a little when the Lion told me that. Looking back, I don't think I was altogether surprised. I should have realized Thiede's mystique went beyond mere charisma. Many hara have that. Thiede was the first. He made us happen: Aghama.

'High-ranking Hara of most tribes are aware of this now,' Ariaric said, looking at the statue.

'Obviously I'm not high-ranking enough,' I said. Ariaric looked at me quizzically.

'I hope you don't mean that.'

'Of course I don't mean that.' I laughed, a forced, harsh sound. 'I have no tribe,' Ariaric winced.

'Downstairs, please,' he said.

So, now it appears that Thiede is truly the guiding force of Wraeththu. A concept that poses more questions as fast as it answers others. How would it affect me? I'd have to think about it.

As we walked together along lofty, panelled corridors towards his suite, Ariaric became formal. He apologized eloquently for the dismissive way in which Panthera and myself had been treated by his staff. 'I hope you weren't insulted,' he said, 'but unfortunately only Fortuny and myself were privy to the information about your journeys in Jaddayoth.'

'You're wrong there,' I butted in, 'there's nothing secret about it. Just about everyone seems to know. They know more than I do, in fact.'

The Lion ignored these remarks. 'Elisyin did not know,' he continued smoothly. 'I had hoped to be back in Sykernesse long before you reached Maudrah, but things have dragged on a little in Natawni.'

'Trying to make peace were you?'

He smiled benignly at my clumsy sarcasm. 'Trying to secure the border actually. Natawni would have the world believe that Maudrah are their wicked persecutors. They prefer to keep quiet about the lightning raids they make upon Maudrah territory, the thieving from Maudrah settlements, the frightening of their inhabitants. Not all Maudrah Hara are warriors, you know. Most are herders, especially in the North.' He sighed. 'However, I hardly think the differences between Maudrah and Natawni can be solved overnight ...'

'There will always be differences, surely, as long as you insist on trying to make all of Jaddayoth Maudrah,' I said. 'How can you blame anyone objecting to that? Although you and your court live like kings, it's rather a different story for the Hara down in the street, isn't it. Do you know how they live? Have you ever seen? Or is that the province of the Niz and beyond your control?'

'Our people are not unhappy,' he answered vaguely. 'When the time is right, their society will blossom. Winter-time is necessary, a time of replenishing. I'm sure I don't need to tell you that most Maudrah came from Megalithica originally, and had to leave it pretty quickly.'

'Who decides when it's spring-time then? The Niz?'

'Yes.' Such a direct reply surprised me. 'Here in Sykernesse, we are privileged; I know that. In Maudrah Hara are expiating the sins of the past. You were there, Cal; you should understand. It's a novitiate state; they are learning.'

'Your education was rather different, wasn't it?'

He smiled ruefully. 'I cannot argue with you, Cal, but you shouldn't really pass opinions on what you don't fully understand, should you. This way ...'.

He assumed I knew a lot more than I did, especially about

himself. I wondered if I could find out what he had heard about me without giving my ignorance away. The last time we had met, he'd had me cast out into the cold night of North Megalithican society – if such chaos could be termed as that. He had been a big fish in a small pond. Now, both pond and fish had grown somewhat. He directed me through an enormous, dark doorway and closed it behind us. As I took in the grand opulence of the room, I was still talking, saying things that perhaps should have been kept for later, but I couldn't wait. The main reason I was there was to say them, after all.

'You've apologized for your people treating us with disrespect,' I said, 'but don't you think that now is the time to apologize for what you did to me in the past? A second-class suite of rooms can't really compare with being ejected into a burnt-out wasteland teeming with blood-hungry psychos, can it!'

Ariaric winced once more. Gracefully. 'You have a long memory Cal.'

'I've lived with it.'

'Have you come all this way just to rake over old coals? The fire has been long cold, surely.'

'Maybe, but I suffered first-degree burns from it, so did Zack.'

The Lion stared at me thoughtfully for a moment. I wish I hadn't spoken; it had sounded so peevish, even if correct. I went to sit on the floor in front of the fire to escape his eyes. The rooms of a king; it showed. 'So here we are,' I said, looking fixedly at a green and gold tapestry hanging above the fireplace. 'It seems Wraxilan is no more. His slate has been wiped clean so that Ariaric the Lifebreather can take his place. Are they that different?'

Ariaric laughed good-humouredly behind me. I heard the clink of glass.

'By Aghama, I really got to you once, didn't I!'

'Dear me, and there I was thinking the feeling was mutual.'

He handed me a crystal glass over my shoulder. I could not feel his warmth; I was too nervous. I drank; a fiery spirit tempered by a cordial of lemon and herbs.

'Cal, I had a lot to learn. I learnt it. There is nothing more to it than that. You've come a long way too, haven't you?'

'Have I? I had hoped to surprise you.' I was deviating from the subject but he went along with it.

'You did. Satisfied? Even though I'd had word you might show up here, the moment I saw you tonight filled me with … what? Terror, shock, awe? Maybe all three. It took me back.' *I know it did.* 'A long way back. I want you to know that the choice you made then was the right one.'

'Oh? Why?' I turned to look at him then.

'Well, after you … left the Uigenna, I chose another to host my heirs. We didn't know enough. I wanted a son too quickly. The Har died. I'm glad you refused me.'

I nodded. 'Yes,' I said.

'Did you ever regret your decision?'

I suppose that was brave of him, or completely egotistical. I wavered. I could not lie. 'Sometimes,' I said.

That must have satisfied him. He smiled. 'Well, it's over now isn't it; all of it. You want me to apologize for kicking you out of the Uigenna? Are you sure? I'd say it was probably a blessing.'

I raised my glass. 'Let's drink to that.' We drank for a moment in silence, then I said, 'Eliṣyin is a perfect consort for you.' I don't know what made me say it; I prefer not to think.

'I know,' Ariaric replied smoothly. 'He's given me three sons. All thoroughbreds like himself.'

'Three? Oh, as many as the fabled spires, of course! How come only two of them were there tonight? Is the third out accruing more land for his noble sire somewhere?'

'Hardly. He's dead.' He smiled gently. 'Don't look like that. The earth won't swallow you, however much you try. I'm not offended. How could you have known? We all have our tragedies to live with.'

'Don't we just!'

We looked askance at each other, over the goblet tops, between shuttered lids. We were strangers who thought that we ought to feel like friends. I was still wondering whether Wraxilan had moulted away from the core of Ariaric or had merely been hidden deep inside. The Cal that he'd once known had shed a hundred skins. Could he see that? I said, 'I thought I was fighting a battle, but I wasn't, was I. All along, I've been doing the right thing. I was want it. I still don't, but I've had no choice.'

trying so hard not to as well. How depressing.'

Ariaric may not have had the faintest idea what I was talking about, but he was too proud to admit it. He smiled only with his mouth and said, 'Learning?'

'Is that what they call it? I've certainly suffered; maybe I've learned. Remember the past and how they used to say that no-one should be dragged onto the Path against their will? I feel I've been tricked, not dragged, but the principle is the same.'

'Oh, come on, don't think you ever fooled me with that superficial, devil-may-care, live for today kick!' Ariaric scoffed. It was so honest; he meant it. 'You've always been there, Cal, if only on the scrubby bits along the side. And the Path is *hard*.'

'You don't have to tell me that. Don't insult me. I just didn't

'Bullshit!'

'It isn't!'

'It is. You could have run away any time, surely.'

'They said I couldn't.'

'They? Who are they?'

I narrowed my eyes. 'How much do you know about me?'

'Not much, but you obviously think it's important, so tell me.'

'You're a bitch, Wraxilan.'

He raised his eyebrows. So I told him. I began by saying, 'You're not the only Wraeththu herd leader who's wanted me firm against their sweaty little flank, you know.' It was the best way to tell it. Now it seemed like only gossip, all those secret thoughts I'd carried around with me for so long. Until I reached Jaddayoth. Shining country; I love you. I must also point out that at no time had I ever envisaged telling any of it to the Archon of Oomadrah. Now the blocks have been removed from my mind, it seems I have to gabble it out at every opportunity.

When I'd told him just about everything, Ariaric said, 'You've never really fought it have you! The Elhmen, the Sahale, the visions, the Jaels. You must have loved it. Every minute. You still do. Why kid yourself? Being the centre of attention has always appealed to you.' Knife straight to the heart, as always. He hadn't really changed.

'Are you saying I'm enjoying this?'

He raised his glass at me. 'Know thyself magician,' he said. 'You haven't spent much time in meditation have you. Why?'

'I have! Every evening once I returned to Jael! You don't know that you're talking about!'

'Oh, I think I do, Cal. Mainly because you haven't seen the blindingly obvious truth. I think you've only been skimming the surface; you're afraid of what you'll see in that beautiful head of yours, that's why. Funny. I never thought self-delusion was one of your faults. Other people, yes, but not yourself.'

I was speechless with anger. Such arrogance! Such conceit! How dare he! I'd poured out my heart to him and he treated it as a self-indulgent joke. What made it worse was the infuriating grin he had on his face.

'Use these rooms as your own for a while,' he said. 'Just sit and think about what I've said. Do more than think about it; face that truth. Recognize it. You might find it will help. I'll be back later.'

Ah, so he was a coward too! Were his observations so flimsy he had to leave the room? Obviously, he was afraid I'd knock holes in them. I seethed with fury. He left me alone for half an hour. I could have gone back to the second floor. I could have left the room. I didn't. I was numb. For five minutes, I didn't think anything at all and then I breathed. Deeply. Rhythmically. Drawing energy from the earth, sending it through my body; travelling inwards. OK, show me the worst, soul of mine. It did. And it hurt. But one thing I learned, that I'd known all along really; the answers weren't outside. No-one else was going to give them to me. *I* knew. It was in me somewhere. And Ariaric was right. A bitter draught to swallow, but swallow it I did. When I opened my eyes, I thought, 'Pell, I want you. I have always wanted you.' Any denials, any fighting I'd thought about were a sham. The truth was, I'd always wanted to go to Immanion, even in Thiede's tower, even on my darkest days in Thaine, but it had to be on my terms. Pride won't let me settle for anything less. I couldn't be the Tigron's lapdog because I knew I was worthy of equality. Pride? Yes, OK. A fault, maybe, but one that I knew. When I'd learned that Pell still lived, my first feeling, after the shock, had been joy. I'd wanted to see him, speak to him, but something had gone wrong, got in the way. What? Just pride? Or something more? Once I knew that I'd have the answer to everything.

Ariaric came in softly. I was still sitting, cross-legged in front of the fire. He put his hand on my shoulder and said, 'You still angry?'

I rested my cheek against his hand and said, 'No.'

He squatted beside me; we embraced. I found myself doing something I vigorously loathe. I was weeping. I said, 'Stop me doing this,' and Ariaric replied, 'No, it is part of you. Live it.'

Live it. We talked and drank and talked about all that happened to us, what we wanted for the future. Ariaric's story was an epic in itself and would take too long to relate. He told me he'd met Pell in Immanion.

'What's he like?' I asked. Here was someone who could really tell me.

Ariaric stretched out on the floor, held his glass to his chest and closed his eyes. 'Let me think,' he said, 'I want to get it right. He's got black hair.'

'No! Really?'

'Indeed. I liked him, even though he was rather cross with me and called me a, what was it?, "menace to all free-thinking Hara". He was right of course. I've learned since then. I was too full of revolutionary zeal and images of Uigenna atrocities. Progression was impossible when I was so full of self-loathing. Pell taught me that. He's frightening in a way because you can't see the steel inside him on the surface.'

'Really? Strange, I would never have described Pellaz as being steely, ever!'

'You must remember many years have past since you last saw him, Cal. Perhaps you should prepare yourself for the fact that he might be a completely different person now.'

'I have thought about that, obviously. I wish I knew more. Prepare me; tell me what you know.'

Ariaric smiled, stroked my hair. 'I don't envy you,' he said.

'That bad is it?'

He shook his head. 'Don't get me wrong. What I'm saying is I'm finding it very hard to equate the Pellaz you've told me about to the one I've met. They seem like entirely different people.'

'You sound like Panthera. He said something similar to me about you.'

Ariaric laughed. 'And have I turned out to be a monster?'

'No, but you used to be. Is that how you'd describe Pell then, a monster?'

'Yes, I suppose I would, in a way. Oh, not because he's fearsome to look at or malign or tyrannical, but because he has such power. You can almost see it, simmering inside him. Of course, I didn't get much opportunity to speak with him alone, but on my last night in Immanion, I was invited to dine with him ... and his consort. Pellaz spent most of the evening talking about Megalithica. Sorry, but your name wasn't mentioned once.'

'The consort ...' I began.

'You'll probably see,' Ariaric said carefully. 'The Tigrina is paying us a short visit very soon.'

'How soon?'

'The day after tomorrow. Of course, you could leave before then if you prefer ...'

'Are you serious?'

Ariaric shrugged. 'You may not like what you see. But you're welcome to stay.'

As if I could leave!

It was nearly dawn when I went back to the rooms I shared with Panthera. My companion was nowhere in sight but there was a note which read, 'Cal, you're so predictable' left on the pillow. I was piqued; it was unjustified after all. Aruna-type thoughts hadn't even crossed my mind when I'd been with Ariaric. I tried to sleep, but my mind was in turmoil. Pell seemed nearer to me. I wanted to see him now, this instant. I wanted to go to Roselane tomorrow, Immanion tomorrow. I also wanted to stay in Oomadrah so that I could see the Tigrina. I wondered if he knew about me too. If he did, it would be a confrontation that I'd relish. My claws were out. What was happening?

CHAPTER

24

The Arrival of the Tigrina

*'Then hate me when thou wilt; if ever,
      now;*

*Now, while the world is bent my deeds to
      cross,*

*Join with the spite of fortune, make me
      bow.'*

William Shakespeare, Sonnet X

Our bags remained packed. Panthera reappeared late the next morning; I did not ask him where he'd been. The news that I wished to remain in Sykernesse for a further couple of days did nothing to dispel the atmosphere of furious gloom that Panthera brought in with him. He did not ask me why, obviously having drawn his own inferences, which were undoubtedly way off the truth. Admittedly giving in to him, I said. 'Thea, the Tigrina is arriving in Oomadrah tomorrow. I want to be here.' He skewered me with a withering, condemning stare. Silence. 'You think I'm wrong then?'

He shrugged. 'Do what you like. I'm only along for the ride. As a matter of fact, I don't mind staying on in Sykernesse myself for a while, perhaps even after you leave for Roselane. If you ever do!'

I realized we were having an argument. 'Thea, I did not take aruna with Ariaric last night, if that's what's bothering you.'

'Not at all,' he replied smoothly. 'I'm in no position to censure you.'

I drew my own conclusions from that, even though they did seem rather unlikely. I wondered who had been the privileged Har to spend the previous night in Panthera's arms. It was not a train of thought that particularly thrilled me. Maybe I'd taken him for granted; my personal property because he was too scared or revolted to seek warmth from somebody new. Ah well, it seemed I'd been wrong. It caused a weird kind of tearing feeling inside me, as if the air was too big to fit into my lungs.

'I was telling the truth,' I said. 'I'm sorry I wandered off like that last night. I had to talk to him. Can't you understand that?'

Panthera did not answer me. He took some clothes into the bathroom to get changed, emerging some minutes later to announce, 'I'm meeting Lalasa now. See you later perhaps.' Then he was gone, and the door didn't even slam.

Ariaric sent for me around lunch-time. I'd spent the rest of the morning mooching about, realizing I really didn't relish having to travel on to Roselane alone. I'd got used to company. Lonely journeys reminded me too much of how I'd been before Thaine, and then I'd been out of my skull most of the time. I thought the hours were going to hang heavily over my head during miles and miles of sobriety. But how could I blame Panthera? Wasn't it entirely possible I'd discard him at a moment's notice should the outcome of all my travelling and soul-searching bode well for the alliance of Calanthe and the Tigron of Immanion? I can be despicable, yes, but not that despicable. Perhaps it would be best if Panthera and I did part company now. I dragged this mood along with me to the Lion's apartments, furiously wishing I hadn't when I saw who he'd got sitting round his dinner table with him. The gracious Elisyin, his two sons and Wrark Fortuny. Elevated company, in fact the best Sykernesse could provide.

'Is your friend not joining us?' Elisyin asked politely when I was shown into the room alone.

'No, I'm afraid he'd already made arrangements for the day when I received your invitation.'

'What a shame.'

'Yes, isn't it.'

I took my allotted place and proceeded to grin and grimace my way through the meal. Ariaric passed me one or two shrewd glances, but made no comment. He probably thought I was worked up about the imminence of the Tigrina's visit. Elisyin went through the whole procedure of apologizing for his dismissive treatment of me.

'I had no idea you were a friend of Aric's,' he said. 'You should have mentioned it.'

'I would have, but I'd been advised against it,' I replied. 'I thought all visitors of suspect origin were swiftly sent on their way.'

'They usually are,' Ariaric agreed. 'Otherwise I'd be swamped with useless Uigenna rejects all hoping for a ride on my back. It's happened before and will no doubt happen again.'

'Would you like to change your rooms?' Elisyin asked. 'We have better suites available.'

'No, it doesn't matter.'

I waited until half-way through the meal until I asked the most important question. 'Was it the Gelaming who told you I might come here?' There was a moment's silence, and then Fortuny cleared his throat. He had hardly spoken before.

'No, it was Tel-an-Kaa,' he said.

I could tell he was waiting for a reaction. The name was familiar, but I could not place where I'd heard it before. 'Tel-an-Kaa? Should I know him?'

'Not a "him",' Fortuny corrected, 'a "her".'

'Of course!' I exclaimed. 'The Zigane tribe of humans and Hara! She was with them in Galhea, before Swift and I travelled south to the Gelaming. I can't see what she has to do with me though. What's the connection? I know she was some kind of messenger and presumed she worked for a high-ranking Harish adept. She wouldn't let on.'

'No, she probably wouldn't have then.'

'She must be very old now, surely.'

Fortuny shook his head and swilled his mouth with wine. 'Not in the sense you mean,' he said. 'Tel-an-Kaa is a parage of the Kamagrian.'

'A what?'

'The Kamagrian are an order of adepts, a parage of one of their number.'

'An order of humans?' I couldn't help scoffing.

Fortuny never changed his expression. 'Far from it.'

'Then what? And what is their interest in me?'

'Your questions will all be answered in Roselane,' Fortuny said mildly, raising his hands at my swift intake of breath. 'Yes, I know. You must have been told that a hundred times, but it is true nonetheless. All we knew was that you were having some kind of ... bother with Thiede and the Gelaming. We often have dealings with the Kamagrian, usually via Tel-an-Kaa. I think we were told about you so your journey wouldn't be inadvertently delayed by misunderstandings.'

'What are the Kamagrian?' I asked again. The Niz and Ariaric exchanged an agonised glance.

'Maybe, after Roselane, you will be able to tell us,' Fortuny said.

'Oh, another secretive lot are they! You know what I really object to?' I waved a fork across the table at him. 'The fact that so many people seem to know much more about me that I do. Why should anyone tell you my business? It was only a spur of the moment decision that I came here at all! It seems like I'm being watched. Is that the case?'

Ariaric burst out laughing and everybody looked at him. 'Was it really a spur of the moment decision, Cal? Was it really? Do you mean to say that someone who knew quite a lot about you couldn't have simply guessed you'd call in here on the way east?' His amusement made me uncomfortable, especially in front of Elisyin who had raised one eyebrow speculatively.

'Well, maybe not,' I grumbled hotly. 'but that doesn't alter the fact that my path through this country seems to have been completely predetermined as if I've had no choice in it at all. Why? It's been like a wild goose chase, a waste of time. Couldn't all my progression have been seen to in Roselane if it's so necessary? I've been played with, cat's-pawed around. Is it unreasonable that I object to it? Even if it has been intimated that it's all for "my own good". That's no comfort! You might think I've enjoyed it all Aric, but there have been moments of hell, sheer hell!' They let me rant on in this vein for several minutes until I exhausted my vocabulary of complaint. It didn't escape me that Ariaric must have spread my life story around his whole family either. Both of his sons were looking very embarrassed, but they knew what I was talking about alright.

'You feel you have to blame someone obviously,' Fortuny said, to break a rather painful silence.

'You know, I actually envy you,' Ariaric said, leaning back in his chair. 'Look at me, trying to carve my name upon the stone of Wraeththu history, whilst yours is there already it seems. Burnt upon it indelibly, and without you even trying!'

'And what does it say after my name do you think? Calanthe: was once a nuisance, but everybody got to hear about it?' They all laughed at that.

'Perhaps, but I think it will say, Calanthe: conscience of kings.' Ariaric decided, pleased with himself.

'Oh, does that explain why I don't have a conscience myself then?'

'Haven't you?' Elisyin asked innocently. It didn't fool me.

'Let him answer that in a year's time,' Ariaric replied for me. He raised his glass. 'A toast: to Roselane,' he said. 'Our hearts will go with you, Cal. Whatever your destiny is, it concerns us all. Isn't that right, Fortuny?'

The Niz smiled slyly. 'There is no doubt of that,' he said. 'No doubt at all.'

All they'd heard were rumours; of that I was sure. Their knowledge was incomplete. I got the strange impression that all these tribe leaders who'd played their part were counting on me for something. What?

I only went back to my room to sleep, the whole day having been spent with Ariaric and Elisyin. I envied their closeness. Sometimes, I forgot entirely who Ariaric had been. It was good to see him again though, the only person, apart from Zack perhaps, with whom I could reminisce about the bad old times. We had been lucky to escape with our lives. Even luckier to escape with our sanity. We had both changed since the days of the Uigenna; perhaps that was why I could forget our last meeting. It wasn't ignored though. We could say, 'Oh, we were children then!' and laugh. If I could have looked into the future back then and foreseen this meeting, I would never have believed it. Panthera didn't come back to our room again that night. He obviously hadn't been there all day either; the place felt deserted. I tried not to feel anxious about it, telling myself there was no point, it was best this way, etc,

etc. I drifted into a sleep crowded by neurotic dreams, in which the lovely Panthera played a very strong role.

I got out of bed early and shot to Ariaric's apartments for breakfast. I wasn't sure what time the Tigrina was expected, but I was going to make damn sure I was by the Archon's side when he arrived. Wonderful lurid fantasies paraded through my mind. The Tigrina knowing who I was immediately. A fantastic argument ensuing with me emerging triumphant, a defeated Tigrina accepting my victory and fading away to some far land. Me killing the Tigrina by poison so no-one could suspect me; him dying horribly in front of the entire court of Sykernesse. Such were the gist of my dreams. Obviously, I have never properly grown up. Ariaric had Elisyin with him; they were breaking their fast in bed together. I waited impatiently, only picking at the food Ariaric's servants set before me. By ten o'clock, the Archon and his consort emerged from the bedroom. I'd been frantically waiting for nearly an hour.

'Don't appear so eager,' Ariaric said to me. 'Knowing your history, I'm not sure whether it's a good idea to let you loose on the illustrious Tigrina ... I hope you won't betray my hospitality by misbehaving.'

Caeru Meveny, consort to Pellaz-har-Aralis, Tigrina of Immanion arrived in time for lunch. To give the people of Oomadrah a fine spectacle, Ariaric had arranged for a lavish procession of horses, warriors and Niz to accompany this visiting dignitary from the south gate of the city to the palace. Ariaric and his court would wait upon a balcony on the outer wall of Sykernesse itself, too high up for the Tigrina to hear him say 'hello', but of ample height for Ariaric and Elisyin to be shown off to their people. It would be good politics for the Tigrina to report the Maudrah's devotion to their Archon back to Immanion. Ariaric would use every opportunity to show how popular he was with them.

I couldn't see very much, having been hustled to the back of the balcony by jostling courtiers. It didn't matter. I wanted my first view of Caeru to be closer than this anyway. Hysterical cheering coming from the direction of the south wall presaged the arrival of the Gelaming party. It came closer and closer, an eery sound, almost like misery rather than joy. To me it sounded like a vast and moaning animal approaching Sykernesse from the south, getting louder and louder, until I had to fight an urge to run. Once the Tigrina was beneath the balcony, the voice of the city had become deafening. It was like a nightmare; all those repressed souls giving tongue, going mad. They weren't allowed to do that very often.

I backed away and descended the dark, stone stairs to the courtyard alone. It seemed deserted, with all noise coming from the city beyond. Only a few whispering servants around. Everyone was on the battlements and the balconies. I stood in the sunshine and watched as guards turned the wheels that opened the vast, wooden gates to the palace. Creaking, turning. They were rarely opened. Smaller doors within the gates themselves admitted daily traffic. First came the soldiers on horseback. The animals hadn't moved faster than a trot, I'm sure, yet they were sweating and snorting as if back from a gallop. This was backstage. Hara dismounting, laughing, calling to each other, lighting cigarettes, away from the public eye. Then came the Niz. They spoke together in low voices, drifting towards the main entrance in clumps. Now the courtyard was beginning to fill up with Hara as the people of Syknernesse came down from the walls. I didn't want to be too prominent. I hung back.

The first of the Gelaming came in through the gates. Huge, white horses, not even faintly damp, gentle eyes sparkling with humour, manes as soft as Harish hair. The riders wore thick leather armour, like insect carapaces, carrying their helmets on their saddles before them. These were Hara chosen for their yellow hair, which they wore loose over their shoulders; the Tigrina's elite guard. All Arahal clones, I thought peevishly. Gelaming always make me feel inadequate. They seem so *big*. Tall, confident, beautiful and brilliant. Still, they fascinate me too. Must be a perversion on my part. The Tigrina came in surrounded by his aides. He looked so much smaller than I'd expected. Perhaps his horse was just larger than the rest. Apart from that, all that struck me was his incredible white-gold hair, a huge mane that Ariaric would once have envied, as light and soft as feathers. I couldn't really see anything else. Ariaric and Elisyin descended from the balcony and the gates were closed upon the city. I watched as the Archon and his consort walked slowly up the wide steps to the palace with Caeru between them. They all looked as if they were very good friends. Caeru was skinny, I decided uncharitably. Small and skinny. I followed the party at a distance.

Caeru

'He that can love unloved again,
Hath better store of love than brain.'

Sir Robert Ayton, To an inconstant one

A banquet had been prepared in Caeru's honour on the second
floor of Sykernesse. I had been lucky to secure a seat in the
main hall because all the rooms were full to capacity. High-ranking
Hara from every Maudrah town appeared to have converged on
Oomadrah for the day. I tried to see if Panthera was around but
that was impossible. Sykernesse being so large, I could have walked
round that crowd all day and not seen someone familiar. No-one
could get near Ariaric or Elisyin, so that it was with relief that I
spotted their youngest son Zobinek speaking to one of Elisyin's
valets at the door to the main hall.

'Will I have difficulty getting in here?' I asked. 'I believe your
father did reserve me a seat.'

'Not if you walk in with me,' Zobinek replied cheerfully.

I felt it would give him considerable prestige in the eyes of his
friends to walk into that room with someone like me on his arm.
I'd done my best in the grooming department for most of the
morning and the results were so stunning I barely recognized
myself. (Would I have to preen myself like this every day if I lived
in Almagabra?) Ariaric certainly had a sense of humour; he had me
sitting right on the top table. I could have easily spat at the Tigrina
and scored a direct hit. Zobinek sat beside me and pointed out the
various personalities of interest.

'See him,' he said, pointing discretely to a venomously glamorous Har further down the table. 'That's Lissilma the Kalamah. He killed my brother Ostaroth.'

'What! *And he dines on the high table in Sykernesse!*' I was amazed.

Zobinek nodded. 'Yes. He was Ostaroth's consort. It's a long story, but my father didn't think Lissilma was much to blame.'

'What does Elisyin think about it?'

Zobinek shrugged. 'He can't dispute Ostaroth asked for it. He treated Lissilma abominably. Kalamah are like cats, you see. You can be tickling their stomachs one moment and it's all purrs, the next ... Psshht!' He clawed the air expressively. 'It's best not to upset them.'

All this was effectively taking my mind off the presence of Caeru, perhaps a deliberate ploy on Zobinek's part. He clearly fancied his chances with me. A well-worn circumstance. Give me a chimaera to pursue any day. Caeru appeared to be utterly at ease with the royal family of Maudrah. I could hear him laughing. We were served the first course; spiced shellfish. Zobinek stopped talking so he could eat. The thought of food in my mouth repulsed me. I was thinking, 'That creature is Pell's. He took my place', but even as I thought it, it didn't seem real. I had been told about the state of their blood-bond; it was ridiculous to feel jealous, except perhaps because Caeru had all the prestige and status that went with being Tigrina. Thiede had said he was good at his job. Could I have carried it off so well? I admit to vanity. Maybe I'd have enjoyed being fussed round, having people think I was important. At least I was being honest with myself now. I know I was staring; I wanted him to look at me. It took me nearly all the meal to get him to do it. He resisted my will, or he ignored it, but eventually, as Ariaric leaned back to speak to one of the servants, Caeru scanned the table and caught my eye. I have hardly ever experienced such a feeling of triumph, even as I realized how grossly I was over-reacting to the whole situation. He looked puzzled. Perhaps he thought he knew me from somewhere. A brief, uncertain smile wavered upon his lips. He had an innocent kind of face, high-cheek-boned pretty, but wistful. I wished he could have been razor sharp like Cobweb, suave like Elisyin or recklessly carefree like

Lahela. Just not this; haunted. I looked away and realized Ariaric had been watching me for some moments. A wary expression. The Tigrina whispered in his ear. It *had* to be about me. Had to.

Later, Ariaric hosted a small (fifty Hara) gathering in his personal suite on the third floor. Zobinek dragged me along, although I was no longer sure I wanted to go. I felt bruised. My journey must be resumed. I must forget this. For a moment, however brief, as I looked into his eyes, I had put myself in Caeru's place. I imagined the pain of fear, of loss. Such eyes as his expected it at any time. Yes, I actually felt guilty. Strange, isn't it. I told Zobinek that I had to find Panthera. 'We are leaving soon,' I said.

'Oh, not yet, surely!' Zobinek replied. 'Anyway, Panthera may well be there. You never know. Come on; let's enjoy ourselves!'

Ariaric's suite was a riot of loud conversation, smoke and laughter. Zobinek forced a drink on me. He had drunk rather too much himself. I was grateful that, because of the crush, I couldn't see the Tigrina at all. With a bit of shuffling, I managed to squeeze Zobinek up against the door, thinking that was the safest place to stand. He obviously misconstrued my intentions, but being a sybaritic creature. I've never objected to having my backside stroked, so it didn't really matter.

'You are like him in several ways,' Zobinek said, with half-controlled slurring.

'Like who?' I humoured sweetly.

'The Tigrina.'

'Oh?' I tried not to sound cold. 'In what way? I'm ten foot taller than him surely, and at least twice as lovely!'

Zobinek laughed. 'You may be right. It's just a feeling, and the hair of course.'

'Same colour. That makes us blood brothers does it?'

Ariaric's son grinned mischievously. 'You want to meet him?'

'No. Do you?'

'I will. Later. Why don't you want to meet him? Aren't you curious?'

'Zobinek, I'm curious about ghouls, cannibals and people who believe they are werewolves, but I can't say I'd want to meet one. Just leave it!'

'You do really though, don't you?'

'Is this irrepressible youthfulness or just crass stupidity?'

'Neither; clairvoyance.'

I rolled my eyes. 'Don't be loathsome, Zobinek. Just get me another drink will you.' He left me standing on my own for some minutes and then pushed his way back through the crowd, beaming happily. As far as I could see, he was not bringing me a drink. I sighed as he grabbed my arm. 'The wine, witless child! Have you forgotten?'

He ignored my remark. 'Come on!' he said, dragging me behind him, me still clutching an empty glass.

'Come on where?' I stumbled, bumping into people as he hauled me along. A drink splashed over my leg; somebody glared at me. Zobinek was relentless. I could see Ariaric standing with a group of Niz behind a vast sofa of black and gold brocade. Sitting on one end of the sofa were Elisyin and Caeru, with a cluster of Hara around them who were all grinning like imbeciles.

'Zobinek!' I hissed. 'Let me go!'

'You wanted to meet him, didn't you?' Ariaric's idiot son said happily. 'I'll introduce you.'

'No!' I hissed again. 'No, Zobinek!'

'Don't be silly! Where are your guts?'

Somewhere in the back of my throat by the feel of it. This was going to be disastrous. I tried to escape but it was too late. Here was I, the beast who had relished the public humiliation of a certain Cobweb years before, struggling like a Harling to escape an embarrassment that was far less harrowing really. Hara slid aside as we drew near to the couch, recognizing the Archon's son. It seemed as if I stood in the centre of an arena.

'My lord Tigrina,' Zobinek began. Caeru turned his startling, blue eyes upon us, smiling mildly. 'May I present a good friend of my father's to you. He's been waiting to meet you.' (Cringe). 'This is Calanthe, formerly of Megalithica, currently of Jael in Ferike, I believe.'

Credit where credit's due; the smile never dropped from the Tigrina's mouth, but his eyes told me he knew exactly who I was. He must have heard my name a thousand times. This was worse than the sick surprise I'd hoped to spring on Ariaric. I should imagine I must be about the last person that Caeru would want to bump into at a party. Whoever else in Immanion knew my every move, Caeru was not one of them.

He said icily, 'How nice,' A flush was creeping up his neck; the atmosphere was electric. Elisyin was looking daggers at his son.

'It is a privilege to meet you,' I said, bowing slightly.

'For me too,' the Tigrina replied, frost still hanging off his words.

Elisyin decided enough was enough. 'Cal's glass is empty Zobinek,' he said, 'Take him to get a refill.'

Gratefully, I let an abashed Zobinek lead me away again. I drank two glasses of wine in quick succession before sneaking out of the room while Zobinek went to the toilet. My heart was pounding. I could have smoked a hundred cigarettes at once, but one would have to do. Shaking, I paused in the corridor to light up. I was shaking too much. Then a considerate hand offered me a flame, which I made use of before looking up. The fact that the flame was offered without the use of match or mechanical means of any kind should have warned me. It didn't. I was in too much of a state. A golden-haired Har with silver eyes blew on his fingers and smiled.

'My lord requests you attend an audience with him,' he said.

Caeru must have reacted the minute I turned my back on him. I shook my head. 'No, I don't think so. Convey my apologies, but it would serve no purpose.'

'My lord thinks otherwise,' the Gelaming insisted. I avoided the penetrating gaze. 'Now. If you would be so kind.' He directed the way with his hand.

'I have no choice do I?'

'No. Sorry, but I have my orders.'

Caeru's suite was the most splendid Sykernesse had to offer. Gifts from the Maudrah hierarchy were heaped on every available surface. I was left in the reception room to take all this in, while my escort went to tell the Tigrina I was there. He kept me waiting. I probably would have done the same. When he walked in, I wondered whether I'd been mistaken about his innocence. This was no melancholy victim. This was a Har of stature who was plainly angry. He stood some distance away from me, hands on hip and demanded. 'Well, was this planned?'

'What do you mean?'

The Tigrina snorted and flung himself into a chair. 'Sit down!' he ordered. 'Omiel, leave us!' His aide left the room quickly. 'What are you trying to do? You think it's clever, throwing yourself at me like that? You think the Archon's cronies haven't heard the rumours flying about this godforsaken country? I don't like being embarrassed ...'

What rumours?

'It wasn't planned,' I interrupted him. 'Just coincidence. At least on my part and your part.' The implications in that only fuelled his anger. He looked ready to explode. 'I'm on my way east. Oomadrah was just a pause in the journey. I had no idea you'd be coming.'

'Of course you didn't! Ariaric has some explaining to do, I can tell you!'

I couldn't reply, sure that whatever I said would only make things worse. Such restraint was doomed to be short-lived, I'm afraid. Caeru saw to that with his next remark. 'Don't think whatever plans you and Thiede have hatched together can ever be successful,' he said.

'Excuse me! There aren't any!'

The Tigrina sneered. 'Oh yes. I've heard all about your lies! I'm not stupid. Recently, yours is the name I'm constantly hearing on everybody's tongue just as I walk into any room. The name I hear before whoever's talking sees me and changes the subject, I might add.'

'That's just as much a surprise to me as it is to you, I assure you.'

'Is it? Well, as a matter of fact, it isn't a surprise to me. What is it you want? Wealth?'

I had to laugh at that. 'That's the most pathetic thing anyone could ever say to me! Do I want wealth. Are you mad? I think we both know what I want.' I regretted that even as I was half-way through saying it.

The Tigrina's face had bleached from red to white. 'I could have you killed,' he said.

I shook my head. 'I doubt it.'

He rubbed his eyes nervously with one hand. 'Why?' he said, and the wistfulness was back. 'Why, after all this time? Can't you let it be? I've always dreaded this moment; you coming back into his life.'

'I'm not. I'm not in his life.'

The Tigrina slammed his fist down on the chair-arm. 'Shut up! You are! You know you are! You always have been! I just can't understand why it's happening now. It's been so long. Is it the position you want? Is that it?'

'Caeru, I have no choice, really I don't. Whoever's behind all this won't let it be, and I don't think it's Pell.'

Caeru glanced up at me. He looked wretched. 'Don't call me by my name,' he said hoarsely. 'That's one thing I can prevent. I am Tigrina to you, for as long as I can be.'

'That's not ... Look, I'm not angling to take your place, if that's what you think. I'm probably as confused as you are. I don't know what's going to happen, or where I'll end up.'

'You're all that he said you were,' Caeru said, unexpectedly. 'I had hoped time and longing had blown up your image out of all proportion. It hasn't. When I saw you at table earlier you intrigued me. I actually ...' He pulled a disgusted face, shook his head. 'I asked Ariaric who you were. "Just an old friend," he said. "No-one important."' He laughed bleakly at the crushing irony in that. 'I can understand what ... people ... see in you now. I wish I didn't. The image Pell has of you lives. Does that satisfy you? It doesn't mean you've beaten me, far from it. My position in Immanion is unassailable.'

'How about your position in Pell's affections?' I couldn't help saying that, because whatever the answer, he was still by Pell's side and I was still the lunatic who'd murdered Orien and had to be kept away. The words struck home. If he hadn't been the Tigrina and groomed for his role, I think Caeru would have physically gone for me then.

'Get out of my sight,' he said, softly, looking at the floor.

'I'm leaving Sykernesse in the morning,' I said. 'You won't have to see me again.'

'Won't I? I hope you die, I really do. Now get out.'

A more depressing, pointless interview is difficult to imagine. I found my way, somehow, back to my own room, my head in a whirl. I felt sure Ariaric would be displeased — no, furious — at the embarrassment I'd caused him. His fears had been justified. Yet it was Zobinek's fault really. I don't think I would have made my identity known otherwise, no matter how graphic my fantasies had been. To throw salt on my tender wounds, I surprised Panthera in bed with Lalasa. It was too much to bear. I just threw myself face-down on the coverlet beside them and groaned, much to their displeasure, I'm sure.

'Fuck the world!' I cried, muffled. 'Fuck it! Fuck it!'

'Shall I go?' Lalasa whispered.

'No, stay and witness my immortal shame!'

'Cal, you're drunk,' Panthera decided wearily.

'I'm not! Just cursed! The Tigrina wishes me dead and I die obligingly!'

'I really think I ought to go,' Lalasa said again.

Panthera sighed. 'OK, I'm sorry about this.'

There was silence for ten harrowing minutes after Lalasa had gone until Panthera said, 'You ask for it, Cal, you really do.'

'Yes, I know. I'm utterly foul. Vermin! Diseased! But I still didn't sleep with Ariaric, Thea, so I don't know why you're angry with me. Or is it just lust for your cousin?'

Panthera sighed heavily again. 'I only have one neck, Cal, and I suspect you're going to stamp firmly across its wind-pipe one day. I must be deranged. You want to leave tomorrow?'

'Desperately. Are you still with me?'

He took my hand, squeezed it. 'Surprisingly, yes,' he said.

Like a coward, I was going to sneak off without saying anything to Ariaric. A note would do; I couldn't face him. But he must have anticipated that because he came to our room in person just after it got light outside. Panthera excused himself and remained locked in the bathroom until the Lion had gone. I tried to apologize, but he didn't want to hear it.

'My fault too,' he said. 'Wasn't it me that suggested you stay? I didn't think Pell would have told Caeru about you. Stupid, wasn't it. Somehow, nearly everyone seems to know about you now. It was playing with fire. I also intend to beat several pints of blood out of my gormless son.'

'Don't be too hard on him; he didn't realize the gravity of the situation,' I said. 'I hope it won't affect your position in the eyes of the Gelaming though. I feel bad enough about it without that.'

He shook his head. 'I really don't know. I'll do my best to butter the Tigrina up, profess my ignorance. It may work.'

'Anyway, it should help not having me around. We're leaving today.'

Ariaric didn't press me to stay. 'You're on a hard path at the moment, Cal,' he said. 'My heart will be with you. We'll all pray things turn out for the best.'

'Thank you.' I stood up and we embraced. It was hard to let go. 'Our reunion started so well. I'm sorry.'

He took my face in his hands. 'Sssh. Don't say that. It's like I said, hard times. One day, all this'll be over and you'll come back here and we can do it properly. OK?'

I nodded. 'You've turned out well, you really have. It gives me hope.'

He laughed at that. 'Cal, Cal, I worked hard, that's all. We were all kids in Megalithica. It's so long ago. Let it go now. It can't be changed. Just let it go.'

'Can I really do that?' Even to me, my voice sounded wistful.

'You can. Don't hoard all that feeling. Release it into something constructive.' He held up his hand. 'See this,' he said. 'It's yours; take it.' Even after all this time, the scar was still there. Overcome by emotion, I took it in my hands and kissed it and kissed it. 'The blood is long-dried, Cal. You can't take it to Roselane with you. Have this instead.' We'd never shared breath. I'd not been worthy of such a caress all those years ago. He gave me strength. I took it eagerly. A true friend is the Lion. He always shall be.

The farewells were nearly done, Sykernesse nearly in the past. But there was one last question. 'Wraxilan, what was your part in this? You did have a part didn't you?'

He stood at the door, smiling. 'Of course I did. What harm can it do to tell you. Tel-an-Kaa said to me, "Tell him my name. Tell him about me, that I know him, but before that, make him see himself." She told me how. I wasn't that clairvoyant.'

'Are you beholden to these Kamagrian then that you obey their orders?'

'No. I did it because of the other thing she said, and that was that Wraeththu's future is in your hands, Cal. Simply that. We need you, and we need you desperately. Could I need another reason knowing that?'

CHAPTER

26

Journey to Roselane

'Whereat I woke — a twofold bliss:
Waking was one, but next there came
This other: Though I felt, for this,
My heart break, I loved on the same.'

Robert Browning, Bad dreams I

From Oomadrah, Panthera and I would travel east to beyond Chane, through a tongue of Garridan territory to Roselane. Our destination was the mountain retreat of Shilalama, high above the world. To speed up our journey, Ariaric kindly offered us the use of one of his private cars, complete with pilot. I was in two minds about accepting this offer. It meant we could be in Roselane within days. Overland, it could take weeks, even months, and that would give me time to think. Eventually, I decided that in my circumstances, time to think would be a bad thing.

We left Sykernesse before most people were even out of bed. It was a misty, chilly morning. I sat moodily in the back of the car, until I could stand Panthera's astute appraisal no longer and curled up, pretending to be asleep. I concentrated on the sigh of the vehicle's mechanisms, the feeling of weightlessness as we drifted slowly over Oomadrah's walls into the true morning, towards the plains of Hool Glasting. A mild humming indicated that the pilot had activated the car's roof. Soon we were cut off from the fresh air and with a shudder the vehicle sprang to life and shot towards the east. This was a much more sophisticated craft than Lourana's. Its speed was determined but effortless. We planned to spend the night in the Garridan borough of Biting; by mid-day tomorrow, if all went smoothly, I would be in Roselane. It was like facing major surgery. I was apprehensive but could not imagine it was really happening. I was still not sure what to expect, but it seemed like a good idea to seek out the cloisters of the Kamagrian, whom Wrark Fortuny had told me had their headquarters in Shilalama. I felt sick about my encounter with the Tigrina. Bad enough to be considered a gold-digging trouble-maker without having twinges of pity for the owner of those opinions. Just where would the Tigrina stand after all this? How could I tell, when I didn't even know what would happen to me? I curled myself around these uncomfortable thoughts and investigated them thoroughly until our pilot brought his vehicle down to land on the plains below, so that we could eat in the open air and perform whatever duties of nature had become pressing. The day had warmed up; now clear sunlight, shining through small, white clouds, dappled the plains with light and dark. I told Panthera in more detail what had happened the previous night. It didn't seem to matter that the pilot was listening avidly whilst pretending not to. My secrets were no longer that. By whatever means, the news had seeped out in Jaddayoth and spread; my alliance with the Tigron was known and it was expected that upheaval would come of it.

It was dark by the time we reached Biting. Our pilot booked us into an inn whilst Panthera and I stretched our legs around the town. Most of the shops were still open. We laughed at the blatant displays of the toxicologists. An establishment named Foul and Fair exhibited its wares in a well-lit window. "Ash-wilt for the successful withering of limbs!" one advertisement boldly claimed. Yes, we laughed, but our joy was false. The performance progressed towards its final act, when the players might say their farewells and go their separate ways, never to meet again. We returned to the inn and took jugs of ale to our room. Now was the time for remembering.

Panthera talked of Piristil. 'I can remember the moment I first saw you,' he said. 'Even then you smelt of freedom, my freedom. Have I ever thanked you?' We undressed and lay on top of the bed. Voices below; other lives carrying on oblivious. Panthera closed the window so that we couldn't hear it. 'We are near the end, aren't we?' he said.

I sighed heavily. 'I suppose we should hope so. Maybe you ought to feel relieved. After this, you can return to Jael and take up your life. You have friends in Maudrah, Gimrah, Elhmen and Sahale now. At least you've gained something from knowing me.'

'Will you ever go back do you think? To the Hafeners, Nanine, the Lyris, Sykernesse … to Jael?'

'I would like to. I hope I can.'

Panthera threw himself across me then, squeezing the breath from my lungs. 'Oh, Cal, Cal,' he said bitterly. 'I wanted to fight for you, fight the Gelaming, the Tigron, whoever was there in the shadows. Back in Jael, I thought I could. But it's all too … big. I have no chance. I cannot lose you because I never really had you. You've given me so much, but if I want to share it, it must be with someone else, not you. That's hard. It's cruel. Why must we suffer? If there's a great power behind all this, why did it let me love you?'

I could feel his tears falling through his hair onto my chest. Part of life is learning to lose, to let go; something I was still learning about myself. 'We must accept it, Thea,' I said. 'Whatever we do comes back threefold, or so they say. For this pain there must be equal sweetness waiting in the future.'

'Do you really believe that?'

'I don't know. It's the best I can offer.'

He laughed weakly, raised his head. 'We must not waste these last hours,' he said.

'No, my pantherine, we must not.' We shared breath to share our souls' grief and in the communion of our bodies beyond that was a vast sea that was time and the Earth, but that sea had a salty shore and it was the salt of tears.

In the morning, we found that we'd adopted a determined good-humour. It must have come to us in the night; a gift from the angels. The ache of tears had become pleasurable, subdued. Now we went to battle with renewed strength. We left Biting immediately after breakfast. The car whistled through mountain peaks of grey and green and white. Clouds were sometimes beneath us. After some hours, the pilot pointed through the window. 'That is Shilalama,' he said. 'Can you see? In the distance.' We peered at the strange, craggy rock towers, catching the light from the morning sun.

'Looks like fungus,' Panthera said.

'How long will it take to get there?' I asked.

'Half-an-hour maybe, not long.'

Half-an-hour. Panthera and I clasped hands like children. I had to say, 'Thea, if you want to go back to Maudrah with the car, I'll understand. Maybe it would be best ...'

'Shut up, Cal,' he said. 'Stop playing the martyr. You might need me here.'

There was no easy place for the car to land in Shilalama. In some ways it strongly resembled Shappa with its vertical streets and tiny plazas. But where Shappa was grey and smooth, Shilalama was pink and russet and yellow, and rugged. We circled the town a couple of times, flying very low. Hara looked up and waved. Everyone was dressed in pale robes like priests. The pilot was concerned. 'This car is too big to land here. I'll have to put you down beyond the walls. Do you want me to wait at all?'

'No. We don't know how long we'll have to stay here,' I answered. We were dropped off on top of a cliff, where a brisk wind whipped away our words.

'Down there!' the pilot yelled. 'There's a track to the town.' We called back our thanks. 'Good luck!' he mouthed and then the car was lifting, dipping, heading west, its transparent roof sliding forwards as it increased in speed. Panthera and I watched it until it had vanished in the distance. No going back now. We pushed our way through stiff knee-deep bushes and scrambled down the stony path, hampered with luggage.

The gates to Shilalama were open; no guards to question travellers or stop us entering. 'Where do we go?' Panthera asked. It was impossible to tell whether the buildings were houses, inns, shops, temples, or just natural rock formations. Two Hara drifted past, heads lowered, hands in sleeves, humming to themselves. They ignored my enquiry about directions. 'Let's just make towards the centre,' I said.

'What centre?' Panthera asked, looking around. 'It's such a jumble.'

'Just keep walking.'

There were few proper streets. Rock buildings seemed to have been hollowed out or thrown up at random. Any Roselane we came across seemed to be on another plane and unavailable for communication. Where were the waving Hara we'd seen from the air? The wind was making such a racket, we couldn't listen out for sounds of activity, but eventually, after an age of aimless walking, we came to a small square where market stalls were set up, and Hara of more alert mien were wandering among them. I went to the nearest stall and asked to be directed to the cloisters of the Kamagrian, though how we'd fare following directions in this place, I didn't know. 'Just keep going,' the stall-holder answered, pointing across the square. 'All paths lead to Kalalim.'

'Kalalim?'

'Your destination. Pause a while and refresh yourselves first. No charge.' He offered us cups of steaming herb tea. Panthera set down his bags and rubbed his shoulders. Mine were numb. As we drank the tea, I tried to extract information about the Kamagrian.

'Is there any particular way we should behave? Any rituals to observe?'

'Just be your own true selves.'

'I see. Do we have to be announced or can we walk right in?'

'There are no locked doors in Shilalama. Have you come far?'

'Very,' I said, darkly.

The stall holder smiled. 'You are tired travellers. The comfort you seek shall be found in Kalalim.'

We thanked him and crossed the square.

Kalalim was unmistakable. The stones of its sheer walls were golden, its crazy towers higher than any other and twisted like cable. Warmth seemed to seep from the very stones, welcome from its open doors and pointed windows. Panthera and I didn't stop to take it in properly, but walked directly up the shallow flight of steps into the golden gloom beyond. A Har dressed in pale lemon robes stood up when we came into the hallway and put down the book he'd been reading. 'Can I be of service?' he enquired.

'I'm looking for a parage of the Kamagrian named Tel-an-Kaa,' I answered. 'I believe she may be expecting me.'

'You have come to the right place.' The Roselane went to a desk by the wall and picked up a heavy ledger. 'May I have your names please?'

'Calanthe and Panthera of Jael.'

The Roselane nodded. 'Ah yes, you *are* expected.' He entered our names on the top of a new page. 'Well, I won't keep you waiting. Come with me please.'

We followed him down a skylit passage that led to a garden sheltered from the wind. Hara were working among the flower beds. Every one of them looked up and wished us good-day. Rather different to Oomadrah beyond the walls of Sykernesse, I thought with amusement. The Roselane showed us into a pleasant, airy room that overlooked the garden. The only furnishings were cushions and rugs upon the floor, a couple of low tables and a book-case next to the window. A brass censer hung from the ceiling, exuding a strong, aromatic smoke.

'If you would like to relax, I will tell Tel-an-Kaa you have arrived.'

Groaning, I eased my bags off my shoulders, slumping gratefully into the cushions.

Panthera went to look out of the window. 'What's going on here?' he asked. 'Why should a woman have such a high position in Roselane? Who are the Kamagrian?'

'We can only wait and find out,' I answered. 'It's probably just a gimmick. I can't see me finding the answers to my problems here somehow. Its unreal. The Roselane seem to have lost touch with the real world. They're incomplete. Perhaps even weak.'

'You are quick to judge, Calanthe!' A warm, musical voice. I turned to look at the speaker, started to stand. 'No, you can stay where you are. I am Tel-an-Kaa. Perhaps you don't remember me.' She came into the light, a yellow-haired waif, very similar to how I remembered her — and that had been quite a long time ago. Either she, or her master, were indeed very adept. To halt the human ageing process requires great power. 'I trust your journey was comfortable,' she said, as if this was some regular visit of no importance whatsoever.

'Very, thank you,' I replied. 'The Lion of Oomadrah provided us with transport ...'

'Yes I know.' Naturally.

Panthera was staring at her quite rudely; to him she was an anomaly.

'You got here quite quickly,' she continued. 'Shilalama can be difficult for strangers to negotiate. Ah, refreshment. Thank you.' A Har came into the room behind her and set a tray down on the nearest table. Wine and cakes. Tel-an-Kaa sat down opposite me and poured the wine. 'Won't you join us Panthera? I won't bite!' Such authority in a human was a little disconcerting. Panthera sat down gingerly beside me. I didn't really feel up to drinking wine (my stomach had enough acid to cope with as it was), but was pleasantly surprised to find it mild-flavoured, gently sweet. 'I expect you've been wondering what this is all about,' Tel-an-Kaa said with a smile.

'Now and again,' I replied.

She laughed. 'All the secrecy, the moving about, it must have been very irritating but necessary all the same. Perhaps you realize this too now.'

'I'm not sure I do. I must confess I sometimes wonder whether you've been picking on the right Har.'

'Oh, we haven't been picking on you! I'm sorry it felt like that. You were in such a mess, Cal. So damaged, so wounded. The healing had to take its course.'

'Well, I'm here now,' I said. 'So what happens next?'

'You must dream.'

'Dream?'

'Yes. You seek answers, but they are within you. They always have been. If this process had begun right after you saw Pellaz being shot in Megalithica, well ... it would have been a lot easier for you. That's when it should have happened, a similar education to the one Pell had.'

'But it didn't, did it! What happened after that seems to have run up a karmic debt that I'm incapable of paying off.'

Tel-an-Kaa laughed. 'Oh dear, always the pessimist!'

'And what are you?' I asked. 'Do I get an explanation for that? Why are you involved in my future?'

'I am Kamagrian,' she replied.

'Is that a tribe? Is it the same one you were with in Galhea, the humans and Hara together?'

'The Zigane? No. Kamagrian is not a tribe. It is a sisterhood.'

'Human!'

Here she paused, uncertain. 'No.'

'Then what? You can't be Harish.'

'Not in the same way that you are, no.'

'What do you mean? Was a way found to incept females after all?' That was incredible; too incredible to be true. If it was true, then all my conceptions about my race were about to be knocked off centre.

'We are not Wraeththu exactly, neither are we human,' she said.

'You're not explaining.'

'I'm trying to. Listen. Wraeththu are hermaphrodite, mutated from the human male body. I say body because, as you know, the soul is androgynous anyway. It was found impossible for human females to be mutated in the same way. No-one knew why. Was it biological? Spiritual? Why? The female has always been the driving force of the universe. The Goddess is life itself, love itself. And as she manifested her love for herself, the Goddess begat the God. He the mirror image of she; her complement. Her son is also her lover. Wraeththu philosophers, once the dust of their inception had settled, wrestled with this concept in respect of their own race. They knew the Earth was female in aspect to the Sun's fiery male. Animals are still divided into two sexes. Everything has its negative and positive polarity. How was this new race to cope with its physical form, to understand it? Thiede tried to outlaw love, but he was wrong and thankfully realized it. Love is the fuel of life, the gift of the Goddess to her beloved son, who sprang from her alone, without father. Wraeththu too are the sons of the Goddess; androgynous, but in the image of the God. Kamagrian are few and far between, but are also hermaphrodite. Made in the image of the Goddess, but as complete as she in light and dark.'

'Can the Goddess reproduce without the God?' I asked, somewhat cynically.

Tel-an-Kaa smiled gently. 'Kamagrian are not blessed with the gift of procreation as Wraeththu are,' she said.

'Then how do you ... happen, if that's not a crass question?'

'Not at all. One in perhaps every thousand Hara is born Kamagrian; a sport, a freak. However, the first was born to a human being, like Thiede was, and round about the same time as well. Her name is Opalexian. She lives here with us in Kalalim. She is our High Priestess.'

'If these Kamagrian are so rare, how do you find them? Do you have to go out and look for them?'

She laughed aloud. 'Oh no! As we have sacrificed the gift of bearing life, we have been blessed in other respects. The psychic powers of the Kamagrian are far greater than those of Wraeththu. Our people find us. We have no need to search. We have also found that it is possible to mutate human females to be like ourselves, although the process is not always successful. However, a failed inception in Kamagrian terms (unlike Wraeththu) does not mean death or imbecility. It simply fails to "take". The woman is as she was before.'

'An advantage, but our way meant we only got the best.'

'And how do you judge what's best? Physical endurance? Isn't that rather masculine?'

'No. I think you'll find the emotional and mental disturbance triggered the deaths, rather than the physical change. Does that screw your pious little theories up? You were human yourself once, weren't you?'

'You thought that did you!' She laughed. 'It was a good disguise, that's all. Kamagrian aren't as obviously inhuman as Wraeththu are. When you met me in Galhea, I was collecting refugees from Megalithica, under the guise of the Pythoness, as they called me. Opalexian has a hand in everything. She is not overt, as Thiede is, more uninvolved, discrete, careful. Wraeththu is Thiede's domain. She has never sought to be a great figure in this new world of ours, but neither is she blind. She saw Thiede making mistakes and, much as she didn't want to, had to intervene. Opalexian sees Kamagrian as here for those that need us, but we do not like to advertise our existence.'

'The Roselane know though. Will you be able to keep it a secret after this?'

Tel-an-Kaa shrugged. 'Who can say? The way the world is at the moment, some Wraeththu may not be too happy learning of our existence. Opalexian wanted them to come of age before we interacted. Thiede has forced this to be otherwise. Never mind. We're survivors. We have to be. The Roselane began from humans and discontented Hara that I gathered together in Megalithica under the banner of the Zigane. We all learn together. Shilalama is a place of contentment. A pity that the outside world needs our attention.'

All of Tel-an-Kaa's disclosures were mind-boggling, to say the least. Wraeththu did not know as much as they thought they did. They worshipped the Aghama as a God, but now we discover he is neither immortal nor infallible. What were the mistakes Thiede was making? What had I got to do with it?

Panthera and I were given a room on the second floor overlooking the garden. It was simple but comfortable, the bed but a striped mattress on the floor, strewn with coloured rugs. Tel-an-Kaa pointed out the shower room to Panthera. 'Someone will be up shortly to show you around,' she said to him. 'I'm afraid I'm going to have to take Cal away now.' She turned to me. 'Unless you want to freshen up first?'

I shook my head. 'No, let's get this over with, whatever it is. I've waited long enough.' Panthera and I embraced in silence. There was little we could say. If and when I ever saw him again, it would be after all this was over. As I let him go, he said, 'I'll wait for you here, Cal.'

'No, not if it seems I'll not be back. Understand?' He nodded, looking so young and beautiful and sad. How could I leave him? Not without touching him again. I held him close and whispered in his ear, 'Whatever else I feel for whoever else, I love you, Panthera. In my own way. I'll not forget you.'

I picked up my bag of notes and small momentoes and followed the slim figure of Tel-an-Kaa down the stairs, across the garden, into a passage that led deep into Kalalim where no light came from outside. If Panthera watched me leave, I'll never know. I couldn't bear to look back. We thought we'd said goodbye, but now I know that this must come later, and with greater poignancy.

Dreaming the Answers

'Farewell, terrific shade! Though I go free
Still of the powers of darkness art though
*   lord:*
I watch the phantom sinking in the sea
Of all that I have hated or adored.'

Roy Campbell, Rounding the Cape

As we walked into the dimness, Tel-an-Kaa asked me if I knew anything about the Roselane. 'They are known as the Dream People,' she said.

'I've heard that. Are the dreams prophetic?'

She nodded. 'They can be, but mostly they are inner visions. Like those of meditation, but the trance is much deeper. This is the state you must achieve, to go into yourself. Usually, it takes years of training; you don't have that much time. The experiences in Jaddayoth, the attaining of Algomalid will help, of course, but I will take you in myself.'

'In?'

'Yes, just in. You'll see. It will be a new experience for you, and I'm not sure how much I'll be able to help you should you run into trouble. You'll just have to try and listen to what I say.'

'Thanks for the comfort! Isn't this rather a long way round though? It seems to me that the Kamagrian must know all about what's going on anyway. Why not just tell me? Wouldn't that save even more time?'

'And how much would you learn from that? You have gained much knowledge during your travels in Jaddayoth, enough to sort this out for yourself with the right help. The visions of Dream show you what is in your mind, as any trained meditator can do, but they will also show you things that are not in your mind as well. Other people's minds. From this you will gain strength, greater understanding. You will need it to deal with Thiede.'

'Deal with Thiede? What do you mean?'

'Veils,' she said. Very illuminating.

She took me to a small room that had no windows. Cushions upon the floor, a single lamp. 'Make yourself comfortable,' she said. I sat down. 'We'll go right in. Is that OK with you?'

'Fine. I'm not very relaxed though.'

'Then we'll attend to it.' She smiled. 'Don't worry. I'll help you.'

It was all happening so quickly. Only a couple of hours ago, I had been sitting next to Panthera in Ariaric's car, flying above the mountains. In any other place, I'd have been given at least a few more hours (if not days) to settle in first. Wraeththu, generally, do not rush things.

'Lie back,' Tel-an-Kaa murmured. She lit a nugget of charcoal in a brass tray and sprinkled it with pungent incense. 'Close your eyes. Get comfortable. OK?'

I could hear the rustle of her robes as she sat down. Her gentle, clear voice talked me through a basic relaxation exercise, disciplined my breathing, opened my mind.

'This is the first stage,' she said. 'Normally you would not need to go beyond it. Let go, I will lead you.' All that caste progression and struggle had borne fruit. My mind slipped easily from reality, through the veil and she was waiting for me. 'Ready?' A voice without a sound.

I am falling, plummeting, down and down, faster and faster, almost catching fire with the speed of my fall. 'Pull up!' Tel-an-Kaa commands. 'Take control. This is not a visualisation.' I 'will' stop, and stop I do. We are in blackness. I cannot see the Kamagrian but sense her presence. 'Make your world,' she says. 'Let it come.'

My world. There it is, spinning slowly, silver and green, spinning, spinning, until it is a shining bullet and there's a horse screaming, flying blood and bone; rain and blood; red and white. No! The image disintegrates in rags, circling round me, still mewing. 'Will you ever face that?' Tel-an-Kaa asks. My core aches with cold.

'Pellaz.'

I hold his head in my hands. On his brow a single star of blood that goes back and back. His eyes staring up at the rain. Rain in his eyes and he never blinks. It was the screaming I hated the most. Those animals. Just mindless screaming. I lay him down on the wet earth and he becomes part of it, absorbed by the life-force. I look up. There's a spinning globe, green and silver, me on a red pony riding through a desert. Pellaz in a doorway ...

We share breath and the link is forged. (I knew he was different, always knew it. Others did too.)

I am walking down a narrow throat of rock, very dark. Doesn't smell too good either. I meet a Har walking the other way, carrying a torch. He is robed in green, red hair, very beautiful. As we pass each other, he puts his hand on my arm. 'You were deceived you know,' he says.

'By whom?' I ask.

'Do you want to know? Then follow me.' I turn around and walk behind him. The light from the torch is like a capsule; beyond it is black space. We come out onto a balcony, high above a city, and the torch in the red-haired Har's hand has become a jewelled sword. 'Take it,' he says. 'This is Phaonica.' (Am I really here? Am I?)

'Where is the Tigron?' I ask. 'Take me to him.'

'Follow me.' We walk along an opal collonade. Hara pass us by, hurrying alone or walking slowly in pairs. 'Thiede has him,' the red-haired Har tells me confidentially. 'He has the part of him that is yours.'

'Who are you?'

'I am Vaysh. The Tigron's aide.'

'Vaysh as I see him or Vaysh as he is.'

'Reality in one context only. There are many.'

We come to a white hall with a statue of glass in its very centre. Within the glass is a figure, bound in black rope. It's head is thrown back, the mouth open wide in an endless scream of impotence. It is Pellaz. Must I free him? How? Obvious really, the tool is in my hands. The torch, the sword. Light and Air. No, I'm afraid. I cannot lift my arm. Around me the room becomes dim, all the light condensing into the heart of the statue. Tel-an-Kaa is at my side, dressed in fish-scale armour. 'You must hurry,' she says. 'Thiede will sense you. He will come. You're not ready for that.'

'Must I break the glass?'

'Do as you feel.'

The sword is heavy in my hands. It takes an eternity to lift it. Then the air is full of chiming, of flying shards of light, stars spinning outwards, my face cut by flying glass and the statue is shattered. I can't remember doing it. I look around for Vaysh and Tel-an-Kaa but I am alone. Alone with the sinuously tumbled form of my beloved lying amongst the glass, cruelly bound. I kneel at his side. His eyes are closed. Black lashes against perfect skin. So young yet so old. This is but a dream. My lips against his brow where there is no scar. I cut the ropes and lift him in my arms. His clothes are dark and dusty. He is heavy. Through a dark doorway and into a garden, but all I am holding in my arms is a web of silk. I look behind me. There is no doorway.

In the garden, beneath a shimmering tree sits a woman. Her appearance changes with every passing moment. 'Thiede fooled you,' she says.

'What do you mean?' I ask and go to sit at her feet.

'You think he didn't want you to leave the tower?'

'He wanted me to return to Immanion.'

'If you believe that, you deserve to be fooled,' she says.

'It's just what I know. He wanted me to join the court.' A wind comes up, suddenly, viciously, and the woman has become a black hag laughing in my face.

'Know this!' she screams 'Thiede has to keep you and his Tigron apart at any cost! You helped him! Fool!'

I put my hands across my face, a reflex action. When I lower them, both garden and woman have gone ...

I am underground once more. I think about what I've heard. The earth groans above me, the cracking of primordial stone bones. Why should Thiede have to keep us apart? Why?

'Because you are part of the same thing,' a voice says from nowhere. 'Light and dark. Malleable and unmalleable. Which is which?'

'And if we are part of the same thing, if we were united, would not our power be greater than Thiede's himself?'

'There would be no place for the Aghama in this world ... *would there.*' The last two words are sly. A covetous longing. Can I trust my own visions? Cal, known for his lies, could lie to himself.

Vaysh appears beside me again. 'Why linger here? He has waited and waited for, oh, so long. He has waited for you.'

'He could have come to me any time.'

'No, it does not work that way.'

Then how does it work? I must tear these curtains of obscurity. Around me, a haze of grey, floating veils. I can barely see Vaysh through them. Just his bright hair, a smudge of green below. Where are we going? Does Pell know what I'm doing? He's so powerful; he must do. In that case, so will Thiede. I grow cold. 'Control your thoughts!' Tel-an-Kaa's voice. She must be near. Vaysh takes my hand and leads me into a temple of light. Tel-an-Kaa is with us, brandishing a drawn sword. Her eyes are wide. I realize that Thiede must have been closer than I thought. 'Where are we?' 'Within you, Cal.' I see a glowing figure robed in star-rays. It is me. But a me beyond all that is possible. This me opens its mouth. A sound peals out that is the music of the world, holding within it all that lives, all that *is*. It takes time and yet no time at all for me to peel the music to its white-hot core. I find inside a moving nest of embryonic thoughts and hold each one up to the light of my being. It is so obvious. I laugh aloud and then I'm weeping and the radiance is raining down like tears. There are no answers because there are no questions. Only what is unseen. And now I see it. Simple because the great purpose is moved by something so small and earth-bound. Greed and jealousy. Wrapped up in clothes of righteousness, but now I see them naked. It is Thiede who should be seeking answers not me. And I know them too. Tel-an-Kaa says, 'It is time' and it is indeed. Beyond the purple, sunset sea and the red sails of an eyed vessel, Phaonica shines on the horizon. It too is waiting. I am ready to fly but the Kamagrian holds me back. 'Not that way, Cal. Earthly matters must be dealt with on the Earth. Follow me back.'

I opened my eyes to a darkened room filled with the smoke of incense. Tel-an-Kaa raised her head, inhaled deeply. 'It is done,' she said.

'Thank you.' It was not enough, but all that I could think of.

She shook her head. 'No need for words, Calanthe. We are all travelling and must offer help to those we meet upon the Path who may need it.' She stood up, smoothed down her robe, brushed back her hair. 'Opalexian wishes to meet you,' she said. 'Later, at dinner.'

'You don't rush everything then!'

Tel-an-Kaa laughed. 'Took your breath away did it? No, not everything. But what point was there in waiting to know the truth? Your companion will be relieved. I think he feared he'd never see you again.'

'A fear I shared. How long have we ... been away?'

'Your friend Panthera has probably not yet dried off from his shower. Come along, I'll take you back.'

She left me outside the door to our room. For a moment or two I lingered outside, almost too scared to go in. It was embarrassing appearing again so quickly. I need not have worried. When I opened the door, Panthera launched himself off the bed where he'd been drying his hair, and hurled himself against me. His pure joy at seeing me was humbling. A Roselane who introduced himself as Exalan came to escort us to dinner. He explained that he was Opalexian's assistant. The spring evening had become quite chilly. I felt cold walking through the garden.

Like Thiede, Opalexian is very tall, but where his hair is brilliant scarlet, hers is rich chestnut. I suppose they are quite similar in appearance though, except Opalexian is not as intimidating. This is quite deliberate on her part, as is the opposite on Thiede's. Dinner was served on low tables; we sat on the floor to eat. Panthera was quiet, almost dazed. I'd told him nothing of what I'd learned. Opalexian's apartments were no grander than any other rooms we had seen so far. Tel-an-Kaa had been waiting for us in the hall. I was grateful that she was there. I was afraid of meeting Opalexian. I was afraid of what she'd look like, but the power I feared merely allowed her to put us at our ease without effort. She greeted us warmly and enquired after my comfort. 'You must not be afraid to tell us if there is a reaction to your experience,' she said.

'I'm sure there won't be,' Tel-an-Kaa added quickly, worried by my expression of alarm.

'You must feel you know me pretty well,' I said.

Opalexian shook her head. 'Not really. I have no desire to be that invasive.'

'Yet you have monitored my every move.'

'You make it sound so dramatic. It wasn't really. Perhaps the most manipulative thing we ever did was to influence the visions of Cobweb the Varr so that his son Swift took you with him to Imbrilim.'

'Is that so! Why did Tel-an-Kaa bother coming to Galhea then if you could influence events from afar?'

Opalexian smiled. 'True, I suppose. But at that time, we could only reach Cobweb. Swift was still grossly uneducated in caste progression. Do you really think Cobweb's visions would have been heeded if he'd ordered the pair of you south? Do you really think Cobweb would even have revealed them if we'd sent them? After all, it was he who wanted to keep you both in Galhea. No, it was too risky.'

'And perhaps too slow,' Tel-an-Kaa added. 'The chances are Swift would have headed south eventually anyway, but we took the decision to speed things up a little.'

'This was mainly because I had misjudged Thiede entirely,' Opalexian admitted. She took a handful of spiced nuts and chewed them thoughtfully. 'Warning signals were coming in thick and fast, so we had to get you to Imbrilim. I believed that once you actually made contact with the Gelaming, Thiede would realize that he should let events take their natural course. He didn't, wouldn't. By then our hands were tied; Thiede had you inextricably in his clutches. I truly didn't foresee all those years of incarceration he put you through. It would have caused too much of an upheaval for Kamagrian to have intervened overtly at that point; counterproductive. For that, I apologize. Thiede's proficient at keeping people in limbo. Mind you, without that talent, it's doubtful whether Pellaz would be alive now.'

'Without Thiede's talents, he would never have faced death in the first place,' I said. 'At least not in the way he did.'

Opalexian smiled. 'Oh never doubt that Pellaz was meant to be Tigron of his people or that the method of making him so was correct,' she said. 'Thiede was right there. It was just you he was wrong about, and for selfish reasons.'

I felt weightless. Suddenly everything was beginning to slide into perspective; everything.

'I can understand a little how Thiede feels,' Tel-an-Kaa said. She turned to me. 'In Galhea, you made me feel very uncomfortable, Cal. I could sense your ungoverned chaos. It frightened me. I kept thinking, "By the Light, I hope I never have to cross swords with him!" I thought you'd see through my disguise and know everything before it was time.'

'No chance of that the way I was feeling during those years,' I said. 'Chaos was a good word to describe me; there was very little else.'

Now the sting was being drawn from my flesh; slowly. It was incredible. I could ask, and Opalexian would tell me. No more mysteries. But where to start? Obvious really.

'One thing you must tell me,' I said. 'How much does Pell know of what I was shown today?'

Opalexian sighed. 'You must understand that Pellaz trusts Thiede more than he should. Mind you, Thiede can be convincing, as I'm sure you'll agree. Pellaz will tell you himself what he believes and it will be up to you to convince him he might be wrong.'

'Does Pell know of the Kamagrian? You seem to know a lot about him. Surely he'd be able to sense your existence.'

Again Opalexian shook her head. 'No, neither Thiede or the Tigron know we exist. Our abilities are greater than theirs. We can hide very well. Only certain high-ranking Hara of the Maudrah know of us and even then, don't know *what* we are. I have eyes and ears in Phaonica though; that was pure chance. Pellaz has a friend, a human female named Kate. He's very fond of her and was concerned about her future. He sent her to a group of ascetics in Almagabra for occult training, hoping she would learn how to prolong the life of her body and mind. It was there that one of our number encountered her and subtly persuaded her to take inception to Kamagrian. It was too good an opportunity to miss.

Nobody female was that close to Phaonica's heart. Kate is not a fool, although at first she was suspicious that we might have been working against Wraeththu. It took a while to convince her. Pellaz does not know what she is. He believes her to be an adeptly trained woman. Eventually, he would have doubted that, as she continued not to age, but it would appear that Kamagrian will soon be out in the open anyway, so that no longer matters. I'm glad. It would have hurt her to move from Immanion as would, of course, have been necessary.'

'Have you been responsible for everything then, all that time I thought the Gelaming were following me?'

Opalexian sat up and poured me more wine. 'There is a lot that has to be explained to you,' she said. 'I appreciate what an enormous relief this will be to you. As soon as we realized Thiede had brainwashed you and let you out of the tower, one of our Roselane initiates was sent to keep an eye on you. It was necessary to watch you for a while to assess damage, to let your troubled mind settle down a little. Strange as it sounds, Piristil was more than we could have hoped for. You began to relax, free from obvious supervision. You began to examine the past, even though Thiede wanted you to forget it entirely.'

'Excuse me,' Panthera butted in. 'Am I to understand that *my* being there was previously organized as well?' He'd gone very pale. I almost dreaded the answer. Opalexian and Tel-an-Kaa both laughed out loud. 'Oh my dear child!' the High Priestess said, 'I can see why you'd think that, but no, it wasn't. Lucky for you that Cal came to the same house. Lucky for us too. We couldn't direct his feet, after all! We were wondering whether we'd have to let our Roselane make direct contact to push Cal into travelling to Jaddayoth. Thanks to you, that wasn't necessary. You saved us an awful lot of bother, Panthera. You took Cal to Hadassah (even provided him with a genuine reason to visit the huyana in Jasminia), you guided him to Elhmen and Sahale. In fact, you effectively did more than half of the Roselane's job for him. That disappointed him quite a lot. He had his own karmic debts to sort out; Cal was part of it.'

'Zack?' I enquired.

She nodded. 'Yes, Zackala is one of us. He joined Tel-an-Kaa in Megalithica, not long after she left Galhea. We considered him a prize when we learned of his connection with you. A bitter young Har, but we managed to sort him out eventually.'

'Is he here?' I asked squeamishly. Somehow I didn't relish another meeting with Zack. More cowardice to be faced, no doubt.

'Oh, he's around somewhere, although I do need him out and about in the world most of the time. There's little chance of you running into him here, if that's what you are worried about! He's one of our best; indispensible.' She leaned back in the cushions, smiling. 'Yes, all the visions you were blaming the Gelaming for came from here. I hope you learned from them as you should. It was a sticky moment when that Mojag oaf had the knife at your throat though. You have Kate to thank for sending Arahal to you. It was difficult for her. She'd been supervising your movements for us from Immanion; they have sophisticated thought amplification equipment, that allows for a much clearer picture of what we wanted to see. Kate was convinced you were going in the right direction. It seemed unlikely you'd run into your pursuers. When you did, she told us she panicked! Zack was too far away to be of any help at that time. Only Gelaming had the ability to get there quickly; to send Kamagrian would have blown everything. We still needed to remain unknown. Kate felt that only Pell himself would send you assistance. There was the chance that if Thiede knew about the situation he would simply rub his hands in glee at such a fortuitous way to get rid of you without dirtying himself. So Kate had to intimate to Pell that you were in danger without giving away how she knew. There was no guarantee Pell would even do anything about it. A sticky moment. She had to act fast. The Gelaming were your only defence. Using the oldest trick in the book she told him she'd had a vivid dream about you and dragged him to the thought transference unit to check if the details were real. Of course they were! He wouldn't look himself, but was concerned enough to send Arahal out. That really put the wolf into the sheep-pen! Arahal lost no time telling everyone you were around again once he got back to Immanion. Rumours were started, a dozen inferences reached. Thiede had wanted to keep your alliance with Pell a secret. Those who'd been in Imbrilim put a stop to that. Now, after everyone thought you must have died or sought a hermitic existence, you were abroad again, in Jaddayoth. Questions were asked. What had happened to you after Thiede had taken you into his custody? Why hadn't Thiede told anyone? Immanion became a hotbed of supposition; poor Caeru caught in the middle of it, no doubt. You have become something of a folk hero to Wraeththu, Cal. You can thank Swift and Cobweb for that. They love you passionately. Swift has never given up trying to find out what Thiede did with you. He is a respected Har; people listened to him. And because of that, many Hara were considering the possibility that you might be a convenient tool to use against Thiede's increasing autonomy with the Hegemony. They all knew Pell was incapable of acting independently. Oh, don't get me wrong; he wants to, but his power is no match for Thiede. He can't do it on his own.'

We all digested these words in silence. I could feel Panthera's agony. Even the sound of Pell's name caused him pain. I found myself wishing he wasn't there, because there were things I had to know, had to talk about, that I knew would cause him further grief.

'There's one thing I must know,' I said, and it was not easy for me to say it. 'If you were responsible for the visions, the pushing around, does that mean Pell himself has had no real interest in me?'

Opalexian answered me briskly. 'One thing you must understand, Cal. Pellaz was under the impression you would seek him out as soon as you made contact with his people in Imbrilim. You didn't. Up until then, Thiede had told him you needed "purification" — whatever he meant by that. That was to keep Pell away from you; it had worked for years. Pell knew you'd suffered penance in the forest of Gebaddon on the journey south. He knew you'd talked with Thiede after that. There was no longer any reason why you could not come back to him. The blood-binding with Caeru was just another of Thiede's smokescreens. It had nothing to do with love. The Gelaming were interested in you, they wanted you with them; you knew nothing of this, but there was no question of you being some underling skulking in the shadows to be summoned to the Tigron's bed when he felt like it.

So, after you didn't turn up, it was easy for Thiede to convince Pell you had no further interest in him. The incident of you leaving the tower was his evidence for this. Pell is too honourable. Assured you wanted to lead your life without him, he let it be. Can you see how Thiede's been manipulating both of you now?'

'I can see it,' I said quietly. 'What I can't understand is why Thiede didn't just kill me. There'd have been no problem then.'

Opalexian laughed. 'Don't think that harshly of him, Cal! He *is* Aghama, and has considerable good sense. He's not a Terzian or a Ponclast who can kill willy-nilly to get rid of nuisances. No, that's not the way Thiede operates. Superficially, it's all above board. He is under the impression that what he's done is right. He believes it is for Wraeththu's sake he's keeping you away from Immanion, not his own. He's blinded himself too much. That's his mistake. It is your task to make him see the light.'

'Your faith in me is frightening!' I said. No way could I imagine being able to convince Thiede of anything he didn't want to believe in, whether it was good for him or not. 'Was it you that came to me in the pool near Jael too?' That was one thing I didn't want to be true.

The High Priestess sighed. 'It was Pell's feelings, certainly, but he wasn't aware of projecting them.' A tactful answer.

Panthera stirred uncomfortably beside me. 'And how did all the rumours that are supposed to be flying around Jaddayoth about Cal get out? Do you know?'

Opalexian shrugged. 'How do any rumours start?! One would presume they originated in Immanion and spread east via traders and travellers. Remember what I said, unbeknown to Cal, he has achieved quite a reputation in the west. No-one can answer your question properly, Panthera. Perhaps if we look upon it as a necessary thing that was bound to happen, we are touching on the truth.' I could sense Panthera thought such a reply was far too glib.

'And have these rumours reached the ears of the Tigron himself yet, by any chance?' he asked.

'If they haven't, they certainly will once Caeru gets home,' she answered. 'Surprise would have been better, Cal. The incident in Sykernesse was rather unfortunate in that respect.' She smiled placatingly. 'Ah, never mind, what will be will be. Rest here for a few days. Such a short delay can't hurt the outcome; it's been waiting for years!'

We talked a great deal more, but now it was all talk of Jaddayoth. What did I think of different tribes? Had I enjoyed Gimrah, Hadassah, Ferike? And what had I learned? Opalexian was not above making one or two salacious remarks concerning Nanine and the Lyris. 'I must admit it was quite exciting to impart these mysterious messages all over the place!' she said. 'We followed your travels with great interest.'

'I'm glad it provided such pleasure,' I said, drily.

'Pleasure for you too in parts, you must agree,' Tel-an-Kaa remarked with a smile. 'The worst bit for us was when I told Ariaric about you. His face went white! For some reason, he was under the blithe misapprehension we didn't know who he really was, or what he'd done in Megalithica. Even when I explained your arrival wasn't going to provoke some wildly embarrassing revelation to us, we still had to argue with him about seeing you.'

'Yes, here's another boost for your ego,' Opalexian added. 'Even for the Lion your image had assumed some strangely avatistic form over the years. Maybe something he couldn't forget, or something he had intense inner fantasies about. He was afraid of facing you again, and I don't think it had anything to do with guilt either.'

'You'll swell my head,' I said.

'No, we won't. You know what you are now, Cal.' I thought about it and realized, for the first time ever, I really did.

'You must remember,' Opalexian said, and now her voice was grave. 'It is wrong to interfere in other people's lives, to try and change their destinies, even if it seems you are acting for the best. What must be must be. Everyone has their own path to follow and, inevitably, the times will come when their way is at extreme variance to yours. Even if you think that someone is acting utterly wrongly, think very carefully before trying to influence that situation. That is their path; they must live it. People may only learn by their own mistakes; you cannot learn for them. For that reason it was very difficult for me deciding whether or not I should take a hand in what was going on out there. Only the fact that

Thiede was being deliberately wayward, and that he had such power, persuaded me. Perhaps I was still wrong, even taking that into account. But it is something I am prepared to take responsibility for. The rest is up to you, Cal. Do what you think is right, but remember what I've told you.'

Later, we began to make arrangements for my journey to Almagabra. Opalexian had Exalan bring out a map. Most of the journey would be by sea. Kamagrian had transport like the Maudrah, but the High Priestess was insistent that once I reached Emunah, a more conventional method of travelling should be pursued. I didn't ask why she should want that, but assumed it was something to do with arriving in Immanion at the right time. That suited me fine. There was no way I wanted to reach it any sooner. I needed time to prepare myself.

Panthera and I returned to our room very late. My companion was silent. As we lay together in the darkness he spoke the words I knew would come. He must have thought about it for ages to say it so quickly. 'Cal, I want to come with you.' I didn't answer at first, so he felt he had to expand. 'Not for the reason you might think; it's not selfish. I just don't want you to be alone.'

'Have you considered I might have to be?'

'For what you have to do, whatever that is, having me along can't make that much of a difference. I want to see you safe, that's all. I couldn't live, not knowing. As soon as all this is resolved, I'll go back to Jael. I promise.'

'It's not like you to plead.'

'It's not like you to act sensibly. I want to be there.'

'Are you sure?'

'I wouldn't have asked if I wasn't.'

There was further silence whilst I examined minutely the relief his suggestion had given me. It was a selfish relief, I know that. If Panthera returned home to Jael now, I could contact him immediately my future was resolved without putting him in danger or the position of suffering further pain. God knows, I should have ignored my feelings, put my foot down and told him to go home. Yet I didn't. I knew what was supposed to happen in Immanion. OK, even with Opalexian's help, there was no cut and dried guarantee that all would go to plan, but there was no way I should take Panthera along. Whatever happened, it was certain we could no longer look upon ourselves as a pair. Ariaric is right about me; I can't let go easily. My pious words to Panthera in Biting meant nothing.

'Count yourself in then Thea,' I said.

He laughed and curled his arms around me. 'Good to see you still can't resist my charm,' he said.

Even as I held him close, even as I wanted him by me, I feared he was going to regret this move.

Aboard the Fairminia
'The foamy-necked floater went like a bird
Over the wave-filled sea,
Sped by the wind.'

Beowulf

The Emunah port of Meris was a lively place, bustling with Hara of many different tribes. It was here that Opalexian moored her personal vessel, a sleek, red-sailed ship with painted eyes upon her prow. It was the ship I'd seen in my Dream. The trip from Roselane had been swift, though dreary; rain, rain, rain. Not a good beginning to such a journey, I felt. By late afternoon, it was almost dark in Meris, rain lashing down on the cobbled streets, shops closing early, Hara hurrying along, muffled in waterproof cloaks, faces down. Tel-an-Kaa had come along to see us off. 'Sail tomorrow,' she said. 'The weather will be brighter then.' We booked into a small, crowded inn up a curling back-street. Tel-an-Kaa was in disguise; she looked Harish. One day, a ghoulish curiosity within me decided, I'd have to find out what the Kamagrian concealed beneath their clothing. Humans must have once felt the same way about us. We ate together in a small back-room in the inn. The Kamagrian kept looking at the door.

'Nervous?' I asked.

She shook her head. 'No, I'm expecting somebody. Opalexian wants one of our people with you on this. Not me, unfortunately. He should be here soon.'

'A Har, then.'

'Yes, one you know; Zackala.'

I was not exactly overjoyed. 'Thanks for telling me. Why?'

'Personal feelings mustn't get in the way of this, Cal. He may be of use to you. The image you had of him in Gimrah was somewhat distorted. Purposely. He bears you no grudge, so don't make things awkward.'

Zack didn't turn up until the morning however. Tel-an-Kaa was beginning to fret. We strolled down to the harbour after breakfast, where the sea was calm beneath clear sunlight. The air smelled fresh and full of promise. The Kamagrian wasn't sure whether she should let Panthera and I continue our journey alone. Opalexian's orders had been that Zack should come with us, but there was no Zack.

'What should I do first when I get to Immanion?' I asked, to take her mind off the problem.

'What? Get to Thiede, I should think. It's your finale, Cal, you decide!'

'Should I go in furtively, or through the front door?'

'I'd go in as if it was perfectly normal. Go to Phaonica; ask to see Thiede.'

'I'm sure his people will let me! He must be more unapproachable than Ariaric, surely, and it wasn't exactly simple getting to see him.'

'Luck was with you in Maudrah, so it will undoubtedly be with you in Immanion as well. Do you think Thiede's going to let you wander about his golden city at will? Just keep your wits about you; he'll attempt to seduce your common sense, steer you away. Remember what you've learned.'

Opalexian's ship, *Fairminia*, was anchored at the farthest end of the harbour. As we approached, we could see Hara busy at work on her decks. One figure waved us a cocky salute. It had to be Zack. My heart sank. I'd hoped we'd miss him. Tel-an-Kaa brightened up considerably when she saw him. Panthera and I watched dubiously as she ran towards him, up the gangway. They embraced; he swinging her around playfully. Oh, it was the Har I'd seen (*thought I'd seen*?) in Gimrah alright. He smiled his crooked, scarred smile at us.

'Good to see you again, Cal,' he said. 'You look well. Better than you did in Gimrah, anyhow!' He laughed. 'Welcome aboard; come on. Our captain wants us to be on our way, and it's a long journey.'

Yes. Just how long, I hadn't really anticipated until I realized I'd have to spend the entire time with Zack. A past thorn. It still made me uncomfortable to recall those days, whatever he felt about it.

And so we left Jaddayoth. Slewing around, the graceful might of *Fairminia* cleaved her way through the waves towards the west. From the west shore of the Sea of Arel, a sea canal divides the lands of Huldah and Florinada. This leads to the Axian Sea and the coast of Almagabra; the way we would travel. Tel-an-Kaa watched us leave. Before her figure was too small to make out, we saw her walk away, back towards the town. Panthera went to sort baggage out in our cabin, leaving me alone to stare at the receding shores of Jaddayoth. I'd enjoyed my time there, made new friends, learnt one hell of a lot. I could no longer isolate myself. It was Jaddayoth that had made me realize life just wasn't going to let me do that. But perhaps the hardest lesson had been accepting I was part of something huge; no amount of hiding or running could change that. Now I must bend to obey its laws, however obscure or beyond my grasp they were. People like Opalexian and Thiede can understand them; people like me just have to accept them.

For most of the journey, I've been catching up on my writing, as you can see. It surprised me that I'd written nothing since Ferike. This journal has been my life-saver in the past; my priest, my confessor. Perhaps I no longer need it. The Har who scribbled the first sentences had no idea what he'd do or become. Will the Har who enscribes the final word in Immanion be as different again? Impossible to tell. But for that reason alone I'll keep writing. It's a record of my metamorphosis. Zack and I are maintaining a polite, if distant, friendship. I get the feeling he's laughing at me sometimes and I hate the way he makes me feel inept. Perhaps it's not deliberate, but personally, I don't think he's forgiven me as much as the Kamagrian think. I can't help wondering, 'What does he think of me? Why does he never mention the past?' I can't believe it's forgotten, yet perhaps it's only me that insists upon raking up the ashes of old fires. Maybe it really is no longer a cause of concern to Zack. How can I tell? We hardly speak. He gets on well with

Panthera though. They've spent nearly the entire journey playing chess.

Panthera and I avoid talking about the future. It's too vague, too vacillating to think about. He holds me tightly at night and once I awoke to find him weeping. Silently. I never let him know I saw that. Zack has strong contacts in Immanion. (The dream I'd had of him on the battlefield with Ashmael was uncannily correct, it seems). As well as Kate, Zack too has infiltrated the Gelaming for Opalexian. He's decided we should go directly to Ashmael's residence once we reach the city. I'm not sure if that's a good idea, but I'll have to trust him. He reckons that Ashmael should help me get into Phaonica. But surely, Ashmael's loyalty lies with Thiede and the Tigron? He'll have been fed the same information about me as Pell has. Zack says, 'Don't worry. Don't make problems.' I can only hope he's right.

Immanion is near. It is nearly dawn, and I've been awake all night. A few minutes ago I was standing on deck, staring at the horizon. Threads of light from the rising sun picked out stars on the spires of a distant city. The jewel of the Gelaming, the Place of Light. It can sense me coming, I know. It understands what I must do to it and I can feel it trembling; half-thrill, half-fear. It is strong; made of stone and Haras' will and desires. Made of souls. But it feels me and its open, glowing streets ripple. Transience; made in a moment, destroyed in a moment. Is that what it fears? Pellaz must still be in bed, perhaps writhing in the grip of nightmare. Unspecified terror. I cannot feel him yet, but he is there, encased in glass. We will soon be there. And now, I crouch in my cabin, hugging my knees, listening to Panthera murmer in his sleep. My fingers are cold. I am afraid; trembling. Have I learned enough? I never wanted to come here, but here I am. I turned my back on the past and found that time is a circle; I'm back there. I think I'm praying, but can only pray to myself. The Goddess and the God are within all of us; that's what they told me in Roselane. A small part or a large part? By Aghama, I hope it's enough.

The Crown
'I drink him, feel him burn the lungs inside me
With endless evil longings and despair.'
Baudelaire, Destruction

Immanion shone far beyond my dreams. We docked in the morning, stepping onto a harbour of sparkling mica. It was so clean. Unbelievably, shockingly clean. The brightness made my eyes ache. *Fairminia* looked tawdry, bobbing alongside the tall, stately craft of the Gelaming, whose colours were white and gold, whose figureheads were of eagles, dragons, plunging horses. From the harbour, tier upon tier of glowing, white buildings reared towards the crown of the city. Here, the coruscating towers of Phaonica, the Tigron's palace, reflected the morning light, visible from any point in the city. Roads were wide, and lined with spreading trees. It was a busy place, but not hectic; alive, but not noisy. Hara moved gracefully; the pace of life was leisurely. Zack led us away from the harbour, heading towards the north of the city. We passed through an open-air market, where food-stuffs from all the Wraeththu countries were available in profusion. Further on, we crossed an avenue where open-fronted shops displayed their wares upon the street. The effect was unobtrusive. Was this an art-display or a gift centre? We saw many other outlanders as we walked northwards; traders, tourists and seafarers. There were also plenty of natives. I felt as if every tall, golden-haired Gelaming we passed could see right into my soul. This caused uncontrollable flinching on my part; probably nobody noticed me at all.

About a mile from the harbour, Zack hailed a swooping hire-car to take us to Thandrello, the borough where Ashmael lived. We skirted Phaonica, high up. I could see figures moving in her tiled courtyards, along her terraces and cloistered walkways. Nervousness made me fearful of looking too closely, but even quick glances assured me of one thing. There was no way the Pellaz I'd once known could ever be comfortable (even convincing) living in a place like that. Why did I still nurture this image of him as he was? Common-sense alone told me not to be so stupid, but I just couldn't visualise him any other way. It was all I knew, all that had kept my love for him alive. God, this situation was a sleeping monster to end all sleeping monsters. The face of the creature was covered; I'd have to wait until it woke up to see whether it was a face I liked. And here I was, having these reckless thoughts, even as I trespassed in *his* city. I'd been warned, told, about his power; surely he could sense me now, close as I was to him. I felt the burn of an unseen gaze at the back of my neck and acted self-consciously because of it. Did he watch me? Did he? Did he already know I was there?

We reached Thandrello in half-an-hour, but Ashmael was not at home. This precipitated an ungovernable sense of relief within me, even though I knew it was only delaying the inevitable. Ashmael's house was fairly modest by Immanion standards, but spacious and comfortable. One of his house-Hara offered to contact him for us, conducting us to an airy lounge, nearly filled with plants, whose northern wall, overlooking the garden, was all of glass. The furniture was low and stylised; not really the sort of place I'd have expected Ashmael to live in. From what I'd seen of him (admittedly only in dreams) he appeared to be the sort of Har who would only be at home in a stable, or under canvas, or in the back-room of an exceedingly seedy inn somewhere. Zack and Panthera sat down; I paced restlessly about the room.

'Calm down, Cal,' Zack admonished mildly. 'You'll be fit for nothing unless you do.'

Easy for him to say. I couldn't remember ever having felt so nervy. I wanted to fight. I wanted to get on with my task. I resented waiting. Affecting a cruel indifference to my inner turmoil, Panthera studiously examined the pictures on the walls. Zack picked up a book to read. I was not feeling particularly warm towards either of them. After all, they had nothing to dread, nothing to accomplish. Their minds were calm enough to look at pictures or read; mine could barely work out which way was up.

We'd only been waiting half-an-hour or so when Ashmael arrived home. His staff must have contacted him straight away. When he walked into that room, I recognized him immediately, which felt odd because we'd never actually met before. He smiled at me and said hello — he hadn't a clue who I was — and seemed pleased to see Zack. They spent nearly an hour swapping pleasantries; Zack was clearly being very careful, gently nudging the conversation along to provide him with a cue. I'd always suspected he'd have made a good politician; very good at manipulating things is Zack. As for me, sitting with my back to the window away from the others, I found it hard to keep my eyes off the star among Gelaming that is Ashmael. In my head, I kept replaying the dream (vision?) I'd had of him with Pell. I wanted to see the scar on his shoulder. He barely looked at me. Was I really there? Everything to fear had come so close so quickly. Only moments ago I'd been in Ferike surely? My thoughts tumbled over each other so swiftly, I could barely keep track of them. Conversation in the room washed over my head; I can remember none of it.

Eventually, Zack mentioned that he'd come, as he tactfully put it, on business. 'Oh? What kind of business?' Ashmael asked him lightly. He'd obviously guessed we weren't there on a purely social call.

'If you don't mind, I'd like to discuss it with you alone first,' Zack replied, not looking at me.

Ashmael shrugged. 'As you wish. I have an office in the next room. That private enough for you?'

Zack nodded, and, excusing themselves to Panthera and I, they left the room.

Silence moved in to take their place. I was still sitting by the window, my forehead upon the glass. I could sense Panthera fidgeting. I felt like saying, 'You still sure you should have come here?' but it would have sounded sour. Panthera couldn't speak. Oh, I was happy to indulge in my own agony; nevertheless, I was not unaware that he was suffering too. After several minutes, he had the courage to say, 'We should talk now, Cal. Who knows when we'll get the chance...'

'No,' I interrupted. 'There's nothing to say. I'm sorry, but there isn't.'

'Are you going to throw your life away then?'

'Thea, be quiet. We can't argue about this. You asked to come here and I believed you when you gave your reason why.'

'I love you.'

'Thea, don't! You'll only make it worse, for both of us.'

If we'd been in a familiar place, he'd have leapt up and stormed from the room. We weren't. He couldn't. So we both fought for breath in that room of thick, heavy air until Zack and Ashmael came back in. It must have been hours.

It was likely Zack'd had some trouble convincing Ashmael he should help me. I wondered how much he'd had to reveal. Quite a lot, I would have thought, at least as much as Zack knew himself. Ashmael was tricksy; you see that at a glance, but he was not stupid. However small the amount of information Zack had been given, I was sure it would be enough for any sane Har to realize what had to be done. Was Ashmael sane? Loyalty does strange things to people. I suspected Opalexian had decided the fewer people who knew everything the better. I was alone in this. I'd got to accept that.

The conversation had clearly been heavy-going. Ashmael's face was inscrutably grim (the only possible way to describe it), while Zack looked worn out. Ashmael went directly to open a window because the room was full of cigarette smoke, and then came to stand before me.

'So, you're the famous Cal, are you?' He stared, shook his head, stared again. I stared back. I wanted to say, 'Yes, I know the feel of you' and perhaps he saw some of that in my eyes. He looked away eventually. He had reached a decision. 'I have just heard the most incredible things about you. Things that are hard to believe. If it's true, then it's my duty to help you. If it's lies then I'm damned forever if I do …' He picked absently at the leaves of a plant by the window. 'Tomorrow, I'll take you to Phaonica,' he said. 'Thiede will be in his sanctum until nine. I will get you there for eight. By Aghama, I hope I'm making the right decision!' This last part was said fiercely. He looked at Zack.

'I've told you the truth,' Zack said, simply, shrugging. 'You must know in your heart what is right.'

'I've worked for Thiede for many years,' Ashmael answered. 'This feels like betrayal. I have only your word that it isn't.'

'You've worked for your race for many years,' I said. 'You won't be betraying them, I promise you.'

He looked at me coldly. 'Damn you for coming here,' he said. 'Damn you for existing.'

'It's not me,' I answered, 'just the Law. There'd be somebody else if not me.'

'Would there?' He shook his head once more. 'I wish I could believe that.'

I made them uncomfortable in that room. The atmosphere was not exactly congenial, not even when the inevitable refreshments arrived, so more out of consideration for others than a desire for personal well-being, I intimated that I wanted to be alone. Now they could talk about me with abandon. Ashmael had me shown to a bedroom overlooking the avenue at the front of the house. I sat on the floor under the window, and the muted sounds of the city reached me in whispers. I stared at the ceiling, but there were no answers there. I was alone, alone, alone. Never had I felt so conscious of it. Not in Megalithica, not in Thaine; nowhere. The world felt vast beyond me, vast and incomprehensible. I was such a small part. A single particle and yet, within me, the whole. I am looking up at the ceiling and there is a point that I must reach. The sun went down beyond the glass and no-one came to disturb me. I drank the water that Ashmael had provided in a glass flask. It tasted like nectar, soothing my throat and the heat inside my head. The bed looked inviting in the gloom, all honey pine and striped rugs, so I went to lie down on it. Now my capricious mind had decided to go completely blank. Could I go downstairs again? A drink of something a little stronger than water would have been welcome, but I resisted trying to satisfy that craving. The end was merely hours away. I must wait here, find strength; I would need it.

It must have been nearly midnight when Panthera knocked on the door. I suppose I'd been expecting something like that happening. He came right in and said, 'I can't let you do this.'

This was the last thing I felt capable of dealing with. 'Panthera, if I'd known you were going to be this way, I'd have left you in Roselane. There's nothing I can do. For God's sake don't take it so personally!' I didn't want to sound so heartless, but it was the truth. Truth often hurts. Perhaps that's why I used to lie so often.

Panthera ignored what I said. 'Cal, I've stuck by you through everything; doesn't that mean *anything* to you?'

'Of course it does, Thea. You know that! But I have to go through with this. There's no way out. I'm not rejecting you, just moving on. We both knew this would happen.'

He seemed caged in a world of his own as, I suppose, I was in mine. I don't think any of my words reached him. 'I know there's something you've got to do with Thiede,' he said earnestly, 'but, for your own good, can't you just walk away after that? Come back to Ferike. You can't live here, Cal. It's not you. It'll kill you!'

'Kill me!' I jumped off the bed and he backed away instinctively. 'What the hell do you know about it? It's me that's the expert on killing, Thea; that's why I'm here.'

'Yes.' Panthera's voice was soft. I sensed an approaching cruelty and was not disappointed. 'I know that. You've been obsessed with it; one killing in particular. He's dead, Cal. Why can't you accept it? The Pell you loved is dead. What lives up there in Phaonica is Tigron. It's power; nothing else. Don't you know that? Or have you just conveniently put off thinking about it?'

I couldn't even bear to be angry with him. I drank some of the water. He knocked the flask out of my hand and it shattered on the floor, water spreading in a dark stain like blood over the pale, wooden boards.

'Thea, you're hurting only yourself. You can't reach me. Not after Roselane. I *know* now. You can't reach me.' The calmness of my voice did not sooth him.

'What do you know, Cal? Tell *me*! If I know too, maybe it'll help...'

'*No*! I can't Thea. I can't.' He looked wild, but he was trembling. I wanted to hold him, tell him everything would be alright. I wanted to strike him senseless so he'd leave me alone. Tel-an-Kaa had told me to watch out for sneaky attacks by Thiede. Was this one of them? I couldn't be sure. 'Panthera, please, you must go. I have to think. Tomorrow's a big day.' I tried a tentative smile. For a moment, he stared at me, full of rage, then he walked to the door. As he turned the handle, it seemed as if someone came and stabbed him in the gut. He doubled up, slid down the door and crouched on the floor, leaning against the wall. I really thought he'd been attacked. Anything was possible here. 'What is it, Thea? Where's it hurt?' I tried to pull him up.

'Here!' he shouted, uncurling. 'Here!' And he was thumping his chest with one hand, right over the heart. His face was wet with tears. Internal agony then; it had been me who'd thrown the knife.

'Thea?'

'I don't know why I'm doing this to myself,' he said. 'I don't know.'

'I'm sorry...' It was all I could say, all I could think of.

'Cal, don't leave me.'

We looked at each other in the half-light. He was so beautiful; it seems almost lame to say it. Why? Why, why, why...

'Don't leave me... *please*!'

My chest ached. My arms ached to hold him, but tomorrow would always be there. I could make no promises.

A long time ago, I'd been chesna with a Har named Zackala. That's very, very close by Wraeththu standards. Some might say an insoluble link that exists even after hearts and bodies have waved goodbye to each other. It was simple to reach out with my mind and call him. Easy to intimate everything, by projecting the very least. He came through my door within seconds. I looked up at him helplessly, crouched on the floor by Panthera, who seemed almost senseless with grief. Zack shook his head, but said nothing. Between us, we got Panthera on his feet. He made an enormous effort to appear normal, perhaps embarrassed that Zack was there.

He did not guess I'd summoned help, perhaps thinking Zack had passed the door and heard something. Before he left he said, 'Goodbye, Cal. I wish you luck.' I pulled a wry face. 'I mean it,' he said.

'Come on Thea,' Zack said, in a horribly cheerful voice. 'Help me make a hole in Ashmael's liquor store! Cal can't afford to have a good time tonight!' He put his arm around Panthera's shoulder and dragged him away. When I closed the door, that white, stricken face was still looking back at me.

Alone, I sat on the floor with my back to the door and stared at the dark place where the water had spilled. I'd have trusted Panthera with my life. He'd trusted me with his heart which had been frozen nearly to death in Piristil. Now, in pursuit of my crazy, half-realized dreams, I was casting him aside like a meatless chicken-bone. (And, oh yes, I'd enjoyed consuming the meat.) I even loved him; but not enough. There was still that bewitching phantom waiting for me, that stranger, that immortal memory. Oh God, am I doing the right thing? Am I? Phaonica … Through the window, I could look out and see those glistering spires. Beautiful, but spiky cruel they are. I want to touch them. It's as simple as that. Beyond the glass, as the hours progressed towards that single point in time, the light gradually changed. I sat on the floor, staring, staring, oblivious of anything but the mystery of Phaonica, and remained like that till dawn.

30

Phaonica

'The agony is past; behold
how shape and light are born again;
how emerald and starry gold
burn in the midnight; how the pain
of our incredible marriage-fold
and bed of birthless travail wane;
and how our molten limbs divide
and self and self again abide.'

Aleister Crowley, Asmodel

Zack was up to see me off. There was no sign of Panthera. Was he making it easier for me or for himself? Ashmael made me eat something but the bread tasted like ashes. I was afraid. 'Remember, we are with you,' Zack said, and I thought of Opalexian. I thought, 'No, I am alone,' but appreciated his concern.

Ashmael and I went out into the brightness of a fair and dreaming morning, walking because we didn't have far to go. Tall trees with glossy, dark leaves hid the palace from general view at first. We passed beneath them and I looked up. Imagine then the tremendous bulk of that fair edifice Phaonica. Effulgence upon shine upon brilliant haze. Darkness without shadow; the crown. And me. Shambling behind Ashmael; a mote of dark within the sphere of light. Dread had made me feel black; from the core out. Oh, I had worked hard to pay for my sins, but that could not erase the fact they'd been committed. Had my shadows any place within this splendour? My heart was aching because it was beating so hard, so fast. I followed Ashmael through the quieter courtyards, where he knew it was unlikely anyone would be about. And then it was deep, deep into the heart of the palace of light; to the inner sanctum of the Aghama. We saw no-one. The spacious corridors meditated in silence, columns and spiralling stairs, galleries and vaulted halls. A place of hushed magnificence. The Tigron lived here. Who was he really? Could he sense my presence? The rooms felt bewitched, enchanted into sleep so I could pass through them unnoticed. I felt Phaonica sigh around me, but there was no sign of Pellaz. We went down a flight of white steps and the light became blue. Thiede's sanctum; the temple in the heart of Phaonica. Ashmael left me at the gateway, and I stepped inside.

It was like being surrounded by floating veils; everything was indistinct. I could smell cinnamon, strong and earthy. Where did the light come from? How big was this place? A single room, a labyrinth? I was stopped, limping towards the centre, shivering like a rat crossing an alley. In Phaonica, I could no longer be beautiful. Ahead of me, an eternity away, I could see a pulsing core of light, solid brightness at its centre. Power radiated out towards me, a slumbering power. It was Thiede, wreathed in blue flame, suspended in the webs of his own thought, contemplating beyond this world. As I approached him (oh, so slowly) the brightness changed colour. Threads of red light streaked its purity. Thiede could sense me. He felt me drawing nearer, a smoking, black-rot presence. At first there was only a dim outrage that something unclean had entered his sacred space, then I caught it; fear! One pure beam of naked fear. He knew. Then I was right up close to him and it was like looking through glass and his burning eyes were upon me, spitting flame. He could not believe it. How could such a worthless beast as I breach his privacy without detection? What power did that mean I owned, or was lent? His face contorted with revulsion. My clothes had become rags.

I stretched a shaking hand towards him and it was caked with grime, so thin, almost mummified. 'I know,' I said, and my voice was the voice of the last doomed prophet. 'I have seen.' He raised his hand to banish me but I spoke first. 'Is the one who would be Aghama afraid to hear what this foul creature might say?' And now it was Opalexian's voice that I spoke with. 'Didn't you always want me to come here, Thiede? Didn't you once ask me to?'

He considered for a moment before saying, 'Speak then,' and there was a certain curiosity in his tone. Thiede still thought he had the ability to get rid of me when he wished.

'It began with a bullet,' I said, 'when the soul of a single Har rose high, transfixed by your radiance, but unable to reach it. Prevented from reaching it. That suited you didn't it? Even the Aghama can know fear. Pellaz could not reach you because he had no complement. Now I know you wanted it to stay that way; always! "Come to Immanion, Cal," you said. "Be the Tigron's plaything." Clever of you I suppose. You knew I'd say no to that. You only had to twist the truth a little to keep us apart. Pellaz and I *are Wraeththu*, Thiede. Fate brought us together, but a very calculating Fate. Pell is Light and I am Dark, but without each other we cannot understand the real Light. Together, we can combine and reach for it. We *become you*, Thiede. We become the ultimate. You knew that, didn't you? That is why it was so necessary to keep me away from here. Oh, I thought you were being so understanding, so reasonable about it all, didn't I? It was Pell who was the villain of the piece, the spoilt child who wanted something, and stamped and screamed until he got it. I know better now. Thiede, you are holding Wraeththu back, stunting their development. There had to be a Tigron, but it wasn't your idea. No, your part of it was to keep the Tigron to being just one person. That way you could keep all your power. Phaonica is but an illusion, Immanion built of dreams. Your dreams. It shines, it is safe, but it is unbalanced. Pellaz lives in glass; you have made him so pure. But there is still the sleeping seed within him that reaches towards me; the seed that shuts the Tigrina from his heart, that keeps his belief in Us strong. You can cage it, Thiede, but you cannot destroy it.'

'No, but I can destroy you,' Thiede answered, and he was calm and unsurprised. One day, all this would have had to come to light. Thiede was not that blind.

'Of course you can, and you must,' I answered. His face flickered with brief, unspecified shadows.

'Have you come here then just to tell me what you know and let me dispose of you neatly?' He smiled. 'I think not, Calanthe. You're a survivor. You won't give in that easily. Are you trying to fool me?'

'Perhaps I'm just playing with words. The Aghama can't kill, can he? If he could, he would have got rid of me years ago. No, in destroying me, you destroy yourself. Life is precious isn't it?'

'What do you want?' His patience was ebbing. He was in no

mood for games, which showed he was worried.

'What do I want? Oh, that's easy. I want you to kill me, as you killed Pellaz. You're going to have to do it, Thiede. You must.'

He smiled wanly. 'And create something more powerful than this world has ever known? Destroy myself?'

'Only in death can you truly become Aghama, Thiede. Why are you afraid?'

'You do not know what I feel. It is not fear as you can grasp it. I have always understood that I am mortal, as we all are. Because of this my weakness is my love of flesh, my love of this world; its people, its earth, its feel. I know that is weakness, but it is also my strength because I can admit it. I also know that I have been fighting against the inevitable. I knew you'd show up here one day, to claim what you think is yours. I didn't believe, for a moment, that I'd managed to get rid of you forever. Don't, in your arrogance, think that I'm unaware of that. If I want to, I can know every thought in every Harish head. I began this race, Cal.'

'Yes, you did, and you must let it go on, Thiede. Wraeththu must progress. The next stage must be initiated. Now.'

'And if I don't? What then?'

'Then Opalexian will make you do it, I'm sure.'

'Opalexian.' The name obviously disturbed him. Perhaps he'd heard it in dreams, banished it from his visions.

'Kamagrian,' I said.

'And what is that?'

I could not believe he did not already know. 'I can show you. It is all inside me. All of it.'

For a moment longer, in those final moments, he stared at me deeply. What did he see? A Uigenna wastrel? A used-up kanene? A murderer? Or did he see Opalexian's initiate? He was afraid.

'Show me then,' he said, and I opened up my mind to let him look within me and learn what I knew. She that taught it lived there. If he'd been ignorant of her existence, as, at last, I felt he must, he did not let me see it. He extended his hand.

'Let me look at you again,' he said, and drew me towards him. He smiled sadly. 'One of my children. Every Har is one of my children. Have I been a harsh father, a useless one?'

'Neither, but you have not been a mother either.'

He shook his head. His last moments. He looked around the temple, loving it, smelling it, absorbing it, afraid he would lose it for eternity. Until the moment of extinction, there is no real proof for any of us that life extends beyond it. 'Pell is waiting to love you,' he said. 'That, in itself, has been an act of worship for him. I envy you. I envy you everything.'

'You shouldn't.'

He smiled more widely, a sparkle coming into his eyes. 'A last fling at carnality, my dear. That's all. I must go back to the beginning, look at it again. Then we will speak some more.'

'In this place, we will speak many times.'

'Conceive your sons here. Bring your love here ...' He sighed and took both of my hands in his own. 'I am not a wicked creature, Cal.'

'I know that.'

'Then let us do what must be done,' he said. There was no way he could fight it, for the only way to fight it was to destroy me, which is what had to happen anyway.

As a column of shadow, I rose towards a vacillating brightness that in the moment of contact exploded into me as a countless number of sparks. At that moment, throughout the world, every Wraeththu Har would shudder, raising his head to the sky, feeling fear, wonder, power. Those that slept would dream my dream, those that were awake would live it. Me, as a mote of the whole, in that instant *became* each of those individuals. And they felt me. And recognized me. But in Phaonica, the Cal that had been was consumed in the fire, spiralling helplessly, at one with the elemental force that held the world together. The walls of that temple trembled. I heard a piercing, agonised shriek that was Pellaz wrenched from the glass, pulled gasping through a crack of infinite sharpness, that cut and tore and ruined. I was high above the city and Immanion shuddered and groaned, black tongues licking its streets, sweeping oily smoke behind it. Buildings listed, fell, twisted, screamed. Hara came out of their homes, still pulling on clothes, dragging Harlings behind them, staring up in horror at a sky that was red and black; a kingdom of flame. I could see all this as I burned and it lasted an eternity. And yet it was just a moment. When the peace came, I was lying on a cold floor in the middle of a vast chamber that was completely empty. For a while I just experienced *body*. I hadn't been sure I'd still have one. Now it was just Harish, panting and winded, with aching guts and scraped lungs, dazed as a small child kicked over by a heavy foot. High above me in the arches of the temple, I could see a spark of light. That was all. I could not reach for it alone.

Phaonica was in darkness, its corridors and halls empty. Everyone was in hiding. I stumbled along the terraces for hours, seeking, seeking. There was no-one to show me the way and I was too confused and drained to use my mind to find him. I came to be standing in a garden and it was evening. I was looking up at a balcony and the open windows beyond it. Here must I climb. Creepers on the walls shook and shed their leaves as I clambered upwards, tendrils losing their grasp on stone. I nearly fell a dozen times, scraping my knees, my knuckles. As I climbed I heard a whimpering that came from above. It was the whimpering of an abandoned child. I swung my legs over the balcony and tried to wipe the dust and twigs from my clothes. Impossible. Easier to tear the rags from my body, even if it was ravaged and unclean beneath. But the filth fell away with the rags and, free of them, I was pale and pure of skin. Reborn. Maybe. For a moment, I stood at the window doors to the room beyond and I was just Cal again. A Cal who had a heart beating fast, whose breath caught in his throat because he faced the thing he desired and feared the most. I walked inside. The canopy was torn from the bed (shredded) and cast about the room. Tall, decorated jars filled with peacock feathers and palms had been thrown at the walls and lay smashed upon the floor. I saw a huddled shape lying amongst all this wreckage and recognized it as Vaysh, the guide of my vision. There was blood upon his forehead, a frown upon his face. Eyes closed. But he was not dead. A single glance told me that. I could feel his life, see it within him. Now I must look at the bed and it took courage to do that. Courage because it was Pellaz lying there, his body scratched and torn and bloodied, tortured in its posture, arms across his face. He was half-conscious, now mumbling, now silent, lying in a tangle of torn sheets and splinters of glass from the long windows that had burst inwards upon him. For a moment longer, I stood and looked at him. Was he different? Older, yes. He was no longer scrawny but lithe. I leaned forwards and uncrossed his arms. This was the moment then, when I looked into the face of the monster. I sat down on the bed, touched his cheek, his eyelids, his lips. The face of the Tigron. Beautiful and, in it, the ghost of my Pellaz. I was afraid to wake him, but knew I must. Standing at the foot of the bed once more, I raised my arms, reaching for the Light. (Here, Thiede, here. We shall reach you.) The bed was strewn with glass. I grabbed hold of the fringed coverlet and pulled sharply. Pellaz rolled onto the clean sheet beneath and groaned. He didn't open his eyes but reached up to touch his face. It's been so long since I touched him. So long. This seems like blasphemy. I lay down beside him.

My body was warm, his was cold. I fed him with heat so that he had to open his eyes and see that I was there. Such bewilderment. From me to the room to me. Confusion to start with. 'What? What ...!' Then he saw Vaysh lying on the wreckage-strewn floor and screamed, 'No!' thinking of Orien. He wanted to leap up, whether to escape or attack me, I couldn't be sure. I had to hold him down. He struggled, tried to bite me, but his struggles were weak because his powers had been disabled by Thiede's passage from flesh.

'Would I be here if it was simply death I was carrying?' I asked and he replied, 'You have always carried destruction. It is you.'

His nightmares, his dreams had been realized. How many times had he yearned to open his eyes and find me there? Even though he had known about Orien whom I murdered, and believed the tales that Thiede had told him, he had still hoped. Now it was true. 'What has happened?' he asked. 'What have you done?'

'Only what had to be done.'

'Thiede has gone hasn't he,' he said. 'You have destroyed us all.' He shuddered in my arms, looking around the room, seeing violation, just violation, too weak to protest any further.

I pulled him from the bed and dragged him over to the window, forced him onto the balcony. 'Look at your city, Pell,' I said and he turned his head away, eyes closed, wincing. 'Look. Really look!' I forced his head around and made him see. On the highest levels, the stone still shone, and there were wide avenues where, in the morning, the light would dance. But now, there were also places where the light would never reach, the dark alleys, the subterranean canals and thoroughfares, where rats would creep and moaning ghosts disturb travellers from the lighter places above. Now, Immanion was whole, a place of softness and harshness, of thieves as well as angels, as all these things should be. Destroyed to be rebuilt. Not Thiede's city, but Wraeththu's. Not just Pell's, but mine too, as we were each other's. I led him back inside. He was still saying, 'What have you done? What have you done?' and protested when I laid him on the bed. 'You are the Destroyer, I'll have no part of you. Where is Thiede?'

'We shall find him,' I said, 'but you must trust me.'

'Trust you?' he asked bleakly. 'As I trusted you to come to me once Megalithica had fallen to our people? In the forest of Gebaddon you encountered the past. I made you ready to come to me, but you never did. Thiede never agreed with me about you, but he tried to help. Even then you rejected me. I was just Pellaz who had died to you. A past occurrence, easily forgotten. It was never like that for me. I never forgot! Now you have returned, and it's like it always was; Cal and the sword of ruin. My city has gone. So too whatever power I once had, I expect.' He sighed. 'Life without you was never easy, but at least it was life. Now what have I got?'

'Everything,' I answered. 'More than you ever had before. Give me your hand.' He pulled a sad, wry face, but did so. I opened up and burned him. He did not pull away.

'You are different.' It was a wary decision. 'How?'

'I must tell you everything,' I said.

'Of course you must.' He smiled. 'So tell me.'

I had rehearsed this scene in my head countless times, anticipating his reactions, his outbursts, his silences. Now he just listened, nodding now and then, his face expressionless; the face of a king. For some reason I didn't tell him about the Kamagrian, feeling that should come later. He had enough to swallow without that. When I finished speaking, he lay face-down on the bed, his chin on his fists, his feet upon the pillow. I watched him digest what I'd told him. I thought about how you did not interrupt the thoughts of the Tigron; you waited until he spoke. I examined the curve of his spine, his black hair, tangled, that covered even his thighs. I looked at his straight nose, his dark eyes; everything. I could never get enough of that. It was like being starved to the point of death and then being presented with a freshly roast lamb accompanied by every exotic vegetable you can think of. One does not interrupt the thoughts of the Tigron, unless one is Tigron too. 'Well?' I said. I think I'd still been expecting him to leap on me with open arms.

He laughed. 'This is crazy. My city explodes, Thiede evaporates and you burst in here naked telling me that now you're Tigron with me! Hell, I'm cut all over! Is this real? Am I going to wake up in a minute?'

'Maybe, but not in the way you think.'

He narrowed his eyes at me. 'Cal, it's been over thirty years! This is just … oh, I don't know.' He shook his head, pressed his brow against his arms on the bed. 'I'm not the same person, Cal. You do realize that, don't you?' There was a hint, just a hint, of a certain wistfulness I'd recognize after a hundred years, never mind thirty.

'Neither am I, Pell, but we're not strangers are we?'

He smiled. 'No. It doesn't feel like that. I don't know how it feels. Maybe we should see. The truth is I've waited a long time for this. Dreams, hopes; oh, I've had plenty of those! Now they are gone. If it's ruins beyond this, then it's ruins! I'll think about it another time.' He turned over. 'Pick the glass from my skin first, Cal. I may be immortal, but not impervious to pain. Here I am; yours. I always have been. Want to come home now?'

There were no shooting stars, no huge explosions. We didn't even know if we were truly in love as we'd once thought; only time would tell us that. We met as Hara and conjoined as Hara, but there was a difference. In the midst of our communion, when we were truly one, we could reach for the ultimate and it was there for us to touch. It was the true Godhead, and when we joined with it we became Three. Divine. It will always be there for us and together we can touch it whenever we want to. The Aghama, a god of all attributes, the sum of our positive and negative, force and meekness, flesh and spirit, love and hate. I am the stone, Pell is the silk and Thiede has become the binding force that makes us mesh. This is what happened in Immanion in the year ai-cara 29. It should have happened twenty-nine years before.

Caeru, the Hegemony and
Beyond
*'If this be error and upon me proved,
I never writ, nor no man ever loved.'*
William Shakespeare, Sonnet XVIII

When we woke the next morning, we knew that it was real because the floor of the chamber was strewn with broken crockery, torn drapes, wind-hurled leaves. We knew that it was real because the smell coming in through the shattered windows was of smoke and destruction. Somewhere a bell was tolling, without urgency, desolately. For a while, we just held onto each other in the fragmented blankets, and we could weep without fear of weakness. A natural reaction; the numbness, the feeling of surreality, had gone. Pellaz asked me, 'What have we become?' and for that first day, it was a wistful, melancholy sentiment, because the easy ways of the past were over. The real work had yet to begin.

We would rebuild Immanion, clear the debris; it was not as bad as it looked. Dreams had been shattered yes, but what would be rebuilt would consist of more than dreams. In that brief, eternal moment when I had become one with the lifeforce of Wraeththu, the truth had been revealed to me. As Immanion had changed, so too had other places, touched by the fire of the Triad. Now there was a small, scruffy town in Thaine known as Fallsend, whose grubby streets would open out into wider avenues where Hara could walk free. I wondered what would be the fate of Piristil and its kind. Would there be a place for them now? Was the force that strong? Somehow I doubted it. One thing I had learned was the utter need for light and dark, nothing can be *wholly* good, but if Piristil still thrived, then to complement it, there would be other houses; places of healing and learning. As Immanion could not be utterly Light, Fallsend could not be utterly Dark. From the mud would come roads, and other travellers would follow them, bringing the warmth of wholeness with them from the south and west. And what of Jaddayoth? I'd only experienced about half of it, but decided that most of the twelve tribes had, in their own way, already balanced their societies. Mainly they had just got on with the business of living. Gelaming, clearly, had just been trying too hard to live up to Wraeththu's potential, their beliefs had been too subjective.

Perhaps it was wrong (*selfish, weak?*) that I actually considered avoiding facing Panthera again, perhaps merely wise, but it was still late in the day when I forced myself to leave Pell's side to go and find him. We'd spent most of the morning trying to sort the Tigron's apartment out with Vaysh, who was nursing a colourful black eye. I had explained to Pell something about my companion from Jaddayoth. At first, he'd been rather unsympathetic with Panthera. 'Why bother seeing him again? It's over, isn't it?'

'We parted messily. I don't like messes. Anyway, I owe him a lot. He deserves more than a kick out the door.'

'Hardly that, Cal, but I suppose you're right. Don't be too long. There are things that need to be seen to.'

It was not an easy mission. There was no guarantee that he'd still be at Ashmael's house although I was confident that he'd stick around to see how everything turned out. Most of Thandrello still stood intact, but a tree had crashed through a window of Ashmael's house, killing one of his staff. Ashmael and his people were in the grounds of the house clearing up, Ashmael stripped to the waist, hauling branches away from shattered glass. He was quite business-like when he caught sight of me walking up the drive. He sauntered towards me, almost as if nothing had happened and casually asked after Pell. There was no mention of Thiede.

'I'll be up at Phaonica shortly', he said. 'You and Pell must call an emergency meeting of the Hegemony; you do understand that, don't you?'

What with all the upheaval, I hadn't really thought about it. Pell certainly hadn't mentioned it, which was odd, because as Tigron, it should be the thing uppermost in his mind, whatever else was going on. 'I suppose you're right,' I answered.

Ashmael laughed grimly. 'You're worried? Don't be! You're lucky in that the Hegemony will be in a bit of a flap; they won't give you their worst. After all, their godhead has ...' He paused eloquently. 'Pell will be able to tell you about how he fared at the Hegemony's hands when he first came here.'

'Pell had Thiede to protect him as well.' I shook my head. 'Oh dear! Will they finish me off do you think?'

Ashmael was stony. 'I doubt it. The very fact that Thiede is no longer ... *appears* no longer to be around will act in your favour. They will look to Pell now for guidance; they will have to. They thought they were *so* democratic, but they're useless without Thiede's brains and common-sense.'

'What makes you so sure they've lost those things?'

Ashmael raised his brows. 'Suspicions, hunches, how the hell will I know until you decide to tell me? Am I supposed to ask? Have you killed him?'

'You've been listening to too many stories about me, tiahaar!'

'Perhaps. Can't help it. They've all been so scandalous. So?'

'So, aren't we rather making light of a very heavy subject?'

Ashmael shrugged. 'I've never been one for those kind of theatricals. If Thiede is dead, let's just get on with what we've got to do.'

'Two days ago you spoke of loyalty.'

'That was a millenium ago! Posthumous loyalty is a matter to be considered seriously. Maybe I will change my affinities in the light of what you know. Come on, tell me.'

I sighed. 'Oh, it's quite simple really. Thiede has become the Aghama.'

Ashmael regarded me quizzically after this statement. '*Become the Aghama*,' he repeated slowly. 'Does that mean he's dead or not?'

'It means that Thiede is no longer a Har entirely of flesh and blood. It means he has become the god he's always styled himself to be. Let us just say that through sacrificing the flesh he has managed to attain the position he has always craved.'

Ashmael did not look convinced. 'Such words slip uneasily from your tongue, Cal,' he said.

'Not my usual style no,' I agreed. 'We will have to talk later. I'm sure many Hara are as anxious to know as you are. Now, I've got business of another kind to attend to. Is Panthera still here?'

Ashmael nodded thoughtfully. 'Round the back. Are you taking him back to Phaonica?'

'Nobody *takes* Panthera anywhere! I expect he'll return to Ferike soon.'

'What a shame.'

I smiled carefully and started to walk away.

'Just a moment!' Ashmael called me back. 'I shall be going to Megalithica next month, to Galhea. You'll have to start getting used to being a celebrity and Megalithica is a good place to start. Perhaps you should come with me ...'

'An inflammatory suggestion, tiahaar! Let me sort out my traumas in Immanion first please.'

'Of course!' He smiled sweetly and ducked a bow. 'Just a suggestion, that's all, but please think about it.'

'I'll think about it certainly. Now, if you'll excuse me ...'

He waved me away, still smiling. I was not blind. Ashmael had talked about Pell having had a rough ride when he first came to Immanion, and I could guess where most of the trouble had come from. I wondered how long Lord Ashmael would consider it necessary to test me.

I found Panthera and Zack together, pausing for a break from the cleaning up, sitting on the trunk of a fallen tree, sharing a bottle of wine and looking very cosy. I sensed a certain closing of ranks as they saw me approaching. A sudden flare of crazy hope kindled in Panthera's eyes, but only for a moment. I went right up to them and took the wine bottle from Panthera's hand, taking a careless swig in an effort to conceal the fact that this was not easy for me. Panthera could not bring himself to stand up and embrace me. It made me realize in an instant that I was now a stranger to him. He hadn't been part of what had happened in Phaonica the day before; all he had experienced was the result. We were both held in an embarrassing kind of silence which Zack had the presence of mind to excuse himself from. We both watched his retreating form in an agony of blank minds. Eventually I thought of, 'Are you returning to Ferike now?'

Panthera didn't look at me. 'I haven't really decided yet. Zackala is travelling to Oomadrah soon. I had thought of going back there with him first. Somehow I think the peace and quiet of Jael would get on my nerves at the moment.'

'Ah, so the "party party" of the Sykernesse court attracts you, does it?'

He looked me in the eye then. 'It would be more healing for me than sitting brooding in Jael, yes.'

I looked away, nervously kicked a fallen branch with my foot.

'You look well,' Panthera said.

'Do you want to know what happened?'

'No, not really.'

'Will you ever come back here?'

He sat there on a tortured, torn tree-trunk, knees apart, strong and young. He'd changed so much since Thaine. Grown, and in so many ways. I considered for a brief moment the ideas I'd once had of shutting myself away with him in Ferike. I still wasn't convinced it wouldn't have been the best thing for me to do. Now it was an impossibility and I had to watch this dear friend walk away from me into the world. He would meet so many new people and inevitably forget the intensity of his feelings for me. It was not conceit to think that. I could see it in his eyes, honest and unashamed.

'Come back here?' he said at last, taking a cigarette from a squashed packet, lighting it and savagely throwing the packet onto the ground.

'Are you serious?'

'Is our friendship over too then?'

'Don't play with me Cal. Not now. OK, you want to hear it? Yes, I may come back here, but it won't be to see you. I don't mean to sound harsh, or petty or jealous, or whatever. It just *is*. Face it. You gave me up the minute you walked out of here yesterday. Maybe you still had the choice then, I don't know. I never will. Just let me get on with my life now.'

'You're bitter.'

'Am I?' He took angry, deep draws off the cigarette. 'This is distressing me Cal, much as I hate to admit it. Would you just leave please?'

'OK, if that's what you want.' I sighed and turned away. He didn't stop me.

Half-way down the drive, I said, 'Dammit!' out loud and ran back to him. He looked up at me, hostile and uncertain, but I still dragged him up off the log and wrapped him in an embrace it would have been difficult to pull out of.

'I never said thank you, you arrogant little shit!' I said, which seemed easier than murmuring something maudlin. He wouldn't relax for a moment, arms stiff at his sides. 'I'm grateful for everything,' I said, 'everything.'

'Then thank me,' he said, and smiled. 'After all, you'll never have anyone as beautiful as me again. Gratitude is hardly enough!' He squeezed me hard.

'Still friends then?'

'I'll think about it. Probably in Oomadrah. Then I might come back and see if you mean it.'

'Yes,' I said. 'Do that. Maybe I'll need a little of your abrasive company after all these high and mighty Gelaming.'

'Just make sure you never truly become one of them.' Wisdom there from my pantherine, which I must never forget. 'Right up until last night I still wanted to fight for you,' he said.

'What made you change your mind?'

He rolled his eyes mischeivously. 'I don't think I'll tell you, or maybe I will. It was Zack.'

'He's always had a way with words,' I said bleakly, rather disappointed.

'Words had little to do with it,' Panthera replied, a brave effort at masking his feelings, which didn't fool me for a moment. If something had changed Panthera's mind it had been nothing to do with mere physical acts (whatever they'd been), but the vast, unimaginable glory of the Aghama's transmutation. It must have touched everybody. Panthera and I shared breath for the last time and sounds around us, which had seemed to fade away, came back as if someone had lifted a veil. I saw Zack wandering over in our direction again and let Panthera go. This strand of the past was now truly over and its frayed ends had been sealed to the best of my ability.

'I'd better get back to Phaonica now,' I said and this time I meant it. Panthera waved and turned back to his work. I did not look back at him, mainly because Zack decided to walk down the drive with me.

'Don't damage Panthera in *any* way,' I said.

'And now you have the power to know if I do, eh?' He kicked a stone. 'Don't worry about him. You're not the only one to change, Cal. Perhaps we should have spoken of the past together during the journey here on Opalexian's ship, but it hardly seemed worth it. That sordid history of ours was so worthless, after all. But perhaps we should mention it. Didn't we think we were so good then? Such a game.'

'And you lost. We both did. At the time.'

Zack shook his head. 'I disagree. What we didn't realize was, that none of it really mattered. I hated you for ages, but then one day realized that I would probably have done the same as you if it had been me up there on the wall with my gun in the next alley. Who knows? We were both foul bastards who got what we deserved.'

'So you don't think I was to blame then? That's great. I'd always been proud to take the responsibility for that as well!'

'Oh, come on, no-one was to blame. It was just the way we were living. Taking risks, scampering along the edge of the abyss with one eye closed. It's conceit to nurture that guilt for so long; it's unimportant. Sorry to ruin your self-indulgent shame, but it's true!'

'Perhaps I should be glad that you think that. I don't know. At the moment it all seems so dim; I can't really care about it.'

Zack laughed. 'No. Why should you? I wouldn't! Enjoy being Tigron, Cal. The title suits you.'

He left me at the gate and I returned to Phaonica alone, scuffing through the streets, somehow tired, somehow sad, somehow relieved. No-one knew me in Immanion; yet. I saw Gelaming sweeping away the past, some with tired, grief-torn faces, some with a smile and determination. They'll learn.

And there was black-haired Pellaz waiting for me, as he had always waited for me and always would. To be able to walk into those luxurious (if currently war-torn) apartments and just take him in my arms as mine was a wonder I was sure I'd never take for granted. He was new to me, yet familiar. Like a shining phantom of the Pell I'd once known. A succubus/incubus, waiting in darkness. But this was daylight and he had a dripping sandwich of spiced ham and savage mustard in his hand, which he thoughtfully pushed into my mouth.

'There is a problem,' he said, wiping mustard from his chin.

'A problem? Surely not!' I gasped, with watering eyes, gingerly putting the sandwich, half-chewed, on a plaster-strewn table. The only available chair was lumpy with clothes so I sat on the floor.

'You will have to deal with it.'

'What is it? And why me?'

'The problem is my consort Caeru, and you will deal with it, because now you are my partner, my twin, and therefore I feel guiltless burdening you with it.'

'Ah, yes. Caeru. We have met.'

'Yes, I know. I heard all about it in extravagant detail. Several times.'

'Did it worry you?'

'Of course. I had no idea what was going on. My Tigrina, being self-obsessed at the best of times, could only rant on about how you must be planning to come to Immanion to roust him from his throne. He had totally ignored the implications of what it could all mean to me, but that's Caeru! You will have to get used to it, I'm afraid.'

'What do you mean?' I asked suspiciously. I had come to see quite quickly in my beloved, a certain deviousness that I'm sure hadn't been there before.

'Quite simply, Cal, I mean this: I am Tigron, Caeru is my consort. Now you are Tigron too, and he is yours.'

'*He is mine*! Have you told him yet?' Horror didn't come into it.

It had already been impressed upon me how popular the Tigrina was in Almagabra. As he had said, his position was unassailable. However, this was a circumstance that I was sure he hadn't thought of. Neither had I.

'No, of course I haven't told him! Sometimes we don't speak for weeks! I haven't seen him since the day he got back from Maudrah.'

'That was ages ago.'

'Caeru's moods can last longer than that.'

'*Caeru*'s moods?'

Pell sniffed impatiently. 'Alright, *our* moods. You can tell him. I'm sure he'll be delighted. After all, he was under the impression that you'd arrive here with a gang of mercenaries and run him through with a sword. Run him through, by all means, but simply to show him his position.'

'Pellaz, you can be foul.'

'I thought I was supposed to be sometimes. You did that.'

'I did not bond you in blood with Caeru, did I. That was your decision.'

'You think so? I had little choice. One day I'll, *we'll* need heirs. Thiede chose Caeru for that function.'

'How callous. Can't we make our own now?'

'Caeru is Tigrina, Cal. That's not something that can be taken back. Unless you really want to run him through with a sword. Think we'd get away with it?'

I sighed. 'Where is he?'

Pellaz smiled triumphantly. 'I'll have Vaysh take you to him. Vaysh!'

I must admit, I found it quite amusing how far Caeru's apartments were from Pell's. Clearly they didn't need the convenience of proximity. I was finding it quite difficult equating the Pell who could treat someone so dismissively with the compassionate young creature I had known in Megalithica. I told myself, 'Of course he had to change. Nobody could be in his position and remain so ingenuous', but it still made me feel a little uneasy. Selfish of me really. Had I really expected the young Pellaz to have been preserved in entirety just so that I could happily relive fond moments of the past?

Gazing in wonder at the tarnished splendour of Phaonica, I followed Vaysh through halls and corridors, stepping over tumbled furniture and tapestries that had fallen from their hangings. Vaysh told me, 'Caeru will be at his wits end. Probably demented.' He smiled. 'Maybe even dangerous. May I stay and watch this?'

'It is my opinion that you and Pell encourage each other in a rather harsh treatment of the Tigrina,' I said, which was meant to sound serious, but came out rather mocking.

Vaysh shrugged. 'You're probably right. But you haven't had to put up with him.'

'Isn't it rather sad? I can't help feeling sorry for him.'

'Oh, Cal, you disappoint me! Pell always admired your clever sarcasm. Don't feel sorry for Caeru, just let your talents rip!'

If Pell had learned to be hard, I at least had learned to be somewhat more understanding. 'Tell him I've come for dinner,' I said.

Vaysh grimaced, pushing aside an obscuring torn curtain, and knocked upon a high, studded door.

The nervous face of a servant appeared round the door. 'Tell the Tigrina the Tigron is here to see him,' Vaysh ordered imperiously. He looked at me and repeated with jarring sincerity, 'Tell him the Tigron has come for dinner.' We walked inside. The place was a mess, dark with an air of desperate desolation.

'Vaysh,' I said. He raised an eyebrow in anticipation.

'OK, I know. I can go now. You don't have to say it, although I must point out that I don't often take orders from the Tigron.'

'I didn't say a word.'

He smiled. 'No, you don't have to. Have fun.'

I wandered alone further into the room, a small, once-elegant ante-chamber with many doors leading off. One was open and I could see a lean, black-haired Har in the room beyond picking stuff up off the floor. His face seemed somehow familiar, so I went and stood in the doorway.

'Need any help?' He looked up at me. I was a stranger, but disaster brings people closer, so he said, 'No, it's OK, I'll manage. I've been away. They called me back today. Is Thiede really dead? What's happened exactly?'

381

'A coming of age,' I answered. 'Destruction, rebirth, you know, that kind of thing.' The Har smiled, wiped his hands.

'You've lost me! I can't get any sense out of my hostling either. Did you want to see him?'

'That depends on who your hostling is!'

'Sorry.' He held out his hand. 'I'm Abrimel, the Tigron's son.' I took the hand and clasped it warily. Stupid of me. I hadn't anticipated that Caeru may have already produced an heir, neither had Pell seen fit to mention it. Probably because, bearing in mind the Wraeththu life-span, by the time Pell was ready to hand over his throne, Abrimel would be too old to take it on. However, the young Har's existence did bring home to me that once upon a time Caeru and Pell must have been locked together in something other than hostilities. I could see the resemblance to Pell in Abrimel's face; that was the familiarity I'd sensed.

'Caeru is your hostling then.'

He nodded. 'Yes. He's around somewhere. Sorry, I don't know you. Should I? Do you want me to fetch him?'

'No, I should already have been announced. My name is Cal. You may have heard of me.' I decided it would be better not to mention my new title as yet.

Abrimel's face clouded instantly, though he was polite enough to try and conceal it. 'You could say your name is familiar,' he said. 'Is my father alright?'

'Yes. Whatever you may have heard, don't judge me until you've spoken to him.'

'My father won't speak of you to me.'

'I think he will now.'

Abrimel pursed his lips and threw down the bundle of clothes he'd been gathering up. Caeru's clothes; elegant and destroyed. 'I hadn't planned to visit the Tigron until tomorrow,' Abrimel said. 'Caeru needs me more at the moment. As I said, I can't get any sense out of him. What do you want him for?'

'I think you should speak to Pellaz about it,' I said, thinking this was something I was definitely not going to deal with myself. This was family business, and although I suppose I should look upon myself as a member of the family, I was just a new member, and therefore exempt from the bulk of internal quarrels. Abrimel was uncertain.

'I'm not going to harm Caeru in any way, I promise you. Please, go and speak with your father.'

'Has he sent you here?'

'Yes.'

'Right!' Abrimel stalked out, his face dark with a hundred bursting questions. I smiled to myself, bent down, picked up the fallen clothes and draped them over a chair. When I stood up, Caeru was standing in the doorway staring at me. From the look on his face, I wouldn't have been surprised if he'd produced an axe from behind his back and run screaming right at me. He didn't. He just said, 'Get the hell out of here. Now!'

'You're not pleased to see me are you,' I said lightly. Imminent attack was still not unlikely. His fists were clenched by his sides, his hair in disarray, his clothes torn and dusty, his face scratched and marked with dry blood. He looked as if he hadn't slept or washed for several days, yet he was still undeniably lovely, possessing the sort of attractiveness that would let him look well-dressed in the proverbial sack.

'I know what's happened,' he said, ignoring my remark. 'You think I'm stupid, don't you. Both of you do.'

'I'm here for dinner,' I said. 'Do let's try to be civilized.'

'Civilized! You've wrecked my home!' he screeched, waving his arms at the torn room. I instinctively backed away as he advanced towards me, still shrieking his displeasure.

'Look!' I said, when he was just inches away and I was pressed against the wall. 'Cut the crap, Caeru. I'm Tigron, Pell's Tigron, not you. We have to talk. No-one's telling you to pack your little spotted hanky and leave. So calm down, remember who you are and get your people to serve us dinner, OK?'

He snorted in a fit of repressed, seething rage. 'It'll have to be on the terrace,' he said in a strangled voice. 'The rest of this place is just ruins.'

'Oh, come on, it's not that bad. Just a little messed up.'

'The terrace,' he said. 'Would you care to follow me?'

It was evening out there, warm and fragrant. All the tiles

turquoise beneath my feet. From the balcony we could see the half-tumbled towers of Immanion stark against a blood-red, smoky sunset. The sea beyond them gleamed like polished metal. A wrought iron table had been set out hurriedly, draped with a fringed cloth. Huge, cushioned chairs from some forlorn salon inside had been arranged on either side and looked rather incongruous. One of the clawed, wooden feet was broken.

'You'd better learn to be friendly,' I said.

'Is that blackmail or just a simple threat?' Caeru responded, sitting down gracefully.

'Neither. Get it into your head, Tigrina, if you are the Tigron's consort, in view of all that's happened, you are now also mine.' I let this statement sink in before sitting down. Caeru remained silent, probably stunned. I admired the view, wafted a napkin over my knees. The servants brought us wine, offered a glass to Caeru to taste which he waved away. I took it. 'Very good,' I said. 'Pour the Tigrina a large glass.'

Caeru stared fixedly at the table, at his servant's shaking hand. Wine splashed onto the cloth. 'This is a farce. I cannot eat,' he said. 'Did you mean what you said? It's too disgusting to contemplate.'

'More disgusting than what you've been living before?' I enquired delicately.

Caeru put his head on one side and sighed. 'OK, I'm tired, I'm exhausted; I cannot fight. If it's going to save time and agony, I give in. I give in! What is it you want me to do?'

'Nothing. Just drink your wine and eat. Ashmael wants to call an emergency meeting of the Hegemony. That'll be tomorrow now, I suppose, although it's leaving it rather late ...'

'No, that'll be tonight,' Caeru corrected, looking at me thoughtfully. 'They don't waste time. I expect they'll send for you when they're ready.'

'You mean after they've finished talking about me behind my back.' (*Aha, a suspicion was forming; an unpleasant one.*)

'Yes.' (*That confirmed it.*)

'Do you attend such meetings?'

'If it concerns me, yes. If it doesn't, no. Same as everyone else. Tonight I will definitely be there.'

And so would I! I'd had some vague ideas floating around in my head concerning the Tigrina ever since my confrontation with Thiede, albeit abstract ones. I gave in to a warm feeling of resentment that my beloved had shooed me off to deal with Caeru, thus getting me out of the way, so that he could call the meeting of the Hegemony and start it without even telling me. The old Pellaz would never have done that. OK, at times his naive honesty had grated on my nerves, but at least I'd always known what was going on in his head. Now, I was not so sure. Cue *déjà vu* concerning my observations about beautiful Hara being clever, cunning or powerful. Pellaz was frighteningly beautiful and I was no longer sure I could strike any of the other qualities from his list of characteristics. Now, he must think me naive! If we were to exist together, as we must, emotions must be put aside. Clearly intense wiliness was called for. I still had the ace up my sleeve. No my darling; you will not push me around. Not completely.

The first course was served. Spiced fish in aromatic sauce with wafers of toast. Caeru sucked a slice of lemon, but wouldn't eat.

'Don't you trust me?' I asked. The food was very good.

'What a stupid remark!'

'Why? I can make life a lot better for you if I want to, and, of course, if you want me to.' I'd already swiftly knocked back two glasses of the wine which was extremely potent.

'Oh, can you indeed! I'm very grateful!'

'Yes, you should be. If Pell is a beast to you, it's because he's been bitter and misled, that's all. There's no reason why things can't improve between you now. It can't always have been this bad, can it? Conception, for example, demands more than mere lust to achieve.'

Caeru's lips had gone pale with rather more than just lemon-juice. 'I expect the ability to shock people is one of your more outstanding talents is it? Am I supposed to be impressed? What happened between the Tigron and I in the past is none of your business, and as for you being able to improve things between us, which in itself is a conceit beyond comprehension, haven't you forgotten just one thing? Doesn't he now have you here for him to love?' Caeru put up his hand and shook his head as soon as he'd finished speaking as if to negate that last remark.

'Ah, but as I said earlier, Pellaz and I should be looked upon as one entity now. Don't you think I have a say in our emotional life as well as our political one?'

Caeru shook his head again in confusion. 'Cal, are you just stupidly romantic, or do you know something I don't?'

I smiled secretively. 'Just eat,' I said, 'then go and have a wash and comb your hair. Come with me to the Hegalion. Let's surprise them.'

The Hegalion stood unmarked, a vast, imposing building, about half a mile from Phaonica. As Caeru had intimated, the meeting of the Hegemony was well under way by the time we got there. Perhaps the place had been cleaned up before the meeting started; there was no sign of debris. Polished columns and dark, carpeted stairs lent an air of solemnity. As soon as we were noticed standing in the hall, an usher in black livery hurried noiselessly forward, bowed to the Tigrina. He conducted us up a sweeping flight of stairs and through the main door of the grand chamber. I saw Pellaz sitting at the head of a long, low polished table, his chin resting on his fist. A number of Hara were spaced out around the table listening to someone who was standing up to speak. Surprise, surprise. It was Ashmael. The public gallery was full to capacity, with fidgetting Hara all dressed in what was left of their best clothes. Pell looked up and saw me, instantly alert, perhaps wondering how I'd got there. Then he glanced briefly at the Tigrina who was standing a little behind me and a barely perceptible sneer crossed his face. I could tell what he was thinking. He had decided that Caeru wanted to cause him discomfort by bringing me here. Let him think that for a while. It didn't matter. All went silent. Then someone offered to show me to a seat, and a ripple of whispered conversation travelled round the gallery.

'No,' Pell ordered, as I went to sit down, 'he sits here by me! Cal?'

Caeru was already seated, staring at his fingers on the table. I took his hand, hauled him from his seat and dragged him up the room with me. I think he was far too mortified to protest. Pell looked me in the eye, speculatively. He was trying to imply: 'No, the Tigrina sits down there with the others,' without actually saying it. He also knew I was going to ignore it. The sussuration of noise had ceased, and now a profound silence filled the hall of the Hegalion as everyone held their breath in anticipation. They were all watching me, all waiting, wondering what was going to happen next. Pell's chair was higher than the rest. Now he was watching me wearily, but there was a slight smile on his face. I could tell that in a way, he was proud of my independent action, but he would still try to fight me. I wouldn't let him. Pell had had his taste of power; he expected to be obeyed by all but Thiede.

I stood up on the dais, Caeru at my side. I turned my back on the Tigron and faced the Hegemony. Ashmael was smiling widely with sheer delight. I addressed them all. I said, 'I am disappointed that you have all seen fit to begin this meeting without me. Especially after I have come such a long way to be here, and accomplished so much for our race in such a short time. For that, I am indebted to our sister race, the Kamagrian, especially their high priestess Opalexian, without whose help the progression of Wraeththu would not be possible.' A fierce grumbling of surprise echoed round the chamber at those words. Someone, whom I did not know stood up, near the end of the table.

'Would you care to expand on that statement tiahaar? Are you implying that unbeknown to anyone another race has been developing somewhere and would I be right in assuming these *Kamagrian* are female?'

'What have they to do with us?' someone else called out.

I could detect a tiny, niggling thread of panic in those questions. Let them wait for the explanation. I put up my hand to silence them and shook my head. Behind me I heard Pellaz exhale, slowly, deeply. A sharp dart of mind-touch reached me: 'What the hell are you doing. Sit down and shut up before you embarrass yourself beyond redemption!'

I ignored it. 'There will be plenty of time to explain fully about the Kamagrian, their relationship to Wraeththu, and their future relationship with Wraeththu. What matters most now is something entirely different, but it is still something that must be explained before all else. As you all doubtless know by now, the Aghama is no longer completely a creature of this Earth. But that does not mean that he has left us; far from it. Thiede is now *above* us; trine in power with Tigron Pellaz and myself. Perhaps it would be to insult your intelligence to point out that what is spiritual must also be reflected in the matter, so I do so, not to inform but merely to place what I have to say in context. Simply; as above, so below. Three in one. Whatever any of you thought about my coming here, I can assure you it was not to remove Caeru Meveny from office. He has his part to play, as do we all, and it is a vital part, as the mundane counterpart of the Aghama. I just wanted to make that clear.'

'To who?' Ashmael mouthed, for me alone.

'To me,' Pell answered resignedly, under his breath, having known that Ashmael would say something like that.

I turned to Pellaz and reached for his hand. He pulled a face at me, but gave it willingly enough. Then I turned to Caeru. 'Three in one?' I said, holding out my other hand. He took it as if he expected me to burn him; his flesh was icy. 'Pellaz?' For a moment, I thought he would refuse. He smiled at me cynically. 'It seems you insist,' he said, knowing full well he had no choice. He took Caeru's free hand in his and closed the circle.

'Remember the past,' I said. 'The good bits.'

'Whose past?' Pellaz asked, but he knew. We opened up to each other and the essence of Tigron/Tigrina whirled into a spectral cone of light above our heads. For Pell, it was so effortless, trained as he was by Thiede. There were still some things that Caeru and I would have to learn, but, one day, we would raise some fearsome power together alright. This was the earthly Triad. Not even Pell could dispute it. Above us Thiede, below us Caeru. Absolute necessity. From us would have to come the strong heirs to lead this confused and potentially great race into the future. We raised our hands to spin the light and Ashmael was the first to stand and applaud. Within seconds, everyone had joined him.

In comparison to that, the rest of the meeting just seemed like small-talk. Oh, there was much to speak about. Rebuilding, reality. What should be, what *was*. What had started as a tense and formal affair, became a relaxed discussion. The minute-keeper was hard-pressed to keep up. I created a storm when I stood up and suggested that the people of Immanion sitting in the gallery should be allowed to have their say. From being normally quite a reserved race, the Gelaming suddenly seemed eager to put their views forward, in some cases at the same time as several other Hara. Caeru suggested that Abrimel was now responsible and old enough to be allowed to sit with the Hegemony. Permission for this was granted. It was also decided, at the instigation of one particular forceful voice from the gallery, that three members of the public should yearly be elected to take their place in the Hegalion. It was politely hinted that perhaps the current Hegemony was somewhat divorced from common life, and that such new members might give a wider perspective of things. The Council of Tribes would also have to be re-organised. It was agreed that the working future of Wraeththu certainly seemed to be taking root in Jaddayoth, and representatives of the twelve tribes should be invited to help in the reshaping of Megalithica, which was really too vast to be coped with solely by Galhea, even though it did have the backing of Immanion. I found that an excellent time to reintroduce the subject of the Kamagrian. Everyone seemed a little squeamish about it at first, which Pell deftly pointed out was a human fault and one which should be discarded.

'If it is so that we must share our world with a race of androgynes more feminine in aspect than ourselves, then we should rejoice,' he said. 'For a long time I tried to reconcile myself to the fact that Woman as a divine form must necessarily become extinct. Now I am glad that it is not so. Are we still so attached to human failings that we shun those that are different to ourselves? Haven't we learned the price Man had to pay for such foolishness? Surely as true Wraeththu we should embrace Kamagrian as the sisters they are and work together with them. As Cal pointed out, without their help we, Thiede included, would have been wandering up the wrong path for a long time. Perhaps forever, or until some other race came to take our place, as we took Mankind's. Think well on this, tiahaara. To be great, don't we also have to be humble? Serve as well as be served? If the power of the

Kamagrian is greater than ours, then we should not resent it, but see it as it truly is. A great opportunity for learning.'

Enterprise was another new facet of Pellaz I'd have to get used to. I didn't think it would be a good time to tell him that Kate, his good friend, was Kamagrian, nor that she had been Opalexian's eyes and ears in Immanion. Perhaps she would want to tell him herself. I still had not seen her. From what I could remember, the last time we'd met (a long, long time ago), I'd been a little bit rude to her. That was when I'd hated women because, deep inside, I'd envied them. Strange to think that I can admit that now. Perhaps it is because I have learned to be truly Wraeththu, to see myself as male and female, as I should, and not just a modified male. A lesson that had to be learned by many I think.

And now my story is just about up to date. It will all take a lot of getting used to. Sometimes, I am sure, Pell and I will hate each other's guts because we have both changed so much. This is necessary because we could not function as a pair if we'd remained the same, but it is still hard. Sometimes he is a stranger and I have to fight a certain fear of him. Sometimes I find myself going to Caeru to escape that fear, that power, but less and less as time goes on. We have learned how to love again. That makes up for all the bad times.

The other night, after a ritual in the temple, Pellaz, Caeru and I ate together on Caeru's terrace and the atmosphere was congenial between us. We were talking about Galhea. Swift, once he'd learned what had happened to me, had lost no time in contacting me. He suggested that we should meet in Immanion before I went back to Forever myself. (Still having trouble with Seel over me, I wonder?) He also said that he'd very much like to bring Tyson with him. It was a request more than a statement. I'd asked how Ty felt about it. My son was now about thirty years old; a disorientating thought. 'He is like you,' Swift had answered, which probably meant he and Cobweb were still trying to force Tyson to agree to it. I'd said OK, but a little reluctantly. Ty doubtlessly felt the same about it. I wanted to see him, but anticipated difficulties in communication at first. He might still hold a grudge against me because I'd left him in Galhea and never bothered to get in touch. I was telling Pell and Caeru all about Galhea, making them laugh with tales of Cobweb's often absurd behaviour which I expect they thought I'd exaggerated. I hadn't. I told them, 'Cobweb hated my guts for ages! Can't blame him, I suppose.'

'Yet you ended up quite close,' Caeru observed wistfully. A certain awkwardness materialized. Relations between Pell and the Tigrina were still cool more often than not.

Pell said, 'Rue, do you want to know why I hated you?' and the air went cold.

Caeru rubbed his arms. 'If you want to tell me,' he said, meaning, "no".

'It was because I wanted you to be Cal, and you weren't. I felt you were taking his place, and if I let myself grow to love you, I would be reinforcing that belief, doing what Thiede wanted me to do. In a way, it was pure stubbornness on my part. It must have hurt you a lot. I won't apologize because it would sound pathetic after so much mental cruelty, so let's just open another bottle of wine and talk about something else shall we.'

But it was said; that's all that matters. I caught Caeru's eye and winked. He smiled back. Sometimes it would be necessary for us to join forces against Pellaz and keep his ego under control. Not too often I hope.

Eventually, it got too cold to sit on the terrace. We stood up to go inside. One of Caeru's attendants was going round drawing the drapes, lighting the lamps that would show the rooms off to best effect.

'It's quite cosy here, isn't it,' Pell remarked. I thought we'd be leaving but he threw himself down in a chair. 'Have we exhausted your wine, Rue?'

'Er, no. I'll have someone bring us more.' The Tigrina was as surprised as me. Usually Pell couldn't wait to get away from him.

Left alone with Pell for a few moments, I said, 'What are you up to?'

'What do you think of Caeru?'

'Why?'

'Just answer.'

'Why?'

Pellaz sighed. 'OK, you think our communion should become more than spiritual?'

'I can't believe I'm hearing this!'

'Do you?'

I shrugged. Caeru came back in, trailing a servant carrying a tray of wine. Caeru was smiling; he was happy we were still there.

'Yes, I think it should,' I said.

'What's going on?' Caeru asked.

Pellaz sat up in his chair, smiled wolfishly. 'Rue, I want you to think back,' he said. 'I want you to remember Ferelithia. Remember a romantic young Har and the time you spent with him. He's not that far away. Think you can manage that?'

Caeru has a good memory; it wasn't that difficult for him.

Someday soon, the stories of our lives, Pell's and mine, will snuggle together on the shelf beside our bed, and that will be an end to all the frantic soul-searching we went through writing them. We have the future now, no need to cling to the past. When we go to the temple to join with the Aghama, we can see it before us. Thiede will always be with us. Not just in memory, but in each Harling that is born, every decision that is made, every worship we make to the power that is within us. We call that power God and Goddess. Once it lived in man, but men and women couldn't experience the light and dark of their natures without fear. Perhaps Kamagrian and Wraeththu are the answer. We shall certainly try. Our races as we know ourselves are just the beginning; there is so much more to come, and if we are wise, we shall greet it gladly.

THE HISTORY OF THE
TWELVE TRIBES
OF JADDAYOTH

The country that became Almagabra was initially colonized by the Gelaming who came over from Megalithica. They found human society in a state of collapse, mainly through the effects of strange, incurable diseases, inner conflict between peoples and a marked increase in the suicide rate via mental disturbance.

After settlement, various splinter groups split off from the main body of the Gelaming and travelled east. Although the Gelaming did not exactly sanction these moves, no overt action was taken to stop them. There are twelve acknowledged tribes of Jaddayoth, varying in size from the powerful **MAUDRAH** (MAW-druh), **HADASSAH** (HAD-uss-ar), and **NATAWNI** (Nat-AW-nee). to the smaller, but mystically influential tribes, such as **ROSELANE** (ROZ-uh-larn) and **FERIKE** (FER-i-kuh).

Hierarchies vary within the tribes, but most have governing families that have either seized power or been elected to govern by the rest of the tribe. Among the tribes, alliances may be formed by the mixing of blood through mating. Hara such as the Maudrah may want to improve their royal bloodlines by breeding with Hara known for their intelligence, such as the Ferike. The sale of harlings between tribes is not uncommon.

Some tribes are city builders, often cannibalising what mankind has left behind to construct their own towns, whilst others live in scattered, smaller communities. The main interaction between tribes is for trade. The Garridan deal in toxins and stimulants, the Emunah (besides being brokers for many other tribes) deal in perfumes, carpets, household commodities, the Gimrah deal in livestock.

Religion among the twelve tribes is as varied as their systems of government. The Maudrah's priesthood, the Niz, are basically political, although the Maudrah do have a king, the Archon Ariaric. However, it is suspected that the Niz put Ariaric on the throne themselves and that he is answerable to them. Before the Confederation of Tribes was initiated in ai-cara 14, skirmishes and raids between the tribes were common, especially along the boundaries of territories. In ai-cara 13, Ariaric of the Maudrah commenced hostilities with the Natawni over some trivial offence, and the Natawni applied to the Gelaming for assistance. Once the Gelaming forces arrived from Almagabra, Ariaric claimed that Natawni warriors had been raiding Maudrah settlements along the border (which was still indistinct), stealing livestock and burning farms. The Gelaming proposed that proper boundaries be marked out, and suggested that a permanent peace-keeping force from Almagabra be stationed along this boundary. Thus, the Gelaming inveigled their way into Jaddayoth; a situation regarded with mixed feelings by all tribes. At this time, the Confederation of Tribes was also formed; an attempt to prevent further incidence of hostilities occurring. Another outcome of Gelaming intervention was that slavery was outlawed in Jaddayoth, whether of remaining humans or hara. Slavery has always been abhorrent to the Gelaming, and they stated that allowing such a practice to continue would be a step backwards for Wraeththukind. Healthy respect for the power of the Gelaming meant that this request was complied with, but the ensuing systems of bondharing are little other than slavery, and it is clear there is still a black market for slaves, if one knows where to look for it.

THE TWELVE TRIBES: A TRAVELLER'S GUIDE

The Maudrah

The Maudrah are the largest tribe of Jaddayoth, many of whom are hara who fled Megalithica at the time of the Varrish defeat in that continent. Their society is governed by many strict codes, one of which is their religious cult connected with the Aghama, the first Wraeththu. To the Maudrah, the Aghama is a ruthless and vengeful entity, whom it is necessary to placate in numerous ways. The Aghama may be offended by deviations from custom, such as wearing the wrong mode of attire in any situation, or utilising incorrect modes of address to other hara. If any har should invoke the displeasure of the Aghama, he is obliged to make the correct penance. Mistakes made by strangers to the region are barely tolerated, but small allowances are made for visitors who may be unfamiliar with the Maudrah codes. Repeated aberrations do tend to inflame the tempers of the Niz, however, so it is inadvisable for Hara unfamiliar with the region to spend too much time in Maudrah. The capital city of Oomadrah is probably the most lenient. An efficient police force, known as the Aditi, are employed by the Niz to supervise the streets of towns and cities. They may invite transgressors to 'partake of the hospitality of the Niz'. It is strongly urged that any traveller receiving such a suggestion resist it strongly. Fleeing abruptly from Maudrah territory is the recommended manner of replying to it.

The Maudrah attitude to aruna is one shrouded in mystery as few have ever spoken of it outside of the country. It is safe to conjecture, however, that it is bound by the same set of rigid rules as govern all aspects of Maudrah activity. Not recommended to be sampled.

Within the palace Sykernesse, seat of the Archon in Oomadrah, it is rumoured that the restrictions adhered to by the Maudrah community at large do not apply. This may be because Ariaric's consort, Elisyin, is of Ferike origin and has considerable influence within Sykernesse itself. The court of Sykernesse is on very intimate terms with the court of Phaonica in Immanion. This too may be a reason why regulations are relaxed within the palace. Visitors from Almagabra are frequent, and would no doubt be offended if asked to behave in any manner other than that of a respected Gelaming. The only other reason why conditions in the palace are as they appear may be because Ariaric and Wrark Fortuny, High Priest of the Niz, are happy to dole out laws willy-nilly to their people but can't be bothered with such things themselves. Conjectures abound, but surely only the most cynical Har would suggest the latter.

The Hadassah

The Hadassah are the second largest tribe of Jaddayoth. They are also the complete opposite of the Maudrah, possessing a far looser social structure. In fact, they have an almost morbid hatred for the Maudrah and utterly despise that tribe's traditions. The governor of the Hadassah is a har known as the Lexy, who resides in the capital town of Camphadal, close to the Natawni border. The Lexy is chosen every five years by means of a strenuous competition which comprises tests of strength, intelligence and magical prowess. The current Lexy has been in office for six years, having won the competition twice. He is highly regarded amongst his people. The Hadassah also worship the Aghama, but the idea rather than the har. They do not worship the image of Aghama, but believe that the Aghama's presence is inherent in every har and that to abuse yourself (or any other hara) is to abuse the Aghama. Thus, when having to engage in battle, for whatever reason, every Hadassah has to make amends to the Aghama. Conveniently, this is usually expressed through sanctified aruna with temple soumelam, known as Huyana, who must also be offered gifts in the form of food, money or clothing. As the Hadassah are a race fond of drinking, conquest and brawling, the Huyana make a comfortable living from this practice. The Hadassah welcome travellers as they are gregarious people and also because they seek to make profit from any visitors. As opposed to the Maudrah, who dress only in sombre grey, black or brown (except for the Niz who wear robes of purple), the Hadassah affect clothing of the brightest colours. They are fond of adorning their costumes with scarves, jewellery and tassels. It is customary for most hara to accentuate their features with cosmetics and they import many exotic perfumes from Kalamah and Emunah. The Hadassah attitude to aruna is more or less the same as that of the Gelaming, in that they believe successful aruna is beneficial both spiritually and physically to whoever indulges in it.

Travellers may expect to receive excellent accommodation and service in any Hadassah town, especially so if they advertise the fact that money presents no problem.

The Natawni

The Natawni, found in the north of Jaddayoth, between Hadassah and Garridan, are also known as the People of Bones. This is because they use bones, the primal building block, for ornament, scrying, and even in the construction of their temples. Bones are built into the walls and foundations of dwellings and the Natawni have also developed a deadly weapon in the form of a bone needle steeped in poison purchased from the Garridan — the tiek. Notably fearless, and not unwarlike, the Natawni nevertheless possess one of the more democratic societies in Jaddayoth. Whilst having no tribe overlord, each community has its own leader, the Askelan, elected from a council of ten individuals, known as the Taima. Natawni has a good relationship with Immanion, but one of severe bad feeling with Maudrah, whom they despise. While they are wary (often bordering on hostile) to strangers in their lands, once satisfied that newcomers are not Maudrah spies or trouble-makers, the Natawni are happy to let them come and go as they please. All travellers wishing to explore Natawni territory are recommended to seek an audience with the nearest Askelan to obtain written authority. This is usually granted at a nominal cost of twenty spinners or thereabouts. More adventurous wanderers may wish to save their money and risk unpleasantness.

The Natawni do not worship the Aghama as a deity, but instead revere a god of their own invention - the Skylording. This deity is hermaphroditic, as themselves, but changes his affinity with the seasons. The warrior caste of the tribe are obliged to follow this custom, hence they may only be soume during Spring and Summer, ouana during the colder season. Breaking this code threatens to bring disaster to the tribe's fertility. Two religious festivals are celebrated each year. The Spring rites are known as the Greening, when harlings are ritually conceived upon the warriors, Feybraihas celebrated and the land blessed for fertility. The Autumn Festival, the Musting, celebrates the Harvest, the birth of new harlings and caste ascensions for the warriors. (N.B. Conceiving children and caste ascensions may take place at any time of year for tribe members other than warriors). The Skylording's priests are known as Skyles, hara chosen for their beauty and tranquillity.

Natawni wear clothes of forest colours, dark brown, green, russet and gold. They plait their hair with moss and leaves and scent their skin with the essential oil of pine and cedar. Their magic is of the earth which they look upon as the feminine aspect of their god. To take aruna with a Natawni is to experience the forest as a living force, to breathe earth and become at one with it. Those towns to be found along the Hadassah border are most receptive to strangers.

The Garridan

Inhabiting the northeastern mountains of Jaddayoth, bound on three sides by Roselane, Maudrah and Natawni, stretching a toe of crags into Mojag, Garridan is perhaps the land most feared by strangers to the region. Incorporating many rogue hara of the Uigenna tribe who had to flee Megalithica during the time of conflict (and who were rejected by the Maudrah — a warning note), the Garridan are a tribe well versed in the esoteric lore of Wraeththu toxins. The Uigenna were a byword in Megalithica for heartless cruelty, and were famous for their ability to devise poisons fatal or painful to harishkind, whom most toxic elements cannot harm. It is rumoured that the Garridan salvaged much of man's technology, which they now utilize in the manufacture of their venoms. Needless to say, poison is the main export of

Garridan, finding its way west, through Jaddayoth, to Thaine, Erminia and beyond. A death through poisoning was reported in southern Megalithica two years ago. It was thought that all Uigenna hara had been expunged or driven from the land at the time, which brought about the conjecture that the toxin responsible may well have originated in Jaddayoth, Garridan in particular. Whether Garridan exports are this far-reaching has never been substantiated.

The Garridan are a notoriously handsome race, inclined to tallness, long-limbed and grey eyed. Their ruler is the Archon Hillelex, their capital city the mountain stronghold of Nightshade. Nearly all Garridan towns and cities are named for various poisons; they have a rather mordant sense of humour. More than most of the tribes of Jaddayoth who have deviated from the habits and customs of Megalithican Wraeththukind, the Garridan have stuck more keenly to their origins, still instituting the exact same caste structure as the homeland, naming their temples Nayatis, their priests Hienamas, their marriages and alliances chesnabond. Though they pay lip service to the Aghama as a deity, most Garridan have little time for religion. This is because the Uigenna were one of the first tribes of Wraeththu and have passed to their descendants a strong sense of what it was like clinging to the ruins of human civilization, regarded as a dangerous freak, having to fight just to live every day. Most tribes nowadays have a far more diluted bloodline from the original strain than the Garridan, owing to interbreeding between different districts and tribes. Hence, the racial memory is perhaps blunted or at least distant enough to ignore. The Garridan are a one-generation descent group away from the Uigenna. Some part of them still lives in the burning cities of fifty years ago. There were no gods then; Garridan see little need for them now.

The Garridan maintain a cursory alliance with Mojag and Maudrah. They are strongly opposed by the Natawni, who disagree with the majority of Garridan customs and creeds. Emunah, however, never fussy with whose money it takes, maintains a healthy trading arrangement with Garridan.

Visitors to the region are not discouraged or hassled in any way, yet there are surprisingly few that brave the journey. Visitors to Nightshade report that the Garridan are excellent hosts, Lord Hillelex especially, but it is advised to examine carefully any food that you are offered, unless you are sure your visit is welcome!

The Gimrah

Known among the tribes of Jaddayoth as the Horse People, the Gimrah (GIM-rar) occupy the vast southern plains to the west of Maudrah and a long stretch of the coast of the Sea of Shadows. Famous for the quality of their animals, many Gimrah can boast that their steeds can be found in the stables of all the noble houses of Jaddayoth. Four different types of horses are bred in this region. Firstly, the working beasts; heavy, muscled brutes, found on all the richer farms in the area. Secondly, riding animals, famed for their elegant appearance, reliability and zest. Thirdly, racehorses, exported to Almagabra, Thaine and as far as Megalithica, and finally, Faraldiennes. These animals are bred from two Gelaming horses presented to Gimrah by Immanion itself. Faraldiennes are far more than just animals, being able to travel through the otherlanes, out of this plane of existence, thus enabling an experienced handler to cross vast distances of land in a very short space of time. The Gimrah have several small herds of these animals, but their sale is controlled by the Hegemony in Immanion, to prevent them falling into the wrong hands. Obviously, there are many brave attempts by would-be thieves to steal from the herd, but the Gimrah guard them with outstanding zeal and happily kill anyone stupid enough to try. Any Faraldiennes sold to other tribes are geldings, preventing any illegal breeding of the strain.

The Gimrah are solely a farming community, and have no cities. Each farm is really a large village, presided over by a headhar known as the Tirtha. All Gimrah Tirtha meet six times a year to discuss tribal matters and to show off the best of their stock. The Tirtha acts as law enforcer within his own community, usually assisted by his family.

The Gimrah worship the Aghama in the form of a white horse

who may sometimes take the form of a Wraeththu har. They believe that on the eve of the new year, the Aghama may be seen galloping over the fields beside the herds, ensuring their fertility for the coming Spring.

Of all the tribes of Jaddayoth, only the Gimrah have any dealings with humans. Whereas Mojag, Garridan, Maudrah and Natawni successfully exterminated, or drove away, any lingering human communities, the Gimrah allowed men and women to remain on their lands, offering them employment and aid. This was sorely needed at the time of settlement as all humans were desperately clinging to the last threads of life at the time, never mind the territory. The Gimrah assisted by using their power of healing over the minds and bodies of the humans, managing to halt the deadly advance of mental illness, ravaging disease and sterility. Because of this, the relationship between humankind and hara in this district is uncommonly good. Many humans now live better lives than before the Wraeththu came. Naturally, this situation invites censure from the less tolerant tribes, but as the Gimrah have the sanction of the Gelaming, both human and har can live together without fear of reprisal. The only problem that arises from this circumstance is that all male children, upon reaching puberty, want to be incepted into Wraeththu. Obviously, if this was allowed to occur without supervision, the humans would inevitably become extinct. To preserve the race, the Gimrah have stipulated that no young man may take inception until he has successfully sired a male child. Therefore, humans tend to breed at a very young age and all of the adult community is female.

Visitors are always welcome in the estembles (as the farms are called) of Gimrah, although they may be expected to pay for their keep with labour as well as money. The best time to visit the region is during the summer months when there are many colourful horse fairs to look around.

The Ferike

Other tribes describe the Ferike as a race of scholars and artists, and it is true that they are a people that devote themselves to learning and creativity. The noble families live in high castles in the hilly, forested districts of Western Jaddayoth. The rest of the community live in small towns, generally along the shores of the many lakes found in Ferike.

Rich hara from other tribes often buy harlings off the Ferike to breed with their own sons, hoping, thereby, to increase the intelligence and artistic natures of their own families. Ferike hara are fey and pale with large eyes. Their pastimes include writing long, fabulous poetry and poignant, convoluted stories. Ferike books (always beautifully bound and illustrated) often appear in Emunah markets, but selling at massively inflated prices. It is said that Thiede of Immanion possesses an entire library of Ferike literature. The Ferike are also renowned for their brilliant artists and musicians, but it is a rich har's hobby to try and collect any of their works.

Time spent in a Ferike castle is supposed to be sublimely relaxing. The occupants are ethereally lovely, soft music enchants the ear, splendid paintings welcome the eye and the food Ferike cooks prepare is reputedly the best in the world for its subtlety of flavour. Surprisingly, not that much is known about Ferike social customs, for they are a private race, but there are many tales about the fabled Elisyin, a Ferike legend whom Ariaric of the Maudrah took as a consort. Between them, they produced three sons of biting, shrewd wit, all the more deadly because of their deceptively pretty appearance. Those wishing to learn more of this history should look for the Ferike book on the subject called 'The blade, the reed and the shadow'. Because of the difficulty in obtaining any Ferike works, serious students are advised to obtain permission from the Hegemony of Immanion to examine those volumes held by Phaonica's library. Although the Gelaming are sympathetic to researchers, and happily open their archives to anyone willing to pay for the privilege, it must be stated that the cost may turn out rather higher than expected. Accommodation does not come cheap in Immanion. Travel in Ferike, however, is not quite so expensive. It is recommended that any visitors to the region find a comfortable inn and pay one of the locals in ale to tell stories of Elisyin and his sons. This works out considerably cheaper than using the library in Immanion and is far more entertaining, even if the stories are rather less accurate.

The Elhmen

The Elhmen (ELL-mun) are a mountain race found northwest of Ferike. They prefer to keep themselves to themselves and can be most unpleasant to strangers if the mood takes them. Whilst hardy and fond of a colder climate, they are markedly more feminine in appearance than most Wraeththu. This is not through sublimation of the male principle, but because of their religion, which is a celebration of water magic. They harness the power of the mountain falls and their appearance is uncannily nymphlike. Elhmen are mischievous and fond of playing tricks upon unwary travellers. They do not often show themselves, but it is said that if a wanderer should catch hold of an Elhmen har, he can ask for a wish to be granted. This is more likely to be a romantic rather than realistic premise, and probably a tale started in Ferike!

Although the Elhmen are not warlike in nature, they are quick to defend themselves and their privacy. This is usually effected by sending any interloper into an enchanted sleep before moving them to the boundary of their territory. The Elhmen also guard the entrances to the underground kingdom of Eulalee, home of the tribe of Sahale. Sometimes the Sahale and Elhmen interact for religious or magical rites, for the Sahale are also known as the Fire People; thus the two tribes' magics are complementary.

The Elhmen live mainly in small communities scattered among the peaks, and have only one city — Shappa. This is built high in the mountains, a dazzling creation of stone towers and vertiginous streets. The Elhmen have no overall ruler. In fact, whoever does govern the Elhmen (*if* anyone does), does so in utter secrecy, for nothing is known about social administration within the tribe. Holy hara, who are definitely something more than mere priests, but no-one except the Elhmen know what, are called Esh. Travellers with money are generally welcome in Shappa, and it is worth the visit if one is prepared to put up with antisocial treatment on the journey to reach it.

All Elhmen grow their hair very long, are generally fair in colouring and have ice-blue or cloud-grey eyes. Their faces are ascetic, their expressions dreamy, hinting at a secret smile. It is said that their touch is always cold. Whilst they are totally unaffected by cold conditions, and often go naked, clothed only in their magnificent hair, the Elhmen usually prefer to appear before strangers clothed in flimsy, floating robes. Another legend about this tribe is that taking aruna with an Elhmen har automatically raises one's caste by one level. As with many such pretty stories, the facts remain unsubstantiated.

The Sahale

As has been mentioned in the previous entry, the Sahale (SARL) are known throughout Jaddayoth as the Fire People. They live underground, beneath the mountain ranges of Elhmen and beyond, emerging only rarely for religious ceremonies. As befits their chosen religion, hara of this tribe habitually dye their hair red, but of varying shades to signify their position within the tribe, and their caste. Young harlings, until feybraiha, have hair of a strawberry pink colour which changes to vibrant scarlet once they have come of age. On reaching first level Ulani, the hair colour becomes crimson, whilst hara of Nahir Nuri level have hair that is so deep a colour it is almost purple. Subtle shades within these four groups denote abilities, social standing and intelligence.

The capital city of Eulalee is Sahen (SARN), situated next to a vast, underground lake, framed by breathtaking stalactites, stalagmites and curtains of gleaming, mineral deposits. Other settlements on the same level as Sahen include the religious retreat of Pir Lagadre, visited by pilgrims from as far away as Megalithica. Of the lower levels of Eulalee, little is known by outsiders. There are rumours of strange, supernatural creatures living in caverns of fire, and of ancient shrines where lost gods live on unaware of the changes wrought upon the surface of the earth. Again, stories. There are many stories to be heard in Jaddayoth. The fires of Sahale heat sacred springs, where bathing in the water is said to promote health and beauty. Anyone brave enough to bathe in the actual flames can try and prove the myths that doing so gives unparalleled wisdom, never mind unparalleled third degree burns.

The ruler, or Lyris, of the Sahale dwells in the city of Sahen, attended by priest figures known as Lithes. Although, as a complement to the Elhmen, it might be expected that the Sahale present a predominantly masculine mien, this is not the case. They are typically harish in every respect, their only peculiarity being that, in spite of living underground, they all have rather dark skins.

The Emunah

Although the Emunah (Em-OO-nah) are principally a non-productive tribe, they act as very efficient brokers for the other Jaddayoth regions. Emunah hara are a mixed bag of many different tribes. They inhabit the eastern coast of Jaddayoth, where their river- and ocean-going vessels can have easy access to other areas of Jaddayoth, the northern coast of Huldah and the sea canal to Almagabra. Law in Emunah is half-heartedly presided over (i.e. it can be bought) by a group of elected hara known as the Nasnan. They are presided over by a grand judge entitled the Garondel. It would appear that the only way to break the law in Emunah is to steal from Emunah subjects or to attempt to defraud the Garondel's authorities, which are concerned with the administration of trade. Therefore, all travellers are advised to arm themselves well in Emunah towns. The advantages of visiting this region are that strangers are never questioned (or even noticed for that matter), and can come and go as they please. Visitors bearing produce to trade are welcomed with open arms and entitled to reduced rates at many Emunah inns. The principle towns are Oriole, Meris, Gaspard and Linnea. The Garondel and his committee reside in the capital town of Oriole.

In this region, little importance is attached to religion, although shrines may be found to many of the Aghama's different aspects deified in Jaddayoth. This is mainly for the benefit of travellers. Native hara use their innate talents for telepathy and illusion to secure prosperous deals for themselves and, unfortunately, to outwit unwary traders from abroad. Emunah are notoriously untrustworthy, but not cruel. If found out in their machinations, they will apologize with a smile, and perhaps offer to make amends by buying the offended party a meal (thus presenting themselves with the opportunity to get the unfortunate victim drunk and doublecross them again). However, once an Emunah har's respect has been earned (which is never easy for a stranger), they can reveal a deep and surprising loyalty. It is said that an Emunah friend, if indeed such a creature can exist, is a friend for life.

The Kalamah

Known among the tribes as the Cat People, the Kalamah (KAL-uh-mar) live in the east of the region in elegant cities of rose and cream stone. At present, most of these are still in the process of construction, for the Kalamah work slowly and precisely, stopping their labours often for refreshment, rest and appraisal of their craftmanship. Even so, the architecture found in Kalamah is unbelievably lovely.

The Kalamah are a philosophical race and have made a thorough study of the feline mind, which they strive to emulate in numerous ways. They are fond of luxury and comfort, good food, excellent wine and soothing music. One of their main incomes is derived from the export of their wine, subsidized by the industries of carpet-making and perfumery.

Their religion, as most other tribes, is worship of the Aghama, but naturally mutated to fit in with their own particular beliefs. Here we have the lion-headed aspect of the god, upon whose statues is to be found the legend, 'To be cunning without beauty and style is to light a fire next to an open door in winter.' It has been said that all the most enchanting and destructive of human female souls have reincarnated in Kalamah. Perhaps that is a little too harsh; Kalamah never kill for sport, but have been known to make a hobby of breaking hearts. Whilst they are a race not easily provoked into a rage, it is strongly advised not to aggravate any Kalamah har to extremity, for once roused, they can continue an argument beyond any reasonable point, or avenge an offence with horrible suffering. As with the Ferike, harlings of this tribe are often sought after by the Maudrah and the Garridan (the only tribes who can cope with Kalamah temperament perhaps), so that harlings born of a union between the tribes may be blessed with the gifts of stealth, cunning and agility, as well as languid beauty. The fabled Ariaric of Maudrah, who is renowned for enriching his family's blood with the best stock, procured a Kalamah consort for his eldest son, Ostoroth. Unfortunately, this union was not destined to thrive. After being on the receiving end of some cruelty or another from his partner, the Kalamah Lissilma murdered Ostoroth in cold blood and, furthermore, effortlessly massacred a great number of the palace Aditi before he was overpowered. Ariaric was so impressed by this feat that he claimed Lissilma for his own son, professing that Ostoroth had embarrassed him dreadfully by allowing himself to be killed by a concubine. How Lissilma reacted to this remark is not recorded, but, being Kalamah, he probably settled comfortably into this new elevated position and overlooked the insult. Ostoroth was not fit to be remembered. His body was burned without ceremony, while Lissilma came to sit at the Archon's right hand, where he was professed to have caused much catastrophe among the other noble houses of Maudrah. A book, written by the Ferike on this subject and entitled, appropriately, 'The claws of Lissilma', describes many of the intrigues initiated in the Kalamah's name.

Visitors to Kalamah are urged to end their journey in the city of Zaltana, where, it is said, if the claws of the Kalamah embed themselves in your skin, you will never want to leave. It is true, the place is breathtaking, and if one is strong-willed, not too dangerous.

The Mojag

The Mojag (MO-hag) are regarded as cultureless barbarians by most of the tribes of Jaddayoth, although it would be a fool who did not regard them with healthy respect. Occupying only one small village on their arrival in Jaddayoth, within only a year or so, they had soon secured for themselves a huge area of land among the eastern mountains of the country. Only the formation of the Confederation of Tribes halted their advance towards other territories. This no doubt caused the tribes of Kalamah, Emunah and

Roselane to give a sigh of relief, and those of Garridan and Maudrah to slacken their defences along the borders with Mojag.

Being a tribe dedicated to conquest and troublemaking of all kinds, the warrior castes of Mojag are generally found among the armies of other countries as mercenaries. Even the Gelaming have a troupe of Mojags, which they use for restoring order in any troublesome areas, and also as escorts for Gelaming personnel venturing into countries further east than Jaddayoth, or south into Olathe. Mojags are totally fearless and seem to regard themselves as indestructible. Because of the strength of this belief, they usually are!

The Princelord of Mojag is a har known as the Wursm, who resides in the capital town of Shuppurak. It is said that he has killed a thousand living beings, both human and har. Because Mojag make little concession to their feminine sides, one wonders how they manage to reproduce successfully. There is no record of them taking hara from other tribes for this purpose, so the subject remains shrouded in mystery. Because of the belligerent nature of this tribe, few scholars have been able to make a study of them. Mojags cannot see the point of hospitality unless it is extended to a possible ally in combat. Not an area recommended for travel.

The Roselane

The Roselane are a tribe of mystics, whose aid may be enlisted by hara of other tribes seeking guidance in spiritual matters. Often called the Dream People by other tribes, the Roselane have control over dreams and visions of the future; solutions to waking-life problems may be interpreted from their dreams. Their religion is based upon the essential male/female polarity within themselves; they have no desire for external gods. Their most respected hara are the most influential dreamers; they are known as Frodinne. These hara have incredible control over their dreams and can even influence the future, in some cases, by dreaming it. Roselane harlings are taught at an early age how to confront enemies or objects of fear in their dreams and overcome them. On reaching feybraiha, all Roselane hara have learnt this technique. If, at this stage, they appear to be unusually proficient at dream control, they may be trained further to join the ranks of the Frodinne. Otherwise, they will take up some other profession, using their dream powers only for personal benefit. It is said that the most powerful Frodinne spend most of their lives asleep, dreaming, although periodically they may take holidays from this function, when they are termed as being 'on adinne'. Some Frodinne have achieved remarkable fame in the country of Jaddayoth, and hara travel from afar to seek their advice. The most celebrated of these is Edolie the Ighted, who has dreamed for many of the royal houses of Jaddayoth. It is rumoured that he may sleep for weeks at a time when working on a particularly sticky problem and that his appearance is 'seraphic'. As few hara outside of Roselane have ever seen Edolie the Ighted in the flesh, this cannot be verified.

The Roselane share their territory with another group, known as the Kamagrian. Little is known about these people, whether they are a separate tribe or an offshoot of the Roselane. The Kamagrian have their headquarters, a kind of temple-school, in Shilalama, the Roselane capital town. This temple is named Kalalim and it is said, in Shilalama, that all roads lead to it. Certainly the Roselane regard the Kamagrian with the highest respect. It has been reported that the Kamagrian have human females in their employ which has led to the assumption that they may, in fact, be some kind of disguised human remnant. This seems unlikely, unless the Roselane are shielding them in some way. Though privacy is a byword in Roselane, visitors are not discouraged. The journey to Shilalama is hazardous and uncomfortable, but the city itself is splendid, appearing almost as a natural rock formation eroded by winds. Other Roselane settlements may be less inclined to be interrupted by travellers, so it is advised to head for the capital.

A guide to the countries and characters

| Calanthe (Cal-An-thee) | A traveller (was once a nuisance, but everybody got to hear about it.) |

THAINE

Fallsend

Jafit	Owner of the musenda 'Piristil'.
Astarth	
Ehzno (EJ-Noh)	
Salandril (Sal-AN-dril)	
Rihana (Ree-ARN-a)	kanene of Piristil
Yasmeen	
Nahele (Na-HEE-lee)	
Flounah	
Lolotea (Loll-uh-TEE-a)	
Orpah	
Wuwa (WOO-wa)	servants of Piristil
Jancis (JAN-kiss)	
Kruin (KROO-in)	a client, trader of the Natawni tribe
Panthera (Pan-THEER-a)	a slave, son of royal house of Jael in Ferike.
Outher (OW-thuh)	guard of Panthera, of the Mojag tribe.
Arno Demell	a client of Piristil
Liss-am-Caar	a dealer in toxins of the Garridan tribe.

JADDAYOTH: LAND OF THE TWELVE TRIBES

In the land of the Hadassah

Jasminia

Lucastril (Loo-CASS-tril)	a huyana of the Aghama's temple

In the land of the Gimrah

Lemarath

Cora	human female, farmer and lodging-house keeper

Jasca	her daughter
Natty	her son
Elveny	a young woman of Cora's household

Gasteau Hafener	Tirtha of Lemarath
Lanareeve Hafener	his consort
Jubilee Hafener	
Danyelle Hafener	their sons
Onaly Doontree (ONN-a-lee)	Danyelle's consort
Wilder Hafener	a relative

In the land of the Ferike

Jael

| Ferminfex Jael (JAY-el) | Castlethane of Jael, father of Panthera |
| Lahela (La-HEE-la) | his consort, of the Kalamah tribe |

In the land of the Elhmen

On the road to Kar Tatang, the gateway

| Arawn | an enchanter |
| Nanine | his brother |

Shappa

| Kachina (Ka-CHEE-na) | a guide |

In the land of the Sahale (Eulalee)

Sahen

The Lyris	ruler of the Sahale
Zhatsin	under-valet to the Lyris
Iygandil (Ee-GAN-dil)	First Shriever of the Lyris
Tatigha	
Loolumada (LOO-luh-MAR-duh)	attendants of the Lyris
The Fire Hound of Shere	
Zaghara	an oracle

In the Land of the Maudrah

Morla

Asvak	Captain of the '*Auric Wing*', of Ferike tribe
Lourana	Maudrah har, a guide

Oomadrah

Ariaric, Lion of Oomadrah	Archon of the Maudrah
Elisyin (El.IZ-ee-in)	his consort, a Ferike
Lalasa (La-LASS-a)	a Kalamah, valet to Elisyin cousin of Panthera
Wrark Fortuny	High Priest of the Niz
Zobinek (ZOB-in-ek)	son of Ariaric and Elisyin

In the land of the Roselane

Shilalama

Tel-an-Kaa	a parage of the Kamagrian
Opalexian	High Priestess of the Kamagrian
Zackala (ZAK-ARL-a)	one of Opalexian's aides, a Roselane
Exalan	one of Opalexian's aides, a Roselane

ALMAGABRA

Land of the Gelaming

Immanion

Thiede (THEE-dee)	The Aghama
Pellaz-har-Aralis	Tigron of Immanion
Caeru Meveny (KY-roo MEV-EN-ee)	his consort, Tigrina of Immanion
Abrimel (AB-ree-mel)	son of the Tigron and Tigrina
Ashmael (ASH-may-el)	a Lord of the Gelaming
Arahal	commanding officer in the Tigron's army
Vaysh	a courtier

I

Wraeththu caste system

Wraeththu Hara progress through a three-tier caste system; each tier consisting of three levels.

KAIMANA (Ki-ee-marna)

Level 1: Ara (altar)
    2: Neoma (new moon)
    3: Brynie (strong)

ULANI (Oo-lar-nee)

Level 1: Acantha (thorny)
    2: Pyralis (fire)
    3: Algoma (valley of flowers)

NAHIR-NURI (Na-heer Noo-ree)

Level 1: Efrata (distinguished)
    2: Aislinn (vision)
    3: Cleatha (glory)

Natural born Hara have no caste until they reach sexual maturity, when they are initiated into Kaimana. The majority of them rarely progress further than Level 2 Ulani: Pyralis. Wraeththu of Kaimana and Ulani caste are always known by their level, i.e. someone of Acantha level would be known as Acanthalid, of Pyralis, Pyralisit. Once Nahir-Nuri has been achieved, however, the caste divisions (mostly incomprehensible to those of lower caste), are no longer used as a title of address. Wraeththu of that caste are simply called Nahir-Nuri.

Caste Progression

Training in spiritual advancement must be undertaken to achieve a higher level. Occult rituals concentrate the mind and realize progression. Progression is attained by the discovery of self-knowledge and with that knowledge utilizing the inborn powers of Wraeththu.

II

Wraeththu special abilities: a comparison to Man

The differences between Wraeththu and humankind are not vast in number, and not even apparent (in most cases) to the naked eye. Biologically their functions are similar, although in the case of Wraeththu many basic design faults present in the old race have been removed.

A. Digestion

Wraeththu digestion is not wildly disparate from that of humankind, although it is unknown for Hara to become overweight whatever amount of food is ingested. Their bodies are so well-regulated that excess of all kinds are merely eliminated as waste. Perfect bodyweight is never exceeded. This thorough system cleansing also extends to most intoxicants or stimulants. Narcotic effects can be experienced without side-effects. Because of this, few poisons are lethal to Wraeththu. It has been rumoured that the Uigenna tribe of North Megalithica are fluent with the use of poisons effective against their own kind, but this has yet to be proved.

B. The Senses

Wraeththu senses of touch, sight, hearing, smell and taste are marginally more acute than those of mankind. But the sixth sense is far more well-developed. This may only be due to the fact that Wraeththu are brought up (or instructed after inception) with the knowledge to glean full use of their perception. This is a quality which has become dulled in Man. Some Hara can even catch glimpses of future events or atmospheres; either by tranquil contemplation or in dreams.

Again, it must be stressed that this ability is not a fundamental difference from humanity, as all humans possess within themselves the potential to develop their psychic capabilities. Most humans, however, are not aware of this.

C. Occult Powers

This is merely an extension of becoming acquainted, through proper progression, with one's psychic senses.

Magic is will-power; will-power is magic. Self-knowledge is the key to the perfect control of will.

Obviously, this particular talent may be used either for the benefit or detriment of other beings. As all Eraeththu are firm believers in reincarnation and the progression of the soul, most are sensible enough to realize the dangers of taking 'the left hand path'. Others, however, still motivated by the greed and baser emotions of human ancestors, are prone to seek self-advancement through evil means.

D. Life-span

In comparison, to Mankind, Wareththu appear ageless, but this is not strictly the case. Har bodies are not subject to cellular deterioration in the same way as human bodies, but on reaching the age of 150 years or thereabouts, they begin to 'fade', vitality diminishes and the dignified end is welcomed as the release for the soul and the gateway to the next incarnation.

III   *Wraeththu sexuality*

A. Reproduction

Wraeththu are hermaphrodite beings, any of whom have the capacity to reproduce on reaching the caste of Ulani. This is mainly because Hara of lower caste have insufficient control of the mind, which is required to attain the elevated state of consciousness needed for conception. Experienced Hara can guarantee conception whenever it is desired.

Conception can only occur during the act of aruna (Wraeththu intercourse); Hara are unable to fertilize themselves. The inseminating Har is known as Ouana (Ooow-ana), and the host for the seed, soume (Soow-mee). This corresponds roughly to human male and female, although in Wraeththu the roles are interchangeable. When conditions are propitious (i.e. when desired state of consciousness is achieved through the ecstasy of aruna), ouana has the chance to 'break through the seal', which is the act of coaxing the chamber of generation within the body of the soume to relax its banks of muscle that closes the entrance, and permit the inner tendril of the ouana phallus to intrude. This act must needs be undertaken with patience, because of the inner organ's somewhat capricious reluctance to be invaded by foreign bodies or substances. Aggression or haste on the side of ouana would cause pain and distress to soume (or possibly to both of them) caused by the inpenetrable tensing of soume muscles.

Once the seed (aren) has been successfully released, the chamber of generation reseals itself and emits a fertilizing secretion (yaloe) which forms a coating around the aren. Only the strongest can survive this process, weaker seed are literally burned up or else devoured by their fellows. During the next twelve hours or so, the aren fight for supremacy, until only one of them survives; this is then enveloped by the nourishing yaloe which begins to harden around the aren to form a kind of shell. By interaction of the positive aren elements and the negative yaloe elements, a Wraeththu foetus begins to develop within the shell.

At the end of two months, the shell is emitted from the body of its host, resembling a black, opalescent pearl some 6″ in diameter. Incubation is then required, either by the host or any other Har committed to spending the time. After 'birth', the pearl begins to soften into an elastic, leathery coating about the developing Harchild. Progress and growth are rapid; within a week, the pearl 'hatches' and the young Har enters the world.

Wraeththu children, on hatching, already possess some body hair and have moderately acute eyesight. Familiar Hara can be recognized after only a few days. Though smaller in size, the Har-ling at this time is comparable in intelligence and mobility to a human child that has just been weaned. Wraeththu children need no milk and can eat the same food as adults within a few hours of hatching. Development is astonishingly rapid within the first year of life. Har-lings are able to crawl aroound immediately after hatching, and can walk upright within a few days. they learn to speak simple words after about four weeks, and before that, voice their demands by exercising their voices in a series of purrings and chatterings. Sexual maturity is reached between the ages of seven and ten years, when the Har-ling is physically able to partake in aruna without ill effect. At this time, caste training is undertaken and the young Har is also educated in the etiquette of aruna. Sexual maturity is recognized by a marked restlessness and erratic behaviour, even a craving for moonlight. Aruna education is usually imparted by an older Har chosen by the child's hostling or sire. This is to prevent any unpleasant experiences which the young Har could suffer at the hands of someone who is not committed to its welfare.

(N.B. Those Hara who are not natural born, but incepted, are instructed in aruna immediately after the effects of althaia (the changing) wears off. This is essential to 'fix' the change within the new Har.)

A physically mature Har, when clothed, resembles closely a young, human male. Hara do not need breasts for the production of milk, nor wide pelvises to accomodate a growing child. They are, whilst obviously masculine, uncannily feminine at the same time; which is a circumstance difficult to describe without illustration.

B. Aruna

The act of sexual intercourse between Hara has two legitimate types. Aruna is indulged in either for pleasure; the intimate communication of minds and bodies that all Hara need for spiritual contentment, or else for the express purpose of conceiving. Although it is a necessity for Wraeththu, the amount of physical communion preferred varies from Har to Har. Some may seek out a companion only once a year, others may yearn for aruna several times a week. It is not important whether a Har enjoys most performing ouana or soume; again this varies among Hara. Most swap and change their roles according to mood or circumstance.

The phallus of the Har resembles a petalled rod, sometimes of deep and varied colours. It has an inner tendril which may only emerge once embraced by the body of the soume and prior to orgasm. The soume organs of generation, located in the lower region of the body in a position not dissimilar to that of a human female womb, is reached by a fleshy, convoluted passage found behind the masculine organs of generation. Self cleansing, it leads also to the lower intestine, where more banks of muscle form an effective seal.

C. Grissecon

Grissecon is sexual communion for occult purposes; simply — sex magic. As enormous forces are aroused during aruna, these forces may be harnessed to act externally. Explanation other than this is prohibited by the Great Oath.

D. Pelki

There are only two legitimate modes of physical intercourse among Wraeththu. Pelki is for the most part denied to exist, although amongst brutalized tribes it undoubtedly does. It is the name for forced rape of either Hara or humans. The latter is essentially murder, as humankind cannot tolerate the bodily secretions of Wraeththu, which act as a caustic poison; pelki to humans is always fatal. Because aruna is such a respected and important aspect of Wraeththu life, the concept of pelki is both abhorrent and appalling to the average Har. Unfortunately, certain dark powers can be accrued by indulging in these practices and this only serves as a dreadful temptation to Hara of evil or morally decadent inclinations.

GLOSSARY OF WRAETHTHU TERMS AND MINOR CHARACTERS

ACANTHA   See appendix one

AGHAMA (AG-am-ar)   Title of the first Wraeththu, worshipped as a god

ADITI (A-DEE-tee)   Military arm of the Niz in Maudrah

AI-CARA   Wraeththu calendar; years since Pellaz-har-Aralis became. Tigron

ALGOMALID   See appendix one

ALMAGABRA   Country of the Gelaming

ARCHON, THE   Title of the lord of the Maudrah

ARUNA (A-ROO-na)   Sexual communion between hara

AURIC WING   Merchant vessel out of Ferike, on which Cal travelled to Maudrah

AZRIEL   Son of Swift and Seel

BETICA   Cheap, strong liquor

CASTLETHANE   Lord of Jael

CHAITRA (CHAY-tra)   Simulated rape performed by kanene for client

CHESNA   A close relationship between hara

COBWEB   A Varr, consort of Terzian (q.v.), hostling of Swift; a mythic and legendary beauty

DIAMANDA   Soporific drug

ESTEMBLE   Gimrah stud farm

EULALEE (YEW-la-lee)   Subterranean land of the Sahale tribe

EXALAN   A Roselane, aide to Opalexian

FAIRMINIA   Opalexian's ship on which Cal travelled to Immanion

FALLSEND   A town in Thaine

FANCHON, THE   Lord of Zaltana, a city of the Kalamah

FEYBRAIHA   A harish coming of age, and its attendant celebration

FILLARET   A coin of the Thaine/Jaddayoth currency

FLICK   A bar from Saltrock, Megalithica

FOREVER   See We dwell in Forever

FULMINIR   Varr city in Megalithica, stronghold of Ponclast

GALHEA (Ga-LAY-uh)   Formerly a Varrish town governed by Terzian, now capital city of central Megalithica.

GEBADDON   Forest of nightmares and consciences in Megalithica

GELAMING (JEL-a-ming)   Superior Wraeththu tribe, originating in Almagabra

GLITTER   An area of Fallsend, famous for its musendas

GRISSECON (GRIS-uh-con)   Sexual communion between hara to raise power; sex magic

HAR   Wraeththu individual (pl. hara)

HARLING   Young har until feybraiha

HEARTSTONE   House of the family Hafener, in Gimrah

HEGALION   Chambers of the Hegemony in Immanion

HEGEMONY   Ruling body of the Gelaming

HIENAMA (hy-en-AH-ma)   Wreaththu priest

HOSTLING   Bar who carries the pearl (Wraeththu foetus), who hosts the seed of another

HUYANA (HOO-ya-na)   Priests of the Hadassah tribe

IMBRILIM   Gelaming camp headquarters in Megalithica

IMMANION   Capital city of Almagabra

KAKKAHAAR   Desert tribe of Southern Megalithica

KALALIM   Palace of the Kamagrian in Shilalama

KAMAGRIAN (Ka-MAG-ree-an)   A sisterhood of adepts, female complement of Wraeththu

KANENE (Ka-NEE-nee)   A harish whore

LIANVIS   Leader of the Kakkahaar tribe

LION OF OOMAR   See Wraxilan

MANTICKER THE SEVENTY   Leader of the Uigenna tribe at time of Cal's inception

MEGALITHICA   Western continent taken from the Varrs by the Gelaming

MORASS   A settlement in Thaine

MUSENDA   A whorehouse

NAHIT-NURI   See appendix one

NAMIR   Cousin to Panthera, and his intended consort. A har of the Kalamah

NAYATI   The temple in Saltrock

NIZ   Priesthood of the Maudrah

ORIEN   A Saltrock shaman, murdered by Cal

OUANA (Oo-ARN-a)   Masculine principle of hara

OUANA-LIM   Masculine generative organ of hara

PARAGE (Pa-RARJ)   Any member of the Kamagrian, an adept

PARASIEL (Pa-RASS-i-el)   Ruling tribe of Megalithica, governed for the Gelaming by Swift. Once known as the Varrs

PEARL   Wraeththu embryo

PELCIA   Simulated resistance to rape, performed by kanene for client

PELKI   Rape

PHAONICA (Fay-ON-ick-a)   Tigron's palace in Immanion

PIRISTIL   A musenda in Fallsend

PONCLAST   Former leader of the Varrs

PYTHONESS   A title of Tel-an-Kaa

SALTROCK   Wraeththu settlement in Megalithica where Pell was incepted

SEEL GRISELMING   A contemporary, and early friend, of Cal's; now a Gelaming har, associated with the Hegemony and consort of Swift.

SHARING OF BREATH   A kiss of mutual visualisation

SKYLORDING   A god of the Natawni tribe

SKYLES   Priesthood of the Skylording

SOUME (SOO-me)   Feminine principle of hara

SOUME-LAM   Feminine generative organs of hara

SPINNER   A coin of Thaine/Jaddayoth currency

SWIFT   Leader of the Parasiel (once Varrs), son of Terzian and Cobweb

SYKERNESSE   Palace of the Archon in Oomadrah, Maudrah

TERZIAN   A Varr, autarch of Galhea, master of Forever, father of Swift (deceased)

THAINE   Northerly region of Almagabra

THANDRELLO   Borough of Immanion, home of Ashmael

TIAHAAR   Respectful form of address

TIGRINA (Tee-GREE-na)   Tigron's consort; Caeru Meveny

TIGRON (TEE-gron)   Lord of the Gelaming, Thiede's protege, Pellaz-har-Aralis.

TIRTHA   Estemble governor among the Gimrah

TYSON   Son of Cal and Terzian

UIGENNA (EW-i-GENN-a)   Tribe of Megalithica, into which Cal was incepted, warlike and famous for their poisons

ULANI   See appendix one

ULAUME   Consort of Lianvis, originally of the Colurastes tribe, renowned for his beauty

UNNEAH (Oo-NAY-uh)   Tribe of Megalithica

UNTHRIST   Outcast, tribeless

VARRS   Former ruling tribe of Megalithica, before Gelaming takeover. See also Parasiel

WE DWELL IN FOREVER   Terzian's house in Galhea

WRAETHTHU (RAY-thoo)   The race of hermaphrodites that evolved from mankind

WRAXILAN (RAX-i-lan)   The Lion of Oomar, warrior leader of the Uigenna after Maticker the Seventy

ZIGANE (Zig-ARN-ee)   Tribe of wandering humans and hara in Megalithica

BESTSELLING BOOKS FROM TOR

THE BEST IN SCIENCE FICTION

THE BEST IN FANTASY

JACK L. CHALKER

POUL ANDERSON

WINNER OF 7 HUGOS AND 3 NEBULAS

GORDON R. DICKSON

BEN BOVA

PHILIP JOSÉ FARMER